A
GIRL
FROM
NOWHERE

ALSO BY JAMES MAXWELL

The Evermen Saga

Enchantress
The Hidden Relic
The Path of the Storm
The Lore of the Evermen

The Shifting Tides

Golden Age
Silver Road
Copper Chain
Iron Will

A GIRL FROM NOWHERE

THE FIREWALL TRILOGY

JAMES MAXWELL

Text copyright © 2020 by James Maxwell
All rights reserved.

Published by 47North, Seattle

www.apub.com

Amazon, the Amazon logo, and 47North are trademarks of Amazon.com, Inc., or its affiliates.

ISBN-13: 9781542005296
ISBN-10: 1542005299

Cover design by @blacksheep-uk.com

Cover illustration by Larry Rostant

Printed in the United States of America

For my daughter, Evelyn, with all my love

1

Taimin's father always said that of all the intelligent races fighting to survive under the two suns, humans were the boldest. Throughout the wasteland, humans hunted, foraged, scavenged, and stole.

Yet Taimin didn't think that what he was doing was bold. What he wanted was to explore, to seek out adventure far from home. Looking for eggs wasn't the same as hunting.

He dangled from a rope at the top of the cliff where wyverns nested, but as always the sunburned plain below kept distracting him. He gazed down and imagined himself visiting distant places. Despite the fact he was just a short distance from the homestead, this was as far as his family ever traveled. There were other people out there, so his father said, and he longed to meet them. His aunt warned him there were dangers. Still, he wasn't afraid.

Taimin's curiosity grew as his eyes roved over the world. The yellow disc of Dex was rising, which meant that both suns—one close and golden, the other a distant crimson orb—cast their rays on the scorched earth and banished the pale moon. He saw a land under cloudless skies as clear as still water and bounded by hazy red horizons. It was a land filled with fields of cactus, deep ravines, stone formations, and ancient riverbeds. The shades of red were innumerable: ochre and amber, pink and rust. A savage land, a land of contrasts, it appeared completely uninhabitable; yet he knew it contained a bewildering array of life, adapted to the harsh environment, buried within the cracks, nestled wherever water was near.

He searched for movement, or anything to catch his eye, and then his stomach rumbled. At eleven, he was growing fast, and as his brown hair grew thicker, his wiry frame was filling out. He ate as much as his father, Gareth, and his body was reminding him that he was here for food.

"Taimin." It was his mother's voice. "Don't dawdle. Your father can't hold on forever."

Taimin felt a flash of guilt as he pictured his father, standing firm while he held the rope that curled around a hermit cactus and stretched down the cliff face. Taimin wasn't heavy, and his father was strong, but he knew that his father would be anxious. Gareth never stopped talking about the danger they were all in away from the homestead.

He had only been daydreaming for a moment but he forced himself to stop wondering about the mysteries of distant lands and the lives of other people. He rotated his body on the rope and put his back to the view. As he scanned the vertical cliff below the escarpment, he looked for nests; where he saw nests, he might find eggs. Sometimes the wyverns built their nests in caves set into the cliff, other times they found ledges that jutted from the sheer wall.

"Taimin?" the voice of Tess, Taimin's mother, called again. "Can you see any? Are you all right?"

Looking up, Taimin saw her head pop over the escarpment thirty feet above. The wind blew her dark hair over her face and although Taimin could barely see her eyes, he heard the familiar tone in her voice.

"You're not daydreaming again, are you? You know what your father says."

"'Dreams are for the night,'" Taimin muttered. He called up to his mother as he continued to search the cliff. "I'm fine." The harness chafed under his arms and the glare of Dex, the near sun, was hot on his back. He spied the entrance to a promising hollow. "I need to go down . . . another ten feet."

Tess nodded and her face vanished from view. Taimin braced himself in the harness, expecting to feel the familiar yet nerve-wracking sensation of being dropped down the cliff. He was light, but that didn't mean his father lowered him at a snail's pace.

Instead, he made a sound of surprise when, rather than drop, he felt himself pulled up. As he drew closer to the summit he again saw his mother's face. This time when she spoke he didn't hear concern, he heard fear.

"There's someone here," she said in a low voice. "Quickly, climb up."

Tess's head disappeared from view and the upward force on the harness ceased. Fortunately, the last part of the ascent was an old rock fall, and by clambering up the boulders, Taimin soon reached the top of the escarpment on his own.

Taimin's parents stood side by side, shielding their eyes and staring toward the blazing sun Dex; the softer crimson sun was on the opposite side of the sky. Taimin's father had tied off the rope around the broad hermit cactus, which explained why Taimin had stopped moving. As Taimin wriggled out of his harness, he looked in the direction his parents were watching but saw nothing. He then noticed something that caused a lump of fear to form in his stomach.

Gareth, a lean man with gray threads in his black hair, had drawn his sword. Tess's left hand gripped her bow and she had an arrow nocked to the string. The obsidian arrowhead glinted in the morning light.

Taimin couldn't tell what his parents were thinking. Were they just being wary? Was there real danger?

3

"Are you sure they're humans?" Gareth asked Tess. Taimin thought his father sounded more excited than scared.

"I'm sure," Tess said. "They're riding wherries."

"By the rains, people . . . How long has it been?"

Tess looked over her shoulder at her son. "Taimin, coil the rope and pack up the harness. Then go and hide behind one of the big boulders until we call you out."

"What about the eggs?" Taimin asked. "We still don't have any."

"Forget the eggs," Gareth said. "Do as your mother says."

Taimin felt a thrill even as he unwound the rope from the hermit cactus. People! He had never seen other people, only his mother, father, and Aunt Abi. What would they be like? His father seemed confident, but looking at his mother, Taimin sensed her uncertainty and wished his aunt were here.

"Should I go and fetch Aunt Abi?" he asked. "She was going to join us."

"There's no time," Tess said.

"They'll certainly want to trade. Don't worry." Gareth glanced back at Taimin. "Your aunt will get to meet them soon enough."

"They're approaching," Tess said. "What are they doing so close to the firewall?"

Taimin wondered if he was supposed to hide now. But he wanted to see the people. His mother said they were riding wherries. Taimin hadn't known people could ride wherries.

He turned toward one of the stacked red boulders dotting the landscape. Then he forgot all about his instructions to hide as he heard the rumble of heavy feet pound the earth. Two broad-shouldered men came forward; with the yellow sun behind their backs they appeared as black shadows astride four-legged creatures. They reined in a short distance from Taimin's parents, before one of them kicked his wherry forward.

4

"We meet in peace," the nearest stranger said.

"Trade brings civilization to the waste," Gareth said. The words had the quality of a ritual, and Taimin was again curious about all the things he didn't know. "It's good to see humans after so long. We haven't seen people in what . . . five years? Five years at least. What are you, rovers?"

The stranger nodded and made a grunt of assent as he dismounted from the back of his wherry. His shoulders blocked the blinding sun and now Taimin could see his face.

Taimin looked in fascination at the stranger his father had called a rover. The man had white hair, close-cropped, and was younger than Gareth. His features were angular, as if cut from stone, and he was tall, standing much higher than the broad back of his sand-colored mount. The wherry snorted and shook its floppy ears in an attempt to dislodge the reins from the rover's grip.

Ignoring Taimin completely, the rover gave Gareth and Tess his own inspection. Taimin noticed that his dark eyes were cold and calculating. "Can I call my brother forward?" the rover asked. Without waiting for a reply, he turned and gave a short wave. The second rover dismounted and led his wherry forward.

"Wait," Tess said. "We haven't worked out the terms of this meeting."

The second rover continued to approach.

"Please, tell your brother to wait," Gareth said.

Taimin focused on the leader's brother, a man with long blond hair almost as white as the leader's. He was obviously younger, with a leaner build. His face was tanned to a deep brown.

Gareth and Tess took a step back. Taimin's fascination became something altogether different as the realization struck him with force: his parents were afraid. Uncertain, Taimin stood just behind them.

"Where is your homestead?" the tall leader asked. "It can't be far. You don't have supplies with you. You've even brought your brat." The rover's eyes flickered to Taimin. The emotionless stare sent a chill up Taimin's spine. "Thought no one could find you this close to the firewall, did you?"

Gareth and Tess continued to walk slowly backward, never taking their eyes off the two rovers. The brothers spread out, bringing their mounts with them. The leader took hold of something near his saddle and pulled.

Taimin heard a whisper, like the hiss of a snake, and the white-haired rover suddenly held a shining sword. Unlike Gareth's blade of pale basalt wood, this sword was made entirely of metal. It looked sharp and terrifying.

Gareth and Tess continued to increase the distance between themselves and the rovers. "What do you want? We can trade," Gareth said.

"We have nothing to trade," the white-haired rover said. His lips thinned. "But we need your food and water."

The leader's brother drew a sword of glossy hardwood, similar to Gareth's. Gareth held his weapon defensively in front of him. Tess drew an arrow to her ear.

The distance between the rovers and Taimin's parents had shrunk. Taimin was frozen in place, watching his parents' retreating steps. Gareth stopped directly in front of Taimin.

"My wife is an expert shot," Gareth said. "Neither of you have bows." He met the eyes of the tall leader. "You'll be the first to go."

Under her breath, Tess whispered, "Taimin, climb down the cliff. Go!"

As soon as she finished speaking, a flash of motion saw an arrow shaft sprout from her cheek and lodge itself in her skull. Taimin screamed. He heard his father roar and a strong hand shoved him.

Taimin broke into a run. He took short, sharp breaths as he raced for the cliff. But he couldn't stop himself looking over his shoulder. He saw his mother lying completely still on the ground. A third man revealed himself from behind one of the boulder stacks, bow in hand. A second arrow darted through the air, this time aimed at Gareth. The shot went wide.

Gareth clumsily blocked a blow from the younger swordsman, and then gasped as the tall white-haired rover thrust his metal blade. The point entered the center of Gareth's chest.

"Father!" Taimin cried. He came to a halt and wavered. He had to help his parents.

Gareth turned to face his son. "Go!" he cried. He shuddered as a thrust from the wooden sword pierced his side.

The white-haired rover called out to his companions as Taimin resumed his sprint. "Leave the man breathing. We need to find his homestead. Stop the boy."

Taimin reached the cliff. Something clattered against the rock at his feet and he saw a wooden arrow with feather fletching. He faced the precipice and blanched while he teetered on the edge of the escarpment, forced to choose between two horrors.

Another arrow shot past his head and he lost his balance. He fell and rolled, legs slipping and scrabbling as they sought purchase on what had become a rockslide. The drop beckoned, a fall of over a thousand feet. Taimin took hold of a big rock with both arms to slow himself, but then it began to move.

The rock tumbled with him as he fell.

Taimin's breath was knocked out of him as he hit a ledge, feeling the twigs and branches of an old wyvern's nest arrest his motion.

Then the big rock smashed onto his foot. Half his size, he felt it crush the bones together as his ankle twisted to an impossible angle. The pain sent stars exploding in his vision.

Taimin moaned, too shocked to scream. He couldn't even think of moving his leg, but when the stars faded he gritted his teeth and looked at the top of the escarpment.

He was only twenty or thirty feet down, but it may as well have been a hundred. He knew his mother was dead; his chest squeezed as he thought of it. His father had been badly hurt; the rovers wanted to question him. Taimin tried desperately to hear what was happening.

He realized there was no sound except for the howl of the wind. The clash of arms was gone. Then he heard a loud voice he recognized as that of the white-haired rover.

"Where is your homestead, settler?"

"Burn you."

Taimin stared up to the top of the cliff. Tears welled around his eyes.

"Ask him about the city." It was a different voice.

"We're looking for the white city. It's supposed to be full of people, so maybe you've met someone who's been there. Well, settler? Anything you can tell us?"

Then Taimin heard a man shout. "There's someone else out he—"

The cry broke off.

More shouts came, one after the other. Taimin wished he could see what was happening. He fought the pain as he gripped the boulder with both arms and tried to move it off his crushed foot.

As the thunder of wherry feet filled the air, Taimin grabbed onto the boulder's sharpest edge and pulled. His muscles strained with effort as he tried to get the weight off his damaged foot. His mother had always called him brave when he hurt himself.

His mother.

He struggled not to cry. She was dead.

The boulder rocked to the side. He renewed his efforts and grimaced. His hands found better purchase. Heaving with all his strength, he screamed when he rolled the boulder off his foot and it tumbled down the face of the cliff.

"Taimin?" He knew the voice calling from above. Aunt Abi's face appeared at the top of the cliff. The big scar on her cheek matched the color of her wild red hair. Her disfigurement was old; Taimin had never known her without it. "Hold on a moment. I'll get the rope."

The coarse rope soon tumbled down the cliff and Taimin held on, his face contorted with pain while his aunt dragged him over the rockslide and up to the escarpment. Abi's eyes widened with surprise when she saw his crushed foot, twisted with the bones crunching together like gravel in a sack. Her face registered surprise and something else . . . Sorrow.

She helped him up until he was sprawled out in the area that had recently been the scene of such violence. As she walked away, Taimin lifted his head. He saw his father, groaning as he gazed up at the sky. The rover with the bow lay dead with an arrow in his chest; his lifeless eyes stared without seeing. The two swordsmen were nowhere to be seen.

The realization that his father was alive sparked a moment of hope, but then Taimin saw his father's gray face and the way he held his hands over his chest. A red stain had spread all over his torso.

Taimin tried to crawl closer, but every time his legs moved a jolt of agony pulsed through his body. He wanted to call out but was forced to grit his teeth against the pain.

"The rovers have gone," Abi said. Taimin involuntarily turned his head to scan the area; he knew he would never forget the two cold-faced brothers. He focused once more on Abi as she crouched beside Gareth. "You fool. You should have run as soon as you saw them."

Gareth coughed and blood spluttered from his mouth. He tried to speak. Taimin could only just hear him. "Taimin?"

Abi looked over at Taimin and then back at Gareth. Taimin's father saw something in her eyes.

"No . . ." Gareth croaked.

"His foot's ruined. He'll never walk again. A cripple can't survive the wasteland."

"Please . . ."

Taimin realized they were discussing his life. Abi took a few moments to reply. "I can't promise anything except that I'll do what's right for the boy."

Gareth gave a sharp groan. Taimin couldn't bear how much pain his father was in. Gareth's face screwed up as his entire body shuddered.

Abi lifted her head. "Look away, Taimin." Her bone knife was in her hand. She leaned over Gareth. "Are you ready?"

Gareth gave a slight nod and turned his head so that he was looking at Taimin. He struggled to raise his voice. "Taimin. Be strong!"

"Father!" Taimin cried out. He pushed at the ground to raise his head; his eyes were fixed firmly on his father.

Abi's arm thrust forward as she plunged her bone knife deep into Gareth's chest. The breath left Gareth's body. Taimin's heart gave strong, savage thumps inside his chest.

Abi looked up and saw him staring. "I'm sorry, but he was suffering." She rose from her crouch and glanced at her brother and his wife. She shook her head. "You heard what we were discussing?"

"Yes," Taimin whispered.

"The wasteland is too dangerous for a cripple. It might have been better if you'd fallen to your death down the face of that cliff. It all depends on your determination, and how you heal. But you can only control one of those things. Do you understand me, Taimin?"

"Yes."

"Good. I'll take you home first, and then I'll fetch the bodies of your mother and father before the scavengers come."

Aunt Abi was a fighter, stronger and tougher than Gareth and Tess put together, but as she admitted herself she was no healer. She massaged the bones in Taimin's foot and then wrapped a cloth tightly around the whole thing.

For the next three days, Taimin writhed in agony. Abi fed him water but he couldn't keep food down and she didn't force the issue. Meanwhile, she went about her usual routine: checking the homestead's defenses, looking to her snares, tending to her garden. She also prepared the bodies of Taimin's parents for their final journey.

Abi seemed angry as she moved about the homestead and Taimin wondered if she was mad at him for not helping his parents fight the rovers. She cursed and muttered to herself as she made a litter for Taimin's father and cast frowns in Taimin's direction. Taimin did his best to stifle his groans.

At the end of the three days, Abi disappeared for a time, and when he could think clearly, Taimin saw that his father's body had vanished with her. While he was sleeping, she took Tess's body too, and when Taimin woke he saw Abi looking down at him.

"You're coming with me," she said. "I'm going to carry you, but this is the last time. Do you understand me, Taimin? For good or ill, this is the last time I will do it."

Taimin nodded, uncertain what to say.

Abi grunted as she picked him up, carrying his slight frame easily in her arms. She took him out into the open and Taimin blinked as he saw the two suns glaring down at him. Abi disarmed the traps around the gate in the fence and then reactivated them behind her.

She walked in a direction they didn't usually travel in, and he realized she was taking him to the firewall.

She stepped over rocks and climbed down hills before making her way up more rises in the land. Taimin was jolted time and time again, but he choked down any cries. His foot was in agony, but Abi's bold strides and tosses of her fiery hair told him she was in no mood to talk. He had always been a little afraid of her, and he wasn't sure if she wanted him to live or die.

The firewall was ahead, a place where the sky became steadily pink and then deepened to red, and the air became hotter and hotter until it reached a point where it was unbearable. Abi kept walking.

Then, when they reached a knoll looking down at the landscape beyond, Taimin saw the blackened land where it was impossible for anything to survive.

He knew that some quirk of the twin suns scorched most of the world, leaving just one portion inhabitable—the wasteland. The boundary, where Taimin now found himself, was called the firewall. Gareth once said that the firewall would one day close in and extinguish all life, while Tess disagreed, and said she had heard that long ago there was no firewall, and all the world was filled with forests of trees and oceans of water. Aunt Abi had never weighed in, and Taimin didn't know what she believed. What he could see with his own eyes was that the sky was red and hazy, and the air above the rocks shimmered. He wanted nothing more than to be gone from this terrible place, but instead Abi sat Taimin down next to the bodies of his mother and father.

"Say goodbye, Taimin," she said.

Taimin looked at his father, now wrapped from neck to toe in white cloth. "Goodbye, Father," he said. He knew that his life had changed forever. Abi's watching eyes made him conscious that he had to show her he could be strong.

"Goodbye, Mother," he said to his mother's body. Her eyes were closed and her face looked calm. The cares of her life were now washed away in death. He bit his lip and glanced at Abi, who scratched at the wide scar that ran from her forehead to her neck. "What about you?" he asked.

"I've said my goodbyes." She let out a breath. "This isn't easy on either of us."

Without another word, Abi picked up Taimin's father and grunted with effort as she hefted him over her shoulder; her frame was wiry but she was stronger than she looked. Abi walked down from the knoll. In moments she had plunged through the firewall and into the heat beyond.

She walked a surprising distance before setting down Gareth's body. Taimin wondered how she could stand it. When she returned, her face was red, making her blue-grey eyes look wild and manic. She then took Taimin's mother's body and laid it beside his father's. Abi was panting when she rejoined him; he could tell that even she was exhausted by her battle with the oven-like conditions.

"We should always give our dead some kind of farewell," Aunt Abi said. "Watch."

She sat down next to him. Time passed, and then smoke began to rise from both bodies. Taimin was glad he couldn't see them up close anymore. Slowly, gradually, they blackened, and the white cloth charred to gray and flittered away. A while longer and the smoke stopped rising. The bodies were now just two piles of ash on the ground.

Abi stood up. "There we have it. Their spirits have gone to Earth, if you believe in that sort of thing. No reason why not to, if it makes you feel better." She scratched again at the scar on her face. "Now, Taimin, it's time for you to make your choice." She met his eyes. "You're crippled. You know what that means, don't you? You're going to be a burden to yourself and to anyone you depend on. You likely won't be able to pull your weight, and I won't be around forever. You don't have a good life ahead of you."

Taimin looked out at the charred remains of his parents. He wondered if Abi intended to take him out there to die.

"This isn't just about you," Abi said. "I know it's hard for you to understand." She stared into the distance. "I remember when you were little, you were shivering with the fever. I wanted to take you past the firewall and blast the fever out of you. Seemed like a good idea at the time." She laughed without humor. "Your mother was right. It would have killed you. The fact is, I've never liked children. Too dependent. I know nothing about how to give you the things you need. And as for a crippled child . . ." Her mouth twisted. "I don't know if it's the right thing for both of us, for me to take care of you. So here's what I've decided."

Taimin watched her and held his breath as he waited for her next words.

"I'm going to leave you to make the choice yourself," Abi said. "I'm heading back, and you can either drag your body to the homestead, or you can go out there to die. If you make it back alive, I'll know you have the determination to carry on, and maybe you'll be able to survive, even with someone like me to take care of you. If you take yourself into the heat, well . . . that's your choice."

Abi squeezed Taimin's shoulder, and then left him alone beside the firewall.

Much later, as the crimson sun Lux rose above him, Taimin moved inch by inch over the rust-colored landscape. His mouth was dry and he was covered in dust, but as soon as he saw the distant shack and the tall fence surrounding it, he narrowed his eyes and shuffled even faster. A surge of victory coursed through him. He knew he had learned something about himself.

The wasteland was harsh. Only the strongest survived.

He might be crippled, but he had passed his first test. He had the determination to keep going.

2

"Your father was too soft," Abi said to Taimin as she snipped leaves from her nursery plants. "He didn't push you hard enough."

Taimin thought back to the sword practice with his father, the archery instruction from his mother, and the care both his parents took when explaining the harsh rules that governed the wasteland. Taimin had always woken up before the true dawn of Dex and worked as hard as anyone around the homestead.

Yet it was true that Aunt Abi was different. Taimin's parents had always held her abilities as a fighter in awe. Taimin often wondered how she became so skilled, but she rarely spoke about her past, even when asked directly.

As was sometimes the case, Taimin didn't know how to respond to his aunt, so he said nothing as she worked her way around the nursery. He knew better than to try to help her; the fenced section of the homestead was small, with makeshift shelves for the gnarled shrubs, cactuses, tubers, and herbs, and it was always his aunt's place.

"You probably think he was teaching you all he could. If that's what you think, well, you're right. But the fact remains that he couldn't teach you much. I saved your father's life too many times over the years, and his weakness was always going to catch up with him one day. That day came six months ago, and here we are."

Taimin had never heard Aunt Abi speak to him in the way she was now. She had generally left him alone while she watched over the homestead, keeping her thoughts to herself.

She wiped her brow, setting the snippers on a hook. She glanced at him and then looked away, muttering to herself. He only heard the words, ". . . fool of a child."

Taimin leaned on his crutch, keeping the hilt buried under his armpit, as he followed Abi out of the nursery, past the water collector, and through the only door out of the shack. He hurried to keep up with his aunt's purposeful strides, controlling the pain in his ruined foot and keeping his face like stone.

He watched Abi check every inch of the tall, protective fence, squeezing several thorns to eject fresh tips of purple poison. Nodding to herself, she then carefully peeled aside the gripper vine before exiting the gate. The deep ditch outside the fence was filled with sharp wooden stakes, and only the plank Abi carried under one arm would enable them to leave the homestead. She laid the plank over the ditch and then walked over. As always, she didn't help Taimin to cross; instead she waited impatiently for him to hobble over the makeshift drawbridge.

Out in the open, there was only a light breeze. Both suns shone fiercely on the reddened landscape. A few pricklethorn bushes and twisted spider trees broke up the vista. Birds, possibly raptors, wheeled in the distance.

Abi turned to face the homestead. "I've brought you here to make a few things clear," she said. "Look at our defenses. Tell me what you see."

Taimin gathered his thoughts. "The homestead has a ditch around it, and a fence behind the ditch."

"How deep is the ditch?"

Taimin hesitated. "About twelve feet."

"How tall is the fence?"

17

"About the same," Taimin said.

"Out in the waste, which creatures grow taller than twelve feet?"

Taimin reflected. He once saw a group of bax in the distance, and with his father he had seen tracks from a passing pair of snub-nosed trulls. He wasn't sure how tall skalen were, but his father had said they preferred to live underground so he doubted they were big.

"I don't know," he said.

"You should," Abi growled. "You can't build defenses if you don't know what you're defending yourself from. Your life depends on knowing your enemies." She shook her head. "Your father was remiss, but I wonder if it's my fault." Abi pointed at the angry red scar that parted her face from her brow to her neck. "Look at this. No, I said look at it."

Taimin forced himself to look at the ugly gouge.

"Your father did this," Abi said. Taimin's eyes went wide. He had always wondered how Abi got her scar, but the one time he had asked his father, Gareth went silent. "No, I don't mean he did it himself." She scratched the scar. "Blasted thing itches. Before we built this place, while you were still inside your mother's belly, we had a camp not far from here. This close to the firewall you get fewer predators, but that doesn't mean there's none at all." She met Taimin's eyes. "During the night, your mother went into labor, and we were attacked by firehounds. No doubt they came when they heard her cries. I needed Gareth beside me, but he said your mother needed him, which was a lie. What did he know about childbirth? So I stood alone and fought them off."

Abi shook her head. "I begged him to help me. With two of us fighting they would have been wary, but with just me, the fire-hounds grew bold. One of them knocked me over while another gored my face with its horns." Her voice became filled with regret.

18

"I drove them off, but from then on, my life wasn't my own. I'm no fool. No man would ever want a woman with half a face."

Taimin had never thought of his aunt ever wanting to find love in the same way his father had found his mother. She was transformed into something more human.

Abi's manner changed, as if she were shaking off the life she never had. "Despite the attack, this is a good place," she said. "There's hunting at the cliffs and deep water if you know how to find it. We built this homestead, close to the firewall where few others go, but I'm the one who knew how to fortify it. Your parents and I fought off attacks over the years, but I was always the one in front." She stared into the distance. "Tess was a good person, as was your father, but they weren't suited for this world." She then looked down at Taimin. "And now I don't know if you've got your father's spirit."

"I can be strong, Aunt Abi," Taimin said in a small voice.

Abi's lips thinned. "I've been thinking about this long and hard. I see strength in you, but you're a dreamer, and you've got a sensitive side. You're also a cripple." She gave him a firm stare. "At any rate, I don't think your future is for me to decide."

Taimin watched his aunt's face and felt a chill. The last time she had asked him to make a choice she had left him at the firewall. "Decide?"

"I won't live forever and you might be better off surrounded by other people. The journey would be tough—you have no idea how tough—but I can take you to a larger group of settlers, if that's what you want."

Taimin swallowed. He realized that the choice he was being asked to make was momentous. He remembered dangling on the rope as he gazed out from the cliff and wondered about the lands that lay out of view. In that moment, he had thought that his parents were too cautious. More than anything, he had wanted to meet other people.

But then he had met other people . . . ruthless men who had killed his parents.

Something snagged in his memory. "The rovers . . . They asked Father about a white city . . ."

Abi's face curled in a scowl. "There is no city, boy. It's a myth. People live in caves and homesteads. Well? Do you want to go? You might be too young to think about finding love, but you won't stay young. There might be someone out there compassionate enough to love a cripple. It's unlikely, but sometimes people fit together and we don't know why. There's no chance of it at all out here."

Taimin longed to find other people, but he didn't want his aunt to abandon him forever. He didn't know what was out there, and he was afraid. "I want to stay with you. You don't have to get rid of me."

"We'll see," Abi said. She nodded. "You've made your choice, then." She inspected him and frowned. "Stand tall."

Taimin straightened but gave an involuntary wince of pain. Abi looked at his crutch and then, without warning, reached forward and pulled it out from under him. He nearly fell before he managed to right himself.

"It's been six months," she growled. "By now your bones have knitted together into some sort of blasted arrangement. The healing is done. I've got bad news for you, boy. Whatever you feel now is what you're going to feel for the rest of your life."

Abi broke the crutch over her knee and tossed the pieces into the ditch. Taimin watched as the bits of wood disappeared. "You're going to have to learn to move without a crutch. You'll never be able to fight if you depend on something like that."

Taimin nodded. He took a deep breath. "I understand."

Her mouth tightened. "I hope you do. Because you're going to have to be more than strong to survive. You'll have to be stealthier than a skalen and tougher than a bax. Mantoreans are good archers; you'll have to be better. Trulls are big; you'll have to strike them down anyway. You'll need to use your head and know more about the creatures of the waste than you know about yourself. Most important of all, you'll have to know how to find food and water in the driest desert."

Taimin nodded again and gave his aunt a determined stare.

"If you're going to stay with me, you'll have to learn all that and more. Now come on, let's get inside before Dex goes down."

Taimin followed his aunt back into the homestead, and when they reached the kitchen she told him to sit down at the table. A few moments later, she came to him with a pair of boots. Curious, he recognized the soft leather she had been saving for a new vest to replace the tattered thing she wore now. The boots were dark red, the same color as the wyvern's hide they had come from, and were made with the same care Abi brought to everything she did.

"Here," Abi said. "Take off those sandals and put these on. Let's see if they fit."

Taimin slipped out of his crude sandals. He yanked on the left boot, feeling it grip his toes. "It fits well."

"And the other."

Looking askance at his aunt, he turned and examined his crippled right foot. Rather than the healthy, familiar shape, the outline was more like a right-angled triangle. The small toes were squished together, and the big toe stuck out like an anomaly. It was as if a foot made of mud had been flattened from above, which was exactly what had happened, except that it was his flesh and bone that had been forcefully reshaped.

"I don't know if I can," he said.

Aunt Abi gave him the look that made him feel like a stupid child. With a sigh, he inserted his crippled right foot into the opening and started to pull.

She left him to it for a time, occasionally glancing at him as if measuring his level of determination. Finally, with a growl, she came over and started to push, pull and twist, regardless of his discomfort. "The leather will shape itself to your foot," she grunted. "Provided we can get the boot on in the first place."

At last, it was done. Taimin looked down at his feet. For the first time since the death of his parents, he felt something akin to pleasure. He looked whole. He didn't look like a cripple anymore.

"Good," Abi said. "Now stand."

Taimin rose to his feet. He wobbled but resisted the urge to grab hold of the table. He took deep breaths as he fought the pain and struggled for balance and control. He wavered, and nearly fell, but in the end he stood tall and looked at his aunt proudly.

"Well done," she said. "Now follow me."

Walking was altogether different from standing. Abi waited impatiently outside the front door, in the cleared area between the fence and the shack, while he bounced and jarred his way over to her.

Abi indicated two hardwood swords at her feet. "Pick up a weapon."

Taimin crouched and grabbed the hilt of a sword. As he straightened, he lost his balance and leaned on the sword, and felt a strike on his head that caused him to cry out.

"Never, ever, use your sword for a crutch," Abi said. "It is your weapon, and your life depends on it."

Taimin put his hand to his head, rubbing the tender spot where his aunt had struck him. "I understand," he said.

"Now," said Abi. "Show me your guard. Let's see what Gareth taught you."

———

As the weeks became months, and months turned to years, Taimin felt the wound of his parents' passing slowly heal, although he never forgot the manner of their deaths.

Abi taught him all she knew, and whether she pushed him harder because of his disadvantage, or whether she was just instructing him as she would have instructed her own child if her life had worked out differently, he would never know.

He learned to manage with his boots, and could eventually walk with only the slightest limp. He would have been useless as a swordsman if he couldn't leap, or duck, or lunge, so he learned to move his body in deft, unpredictable ways. But he couldn't run. When he tried, he lumbered at a pace easily outmatched, and never managed more than a dozen paces before stumbling. It was the best he could do, even with Abi pushing him, and eventually she understood that anything else was impossible.

Taimin learned the limits of his dexterity, but to do so he had to defeat the pain. He felt the bones jangle together whenever he pushed himself. Controlling the pain was the key to his freedom of movement, and learn to control it he did, even if after hard practice it kept him awake at night, sweating and shivering.

Abi taught him to wield a sword, and built cactus dummies for him to practice on. By the age of fourteen, he could block his aunt's blows, and she had to actually work to make a strike. At fifteen he landed his first blow. Then he realized his aunt had been holding back after all.

He learned marksmanship with a bow. At sixteen he could hit a nesting raptor from seventy paces. As Abi always reminded him, a good archer rarely went hungry.

Even as his skill with weapons improved, Abi said there was more to survival in the waste than fighting, as important as it was. He learned how to make a sword from the limb of a basalt tree—the pale wood so hard it had to be burned from the trunk—and to construct a composite bow from firehound horn, spruce, and raptor sinew. He fashioned arrows with obsidian heads, learning to value each and every one and retrieve them whenever he could.

All of his instruction centered on the daily struggle to stay alive. One year, Abi's precious nursery was ravaged by plague beetles, and for six months Taimin hunted from dawn to dusk so that they had enough food to eat. He learned that survival in the wasteland meant focusing on the one thing no creature could do without: water. He became adept at finding water beneath ancient riverbeds and in the hearts of lifegiver cactuses. He used the tracks of the wherry and the firehound as a guide, following them to shallow pools in caverns where water seeped up from subterranean sources. Where he found water, he inevitably found food. Sometimes he had to escape becoming food himself.

Always, his inability to run threatened his life.

The homestead was protected by cliffs and close to the firewall, but the creatures of the wasteland still managed to harass Taimin and his aunt. Twice Abi and Taimin fought off curious wyverns, the big flyers a regular presence as a result of the homestead's proximity to their nests. Raptors, scorpions, and snakes were a constant menace. Once a pack of firehounds called to each other in the night and kept the two humans in the homestead awake for hours.

But there were also much more dangerous threats Taimin might encounter—potential enemies possessing intelligence. Abi made sure he knew about each and every one of them as she smashed her larger weapon against his hardwood sword again and again.

"What's a trull's weakness?"

"They're slow," Taimin would gasp. "They can be goaded to anger."

"Where are the soft parts on a bax?"

"Under the chin . . . but not the throat," he puffed. "Under the armpit . . . slanting down."

"How do you know when to fight, and when to run?"

"I can't run," he would say. "I have to avoid battles I can't win."

One day, he asked his aunt again how she knew all these things.

"I can fight." She shrugged. "It's what I'm good at."

Taimin sensed there was a lot she wasn't saying, but she was reticent at the best of times. He changed the subject. "What was that sword the rover had? The one who killed my father. It wasn't made of wood."

Abi looked surprised. They rarely spoke of the event.

"He had white hair—" Taimin began.

"I remember," Abi interrupted. "You don't see steel swords very often, and you tend to remember them."

"Steel?"

"It's a metal. Red ore is dug up from the ground and when it's heated to very high temperatures it melts. Coal is added to the melted ore to form steel when it cools. Steel is harder and can be made much sharper than the wood of the basalt tree."

"We already have coal. Should I look for red ore?"

Abi snorted. "Leave it, Taimin. There's more to it than my simple description. Steel swords are rare and valuable. Men will kill you for them. That rover probably killed someone to get his hands on that weapon, just like he killed your parents."

Taimin again experienced the frustration he'd felt that day. He now considered himself a man, and he wished he had been able to tip the balance in his parents' favor. Sometimes he had vivid, savage dreams, where he took his vengeance upon two tall rovers with hard faces and pale hair. If he ever saw them again, nothing would stop him.

Seeing his expression, Abi spoke. "Taimin, one thing you should know . . . Those rovers are probably long dead. Even if they're not, you'll never see them again. Here, close to the firewall, we have a life of safety, but also solitude. We might as well be the only people alive."

3

Taimin dangled his feet over the edge of the cliff, close to the place where he had watched his parents die. Wyverns wheeled in the sky, high above the plain below. The yellow sun Dex hung low on the horizon, casting slanted morning rays over the towers of rock, clumps of green cactus, and dried riverbeds.

He was nineteen. Eight years had passed since he had looked out over this same view and wondered what lay beyond the cactus fields. He had now followed the steep trail to the foot of the cliffs, and explored some of the caves at the bottom, but he couldn't travel much farther and still make it back to the homestead before nightfall. He still knew little about the wider world.

He looked down at his right foot, which appeared much the same in the boots as his left. He had outgrown the pair Abi made him after a year but she had made him another. This pair, he had made himself, with the skin of a wyvern he had hunted down on his own. Only just undergone metamorphosis from its wherry state, the wyvern had been uncertain with its new wings and fallen prey to his arrow.

As he took in the view, Taimin dreamed.

He wanted to explore. He wanted to meet other people. Yet with his slow speed, any travel would be risky.

He watched one of the soaring wyverns as it circled and looked for prey. Then he thought about the four-legged creatures the rovers had been riding on that fateful day.

An idea struck him with force.

He climbed to his feet as he recalled everything he knew about wherries. Wyverns laid eggs on the cliffs. The eggs hatched, and while the wherry young were small, the location kept them safe from predators. Then, when the wherries grew too big for the nests, the wyverns transferred them to the ground below so they could hunt. The strongest wherries, the healthiest, grew in size until they underwent metamorphosis. Wings sprouted from their shoulder blades and their strong forelegs shrank and tucked in under their bodies. They became wyverns, mated, and the cycle repeated.

Wherries were as fast on land as wyverns were in the air. Taimin looked down at his foot. He couldn't run but, with a wherry, he could ride. On the back of a wherry, he wouldn't be a cripple anymore.

———

Taimin wiped blood from his forehead and grimaced as he examined the smear of red on his fingertips. He had just lost the wherry as it darted from under his net, and then tripped and fallen hard. He now watched the four-legged animal bound away, scampering over the rocky terrain until it disappeared from view.

Abi thought him a fool but left him to his own ends, muttering to herself as she trimmed the leaves on her plants, caressing them with a delicacy she never displayed in any other task. Now he was starting to believe her; after months of effort clambering around the rocky terrain below the cliffs, he hadn't even come close to success.

Shaking his head, he decided to give up for the day, and perhaps for good. He gathered his net and put it into his pack. As he scanned the irregular cave mouths that peppered the bottom of the cliffs, his gaze alighted on the cave where he had left four brown lizards he had killed earlier. He would collect them before heading for the trail that would take him up to the summit. Bow in hand, he walked warily, the way Abi had taught him, checking the sky and the rust-colored rock in all directions.

He frowned as he approached the cave where he had left the lizards. He had hidden them well, but something else had drawn the attention of some raptors. Dozens of the lean, leathery birds had focused their attention on a different cave, and were darting in and out of the entrance. They shrieked at each other in the way they only did when they had some prey to torment.

Taimin knew he had to be careful. If he couldn't clear the raptors, he wouldn't be able to fetch the lizards; the raptors would smell the meat and undoubtedly attack him.

Raptors didn't like darkness and they took turns plunging into the cave. They were small compared to wyverns, but they could still be deadly as a group. Their crimson eyes glared and leather gullets twitched as they shrieked. Blood stained their hooked beaks.

Taimin reached for an arrow from the bundle strapped against the side of his pack. He kept a wary eye on the raptors and when a bird came screeching toward him he let an arrow fly. The raptor spun several times in the air as his shot took it clean through the wing.

He retrieved his arrow and continued to watch the raptors dart in and out of the dark opening. More of them had blood on their beaks or talons. Whatever they had found, he soon wouldn't be able to scare them away before hunger drove them mad.

He shot at another raptor and cursed when his arrow lodged in its body and the bird fled, wounded yet taking his arrow with it. He decided to forgo the bow for his sword and crouched to make the exchange. With the wooden grip in his hands, he neared the mouth of the cave. If he could find out what was attracting the raptors, he might be able to drive them off.

He batted away several of the birds. They became wary of his sword and regrouped to hover in the air, wings flapping as they cawed in frustration. He stood just inside the cave's entrance, knowing he would be outlined in Dex's bright light but risking exposure to give his eyes time to adjust. He heard the flutter of wings just behind his head and cut at the air to strike a screeching bird and cause the rest to scatter. Still unable to see what was inside the cave, he entered.

There were hundreds of caves set into the cliffs and this one had the jagged walls and graveled floor he had seen before. He walked forward cautiously but shot a glance over his shoulder when he heard shrieking. At the mouth of the cave the raptors were screeching, trying to summon the courage to enter and attack.

Then Taimin heard a different sound, somewhere between a growl and a whimper. It was accompanied by a scuffle.

He moved deeper into the cave, sword held out in front of him. Hidden by shadows, a large shape twisted and growled at his approach, causing him to raise his sword, but then the shape gave a sorrowful whine. Taimin moved to allow light to pass his body. His eyes widened.

He was looking at a wherry—a male—with the typical strong legs, soft, wrinkled skin, and floppy ears. The raptors must have hounded him, forcing him into the cave, where he had obviously been penned for a long time. Taimin's heart went out to him; the wherry was young and would have been frightened as more raptors joined in and braved the darkness to peck at his soft spots.

The animal was in a bad state. Blood ran in rivulets down his leathery hide, contrasting with his sandy color, and as Taimin came closer the wherry looked up at him with pitiful eyes framed by long eyelashes.

If the wherry ever underwent metamorphosis and became a wyvern, his floppy ears would straighten. The jutting ridges at his shoulders would erupt into wings, and his legs would become smaller. But given his size, Taimin wondered if he was a runt, one of those that never changed, spending their entire lives in wherry form.

Taimin glanced back at the mouth of the cave. It was late in the day and he knew he shouldn't stay out much longer. He wanted to help, but he also knew that the wherry was a dangerous creature. The animal was obviously exhausted and starved. But he weighed perhaps five times what Taimin did, and his teeth and claws were sharp.

"Shh." Taimin made soft sounds as he approached, but he wasn't taking any chances and still held on to his sword. The wherry tried to snarl but it finished in a whimper. Taimin saw peck marks on his belly, neck, and beside one of his drooping ears. The blood attracted flies, and Taimin waved them off, relieved when the motion didn't enrage the animal.

Deciding to take a risk, Taimin leaned down and laid a palm on the wherry's neck; the creature stirred but didn't have the strength to fight. Making low tones of encouragement, Taimin held his breath as he put down his sword and continued to hold a soothing hand against the animal's skin. The wherry lowered his head to the ground, and Taimin became more confident.

Taimin watched the wherry's sad eyes as he slipped his pack off his shoulder. He froze as he saw a hind leg twitch, but it was just the creature stretching. He grabbed his water flask and poured some water into his cupped hands. Trying not to show his fear, he brought his hands close to the wherry's strong jaws. A moment later the wherry was lapping from his hands, his tongue gliding over Taimin's palms to get to every last drop.

Taimin glanced at the cave's mouth and breathed a sigh of relief. The raptors had given up. The wherry gave another whimper.

"Wait here," Taimin murmured. "I'll get you something to eat."

As Taimin left the cave, he saw the exhausted wherry follow him with his eyes. He already felt responsible for the animal's fate. He wanted the wherry to heal and be well. Some food would lift his spirits.

Taimin smiled.

"We're going hunting," Taimin called to his aunt.

Taimin held the reins as Griff trotted beside him and grinned with pent-up excitement. Abi grunted in reply, completely focused while she checked the boundary fence.

Taimin didn't know why he had chosen the name, it just seemed to suit. Griff was too big to sleep in the house, so Taimin had built him a stable alongside the shack. Even so, Griff preferred to sleep on the threshold, much to Abi's annoyance as she kicked him out of the doorway each morning.

"That wherry runt," Abi called him, which was true; Griff was much smaller than the wherries that belonged to the rovers. He tired quickly with Taimin on his back and cast reproachful looks over his shoulder every time Taimin climbed up. Nonetheless, when the mood took him he could bound along with speed.

Taimin patted Griff's flank as he and the wherry left the homestead behind. He glanced back one last time at his aunt, and with a start realized that her once-red hair was now entirely gray. When had that happened? While he had grown, Abi had seemed to shrink. She hadn't, of course; he had just become bigger. Taimin could now best her with a blade, although she was still his superior at tracking and archery. Their relationship had changed. Abi now spent more time with her plants, while Taimin roamed the plains, hunting with Griff.

The wherry had a sixth sense for finding game, and even Taimin was surprised by how much extra meat they were able to bring home at the end of a day. Taimin still worked to keep the homestead safe and carry water from the spring, and was always exhausted by the time he went to sleep. But with a surplus of meat, and Abi bringing more vegetables to the table, he was now a few inches taller than his father had been. Abi's constant lessons and his own exertions had given him broad shoulders and strong limbs. Dark stubble covered his cheeks.

He followed the escarpment for a time and made absent sounds of encouragement to Griff as he walked. Reaching the steep trail that led to the plain below, he began his careful descent, and with Griff far more surefooted Taimin held on to the saddle for support. The cliff cast a long shadow on the plain, but slowly the darkened swathe shrank as the golden sun climbed higher. A warm, dry wind blew against Taimin's face and rustled his dark hair. Distant specks dotted across the terrain became cactuses and rust-colored boulders. Raptors and smaller scavenger birds hopped around on the branches of withered trees.

Completing the descent, Taimin reached the row of caves where he had found Griff. Hot air shimmered over the plain, causing everything but the largest rock formations to waver. He scanned the sky, and looked both ahead and behind him, always searching for threats, the way he had been taught. Satisfied, he walked a little farther until he found a hollow in the rocky ground. He then poured out a small amount of water, which Griff greedily lapped up. While Griff drank, Taimin checked the wherry over, pleased to see that the peck marks on the sand-colored hide had healed.

"You ready?" Taimin asked, but he could already sense that Griff was eager to run. As he felt his own excitement rising, he gripped the horn at the front of the saddle he had made, and mounted.

The wherry immediately bounded forward, eager for the hunt and the chance to stretch his legs. Taimin leaned forward and held on hard. Air rushed past his ears, but he easily kept his seat. Griff pulled toward the cactus field, and Taimin let him choose the direction. The pace settled to a steady run, and Taimin readied his bow, on the lookout for raptors and rock lizards.

Griff soon hunted down two big lizards on his own before wearing himself out chasing a third. Taimin let him rest near a basalt tree crowning a knoll where he had a good view of the plain, but Griff wouldn't settle while the raptors in the tree shrieked down at him. Taimin shot one of the ugly birds and tied it to his pack while the rest fled. He smiled to himself as he dragged Griff away; the raptors would return, and Griff hated raptors.

Lux finally rose, giving the terrain another shade entirely, adding the color of blood to the landscape. With the golden sun close to the middle of the sky, Taimin decided to find somewhere to escape the heat.

He led Griff by the reins and directed the wherry to a ravine they had sheltered in previously, with steep walls that cast the interior in perpetual shade. Griff's calm demeanor made Taimin confident there was nothing dangerous hidden within, but he still scanned as he descended, before allowing himself to settle in and slip the pack off his back.

Griff ate the raptor, crunching the bones in his strong teeth while Taimin drank sparingly from his water flask. It was still too hot to resume the hunt, and Griff finished his meal and sprawled out on the ground. His eyelids closed, and the wherry's broad chest rose and fell while he slept.

Taimin sat with his back against the rock wall and thought about his aunt. He remembered seeing her gray hair and realizing that she was getting old. She had always taken care of him, but now he was beginning to worry about her. She was still spritely, but her movements weren't as swift or sure as they once were. If something happened to him, she wouldn't have anyone.

Thinking about his aunt made him reflect on his parents. One thing he was sure of was that Gareth and Tess had loved each other. He knew he was now a full-grown man. Abi would die one day, and he didn't want to be alone. He wanted to have a companion to share the red and gold sunsets with. Someone to travel with. Someone his own age, who shared his curiosity about the wider world.

The time had come. When he returned to the homestead he would talk to his aunt, and they would both make the journey to find a group of settlers. The homestead's location made it safer than many other places, but there would also be safety in numbers. Abi was something of a loner, but she was practical enough to face facts.

His thoughts were interrupted by a sound.

Griff immediately lifted his head. His floppy ears pricked slightly and his eyes narrowed, as if he had never been sleeping. A low growl came from deep within his chest.

Taimin carefully set down his water flask. He picked up his bow and nocked an arrow to the string. As he listened intently, he soon heard multiple voices with a gruff, sandpaper quality to them. The coarse throatiness was something he had never heard up close, but his aunt had described it to him, drilling him so that he would be wary of the creatures he might one day find himself fighting in the wasteland. The voices belonged to bax.

Taimin's pulse began to race. His immediate impulse was to lift his head out of the gully, but he told himself to stay still and instead cocked his head as he tried to estimate how many there were. It was difficult at first, but the harsh voices were coming closer, and he soon knew that it was far from a small group. Bax hunting parties were usually no larger than a few warriors. This was four or five times as many.

Griff climbed to all fours and his growl became louder. Taimin laid a hand on the wherry's flank. He shook his head and met Griff's eyes until he stilled. Taimin was tense as he wondered what so many bax were doing on the plain, dangerously close to the homestead. He wished his aunt were with him. He couldn't tell from their voices whether they were traveling with females and young. One thing he did know, from the growing volume of their calls and the thudding of their footsteps, was that they were traveling with speed.

He made sure Griff knew to stay where he was and then left the deepest part of the ravine to climb closer to the surface. He was already aware that the bax were on their way toward the gully. He kept his head down and body low while the rasping calls became louder. They were still a reasonable distance away when the sound changed. The bax were now past the gully and heading away. He waited until he was sure they would have their backs to him. He then raised his head.

The bax were in a hurry and didn't see him as he watched their departing group. They were ugly creatures, man-sized but shorter and broader, with thick, knobbed skin and a ridged spine that jutted out from their backs, just below their necks. Taimin couldn't see their faces, but he knew that their noses were small compared to their squared jaws.

His eyes widened as he realized he was looking at a war party. There were over a dozen male warriors burdened with packs, and all carried clubs, bone axes, and sharp spears. They wore leather armor but their splayed feet were bare as they ran and called out to one another. One had a bandage wrapped around his arm, which he held awkwardly at his side. Another warrior's torso was strapped tightly with a strip of linen. The bandages were fresh. They had been in a recent fight.

Taimin's heart beat out of time.

He forgot about the fact that at any moment one of the bax might turn around and see him. The water sack poking out of a warrior's pack was frayed at the seams. It looked familiar. Another bax was carrying a well-crafted spear. It was Abi's. A bundle of kindling looked like poles from the barrier fence.

In moments the bax were gone. The shock was so strong that Taimin felt sick. He gave a piercing whistle and Griff bounded out of the ravine. Taimin immediately threw himself on the wherry's back and dug in his heels. He headed directly for the homestead.

The plume of smoke added to Taimin's horror. Sensing his urgency, Griff flew over the uneven ground, bounding over gullies and swerving past boulders, kicking dust behind him.

Taimin roared at Griff to hurry. He passed the first body, hundreds of paces from the homestead. He barely registered the bax warrior other than to note that he had two of Abi's arrows sprouting from his chest. He saw a second body, and then a third. Abi had encountered them while away from the protection of the barrier fence. She had fought a retreating action, sending arrows at the bax while they tried to outflank her.

As Taimin approached the homestead he pulled up sharply. Part of him read the tracks and scanned for threats. Meanwhile he gripped his bow with white knuckles, desperate for a sign that his aunt was still alive.

The homestead was destroyed beyond recognition.

The barrier fence was in ruins. Most of the shack was burned. The bax had penned Abi in the shack and used fire as a weapon against her. She had been forced to put the fire out, which distracted her and gave the bax a chance to lay planks over the ditch and storm the gate.

Such a large war party must have been heading somewhere. They had clearly been following the firewall's edge, and would have needed food and water. The homestead was too tempting to resist. The attack had come with a cost, but they had succeeded in the end.

Taimin dismounted to stand at the edge of the ditch and stare at what was left of the homestead. Abi's body was just outside the door, in the place Griff liked to sleep. Her gray hair fluttered in the slight breeze. She was utterly still, eyes open wide, with a broken spear embedded in her chest. Her sword had taken two more bax before their numbers overwhelmed her.

The smoke was dissipating, leaving behind the sour stench of char. The bax had ransacked the homestead, taking the water sacks from under the collector, before they passed Taimin on the plain as they continued their journey.

Griff whimpered and sank to his haunches, staying where he was. Taimin walked alone across the makeshift bridge that the bax had used to span the ditch.

Taimin reached Abi's body. The smoke in the air stung his eyes and he wiped them with the heels of his hands. He crouched down beside his aunt.

His guilt and grief mingled as he bowed his head. While he had been resting in the shade, Abi had been fighting for her life. He wasn't sure if he could have made a difference, but he would never know.

With a start, he lifted his head once more. Time had passed; he had no idea how much, but the suns had shifted position. His aunt was dead, but her voice still spoke inside his mind, telling him he should be thinking about survival. He brushed some gray locks aside to kiss Abi's forehead. His instincts took hold as he straightened. It was unlikely, but he needed to see if the bax had left behind any water.

He ignored the heat as he kicked aside timbers where once he and his aunt had prepared meals. The nursery where Abi had tended her plants was completely destroyed. All the food was gone. The bax had even taken the skins they were preparing to make leather. There was no water at all.

Still Taimin searched, knowing that the things he found could aid his survival. He discovered a dirty blanket and a sturdy pot. He collected splintered wood and bundled it together; it would be useful as kindling.

Last of all, he came to the chest at the foot of his aunt's bed.

The chest was on its side. It had been emptied out, of course, but the fire hadn't spread to the area. His aunt's clothing had been discarded and tossed aside to form a pile on the floor. Anything of value was gone. He glanced inside the chest anyway.

Taimin frowned as he leaned forward. There was something inside, at the very bottom. He bent down and his fingers closed over a folded sheet of fibrous paper.

He unfolded the piece of paper and held it up, to find himself looking at a picture. The image was initially confusing. He had never seen anything like it.

The picture was well drawn, and depicted a high wall that surrounded a collection of buildings. Not just a dozen buildings, or a hundred, but more than could be real. It was a city, with a tall, graceful tower in the very center.

Taimin again heard the voice of the pale-haired rover who had questioned his father. *We're looking for the white city.*

It was just a drawing, Taimin told himself. Abi had said the white city was a myth.

A nagging doubt remained. But what if it was real?

He shook his head and quashed the doubt. If the white city was real, and his aunt knew about it, there was no way she would live in a remote homestead near the firewall. If a walled city full of people actually existed, Taimin might have grown up there, and his aunt and his parents would be alive today.

He folded the piece of paper and put it in his pack along with everything else. He realized that it was all he had of his aunt, and his parents too, for that matter. In fact, he had lived with Abi his entire life, but knew little of hers.

His search complete, he left the clothing chest behind. Clambering over the charred remains of the homestead, he returned to his aunt's body. With a catch in his throat and feeling numb all over, he looked down at her and cast his mind back. He remembered when he had watched his parents' bodies smolder beyond the firewall. His aunt had taught him that the dead always deserved some kind of farewell.

Taimin gathered the last of the shack's timbers and stoked up the fire once more, so that the flames could send her spirit into the sky.

When he was done, he stood with Griff and watched his aunt's funeral pyre. His grief shifted to anger as he thought about the bax who had destroyed his home. They had taken his water and food, enough to survive for a long time. They had been traveling quickly, but they were on foot, and hadn't bothered to conceal their tracks.

Abi had cared for him, trained him, and taught him about the world. She was gone. He was all alone.

Yet he already knew what Abi would tell him to do. He had his weapons, and he had his training. If he was going to survive, his first objective was clear. He would pursue the group of bax and get his supplies back.

Taimin realized he was about to go out into the wider world. And whether or not the white city was real, if he searched for it, he might find the two pale-haired brothers who had killed his parents.

He wasn't sure, but perhaps Abi had reacted strangely when he had asked her about it. He didn't know about his aunt's past, but the drawing had meant something to her. It was a start.

But first, he had to survive.

4

"Is she faking?"

"Looks pretty real to me."

"Jab her in the ribs. If she's faking, she won't grab her head like that; she'll protect her body."

"Vic, Sully, stop it! She's in pain."

"C'mon, Lars. You know we can't trust her."

"Vic, I said let her be."

Selena heard the voices as muted, muffled, as if she were standing at the mouth of a cave, listening to people talking deep within. Vic's jab in her side was nothing compared to the pain in her head. She felt each beat of her heart as a single, isolated event, sending blood from her veins up into her skull, where the throb of its pulse detonated with a furious blast before the next beat repeated the agony.

She rolled on the ground, her hands at her temples as she tried to let the pain drive her into unconsciousness. It never did. It always kept her sharp, aware of her surroundings and what was happening to her while able to do nothing about any of it. She knew the gravel under her back was hard and piercing. Three men stood over her. Her eyes wildly flashed from one face to the other, seeing no pity in any of them, only fear and distrust, the same emotions she had seen on people's faces her entire life.

"We should leave her," said Sully, a wiry man, perhaps forty years old, with black hair and a talent for complaint. "Look at her. She's useless to us."

"Sully's right. Who's to say she's not leading us round in circles?" Vic scowled. He was a stronger and tougher man than Sully but with half the cunning.

"You two can go if you want. She stays with me. I haven't come this far for nothing. It's out there, and she's going to take me to it."

The last man to speak was Lars. He looked about fifty, perhaps even older. It was hard to tell because he scraped any vestige of hair from his head with his sharp skinning knife. The rest of his body contrasted with his bald head, for he was hairy from his ankles to his thick black beard. Lars wasn't as big as Vic, but the other two skinners were wary of him. Lars's eyes were dark and moody, but he had spoken up on Selena's behalf more than once.

Selena gradually felt the pain lessen. Her rolling slowed, her gritted teeth relaxed, and her breathing began to return to normal.

Lars crouched down next to her and helped her sit up.

"Water," Selena said.

Lars put his hand in the air but first Sully, and then Vic, stepped back.

"She can have yours," Sully said.

Lars unclipped his water flask and dribbled some liquid into Selena's mouth. It was barely a mouthful but she felt her strength return. Compared to the agony of her seizure, she could handle the nagging thirst. Even as she had the thought, she took it back. Thirst could mount until it was its own form of agony.

"Better?" Lars asked.

Selena nodded.

"Did you see anything?" he pressed. "Are we going the right way?"

Selena shook her head. She tried to speak, but was forced to swallow and lick her lips before words would come out. "I can't cast when I can't think." She met Lars's eyes. "I need more water and rest."

Sully snorted. "Absolute mud. Don't let her take you in, Lars. You know what her kind is capable of."

Lars ignored Sully. "You know we're low on water. Can you stand?" he asked her. She held out her hand, and Lars rose from his crouch to bring her up with him. "No rest, not here in the open," he said. "That goes for all of us." Lars glanced at the other two men as he spoke.

"So which way do we go?" Sully asked.

"The horizon's red the way we're going," said Vic, staring out at the plain. "We're heading toward the firewall."

"Which way?" Lars asked Selena.

Selena's mouth tightened. "I've already told you. I don't know."

"Nine skins, she cost us," Sully said, "and all she does is get those headaches. Sure, now and then she points us in a direction. But there's no way for us to tell if she's full of lies. I wish I'd never decided to go along with this plan of yours, Lars."

"Then leave," Lars said bluntly.

"Three of those skins were mine! You have to buy me out."

Lars smiled thinly, and Selena saw him turn his dark gaze on his wiry companion. She knew how cold those eyes could feel. "I've got one wherry skin, that's all. You can take it and you can go. Or you can stay. The choice is yours."

"I want three," Sully said.

"I don't have three," Lars said. "Look, she's said she'll help us find the white city, and that's what she's going to do. Anyone has a problem they can leave, or we can take it up with knives."

Sully scowled at Selena. "If she's no good at guiding us, we should get her to do more. Sure, she can cook, but I'm sick of carrying the firewood. She should do it."

Selena cleared her throat. She held Sully's gaze and spoke firmly. "The reason I cook is because you burn everything. But yes, I can carry the firewood. I can carry your pack and your water and rub your feet at night. Is that as far as your ambition goes?"

"It's a start," Sully said.

Selena turned her gaze to take in all three men as they watched her warily. "You three have got an opportunity you've never had before. I'll take you to the only safe place in the wasteland. Why else did you trade for me?" She combed her fingers through her long black hair as she spoke; it had become tangled with grit as she rolled on the ground. "If you would prefer to have me carry things on my back, or you would rather keep your water for yourself, you will be the fools who never get there. You all know it. We need each other. I'll do my part and get us to where we're going." She directed her words at Sully. "Focus on doing yours."

Lars gave a short laugh. "No reply, Sully? She's got you there." He harrumphed. "She's right. We should keep moving."

Sully grumbled and looked away.

The march in the blazing heat continued.

⌣

The land was featureless in all directions, barely broken up by dead bushes rolling in the wind or the occasional hermit cactus. Boulders large and small clustered in groups. Lizards scuttled underneath rocks when they sensed footsteps. Sometimes the three men and one young woman marched in the eerie crimson light of Lux alone; other times both suns scorched the flat terrain and forced them to hide in what little shade they could find. The pink strip of sky above the horizon became darker. It was clear that the distant mountain they were using as a marker was leading them toward the firewall, which might mean that Selena's earlier directions were wrong.

Selena's headache persisted for days, but she counted herself fortunate to avoid another seizure. The pain between her temples was always worse when thirst took hold, and with Vic and Sully refusing to share their water, Lars's supplies were low. Both Vic and Sully continued to complain about the trade that Lars had insisted they make.

Selena focused her determination on keeping her body moving as the three skinners walked in front of her. This wasn't the first time she had been traded like property rather than a person, but she intended for it to be the last. No matter what the three skinners believed, she knew it had been her decision that had initiated the journey. The wasteland was dangerous. She needed their help to get to the white city.

If there was one thing she knew, it was how to survive.

She remembered nothing of her parents. A girl from nowhere, she had spent her youth being passed from one group of settlers to another. Survival was something she had learned on her own, and her abilities hadn't made things any easier.

At first, as an innocent, she hadn't learned to hide the things she could do. She had told people that visitors were coming when they were still several days away. She had challenged people when they lied to her. One settler even tried to leave her alone in the waste, but she never got lost, and always found her way back. Visions came to her unbidden, and it was hard not to speak out when raiders came to plunder. There were so many threats in the wasteland that she had no choice but to heed warnings, especially when she could save lives. People she thought cared about her began to mutter about her entering their minds, and gave her or traded her to others.

As she grew wiser, she learned to hide the fact that her strength as a mystic was far beyond what people were used to, and then to hide what she was altogether. One benefit of moving around was that she had picked up skills—from foraging for edible plants to nursing a sick wherry—and she earned a safe place to sleep at night in return for caring for children or doing anything else that was asked of her.

But then the seizures came. And the group of settlers she was living with had changed over time. The kind-hearted woman who took her in had been killed by a firehound. The three men remaining gave her stares that made her fear for her safety.

She held on to her goal of going to the white city. Most people thought it was a myth. In the vastness of the desolate wasteland, how could there be a city? It was supposed to be beautiful, built of pale stone, with a soaring, graceful tower in the very center. Tall walls kept the people safe. Water was plentiful. Everyone lived in peace and harmony. A wise leader, the Protector, welcomed all newcomers.

Selena had thought it was a myth too, until, just a few weeks ago, she discovered the truth for herself. The white city was real.

Part of her hadn't known what she was searching for until she found it. The image she farcasted was hazy, like a distant mountain that might be mistaken for a cloud, but there it was. Once she knew that the white city was out there—a faraway dream but real—everything changed.

When the three skinners passed through, she seized her chance. It was a risk, but she revealed what she had seen with her talent. Lars, in particular, had seized on the opportunity. He was the oldest of the three skinners. A rover, with no one to rely on but himself, he knew that his future in the wasteland was bleak.

Yet Selena knew she wanted it more.

The white city would provide the home she had always been searching for. And there was one hope she was holding on to so tightly she would never voice it aloud. If she could only get there, the Protector might know of a way to remove the curse she had been born with.

As Selena walked, she glared at Sully's back. Her mouth was dry. Running her tongue over her lips did nothing. Vic glanced back at her and muttered something to the wiry skinner at his side.

"Can you farcast at all?" Lars asked. He looked worried as he gazed out at the landscape. A long, downward slope ahead climbed to a tall rise, crowned with a hill. "We're exposed out here."

Selena shook her head. "I can barely cast a hundred paces right now."

"That mountain we're heading for is beyond the firewall, I'm sure of it," Sully said. "This is ridiculous."

"We can skirt the firewall and still head in the same direction, can't we?" Vic asked.

"It's risky," Lars said. "We should find shelter until she recovers. The last thing we want to do is go the wrong way."

Selena scanned the plain. She couldn't see anywhere to take shelter, but at least from the circle of boulders on the next hill's summit they would have a commanding view of the area.

She felt a sudden rising dread.

Experience told her that her talent was trying to tell her something. She sensed a presence behind her. Hazy figures in her mind became distinct.

Her hand shot out and she gripped Lars's arm. "Bax," she whispered. "Behind us." Her eyes widened. Dread shifted to fear. "They've seen us."

"Blast it," Lars swore.

Sully drew a long bone dagger. His gaze narrowed at Selena. "You're sure?"

"What do we do?" Vic asked, searching wildly the way they had come.

Selena whirled. She saw a dozen bax crest the ridge behind them, this time with the clarity of her eyes rather than her muddled mind. Light brown in color, they were covered in lumps like desert toads. Their ridged spines made it appear as if they barely had necks and gave them a hunched posture like old men. But they were surprisingly fast, even in their leather armor. They brandished weapons of wood and bone, and fanned out as they ran down the slope, directly toward Selena and the three skinners.

Lars pointed to the tall hill and the ring of boulders on top of it. "We need to get up there. Now!"

Lars had barely finished speaking when Vic and Sully both broke into a run. Putting her head down, Selena sprinted after them. The grunts and rasping calls of the bax followed her. Lars puffed and panted beside her, clearly showing his age. It was hard going, racing up an incline that grew steeper as they approached the summit. She could only hope that the bax behind them found it equally difficult.

The grunts of the bax grew louder, making the area between her shoulder blades itch. Approaching feet pounded at the ground with a rumble that echoed her thumping heart. There was no doubt in her mind. Death was just behind her.

She heard the whistle of something thrown through the air. An instant later, a spear slammed into the center of Vic's back. His momentum carried him forward until he was face down on the hillside.

Then Sully went down in a tumble, and when he stopped rolling, he was coughing blood. He fumbled at the spear in his lower side. His weak movements stopped altogether.

High on the slope, Lars whirled and brandished his big axe. Red-faced and showing the whites of his eyes, he stood his ground and roared like a wild beast. Selena focused every effort on running.

Her foot struck a rock.

As her leg collapsed underneath her, she flung out her arms and saw the hillside coming up to meet her before her wrists crashed into the dirt. With every sense screaming at her, telling her that danger was behind her, she spun so that she was on her back. She faced down the slope and stared at the snarling bax rushing toward her.

Lars stood grim-faced, holding his axe and waiting. Two bax were well out in front. The first reached Lars and gave a cry, attacking with a spear. The bax's nostrils were thin slits and his eyes were dark and deep-set. Lars smashed his axe into the warrior's chest, sending a spray of green blood into the air. The second bax, with a face covered in purple warts, made a sound of rage and raised his club as he charged. Lars chopped at the bax's thick neck. His opponent went down.

More attackers were coming, slowed by the incline but still racing up the hillside. Selena tried to comprehend the rapid pace of events as her breath came short and fast. Vic and Sully were both dead. Lars looked haggard and green blood coated his leather vest.

Selena's eyes darted to Sully's body and she saw the hilt of a dagger in his hand. She threw herself forward, climbing up the hillside. As she tried to pry the skinner's fingers free, she heard a voice and looked at Lars, who met her eyes and shook his head.

"Don't fight," he said. "They might make it quick for you." With his face red and chest heaving, Lars looked much older than he had before.

Selena ignored him, grunting as she freed Sully's bone dagger. She straightened and faced down the incline, dagger held out in front of her.

But then the same awareness that sensed the bax alerted her to something new. An instant later, she saw a shape crest the opposite hill, heading directly for the bax with formidable speed. One of the bax called to his companions and, as a group, they turned to face the potential new threat.

Lars shaded his eyes. "It's a man on a wherry."

Selena waited for the man to slow and prepare himself, or to turn and run, but the wherry kept bounding toward the clustered bax. At the same time Selena realized the man was holding a bow, one of the toad-like creatures fell with an arrow in his chest. A second strike made a bax scream and try to pluck out the shaft that sprouted from his eye until he collapsed. Two more shots close together peppered another bax's body.

Selena had an impression that the man was young and tall, with dark hair. Then he charged, and she found it difficult to make out what was happening. The man threw himself from his wherry and straight into combat, fighting with a hardwood sword. He weaved between his opponents, blocking their blows and countering with savage thrusts that each left a warrior dead. The wherry fought alongside him, growling and using its size to scatter the bax, butting with its head and shoulders.

Selena exchanged a quick glance with Lars, who still stood with his axe in hand and the bodies of two bax at his feet.

As the newcomer dispatched more of his opponents, at first he looked indomitable, but then he moved to evade a bax's club and staggered, falling to one knee. The club whistled over his head, and he straightened, just in time to stab the bax through the torso. A grimace of pain crossed the man's face. His final opponent roared and ran forward, but the man appeared to have recovered, and the last bax went down with a cry.

It was over.

The bax were all dead. The man stood panting, but for some reason he didn't immediately approach.

Selena knew that he had seen her and Lars, but he didn't call out or make any sign of acknowledgment. Walking slowly, almost laboriously, he searched the area, stowing items as he found them and gathering two heavy water sacks. Selena's parched tongue roved over her mouth. The young man then hoisted the water sacks onto the wherry's back and held on to the saddle with one hand while he walked with his strange gait toward where Selena and Lars waited.

Lars gripped his axe tightly and his expression was inscrutable. Selena looked at Sully's long bone dagger in her hand. She then stared at the bodies of the two skinners, sprawled on the hillside nearby.

Lars lowered his axe, but he kept it ready. Selena regarded the man as he drew near. Now that he was close, she was surprised to see that he was young, close to her own age.

He had a sharp jaw, strong nose, and dark, piercing eyes. Close-cropped brown hair coated his head and black stubble covered his cheeks. His shoulders were wide and defined, and his leather vest did nothing to hide his broad chest. Remembering his strange walk, Selena glanced at his legs, but his animal-skin trousers and well-made boots gave nothing away.

The wherry snorted, and Selena turned to the man's steed. The wherry was a male, a relatively small one, with a hide the color of sand, floppy ears, and long eyelashes surrounding gentle brown eyes. Despite his size, his four legs were powerful, and he looked as fit and lean as the man who rode him.

The young man stood with his hand on the wherry's saddle. He glanced at Lars, assessing him, and then focused his attention on Selena. He stared at her for a long time, as if he had never seen a woman before. In contrast with his warrior's build, his eyebrows gave his face a childlike, inquisitive air. Selena was conscious of her tangled hair and the grime on her skin. She was weary, and she looked it.

Lars broke the silence. "Friend," he said with a smile, "I thank you. Those bax . . ." He trailed off.

The young man still remained silent. Then, noticing Selena's eyes on the water sacks, he reached over the wherry's saddle and held out the sloshing bladder.

"Here," he said to her. "Drink."

Selena forgot about everything else as he passed her the water. She struggled with the heavy sack and the young man stepped forward. He was close, but all he did was hold the sack up for her so she could drink. She took out the plug and her shoulders slumped as life-giving liquid splashed into her mouth. She took swallow after swallow, waiting for the man to snatch the bladder away from her, but he said nothing, and she drank her fill.

The young man next handed Lars the water sack. Lars set down his axe, laying it on the ground at his feet, but unlike Selena, he took only a few mouthfuls before handing it back with a grateful nod. The man returned the water sack to the wherry's back.

Lars spoke again. "You saved our lives. Where do you come from? Where are you bound?"

The young man's eyes were tight as he gazed at the bodies he had left behind. "They destroyed my home."

"Disgusting creatures," Lars said with a grimace. "Not so long ago, they might talk or trade, but for whatever reason they now attack humans on sight. War parties like that are everywhere. No place is safe." He cleared his throat. "What's with your leg? Are you wounded?"

Selena glanced at the young man's leg; even now, he was standing awkwardly.

"I'm fine," he said. He met Lars's gaze. "I can take care of myself."

"No one's doubting that," Lars said. "Bax are as tough as basalt wood but you knew how to bring them down."

The young man hesitated. "To be honest, that's the first time I've fought one."

Lars snorted. "I find that hard to believe."

"I was taught how to fight them."

Lars's expression became curious. "By your parents?"

"My aunt."

"A woman?" Lars grinned.

The young man's nostrils flared. "They killed her."

As Selena frowned at Lars, he cleared his throat. "Ahem. Fair enough."

"What's your name?" Selena asked.

Already the young man was becoming something more than a stranger. She had learned that he had lost his home, and tracked down those who had destroyed it. A name would make him into a person.

"Taimin." The word came tentatively, as if he hadn't introduced himself to many people before.

"I'm Lars. And the mystic—"

"I'm Selena," she interrupted.

"So if nowhere is safe, where are you heading?" Taimin asked.

It was Selena who answered. "There's somewhere that will be. We're trying to get there quickly."

Lars threw her a sharp look. She hoped she wouldn't regret her decision to mention their destination, but she knew she needed allies in order to survive the perilous journey to the white city. Vic and Sully were dead. Lars had kept her alive, but it wasn't from any altruism on his part. More than the others, Lars believed in the place she had farcasted, and was desperate to find it. But Lars wasn't a young man. Taimin had water and was a capable fighter. There was something about Taimin. She couldn't explain it . . . Perhaps she felt that if she could trust Lars, she could certainly trust him.

Selena stared into Taimin's eyes. "We're looking for the white city," she said.

Taimin's manner changed. He became completely focused on her. "It's real?" he asked incredulously.

"I've always heard rumors," Lars spoke up, "bouncing around from the rovers to the settlers and back. But the mystic here, she can cast far enough to actually see it. It's beautiful and white, with a tall tower. Newcomers are welcome. There's plenty of water, fields of crops, and safety inside its walls. The leader is called the Protector. He's wise, and watches over his people. It's the only place where everyone can live in peace."

"I thought it was a myth," Taimin said. He looked at Selena, still dubious and waiting for her to confirm what Lars had said.

She felt a flash of irritation. "It's real," she said firmly. She tried to cast now, just to confirm for herself that it was there. But the vision her talent gave her was always hazy, and even having drunk some water, she still needed rest and recovery.

"How can you be so sure?"

When Selena opened her mouth, Lars interjected. "She's a mystic," he said. "And if you've got any sense you'll follow where she leads. One thing I know is that if I spend much longer roaming the wasteland, I'll be dead before my time."

"There might be someone there who could heal your injury," Selena said.

Thoughts visibly crossed Taimin's face. His eyes lit up with hope, but then he controlled his expression. "Do you really think that's possible?" he asked cautiously.

"In the white city, anything is possible," Lars said with a grin. "Well? Will you help us find it?"

"There are people there? More people than in the waste?"

Lars barked a short laugh. "Undoubtedly. The humans in the waste are spread thin. The settlers fortify their homesteads. The rovers kill and trade, skin and hunt. You can go for weeks without seeing anyone. If the city is as big as she says it is, there'll be a chance to build a real life."

Taimin looked pensive for a moment. He then nodded to himself. "I will help you find it."

The serious way he spoke heightened Selena's sense that something important had just happened. She glanced at Taimin and he met her eyes at the exact same time.

"Whether the city is real or not, we should get moving before the scavengers come," Taimin said. "Lead the way."

5

Taimin sensed that Lars and Selena hadn't known each other for a long time. As he headed with his two new traveling companions away from the site of the recent battle, he tried not to let Selena catch him glancing at her. She had long coal-black hair and odd-colored eyes, one brown and the other green. Her features were small but sharp, with high cheekbones and ears barely visible under her hair.

Tearing his gaze away, Taimin turned his attention to Lars. He inspected the bald, bearded older man, still taking his measure. "So you're a rover," he said slowly. "Rovers killed my parents when I was young. Two brothers with pale hair."

Lars gave Taimin a black look. "Not all rovers are killers, lad."

Taimin pictured the white-haired rover's hard, angular face, and saw again the arrow that struck his mother in the cheek. He would never forget his father's pain as he lay bleeding on the ground.

Lars cleared his throat. "I'm a skinner, to be exact," he said. "That's a nice wherry you've got there. I could remove his hide with barely a mark on it."

Griff growled and tossed his head, while Taimin kept a firm grip on the reins. "I don't think he likes you," Taimin said.

"The feeling's mutual," said Lars. "I don't know how you can trust your life to one of those beasts."

"Without Griff I wouldn't be alive to hear you say that," Taimin said.

"Is that his name?" Selena asked.

"That's his name," Taimin said, patting the wherry's flank.

He was surprised when Selena reached out and stroked just behind Griff's head. The wherry even grinned when she scratched his long, floppy ears.

As Taimin walked at Griff's side, he caught Lars looking down at his leg.

"How bad is it?" the skinner asked. "Your leg."

"Bad enough." He saw Selena watching him as he replied.

"Not a good thing, to be a cripple in the waste," Lars said. "Can you run?"

"Not really," Taimin said.

"You can fight, though."

Taimin gave a brief shrug.

"Remind me not to stand too close to you, though, if there's trouble and your wherry isn't nearby," Lars said in a grim voice. "A man who fights but doesn't run is a danger I can do without."

"I was taught to avoid trouble."

Lars tugged at his thick black beard. "Trouble has a way of finding you." He glanced again at Taimin. "And I hope your aunt taught you more than just how to fight."

"What do you mean?" Taimin asked.

"You know . . . How to talk to the different races if you get into trouble. Their habits. Sure, bax have green blood, but they're the most similar race to humans." Listening to Lars, Taimin realized that the skinner must know even more than Abi. "They marry like we do, and when they do, it's for life. But the young warriors can't marry without a warden's blessing, so they have to prove themselves first."

"Warden?"

58

"It's like a chieftain. The lead bax who looks after a territory. One thing's clear: there's a warden out there who doesn't like humans one little bit."

Feeling anxious about the journey ahead, Taimin had a sudden thought. "I've got something to show you both." Reaching into his pack, he rummaged until he found the drawing he had salvaged from the homestead. "Here," he said. He passed it to Selena.

She opened up the folded paper. He watched her face as she inspected the lines that made up the image. She gave an exclamation. Her gaze roved over the high wall that surrounded a collection of buildings, with a tall, soaring tower in the very center.

He leaned toward her. "That's it?" he asked.

Selena met his eyes. "This is it. The white city. Where did you get it?"

"I found it in my aunt's things. I've no idea where she got it." Taimin left unspoken his aunt's reaction when he had asked her about the white city. *There is no city, boy.*

"Give it to me." Lars snatched the piece of paper, and as soon as he looked at it his manner changed completely. He let out a slow, steady breath, and his expression was utterly captivated as he saw the multitude of buildings, so many that it was incredible such a thing could exist in the barren wasteland. He rested his dark eyes on Taimin. "You sure you don't know anything more about who made this?"

Taimin frowned. "I'd tell you if I did."

"Lars, give it back to him," Selena said.

Lars reluctantly handed Taimin the piece of paper, and Taimin folded it and returned it to his pack. The skinner lifted his gaze. "Light's fading. I'll scout ahead."

As he watched Lars move to higher ground, Taimin realized he was alone with Selena.

"How long have you known him?" he asked.

"Lars? Not long."

"How did you know you could trust him—and his two friends?"

Her mouth tightened. "I didn't, but anywhere was better than where I was."

Taimin watched Selena, waiting for her to continue.

"Things changed. Someone I trusted died and a few newcomers joined the group. I thought we had an arrangement. I would help around the homestead in return for a place to sleep, but then . . ." Her voice trailed off. "I get headaches. They've been getting worse and the settlers I was with were becoming tired of me. I'm glad Lars took me away from them. He's using me, but I'm using him too."

Taimin wanted to ask about her family, but he sensed that she had already given him the answer. He glanced at Lars's large figure, visible in the distance as the skinner gazed out from the top of a hill.

"And you're guiding him? How?" His brow furrowed.

Selena's face registered surprise. "You really don't know what a mystic is?"

Taimin shook his head.

"It means I can farcast. It's not as common in humans, but mystics come from all the races. Sometimes I can see things with my mind I can't see with my eyes. I can cast farther than most, which might explain the headaches I get."

Taimin knew he hadn't seen much of the world, but he still couldn't hide his incredulity. "I see," he said slowly.

Selena's eyes flashed. "If you don't like the truth, next time don't ask."

Looking at her, Taimin swiftly reassessed her. Though she was undeniably pretty, she was also brittle. Just because he was trying to understand, she flared up with anger.

"How far can you . . . cast?" he asked, curious.

"It doesn't matter."

Taimin wanted to believe her, to believe that the white city was real and she had somehow seen it with her mind. Lars clearly did. At the same time, he didn't want to allow himself to hope that someday his injury might be healed. "Please," he said. "Tell me. I want to know."

She glanced at him, checking his expression, and then continued. "I see outlines and shapes better than I can make out detail. Sometimes I see things so strange I wonder if they're part of this world. If something isn't close, I often don't know how far away it is."

Deciding to reserve judgment, Taimin thought back to a time when he had gazed out at the lands below the cliffs and wondered about the wider world. "It must be a useful skill to have."

"I hate it," Selena said with venom. "My whole life people have looked at me like I'm a monster. Stories go round about mystics who read people's minds and control their thoughts. No one wants to be near me. They keep me at a distance, or tie me up because then if I try to bewitch someone they'll be able to knock me on the head and end the spell. I've taken my share of beatings for nothing. It's a curse, not a blessing."

"Then what made Lars take you?"

"Like I said, I wanted to get away from the people I was with. I told Lars about things he'd done before he arrived at the settlement. Where he camped . . . when he'd last scraped the hair from his head. I impressed him. When I told him about the city, that's when I knew I had him."

As he saw Lars returning, Taimin inspected the terrain ahead. They were on open ground, on a broad plain where anyone could see them.

"No sign of somewhere safe to camp," Lars said as he approached.

"Camp? Here?" Taimin shook his head vigorously. "This isn't a place to stop."

"I need to rest," Selena said firmly.

"I understand that," Taimin said, "but if we want to stay alive, we need to find somewhere sheltered."

Lars scratched his beard. "The lad has a point."

Selena's expression darkened. "And if we're going the wrong way? We could end up retracing our footsteps. I need to cast so that we know where to go."

"Look," Taimin said. "Even if you can do what you're saying—"

Without warning, Selena strode away. Her voice was cold as she spoke over her shoulder. "You want to keep moving?" She looked meaningfully at Taimin's leg. "Then you'd better hurry."

Lars gave Taimin a rueful grin. The skinner indicated Griff, and Taimin scowled and then pulled himself up onto the wherry's back.

In the end, Taimin found a bowl-shaped hollow where the three travelers could shelter for the night. After a cold camp, he rose early and went hunting with Griff. When he returned with a fat lizard, he found Lars quietly sharpening his skinning knife. Selena sat with her back against the rock wall. Her shoulders were slumped and her eyes stared without seeing.

Lars put a finger to his lips.

Taimin frowned but he quietly and carefully removed the saddle from Griff's back. The wherry sank to his haunches, panting as he spread out on the ground.

"Here," Lars whispered, holding out a hand. Taimin gave the bald man the lizard, and with several swift movements Lars skinned it better than Taimin could ever have done. Soon the tender flesh was separated from the bone while Griff whimpered nearby.

Taimin took some sticks and dried cactus flowers from his pack. He looped his bowstring around one of the sticks and placed the stick into a groove on another. Yanking his bow back and forth, he soon had a fire going. He glanced at Selena, but she was unresponsive. He added some larger kindling, before letting the fire die down to embers.

Lars laid the lizard meat on the coals and murmured, "Got any salt?"

When Taimin shook his head, Lars pulled a small pouch out of his pack and sprinkled a little white powder on the grilling meat.

"White gold." Lars grinned.

"What's gold?" Taimin asked.

Lars laughed, and the booming sound echoed around the rocky hollow. Selena's head moved and Taimin that saw her eyes had refocused.

"Did you see it? The white city? Which way do we go?" Lars asked.

"I saw it," Selena said. She didn't look at Taimin as she spoke. "We're heading in the right direction. The firewall curves, opening more land up ahead."

"Good, good," Lars said. "Dangers?"

She shrugged and shuffled over to take a speared piece of cooked meat from Taimin's hands without asking. "There's always danger," she said as she ate. "Nothing I could see, though. We'll soon reach two tall rocks leaning against each other. When we get there we'll be able to take another bearing."

Taimin saw that the light filtering into the hollow from above was shifting hue from red to gold, indicating that Dex was rising. He ate quickly and then threw gravel on top of the embers to put the fire out.

"We should go," Taimin said.

They swiftly packed and drank a few mouthfuls of water. The golden sun greeted them as they left the shade and began the day's journey.

———⌣———

The three travelers kept the firewall on their left as they walked ever onwards. At first Lars seemed worried that Taimin would tire and barely concealed frequent glances at his leg, but as the day progressed Taimin showed no signs of fatigue. He might not have speed, but he had endurance. His foot hurt, of course, with a pain that grew steadily, but he had learned to control the pain by keeping his mind busy and staying alert for danger. He scanned the terrain with a dedication that Lars said was unnatural.

With the crimson sun below the horizon, the rugged landscape was washed with golden light. As ever the bright blue sky was clear and the slight gusts of wind were hot and dry. Cube-shaped boulders the size of houses clustered in odd arrangements. Every time he neared them Taimin was wary; they would make excellent positions for an ambush.

They followed a canyon between two peaks, which soon opened up onto another plain. Ahead, in the distance, Taimin saw two slanted rocks on a tall hill, each the height of ten men, leaning against each other with a void underneath. Remembering Selena sitting with her eyes glazed, he stared at her in awe.

"You don't need to say anything," she said.

"From all that way—"

"Wait." She cut Taimin off with a stroke of her hand. "There's something there . . ." She hesitated. "Yes, definitely. A group of mantoreans on the hill."

Lars swiftly focused on her. "How many?"

"I can't tell."

"Try harder." Lars scowled.

Taimin squinted but the distance was too far to make out any figures. Giving up, he turned to see Selena's brow furrow in concentration. All of a sudden, she put her hand to her head and swayed. He was walking beside her and she used his shoulder to steady herself.

"Sorry," she said, taking her hand away.

"Don't try anymore," Lars said to her. "The last thing we need is you fainting."

"We're still far away," Taimin said. "If we find another route, they won't see us."

Lars thought for a moment and then shook his head. "We should go up to them. They might even trade. I have a couple of skins I could get some food for."

"Trade?" Taimin frowned. "If they were humans, maybe . . ."

Selena and Lars exchanged glances. "What did your aunt teach you about the other races?" Selena asked Taimin.

He shrugged. "She taught me how to kill them."

"There are good humans and bad humans. It's the same with the other races."

Taimin immediately pictured a snarling bax, eyes deep-set and menacing, ready to kill. "I wouldn't share a camp with a bax," he said.

She gave him a look of amusement. "I've met humans who have."

He blinked. The idea was strange.

"Leave this to me," Lars said. "Taimin, watch and learn."

Taimin's lips thinned but he didn't reply. He and Selena followed Lars toward the hill, and as they neared he shaded his eyes to look up at the two leaning rocks. His gaze kept moving until he saw something nearby, to the right. "I think I can see them. Looks like they're resting."

"Let's go up to them," Lars said. "It pays to show we're not afraid."

The terrain was graveled and devoid of anything except the occasional thorny cactus. Heat waves rolled off the ground. On Taimin's left, the sky near the horizon was red rather than blue—always a sign that the firewall was near. Taimin felt tense; as they climbed they would be visible to the mantoreans on the hill.

Soon they were approaching eight humanoid figures, clustered together near the leaning rocks. Lars turned his head toward Taimin. "No mystics with them. That's a blessing."

"How can you tell?" Taimin asked.

"Mantoreans make the best mystics but they only train females. Don't ask me why. There's none with the group. Females have an egg sack, just below their waist."

Taimin looked curiously ahead. The eight figures had stick-thin bodies and sat on the ground with their limbs folded unnaturally beneath them. Wedge-shaped heads turned to display black eyes. The three humans were nearing the summit and would soon be within speaking range.

"Wait here," Lars muttered. He held his palms out and stepped forward to approach the group resting in the shade cast by the huge leaning rocks. One of the mantoreans rose and left the others, and Taimin had his first good look at the insect-like creature.

Lars had confirmed that the mantorean was male. His body was eerily thin and his head was shaped like an upside-down triangle, with two multifaceted eyes just below his hairless crown. A pair of antennae twitched above his eyes, while two vertical scars formed nostrils halfway down his face. His mouth was tiny, and Taimin knew from Abi that he only ate plants and insects, never large pieces of meat. While the mantorean wore no clothing, a belt at his waist bore an array of tools, and a bow and a few arrow shafts poked from behind his shoulder.

Abi's voice sounded in Taimin's mind. *A mantorean's advantage is speed. Fortunately, they aren't aggressive, and prefer to talk rather than fight. They have a knack for finding water, and the females will do anything to protect their eggs, so some humans keep a female captive for just that reason. They prefer to fight with a bow and arrow, but if you do find yourself in combat, try to cut off its antennae. The pain they feel is unbearable.*

Like Lars, the mantorean also held out his hands to show he was unarmed.

"Greetings with peaceful intent," the mantorean said in a scratching, clicking voice.

Taimin glanced at Selena, who was also watching the exchange. Griff whimpered, and Taimin put his hand on the wherry's back.

"Greetings," Lars said. "Will you trade?" He pulled a folded skin out of his pack, along with the ripe-smelling skin of the lizard Taimin had caught earlier. "I have skins."

The mantorean came forward to examine the skins. Taimin heard Griff growl; the bigger skin came from a wherry. The mantorean rubbed a skin between his fingers. "We have need. Will you add one more skin to your trade?"

Taimin realized the mantorean meant Griff. "Not on your life," he said flatly.

Lars made a pushing motion with his hands. Taimin glared back at him.

"What is it you need?" the mantorean asked Lars.

"It is for you to offer," Lars said.

As the bargaining began, Taimin turned to Selena, who was lifting one of Griff's paws. She plucked out a stone and then patted the wherry on the flank. Griff gave her a grin and butted his head against her torso.

"You've spent time with wherries?" he asked. He glanced again at Lars but had the sense that the trade had only just begun.

She nodded. "He's smaller than some of the others I've seen."

"My aunt said he's a runt. One of the wherries that never become wyverns."

"I've heard it said people can ride wyverns too."

"Ride wyverns?" Taimin was incredulous.

"I've never seen it, but it's what I've heard."

"Who from?"

She scratched Griff in the place he loved, just behind his floppy ear. "One advantage of moving around is that you pick up a lot of skills. I lived for a few years with a hunter and took care of his children. He had a wherry."

"What happened?"

Selena continued to pat Griff, even as she stared into the distance. "I told him I'd seen some trulls heading our way. He didn't believe me. But I knew. He found me with his children, a boy and a girl, five and seven. We were running. I was taking them away." Her eyes were tight but her tone was matter of fact. "He beat me and took his children home. The trulls came. They killed him and his children. I was weak, but I made my way back. I loved those children. I'd watched them grow. I buried the bodies. Then I left and never looked back."

Taimin's mouth was open. "But didn't he know you were a mystic?"

"I didn't know myself. I was only twelve." Selena gave a slight shrug. "It was a long time ago."

"What made you keep going?"

"I have a dream," she said simply.

Taimin opened his mouth to ask her what it was, but she spoke first.

"Now I have a question for you," she said. "What were you thinking when you saved us? Was it just about vengeance?"

Taimin's brow furrowed. "Of course not. I saw you and I knew you were in danger."

"Then why didn't you come up to us right away? You didn't call out or wave. It was almost like we weren't there."

She was deadly serious, and Taimin wondered what he could say that wouldn't sound foolish. "In truth . . ." He hesitated. "I haven't met many people."

Her expression changed as she smiled. "You were shy? After what you just did, you were afraid of talking to some people you didn't know?"

He knew his face had reddened, but a gruff shout forestalled any reply. He saw Lars trying to get his attention.

"Lad," Lars called. The big skinner nodded at the stick-thin figure in front of him. "We're going to be here for a while, but I've learned there's a spring nearby." He indicated a broken cliff perhaps a mile away. "Best if the two of you go together." Taimin was initially surprised that Lars would be willing to let him and Selena out of his sight, but then the skinner spoke again. "Leave your packs here." He gave a dark-eyed smile. "You don't need the extra weight." He glanced at Griff. "Also . . . you don't have far to go. The wherry stays too."

6

"Wait," Taimin said. "I don't think I can do this."

Selena was already poised to gather speed and jump over the narrow crevasse that stretched in both directions. Taimin could see no way around it. She cast him a look of surprise, but then glanced at his leg.

He flushed with shame. If he had a plank or a log he could cross the gap with little trouble, but if his only option was to jump . . . He knew he would never make it across.

The terrain was rocky, stretching all the way to the broken cliff in the distance. Just fifty paces past the crevasse, a dark shadow carved an even bigger gouge in the landscape up ahead. Lars had said they would find the spring at the bottom of this wider, deeper gully.

The problem was that the crevasse made a barrier Taimin couldn't get past.

As he pondered, he heard a rush of footsteps and his gaze shot to the side. He heard Selena grunt just as she launched her slender body from the edge of the thin gap. She sailed through the air to land squarely on the other side.

Once she was across, she moved so that she was facing him. "Throw me the water sacks," she said, holding out her arms, ready to catch.

"And then what?" Taimin frowned.

"What do you mean?" she asked, puzzled. "I'll find the spring."

Taimin shook his head. "No." He looked her up and down. "Do you even have a weapon? Why didn't you bring that dagger?"

"Taimin," she said, lifting her chin. "I'll be fine. If I see anything down there I can run straight back, and you'll be here waiting." She nodded toward the gully, where a far more gentle descent beckoned. "The sooner I get down there, the better."

He wished he could give her his knife but it was in his pack, which was on the ground near Lars's feet. "Can you use a bow?"

"No," she said. "Come on. Throw me the sacks."

He reluctantly tossed her the first leather bladder, which she caught easily, before he followed with the second. But he was still troubled by her heading off alone, where he couldn't help her if there was danger. He had an idea.

"Selena, wait." He glanced over his shoulder to look back at the hill. "I'll go and fetch Lars—"

A crease of irritation formed on her brow. "Taimin," she interrupted. "I'm going."

Taimin felt helpless. He stared into her eyes and put strength into his voice. "Don't be foolish—"

Her mouth twisted. "I've managed to survive for a long time before you came along. I'm dirty and I'm tired. We need water. Lars is busy. You can't stop me."

He scowled at her, but already she was heading toward the gully. Her long black hair trailed behind her, blown by the wind. She lost height as she descended, and then all of a sudden the landscape was empty, and Taimin was alone.

He began to pace, following the edge of the crevasse that looked so narrow any child could jump it, but was much too wide for him. He imagined Selena clambering down the rock as she made her way to the bottom of the gully; it wasn't so big that she

71

would get lost, and she wouldn't take long to find the spring. She would fill up one water sack. That might take her the amount of time she had already been gone. As he waited, she was probably filling the second.

But still the moments passed.

He gnawed at his lip. He kept up his constant search for danger, and walked back and forth, back and forth. As time dragged on, he tried to stay calm, but he kept conjuring up images of something unexpected in the gully: a snake, scorpion, firehound, or something even worse.

He turned to look back at the hill once more, where the two slanted rocks leaned against each other on the summit. He couldn't see the other mantoreans, but Lars and his stick-thin companion were silhouetted against the sky.

As he returned his attention to the crevasse in front of him, and past it to the gully containing the spring, he clenched his fists at his sides. Selena should have been back by now. Something had happened. He knew it.

His eye caught movement.

The direction was unexpected, but long habit meant he never stopped scanning the horizon. He saw a row of squat, brown, hunched figures—tiny but growing larger as they followed the base of the broken cliff. Their path was angled; they were coming closer as their route led them toward the gully Selena had disappeared into.

Taimin's breath caught. Bax . . . and more than a handful of them. His pulse began to quicken. Water was precious. The approaching bax might know about the spring. Taimin could run or hide before they saw him, but Selena was down in the gully.

Perhaps she had sensed them. She might already know.

But what if she didn't?

His heartbeat shifted to a hard thumping. He had to warn her. The bax didn't appear to have spied him—their vision was worse than a human's—but if he shouted loud enough for Selena to have a chance of hearing him, they would hear too.

He had to take action.

He took several steps back, putting distance between himself and the crevasse, far more than Selena had used for her approach. Knowing he was about to test his body, he moved into a lumbering, staggering run.

He gritted his teeth. The bones moved against each other in his right foot, sending flashes of pain up his leg. When he reached the edge of the gap, he pushed hard with both legs. He put his head down and swung his arms as he jumped.

Hard rock approached with speed. He saw the steep chasm coming at him, wrinkled with jagged furrows. He was losing height too quickly.

As he slammed into the wall of the deep crevasse, his hands grabbed at anything they could. Frantic movements held him fast before his body could slide down the sheer face. As he found purchase on the natural seams, he winced: one of his fingernails had torn. His hands weren't the only part of him hurting; he had scraped his arms and torn his vest on the lower side. Lifting his gaze, he saw the lip of the crevasse a dozen feet above him, tantalizingly close.

He groaned and tried to pull his body up. The muscles in his arms tensed as he reached to a different hand hold. Moving from one position to another, he climbed higher and pushed with his good leg. He gave a final stretch and flung out his arm over the top of the wall. His other arm followed. A great heave pulled his body out of the crevasse, and he rolled over on the dirt, until he was on his back, staring up at the sky with his chest heaving.

Thoughts of Selena made him shift into a crouch. His gaze shot to the cliff. The bax were still there, and now he could make out individual warriors as they followed each other in single file.

Taimin burst into a shuffling run, taking the risk now that he was just fifty paces from the gully. The gouge in the terrain opened up in front of him. He began to clamber down the rocky slope.

The gully was crooked, shaped like an arm bent at the elbow. Taimin could only see his section, but as he hurried down to the bottom, he knew the spring must be in the part beyond, after the bend. The shadowed interior swallowed him up, but the air was warm. Soon he was on solid ground, made up of dirt and gravel. He stayed quiet but moved as quickly as he could.

He guessed that if the bax were on their way to the spring, they might already be close. His struggle in the crevasse had cost him precious time. He had to find Selena and get her to leave. If she jumped over the crevasse and rejoined Lars, the bax might decide not to give chase, especially if what they were really after was water.

As sweat broke out on his forehead, he wondered what was taking her so long, and if it would stop her getting away. She might have twisted an ankle. Dangerous beasts needed water too. Anything might have been lurking in wait for her.

He rounded the bend in the gully. Coming to a sudden halt, his mouth dropped open as he stared.

Selena faced a trickle of water that slid down an incline. Two bulging water sacks rested on the stony ground near her feet.

She was naked.

She had her back to him as she splashed water over her torso. Her black hair was wet through and draped between her shoulder blades. Her angular face was in profile, so that he could see a dainty ear and her red lips, and her brow was furrowed in concentration; she hadn't heard his approach.

For a moment, he couldn't believe he was gazing at the same girl who had boldly jumped over the crevasse. Her waist was narrow but curved at her hips, which continued down her tapered thighs and legs, where one of her knees was slightly bent. Her skin was smooth and wet with moisture. She looked fragile but she also had a power, something that made him want her more than he had ever wanted anything.

With a start, he remembered his purpose.

He cleared his throat. "Selena."

She whirled.

Her eyes went wide and her arms went over her body, one covering her chest and the other across her hips. "Taimin!"

He quickly spun so that he was facing away from her. "I'm sorry," he said. "We have to leave."

"What are you—?"

"There's danger," he insisted. "You didn't sense it? Some bax are coming."

"I have to put my clothes on."

"Do it quickly."

He heard sounds of movement and the rustle of clothing but he still didn't turn around, and waited until Selena strode past him with a sloshing water sack in each hand.

"Let me take one," he said gruffly.

Her hair, face, and neck were wet, and her tunic was dark in places that clung to her body. She almost threw the water sack into his arms, and he soon found himself hurrying to catch up with her as she left the spring behind. Her eyes roved over the area before she spoke over her shoulder. "Where are they?"

"You haven't sensed them?"

"It doesn't work all the time."

"We'll either see them as soon as we leave, or we'll know they've left the area. If we see them, we'll have to run."

Her mouth tightened. "I thought you couldn't run."

"I have to try or we'll be trapped here." His voice was grim. "If we do end up running, don't look back."

But when they climbed cautiously out of the gully, the bax were nowhere to be seen.

"There's nothing here," Selena said, turning to scan in all directions. When she looked at Taimin again, her expression was cold.

Taimin made his own careful assessment. "We're lucky. They must have moved on." He turned his attention to the crevasse. "Now I just have to figure out how to get to the other side."

"If you can do it once, you can do it again." Selena frowned. "Come on. I'll help you."

———

Selena knew she was scowling, but she couldn't smooth her expression. She wasn't someone who let anyone take advantage of her, and that meant she had become used to speaking her mind.

The mantorean Lars had been trading with had returned to his group, and the insect-like creatures all sat together, talking in low, clicking voices while they gave the humans the occasional curious glance. Lars was stuffing items into his pack: salt, twine, leather. Taimin absently patted Griff while he hoisted the bulging water sacks onto the wherry's back.

Selena set her mouth in a thin line. Making a decision, she walked toward Taimin with long, angry strides.

"Taimin," she said flatly.

"Selena," he said, smiling as he turned to face her. His smile faded when he saw her face. "What is it?"

"There were no bax."

His brow furrowed. "I don't understand."

"There were no bax," she repeated. "You made them up."

Realization dawned in his eyes. Color came to his cheeks; he was obviously remembering the encounter at the spring. Thoughts visibly crossed his face, but slowly his expression changed.

"That's not true," he said, meeting her gaze. "I wouldn't lie to you. And especially not like that."

"I've been around a lot of men—"

"But you haven't been around me," he said.

Without another word, Taimin led Griff away.

Selena had been prepared for lies or obfuscation. Taimin's reaction wasn't what she had expected. She tried again to farcast, allowing her eyes to become unfocused and her mind to wander. Again, she found nothing.

But her talent could be unreliable. She turned her head, and found herself watching the distant, broken cliff.

The golden sun had moved to a lower position in the sky. The hilltop with the two leaning rocks was high, with a clear view in all directions. Following the bottom of the cliff, where their path would have taken them, she saw a line of shadows. The shadows were cast by tiny figures, walking in single file. Only one race had that strange, hunched posture.

As soon as she saw the group of bax, Selena's eyes widened. She turned back to Taimin. Now that she was inspecting him, she saw scratches on his arms and hands. A few of the grazes looked bad. He had torn his vest low on his abdomen, revealing an angry red patch where he had smashed his body against the rock.

He had risked his life to warn her.

She glanced at Lars. He would have left. If Lars had to choose between putting himself in danger, and leaving her behind, he would go without a moment's thought. Even if it meant finding the white city for himself.

She returned her attention to Taimin. He looked toward her and held her stare. There was depth in his eyes. They were brown and warm. The golden sun burnished his dark hair and made his skin glow.

The moment was interrupted when she saw the mantorean Lars had traded with walk over to Taimin. She was close enough to hear the exchange.

"I saw your supply is low. These are for you, young warrior," the mantorean said.

Taimin's face showed surprise as the insect-like creature held out a bundle of arrows. "Why?" he asked. "I don't have anything to trade."

"They are my gift to you. Not all humans are kind to my race. Please take them and remember. Perhaps you will treat the next group of mantoreans well."

Taimin thanked the mantorean as he took the arrows. His face was troubled, and Selena remembered their conversation when they were approaching the hill for the first time.

Lars's growling voice made them both turn. "Come on, both of you. It's time to go."

7

"Take off your vest," Selena said.

Taimin was leaning with his back against a rock wall, resting in the shade. Not far away, Griff was sprawled out, fast asleep. A rumbling sound came from Lars, who lay snoring on his blanket under the shelter of an overhang. The golden sun Dex blazed from high in the sky. The day was still, without the slightest wind to dispel the heat. Until Dex began to fall, travel was unthinkable.

Taimin stared wide-eyed up at Selena. "What?"

She crouched at his side. Her voice was firm. "I need you to take off your vest." Taimin noticed that she had a clean cloth and a water flask in her hands. When she saw his reluctance, she raised an eyebrow. "You saw me naked, but you're too shy to take off your vest?"

"I didn't choose to see you naked," Taimin said. As soon as he said it, he wished he could take the words back.

"Ah, so you did see me."

"No. Yes."

Cursing his tongue, he stopped talking, and instead gave a sigh and pulled his vest over his head. He glanced down at himself. His chest was lean; there was no soft layer below the skin at all. His abdomen rippled with ridges, and from his navel a sparse trail of dark hair vanished below the waistline of his trousers. The graze on one side of his chest looked bad, but he'd had worse. Black specks on the wound indicated bits of rock or dirt.

"Lean back," Selena said. She inspected the wound for a time, so close to him that a few strands of her black hair tickled his chest.

"Do you know about wounds?" Taimin asked.

She looked up at him. "I took care of children," she said; clearly she thought that explained enough.

Splashing water onto her cloth, she began to scrape against the graze. Taimin drew in a sharp breath and his muscles tensed in the area where she was working. She had to apply pressure to get out some of the deeper dirt. Yet despite the stinging sensation, Taimin's mind was on something else altogether. Her body was so close to his. Her touch was gentle as she finished her task.

"There," she said. "All done."

Taimin pulled on his vest and then cleared his throat. "Selena." He hoped he wasn't going to say the wrong thing. "The white city . . . is that your dream?" He glanced at the sleeping older man. "I know why Lars wants to go there. He's old. Me, I'd do anything to become whole again. Why are you so determined to get there?"

She hesitated. As she sat beside him, he didn't want her to leave. "Perhaps I shouldn't have said anything."

"Please. Tell me."

She looked away for a moment, and he knew that what she was about to say was important to her. After gathering her thoughts, she turned back to face him. He stared into her eyes and waited for her to speak.

"Sometimes things have a place," she said. "They belong in their place; they fall into the same arrangement, time after time." She paused. "It's like when your pack settles on your shoulder, or when you put a knife back in its sheath. At night, a wherry returns to its bed. Do you know what I mean?"

"Like the groove on my bow. When I draw an arrow, it slots into the right place every time."

"Exactly." She reached out. "Give me your hand."

He gave her his hand and she clasped their two palms together. Her skin was smooth. Her hand was smaller than his, but there was no gap between them—they fit together perfectly.

"Like this," she said. "Sometimes, things fit together. Everything needs a place, a purpose. Everyone needs to fit into their place. A home. A life. People who care about you."

The look she gave him was heavy with intent. He still held her hand. He never wanted her to let go.

She gave a last, firm statement. "That's what I want." He felt he had lost something as she pulled her hand away.

"There's more to it," he said. He didn't know how he knew, he just did. "It's something to do with your talent." Her smile faded as soon as he mentioned it. "I'm right, aren't I?"

"I told you. It's not a talent, it's a curse."

"And you want it gone."

Her face was troubled. "Everyone says that the Protector of the white city is wise. He might be able to help me."

Taimin tried to understand. He still thought that what she could do was incredible, and hated to see her despise a part of herself. "Everyone has something that makes them unique," he said slowly. He gave a wry smile. "Even me, with my foot."

"You're not a cripple," she said firmly. "You're a man with a limp, and that's all."

Making a decision, he continued to stare into her eyes. "You want to remove your curse. What if there's another way? It's a part of you, isn't it? You were born with it. You said that you're not the only mystic in the wasteland. What if you could instead find someone to teach you about your abilities?"

His heart sank when she climbed to her feet and stared down at him. "Teach me to do the terrible things I've been blamed for?" Her tone was scathing. "People do stupid things. They lie to each other. They steal. They also don't like to take responsibility for what they've done. So who gets blamed? Who could have bewitched them?" She lifted her chin. "Me."

All of a sudden her face contorted with pain.

"Selena!"

Taimin rushed to catch her as she fell. As he lowered her to the ground, she put her hands to her temples. Then she rolled onto her back and began to writhe.

"Lars!" Taimin cried. "I need help!"

Crouched over her, he saw Selena grit her teeth and press her hands so tightly against her head that her knuckles turned white. He felt helpless.

He could only hope that there was someone in the city who could help her.

───────

Selena's recovery was quick, but her seizure meant she was unable to farcast for days. As the two suns rose and fell over a barren landscape, Taimin wasn't the only one who wondered if they were still heading in the right direction. He walked sometimes with Lars, but more often side by side with Selena. He sometimes glanced at her and thought about her curse, and although he didn't say anything, he felt remorse for ever doubting that what she could do was real.

As the journey progressed, the fear of a deadly encounter drove them on. Lars always reminded them that with bax destroying homesteads and killing humans on sight, nowhere but the white city would be safe.

Now Taimin glanced anxiously up ahead. After a long day's travel, the light was fading rapidly. They were following a snaking gully, an ancient riverbed where the occasional bush or skeletal tree framed what were once the river's banks. The deepening shadows could hide anything.

A low howl might have been the wind, but the air was completely still. Taimin's heart gave a jolt. "Did you hear that?" He cast a swift glance at Lars.

Lars nodded grimly. "Firehounds."

Taimin tried not to look at Selena. He knew she would feel guilty for the erratic nature of her talent.

"We'd be boxed in if they found us here," Taimin said. He became silent for a time, scanning the terrain as he walked with Griff at his side. "There. See it? That big tree with the bush at the bottom. It'll give us something to put at our backs."

"Good idea," Lars grunted.

But as they neared, Selena gave a low exclamation. She stopped in her tracks. "Wait. Look . . . There's someone already there."

The glow of firelight flickered against the gnarled tree that loomed over the gully. Taimin glanced anxiously at Lars. "Bax?"

"Maybe," Lars said uncertainly. He made a decision. "I'm going to get a closer look."

"I'll go—" Taimin began.

"Lad," Lars interrupted. "I might be old but I'm quicker on my feet. Both of you, wait here."

Lars left Taimin and Selena to climb the bank of the dried riverbed. Keeping his body low, the skinner moved closer to the tree, before sinking to one knee and watching for a moment. Once Lars had taken a look at whoever was tending the fire, he scurried back to his two companions.

"A human," Lars said in a low voice. "Looks like he's alone."

"It's risky," Taimin said. "Having a fire."

Another sonorous howl filled the night, louder this time. Remembering the story of how Abi had got her scar from a pack of firehounds, Taimin tensed.

"Or smart," Lars said.

Taimin thought for a moment. "He'd probably be happy to see us. The firehounds will avoid a group."

Selena's expression was wary. "What can you tell us about him?"

Lars shrugged. "He's middle-aged. Got a stack of tinder." He scratched at his black beard. "All right. We'll show ourselves. There's three of us and one of him. Just keep your wits about you."

As they cautiously approached the gnarled tree, they soon saw the stranger. He had been seated as he tended his fire, adding more kindling from a large pile, but when he heard Lars announce himself he leaped to his feet and stared with frightened eyes into the darkness. Dark-haired and slim, with a short beard and an open face, he brandished a cudgel studded with thorns in his left hand. With a start, Taimin saw that the stranger's right hand was missing, cut off at the wrist.

"We meet in peace," Lars said.

When he saw that Taimin, Lars, and Selena were keeping their hands visible, the man's shoulders relaxed slightly, but his eyes were still tight and wary.

The stranger made the same reply that Taimin had first heard as a child. "Trade brings civilization to the waste."

Despite the ritual greeting, Taimin was older now, and wiser. The two brothers had said those words, and then killed his parents. The stranger might be a different sort of man, but he still held his thorn-studded cudgel.

"We saw your fire," Lars said.

"I had to make a choice," the stranger said. "There might be bax around, but there's no use worrying about bax if a firehound gets me."

84

"Makes sense." Lars rested his dark gaze on the stranger. "We heard them too. Can we share your camp?"

The stranger looked from Lars to Taimin, to Selena. "How do I know you won't murder me in my sleep?"

"What would we murder you for?" Lars said bluntly. He cast his eyes over the stranger's camp. "You don't look like you have much."

The stranger hesitated. "You've got meat?"

A familiar calculating expression appeared on Lars's face. The skinner knew when there was bargaining to be done. "That depends. Have you got information?"

"I can tell you where there's a grove of lifegiver cactuses."

Taimin decided to speak up. With Griff at his side, he could always bring in meat. Lifegiver cactuses meant water. "We'll share our meat."

The stranger gave a smile and a nod. "Then you're welcome to share my fire, and I'll tell you where to go. Name's Callum."

Introductions were swiftly given. As Taimin, Lars, and Selena chose places near the fire, Callum noticed Taimin's limp.

"Not easy, is it?" Callum asked. "I've got my own war wound." He displayed the empty sleeve where his hand should have been. "I'm not a rover by choice. Fact is, I won't last long, not fighting with my left hand."

Griff peered up at Taimin and then looked at Callum curiously. Taimin watched in surprise as Callum held out his left hand and the wherry came toward him and nuzzled his head against Callum's abdomen. Callum patted the wherry, scratching him in all his favorite places. Griff gave a rumble of appreciation.

"I had a wherry once," Callum said to Taimin. His eyes became misty. "Loved that creature. I miss him."

Everyone was soon seated. As Selena drank from her flask and Lars rummaged in his pack, Taimin felt glad to be off his feet. He squeezed at his right boot, massaging it, and looked across the fire at the one-handed man. "What happened to your wherry?"

Callum continued to scratch Griff along his belly, while the wherry sprawled out beside him. "He helped me fight off the trulls that took my homestead." He held up his right arm again. "Died saving my life, and the trulls did this."

Taimin felt a strong pang of sympathy. Like Taimin, Callum had lost everything, but at least Taimin still had Griff. Struggling to survive one-handed must be even more difficult than managing with a crippled foot.

Two loud howls interrupted his thoughts, one after the other. Everyone's head turned toward the direction the howls had come from.

Callum climbed to his feet. "That sounded close. I'm going to see if I can catch sight of them."

Taimin nodded. "We'll get some food on."

As soon as Callum was gone, Selena spoke in a low murmur. "What do you think of him?"

"He seems all right," Lars said noncommittally. The skinner laid strips of lizard flesh over a flat rock placed in the middle of the coals.

"It must be hard for him, all alone," Taimin said. "He might want to find the white city with us." He glanced at Selena. "You said we have to keep an open mind."

"I said you can't judge by race," Selena said. "Just because he's human doesn't mean we should trust him right away."

"Don't mention the city," Lars said. "Not yet."

The brief conversation ended when Callum returned. "Five firehounds in a pack." The one-handed man added another stick to the embers. Sparks shot into the air and the fire crackled. As he settled himself, he looked over to meet the eyes of each onlooker in turn. "We'll have to watch in shifts tonight." His voice firmed. "I'm going to have to insist I take the first watch."

Lars's eyes narrowed. "And why is that?"

"Once we make it to midnight there's less chance of an attack. No offence, but I know I can trust myself to stay awake."

"Not so fast," Lars said flatly. He nodded toward Taimin and Selena. "I know these two a lot better than I know you. We'll take the first three watches. You can have the dawn shift. Don't forget, we're the ones with meat."

Callum opened his mouth to retort, but shut it again when Lars met him stare for stare. He gave a sigh. "Have it your way. Dawn watch it is." Lars handed out the hot meat, and for a moment there was silence as everyone ate, hungry after the tantalizing cooking odors. Callum then took a long swig from his water flask. "Hope you don't mind, but I'm going to catch what rest I can. You three can sort out the other watches."

Soon Callum was lying on his side with his back to the others. As the one-handed man's breathing evened out, Taimin realized he hadn't heard a firehound's howl for some time. Nonetheless, he turned to Selena.

"Keep your dagger close by," he said softly. "Get some sleep." He then addressed Lars. "I'll wake you in a few hours."

As Selena spread out her blanket, Taimin sat by the fire with his sword on his lap and bow on the ground nearby. Lars added some more tinder to the fire before spreading out his bulk. Soon Taimin was the only one awake. Griff's snores were the loudest of all.

8

Taimin woke with a gasp. He wondered what it was that had startled him, but then his mind began to clear: he had heard a distant whine, followed by a yelp. He was certain it hadn't been a dream.

He sat up swiftly and scanned the camp. The embers of the fire still glowed. It was close to dawn, with the golden sun gradually brightening the sky. The gnarled tree cast a long shadow. Taimin's gaze went to Selena: she was sleeping peacefully nearby. Lars's chest rose and fell as a low rumble came from his throat.

Callum was gone. And so was Griff.

Taimin's heart beat with sudden fury. He shot to his feet. "Wake up!" he cried.

Without waiting for Lars and Selena, Taimin grabbed his sword and bow. He began to circle the area, reading the tracks in the way his aunt had taught him. It didn't take him long to find Griff's claw marks. He followed the tracks away from the riverbed, toward the open plain.

He searched frantically until he found a scatter of blood and a few specks of raw flesh. Callum had his own meat after all.

Taimin cursed. He shouldn't have let Griff become so trusting. He shouldn't have been so trusting himself.

Griff was always hungry in the morning. It didn't take Taimin long to build up a picture of what had happened. Callum had lured Griff away from Taimin with the promise of an early breakfast. Despite his one hand, the desperate thief was experienced with wherries. He hadn't bothered with the saddle but he had taken the reins. Throwing himself onto Griff's back, he had dug in his heels and forced his will upon the wherry.

Taimin's friend had needed him. Griff had called out, and Taimin hadn't been there.

More tracks confirmed it. Taimin saw Griff's opening stride. He hurriedly followed the trail and saw where Griff had tried to pull round sharply. Callum had savagely turned the wherry onto the path he wanted.

Taimin was finding it hard to breathe. He heard Lars's voice, and turned his head to see Lars and Selena both watching.

"Why didn't he kill us?" Lars asked in wonder. "He could have."

"He just wanted Griff," Selena said. She gave Taimin a look of mingled anxiety and sympathy. "We shared our food with him. He thinks he'll outrun us easily."

Taimin shook his head. "No, he won't." He set his mouth in a thin line. "I'm going to track him down."

"Let me try," Selena said.

As she became still, Taimin began to pace.

His eyes kept returning to Griff's tracks. He threw frequent glances in Selena's direction. The moments passed. He realized he was breathing too fast, but there was nothing he could do to control it. He clenched and unclenched his fists. His jaw was so tight that it felt like he would grind his teeth into powder.

Selena put her hand to her temples. But as Taimin looked at her in hope and desperation, she shook her head. "I'm sorry," she said sadly. "I need more time."

"I don't have time," Taimin said. He returned his attention to the tracks. "I'm going."

"It's a hopeless task," Lars said.

"Taimin, let me help you," Selena called after him.

He ignored them both and strode away as quickly as he could manage.

Taimin stood in the middle of a vast stretch of rock. Like a smooth, rippling blanket, it spread out to coat a great portion of the plain. There wasn't a blade of desert grass or a patch of dirt in sight. The tracks he had been following had vanished as soon as he had reached the area.

Callum was wily. He knew the terrain he had been traveling in. To confuse any pursuit, he had taken Griff to a place where he could change his path and anyone following wouldn't be able to track him.

Taimin's despair combined with his frustration and guilt. His eyes burned. He wanted to scream and cry. As he stood and turned in circles, his entire body ached. Without warning, his right leg collapsed underneath him. He crumpled to the ground and blinked away his tears.

Griff was his last connection to the life he had left behind. Taimin had looked after Griff, and in turn Griff had taken care of him. Griff had helped him to look forward to life. He could still have hope, as long as he had his friend and companion by his side.

He remembered the day he had found Griff. The wherry had been alone and afraid, but Taimin had rescued him and brought him back to health. He knew he would give anything to see Griff's grin and his soft, mournful eyes . . . to have his spirits lifted by Griff's eager, boundless energy.

Taimin had failed. He was alone. A harsh world awaited him. His aunt's warnings about the difficulty of life as a cripple came back to him with force.

More than anything, he missed his old friend.

——— ———

It was almost completely dark when Taimin finished retracing his footsteps. With bowed shoulders, trudging wearily, he approached the gnarled tree. He didn't expect Selena and Lars to have waited for him, but he had no other plan.

Filled with despair, he was surprised to see the cheerful light of a fire. The flames were tall and provided a guide so that even as dusk settled on the plain, he could easily find his way. He hobbled slowly, painfully. Each step made him grimace.

He soon saw the tree's trunk, and the fire nearby, silhouetting two figures.

His eyes widened. He came to a sudden halt.

It couldn't be. There was a third shape, but it was low and sand-colored, with four legs.

As Griff came racing toward him, Taimin's exhaustion didn't stop him from shifting into a lumbering run. He bent down and opened up his arms.

Griff slammed into him. The wherry growled and whined. He pushed into Taimin with his head, and then drew away to circle around Taimin before crashing into him again, as if the wherry was unable to make up his mind what to do. Taimin hugged Griff over and over. He had never seen Griff so excited, but also knew how he felt himself. He realized he was crying, and a surge of warmth kept bursting throughout his body. With wet cheeks, he wrapped his arms around the wherry and tried to pull him close, but Griff was so animated that Taimin could barely catch hold of him.

When at last he looked up, he saw Selena and Lars watching him.

Taimin straightened. "I don't understand," he said. He wiped his face and tried to control his expression. "How?"

Selena smiled. "It's always easier if I know someone. Even a wherry."

"You found him?" Taimin asked in wonder. He glanced at Lars, who still hadn't said anything. "What happened? What about Callum?"

"It was all her," Lars said with a nod in Selena's direction. "Seems Callum was struggling to stop your wherry from turning back. We found them both pretty quickly." He shook his head. "I didn't have much choice. She said if I didn't help her, she wouldn't guide me anymore."

"Selena . . ." Taimin said. "I don't know how to thank you."

"You would do the same for me," she said seriously.

Taimin tried to put everything he was feeling into his next words. "I would."

He would move mountains for her, if she asked him to. In that moment. Taimin realized that he wasn't alone at all. He had Griff. He also had her.

Lars harrumphed. "It's been a long day for us all. Come on, lad. It's time for a meal."

"Callum got away, then?" Taimin asked as he followed the skinner. He still kept one hand on Griff's back. The pain in his foot was bad, but inside he felt as light as a feather.

"Something like that," Lars said.

As soon as the skinner spoke, Selena's face became pale. Something crackled in the fire, and Taimin looked past them both.

He saw an empty pack by the fire, and a thorn-studded cudgel, burning at the edge of the embers.

9

"The key is to get access to the heart," Taimin said. As he spoke he knelt directly in front of the broad green trunk of the lifegiver cactus and used his knife to widen a hole the size of his head. "Watch out for the spikes." He tossed chunks of pale green flesh to the side while he worked. "They're even sharper than they look." He glanced at Selena, standing nearby, to see if she was following what he was doing.

"You make it look easy," she said with a smile.

"It takes some practice, but I'll let you have a go when we find another."

He reached deep into the hole he had made and felt around. There was wetness, but not as much as there should be if he had reached the heart of the cactus. He was forced to focus his full attention on his task as he cut slabs away from the interior of the sturdy plant. Something burst and a gush of liquid poured out. The sweet-smelling water then flowed directly into the depression he had carved near the entrance to the hole.

"Got it." He turned around and grinned.

But then his smile faded.

High in the sky behind her, Taimin saw a pair of spread wings that supported a lean body and a narrow head. Open jaws revealed rows of sharp teeth. The wyvern was already swooping. As the creature plummeted like a stone, its eyes were focused on Selena.

The wyvern's claws would grip her shoulders in moments.

"Look out!" Taimin cried.

Fear coursed through him, heightening his senses. He ran toward Selena as quickly as he could. Wings snapped and cut through the air. He heard a piercing shriek. Grasping talons flexed.

Taimin launched himself forward. He crashed into Selena and threw her down until she was lying on her back. He stayed on top of her while the swooping wyvern cried out in frustration and shot into the air again.

Taimin watched the wyvern and stayed where he was. The winged creature soared through the sky until it disappeared behind a tall peak. Taimin checked for a few moments longer, searching warily, and then he knew it wouldn't be back. They were at the bottom of a cliff that rippled with a multitude of alcoves. The wyvern had probably gone back to its nest.

"It's gone," Taimin said. He focused on Selena. "Are you all right?"

She nodded, and that was when Taimin realized that he was lying over her, with his face just above hers.

Her lips were moist. His heart began to race, and it was nothing to do with the wyvern's failed attack. She stared up at him, directly into his eyes. Her chest was rising and falling, just as quickly as his.

"Anyone hurt?" Lars called out, approaching from the direction of the cliff where he had been hunting for lizards.

"We're fine," Taimin replied. He rolled off Selena and returned to his feet. He put on a smile and held out a hand to help her up.

His heart was still pounding. She had been so close, right underneath him. He looked back at her. She didn't appear to be angry. He cleared his throat. "Selena," he said softly and then hesitated. "Sorry . . ." He faltered, unsure what to say next.

She frowned, perplexed. "For what?"

Lars was now close enough to interrupt. "There's a snake behind you," he said.

Selena whirled. "Where?"

"Ended your conversation, didn't I?" Lars barked a laugh. "Come on. We need to keep moving."

Days became weeks as the three travelers navigated the wasteland. They followed gullies carved by long-vanished water, crossed broad plains under the shadow of mountains, and skirted the edges of escarpments where cliffs dropped away for thousands of feet. Selena farcasted. Taimin hunted and Lars skinned. Griff began to follow Selena around nearly as much as he followed Taimin.

As Selena walked beside Taimin, she was surprised to realize it was now the way they usually traveled. He was the first man to make her feel safe. She liked it when he taught her about survival in the wasteland. But at the same time, they often argued.

"Have you ever wondered if your aunt went too far?" Selena asked. She glanced over at him. "She thought she had to make you strong, so now you think strength is everything."

Taimin frowned. "Perhaps it's safe in the white city, but out here, without strength, a cripple can't survive long."

Selena's lips thinned. "I hate it when you call yourself that," she said. "And strength isn't everything. I can't fight the way you can, but here I am. I've managed to survive."

"By getting other people to do your fighting for you," Taimin said.

She struggled not to flare up. He had a way of making her angry; it was the way he always thought he was right. "Yes," she said. "What's wrong with that? Humans form groups, in case you

95

hadn't realized. If you're strong, but you don't understand people and how to work with them, you won't last long."

"When I'm healed, and within the walls of the white city, then I'll relax my guard."

Selena felt frustrated. She understood what he was saying, that the wasteland was always dangerous, but he wasn't even trying to understand the point she was trying to make.

She let out a slow breath as she focused her attention on the terrain. It had been unnerving in the plains, exposed where anyone could see them, but now that they were in a region of cliffs, canyons, and ravines, threats might come from anywhere. They were following the edge of a rocky slope that climbed and then leveled off. Deep wrinkles carved the treacherous heights.

Then something strange happened. A voice spoke to her. And the voice was inside her head.

Please. Help me.

Selena realized she had stopped. Taimin was calling her name.

"Selena?" His face was alarmed. "What's wrong?"

Rather than reply, she shook her head. She turned toward the graveled slope and then her eyes glazed. An indistinct impression came to her: a stick-thin creature with a triangular head.

The voice came again; it spoke in staccato tones, but sounded female. *I can sense you. Your power is so strong I felt it as soon as you were near. Please.*

"Lars!" She heard Taimin calling.

Selena shook herself and saw that both Taimin and Lars were staring at her. "Someone needs help," she said.

Taimin's face was puzzled, but Lars soon realized.

"Another mystic?" The skinner tugged on his thick black beard and then shook his head. "It could be a trap. Ignore it."

Selena returned her attention to the hillside that climbed and climbed until it leveled out in a plateau. "I think it's a mantorean. She's up there."

"We should stay out of trouble," Lars insisted.

Ignoring Lars, Selena slipped her pack off her shoulder so that it thudded to the ground. She began to walk, and as soon as she reached the treacherous slope, hopped from one rock to the next to take herself higher.

She heard Taimin's voice. "I'm going with her," he said.

"Then you're as much of a fool as she is," Lars growled. He raised his voice to call out to Selena. "How will I find the white city if you're dead?"

Selena glanced over her shoulder and saw Taimin hurrying to join her. He had also left his pack with Lars, and rather than trust his footing, he used his hands to steady himself as he climbed.

"Griff, stay there," Taimin said.

Lars stood next to Griff and called after them. "I'll be here when you get back." His tone became ominous. "If you get back at all."

⁓

The mantorean was stuck in a crevice, her thin body wedged tightly as she stared up at the two humans peering down at her. Selena had no idea how long she had been trapped, but she was in a wretched state. Her antennae drooped. Her bone-colored carapace was covered with dirt and tiny bits of gravel. The expression she gave Selena was pleading.

Selena's first thought was to offer her flask. She leaned over the narrow defile and stretched down her hand, while the mantorean's insect-like limb stretched up to take it. "Here," she said.

The mantorean's multifaceted black eyes gave nothing away but she drank thirstily; her mouth was tiny, but it could open up surprisingly wide. It took a long time until she was done, and then she stretched her limb as high as she could to return the flask.

Taimin was in the same position as Selena, flat on his stomach as he gazed down to assess the mantorean's predicament. "What happened?" he asked. "Have you broken anything?"

"My group was attacked by trulls. We scattered. Anyone who made it probably thinks I'm long dead." The mantorean's antennae gave a swish that Selena instinctively knew was an expression of agitation. "I hold on to the hope that my hatchlings are still alive."

"I think I can pull you out," Taimin said, "but it might hurt."

"Please. I am desperate," the mantorean implored as she stretched her arms toward the sky.

Taller than Selena, Taimin leaned down as far as he could. Rather than clasp hands, he gripped the mantorean's forearms as she took hold of him between the wrist and elbow. Taimin drew in a breath, held it, and then his face began to turn red.

It was too dark near the mantorean's legs for Selena to see, but she heard something shift. The mantorean gave a cry of pain. Taimin froze.

"Do you want me to stop?" he asked anxiously.

"No," the mantorean said with force. "Please. Keep going."

Once more Taimin tensed as he prepared himself. When he began to pull, veins stood on his neck and forehead. Selena bit her lip. She heard rocks moving against each other, and then the mantorean began to move upward. His forehead coated in sweat, Taimin drew in another breath to bring the creature higher, and now Selena could help. She grabbed the mantorean under her arms and heaved.

All of a sudden, the three of them spilled out onto the rocky ground beside the crevice. Then everything became still. A warm breeze blew across the ground. Two suns, one red and the other golden, beat down from overhead. The sound of heavy panting filled the air.

Selena stared up at the sky. She heard clambering, and turned her head to see Taimin standing beside her to offer her his hand. She gripped his palm and he pulled her up. The mantorean's limbs unfolded as she brought herself to her feet.

"Nothing is broken," the mantorean said in her stilted voice. "I am fortunate."

Selena nodded toward the direction she and Taimin had come from. "We have food and water. Will you come with us to rest?"

The mantorean shook her head. "I do not eat the same things you do. I must try to find my hatchlings."

"Then—" Selena began.

"Wait," the mantorean said. She looked from one human to the other. "You saved my life. I owe you a debt. I realize I have little to offer, but there must be something I can do."

Selena opened her mouth to say that she only wanted to help, but Taimin spoke first, forestalling her. He had a strangely thoughtful expression on his face.

"You're a mystic?" he asked.

"Yes," the mantorean said. She rested her black eyes on Selena. "I do not have this one's power, but I have trained since I was young."

"Can you help her?" Taimin asked the mantorean.

She tilted her triangular head. "In what way?"

As Taimin met Selena's eyes, his expression was deadly serious. "Selena . . . Ask her."

Selena finally realized what Taimin was talking about. She knew that when she asked her question, whatever the answer was, it would change everything. "Can you remove my power?"

"Remove it?" The mantorean's voice was surprised. "No, that is not possible."

Selena felt a catch at the back of her throat. For a moment, she didn't trust herself to speak. "Oh."

"But . . ." the mantorean paused, "I can help you to wall it off. To you, it would be as if you had no ability at all."

Hope rose, spreading its way through Selena's body. "The headaches?" she asked.

"Gone." The mantorean gave a swift look up at the sky. "It will take time. An hour or more."

Taimin reached out and took Selena's hand. "This is what you've always wanted," he said softly, giving her hand a squeeze. "I'll find Lars and tell him you'll join us soon."

Taimin sat beside Lars in the shade of a boulder. He stood quickly when he saw Selena's familiar slender figure and long black hair blowing in the breeze.

Leaving Lars behind, Taimin ran toward her until he was facing her. He came to a halt as he searched her face. Just by looking at her, he could tell that something had changed.

"How do you feel?" he asked.

Her serious expression shifted. As if throwing off a heavy weight, a lightness came over her as she smiled. "The same."

"You didn't do it?" Taimin's mouth dropped open. "But it's what you've always wanted."

"If I had, how would we find the white city? If I couldn't farcast anymore, we might never get there."

Taimin couldn't believe the opportunity she had given up. But at the same time, as he gazed into her eyes, one brown and the other green, he could.

"What we're doing is about more than our problems," she said. "It's about a home, and a new life. We're going to find the white city, and we're going to do it together."

10

The sour stench of smoke hung in the air, heavy and cloying, so that every time Taimin inhaled, his mouth twisted. The destruction had taken place only recently. Flies buzzed around the bodies. There were three of them, all adults, but burned as they were it was impossible to tell if they were men or women.

Taimin tried to hide his emotions, but he was seeing the ruins of the homestead with blurred vision. Griff lay near his feet and whined. Perhaps the wherry was picking up on Taimin's mood, or Griff was remembering too.

The homestead had been partially hidden, located in a basin between the hills of the rolling plain. It had been fortified, with a ditch and a tall fence. The settlers had done all they could, but as with Taimin's homestead near the firewall, peril had come anyway.

"Bax," Lars said from a stone's throw away. "Their tracks are everywhere."

The bald, bearded skinner kicked around the timbers, looking for any tools or supplies worth salvaging, although Taimin had known from a swift glance that he'd be lucky to find anything at all.

"Taimin." He turned to face Selena and realized she was standing right beside him. She was looking at him in sympathy. "You're remembering, aren't you?"

He knew his tone was bitter. "How can you say we can't judge them?"

"These bax were bad," she said softly. "Evil. I wouldn't blame you if they were here and you wanted to kill them all. But remember: humans do the same things to bax, to mantoreans, to skalen, and to trulls."

Taimin took a deep breath as he tried to compose himself and smooth his expression.

"Stop it," Selena said. "You can't be strong all the time, or you won't be strong when you need it most."

The burned-out homestead didn't only make Taimin think of his aunt; it was hard not to dwell on his parents' deaths too. He didn't know why the world had to be such a harsh place. All he knew was that this savagery couldn't go on. What if these settlers had sought safety in the white city, rather than face the wasteland on their own? They would still be alive.

"The men who killed your parents were evil too," Selena said, making him wonder if she could somehow read his thoughts from his face. "One day you might find them, and do what you need to do. You need to understand, though, that the world will stay the same."

When Taimin next looked at Selena, he wore his emotions openly, rather than trying to suppress them.

"Come on," she said. "It's not safe here. We should go."

Soon after leaving the burned-out homestead behind, Selena announced that the white city was close, just behind the next range of mountains.

With renewed determination the three travelers pressed on. They worked together, hunting, finding water, making camp, and keeping watch. They talked about what they might find when they reached their destination. Taimin and Selena still argued, but something had changed between them. She made him think about a world where survival depended on more than simple strength. He continued to teach her skills so that, if she had to, she knew she could manage on her own.

As they made camp in a valley between two hills, the area near the firewall where Taimin grew up felt like a world away. The night sky was full of stars. There was little cover, making it too dangerous to build a fire. The cratered moon hung low in the sky, huge and unchanging, silver in color and beautiful in a way that the suns could never be.

Taimin and Selena lay on their blankets and gazed at the moon together while Lars snored a dozen paces away. The mood was tranquil: the white city beckoned, they had plenty of meat and water, and cooperation had kept them safe.

"What are you thinking?" Selena asked.

Taimin felt her eyes on him as he stared up at the sky. "Nothing important."

"Tell me."

"I was just thinking that wherever you are, the moon looks the same. It's always in the same part of the sky, with the same scars where they always are. The suns come and go, rise and fall, sometimes both in the sky, sometimes just one, but the moon is always there. It gets out-shone by Dex, so that you wonder if it's still with us, but it always is."

"I've never thought about it before," Selena said. "But why doesn't it move like the suns?"

"My father told me it's another world, cold where ours is hot. His father told him that it's much closer than Dex and Lux."

"A world," Selena mused. With her head close to Taimin's, she smiled. "I like that thought. I wonder what our world would look like from up there? I suppose it would have lighter and darker shades of red and brown, but the rest would be black—the land beyond the firewall."

"What would we look like, from up above?" Taimin asked.

"Like two tiny ants, who should be resting while they can." She rolled over and softly kissed him on the cheek. Her eyes sparkled in the moonlight. "I'll dream about other worlds tonight, and I'll tell you about them in the morning. Good night."

Taimin's heart gave a strange lurch in his chest. Selena shuffled nearby until she was on her side with her back to him; meanwhile he was still staring at her.

He watched her sleeping form for a long time before he shifted to gaze up at the night's sky once more. As he tried to sleep, he thought about his parents, Gareth and Tess, who had always been close. They may not have been tough like Abi, but they had taught him something of what it meant to be in love. They had loved each other, and they had loved him.

Thinking about Selena's dream of finding a place in the world, he tried to imagine his future. He didn't want to be a settler like Abi, a victim of her defenses, so busy staying alive that she never went farther than could be traveled in half a day. He also didn't want to be a rover like Lars or the men who had killed his parents, living by his wits, constantly struggling to find food and water, dominating those weaker because, in the wasteland, only the strongest survived.

Taimin longed to reach the white city, with a feeling that came from deep inside.

He and Selena shared the dream together.

"More bax," Lars grunted.

The two men lay on their stomachs on a rocky crest, knowing that to stand would be to silhouette their figures against the sky.

"I count at least twenty," Taimin said.

"Blasted creatures. I don't know what's changed. They're supposed to be territorial. But here they are, always heading in the same direction."

"The same way we're going."

"It doesn't bode well. We'll have to be careful." Lars spat. "Disgusting things. I'd wipe every last one of them from the waste if I could."

Taimin knew what Selena would say. "They probably feel the same way about us."

"Eh?" Lars frowned. "What's your point?"

"I just think it's a shame we have to fight for every scrap of meat and every drop of water."

"Sure, lad. It's a shame. It's the way the world is, though. When you're as old as me, you'll see that it's us against them. Humans against bax, trulls, skalen . . . Even mantoreans."

"I suppose so," Taimin said. He started to shuffle down the hill. "We should head back to camp." He had left Griff with Selena, but he still didn't like her being alone.

"Wait," Lars said. "Hold on a minute."

"What?" Taimin stopped.

Lars moved until he and Taimin were again side by side. "It's about the girl."

Taimin bristled. "What about her?"

"Look," Lars sighed, "perhaps I'd best just tell you."

Taimin felt a jolt at Lars's tone. "Tell me what?"

"You're a good fighter and you know how to survive, but you don't know much about the world. And you definitely don't know much about mystics."

Taimin looked back down the hill, even though he couldn't see her. "So?"

"I've told you this, but I'll say it again. Selena isn't just any mystic. You should know what you're getting yourself into. She wouldn't have had the life she's had if she were an ordinary girl. It's because they were afraid of her."

"All she's done is guide us. What's there to be so afraid of?"

Lars snorted. "You really have no idea, do you? A strong mystic can speak from their mind to yours, even from far away, and change a man's thoughts without him knowing he's ever thought differently. Those headaches she gets come for a reason. She can cast farther than any mystic I've even heard of. Think about how long we've been traveling."

"And she's your chance at a new life," Taimin said.

"Yes, she is. If I didn't need her help to find the white city, I wouldn't go anywhere near her."

"But she's never done any of the things you're worried about, has she?"

"She doesn't know what she's doing. But she might one day."

"And what would you do if you believed she was changing your thoughts? Would you hurt her too?"

"I'd do what I always do," Lars said soberly. "I'd run away."

11

Taimin, Selena, and Lars crouched in shadow. Rock surrounded them on all sides. They were in a narrow ravine, the best hiding place they could find at short notice.

"I've never seen so many skalen out in the open." Despite his heavy breathing, Lars spoke in hushed tones. "There must be a hundred or more."

Selena looked up to the top of the ravine. "I doubt they saw us."

Lars rested his dark eyes on her. "Such a big group will have mystics," he said. "They might already know we're here."

It was close to dusk, and the three travelers had been crossing another barren plain. The skalen had appeared from nowhere, approaching from behind. Taimin, Selena, and Lars had run for the steep-walled gully and climbed down before they were spotted. Even as they spoke, they huddled together and kept their heads low. Taimin's heart thudded in his chest as he realized that an encounter might be inevitable.

"There's not much we can do," Taimin whispered. "They'll definitely spot us if we head back up. We either run, and hope they don't give chase, or we wait here until they pass."

Selena's voice betrayed her fear. "If we're worried they've got mystics then we should run, shouldn't we?"

"Why didn't you know about them?" Lars glared at her.

"It doesn't matter now," Taimin said. "Two options: run or wait."

"They're moving fast," Lars said. "If we run they'll know we're here for certain. So many of them . . . It must be an entire clan. They'll probably have flanking scouts." He scratched anxiously at his beard. "If we show ourselves, we lose any chance of them passing us by."

As soon as Taimin had seen the dark, sleek, lizard-like creatures with skin that reflected the low evening light, he had known what they were. He remembered Abi's lecturing voice.

Skalen live in aurelium mines scattered throughout the waste. They don't see well in bright light, although Lux doesn't hurt them like Dex. Just because they like it underground doesn't mean you won't encounter them. They trade aurelium for the things they need. I don't have any, but it's useful for starting fires and bursts into flame if you strike it hard. The tips of their javelins are made from the stuff. Don't get hit. They aren't as aggressive as bax or trulls but they don't like humans much, and they're more likely to fight than talk. Never take on a skalen in darkness; only fight in daylight so you'll have an advantage. Their skin isn't as tough as it looks, so their weak points are similar to those on a human. Make sure you can see them all: they like an ambush.

"So running isn't an option," Taimin said.

"I suppose not." Lars hesitated. "Blast it, we should have scouted them."

Taimin couldn't help but agree. He had been distracted, talking to Selena. Usually attentive, he hadn't realized how exposed they were. There were better routes they could have taken, and high points he could have scanned the terrain from.

Selena gazed up at the sky. "It's going to be dark soon," she said.

"By the rains," Lars cursed. "They'll see better than we will."

"Looks like we have to stay hidden, and stay still," Taimin said. "Moving shapes attract attention."

109

Lars cast his eyes over the ravine. "There's not much protection here."

"It's all we've got."

"All right, we wait then," Lars said.

Taimin, Selena, and Lars wedged themselves into the gully as best they could, while Griff's leathery hide camouflaged him better than any of them. The deepest, darkest part was narrow, forcing Taimin and Selena close together, so that she was nestled into his body.

Taimin wondered how close the skalen were to their hiding place. He pictured their small forms, javelins in hand as they swarmed over the plain, a group so large that few would challenge them, sacrificing stealth for speed.

He fought to still his breathing and settled in.

———

The sibilant voices started as low murmurs, just audible at the edge of hearing. Selena burrowed even closer into Taimin's bigger frame. Taimin felt her reach out and take his hand, squeezing his palm with a surprisingly strong grip. He squeezed back as his fear mounted.

The voices grew in volume. Dex cast long shadows in the gully; soon it would be completely dark, which would increase their chances of being seen with the sharp night vision of the skalen. Tonight would be a false night: Lux would rise soon after Dex set. The most dangerous period would be when both suns were down.

Taimin could hear Selena's fast breathing and wondered if his own was as loud. His heart made strong, pounding beats in his chest as he thought about what he would do if they were caught. He supposed he could take his chances and try to flee. He would have to ride Griff, of course. Perhaps the wherry could also support

Selena. Taimin thought it might work; Selena was slight, and Griff was stronger than he looked. Then he realized the choice he would have to make. Could he leave Lars? There was no way Griff could carry the three of them.

He glanced up and his eyes widened as shapes moved above, on both sides of the gully's steep walls. The darkness was almost complete, and the figures were menacing shadows, walking with more silence than humans, naturally sliding along with sinuous movements. However, their sibilant voices were loud as the skalen called to each other. He saw little pinpricks of green light, bobbing up and down, and realized he was seeing the aurelium that made up the points of their javelins.

His thoughts whirled. He knew that in the same position Lars would leave him; the skinner was a survivor. Abi's voice in his head told him he should see Selena to safety, and together they could continue their search for the white city.

But Taimin knew he couldn't leave Lars behind.

Then he blinked, and three black shapes stood in the gully, directly in front of him, barely paces away.

Lars bellowed and already his axe was in his hands. He cut the air, but the black figures easily avoided his wild swings. Taimin still held Selena's hand and he pulled her behind him as he drew his sword. In the sudden commotion, Griff was nowhere to be seen.

Something green and glowing arced from above to strike the wall of the gully. A burst of flame erupted from the rock wall and sparks shot in all directions. In the flash of light, Taimin saw skalen lining the ravine, each holding a poised javelin. Behind the three skalen in front of him were many more, crowded into the gully with weapons ready.

Taimin's nostrils flared. There was no use fighting. He lowered his sword and even Lars stood panting. As silence filled the air, broken only by heavy breathing, the crimson Lux climbed above the lip of the ravine. In the low red sunlight Taimin felt a stab of fear when he saw the three dark figures in front of him revealed in detail. He had always been curious about skalen, but this wasn't how he had imagined his first encounter.

The centermost skalen, the tallest of the three, tilted his head as he regarded each human with almond eyes. His face was flat, with high cheekbones and a small chin, and a handful of dark feathers sprouted from his scalp. He wore a fan-like metal necklace and a cloth garment covered his torso, gathered in by a wide leather belt. Tight leather trousers were also tucked into high boots. Where some of the other skalen had bronze-colored neckpieces, this skalen's was made of shining steel.

"Definitely humans," he said to his companions. He took a step back and turned to nod at the skalen flanking him. "Kill them."

"Wait!" Lars cried. "I claim trade rights. As a watch leader, you must honor my right to offer trade."

"Interesting," the skalen with the steel neckpiece hissed as he turned his attention to Lars. "You know our customs, human."

Lux's blood-red light grew stronger, and Taimin saw the skalen's tilted eyes cloud over, as if a protective film were falling into place. Taimin risked a glance at Selena. Her face was pale. He had made the honorable choice in not leaving Lars, but it might have been a fateful one.

"I have traded many times with Treesk of Reswith Watch," Lars said, clearly finding the strange names hard to form.

"I know Treesk," the skalen said. "Tell me, human, what do you have to trade? I hold your lives, and my mother, who leads here, commands a hundred warriors. I doubt there is much you can offer that I cannot take for myself."

Taimin knew the look of desperation on Lars's face, but it gradually shifted to a familiar cunning. "You must have close to an entire clan here," Lars said. "We both know that a large group brings dangers of its own. We're not far from the firewall. How many will die if you get caught in a firestorm? You don't leave your mines without purpose. Perhaps you need the help of a mystic where you're going."

The skalen—Lars had called him a watch leader—gave Lars a careful inspection. "You are a mystic?"

"No," Selena said. She came forward. "I am."

The watch leader opened his mouth, displaying rows of pointed teeth. "We already have a mystic. My cousin, Aris." He called over his shoulder. "Aris! Someone fetch him."

A younger skalen pushed through to the top of the opposite wall of the gully. "I am here, Watch Leader Rees."

"Aris, tell me, is this human female a mystic?"

Aris looked at Selena with narrowed eyes. Selena stood her ground and returned his reptilian stare. All of a sudden Aris drew back, his expression fearful. "She is untrained, but she has power, Watch Leader Rees."

"More power than you?"

Aris gave a soft snort. "I can barely cast a few miles."

"So that is a yes." Rees dragged out the last syllable in a soft hiss. "You have my interest, human," he addressed Lars. "You have bought her life. Unfortunately, you have not—"

"Do you think I'll cast for you if you kill them?" Selena interrupted. "You can take me, but let them go."

"Selena—" Taimin began.

She cut him off with a frown. Rees's gaze narrowed. Taimin clenched his jaw as the watch leader pondered; he knew there was nothing he could do. Lars had made his gambit. Everything came down to Selena now.

"First, a test," Rees finally said. "What lies in this direction?" The skalen pointed.

Selena's eyes became unfocused. She had a distant look about her for a time, before clarity returned to her gaze. "A series of mountains and then a vast canyon."

"Past the canyon?"

"A plain."

"You know what I am asking. What is after the plain?"

Taimin tensed as Selena took a long time to reply. "The white city."

"Excellent. You have your bargain," Rees said to Lars. He turned to Selena. "You will cast for us, and we will keep your companions safe from harm. Be careful, though, for we will ask many things from you, and we expect your full commitment to our cause."

"No," Selena said. Her voice was firm. "Let them go."

"And how would I trust you to cast for us?" Rees tilted his head. "Believe me, mystic, there is no other bargain to be made."

"What is your cause?" Lars asked. "Where are you going?"

"We travel to the Rift Valley, the canyon the mystic spoke of, to a meeting with the bax and their warden. A gathering such as this has never taken place before."

"To what end?" Lars persisted.

"We plan to conquer the white city," Rees said. He rested his gaze on Selena. "And with your help, we will do it. You will help us avoid the Protector's patrols, and find the weak places in the walls. A strong mystic is worth hundreds of warriors."

Taimin saw Lars's expression of horror, mirroring the way he felt. It was Lars who spoke, so low that Taimin could only just hear him.

"What have we done?"

12

Taimin and Lars marched.

Their wrists were bound behind their backs. On all sides a large group of strange, sinuous creatures surrounded them. There was no chance of escape.

Sweat trickled down Taimin's face as he concentrated on placing one foot in front of the other. It was his third day with the skalen, and Dex was a sliver of bright yellow just above the horizon. He hoped they would soon rest; the rising heat and fatigue were taking their toll. The fast pace the skalen set made him wonder at the column's urgency.

Taimin often didn't glimpse Selena for hours. The skalen avoided bright Dex and preferred to march either at night or when only the red sun was above the horizon; often it was so dark Taimin could barely see. When he tripped on unseen obstacles, guards yanked him up again without a word. The reptilian eyes of the skalen heightened their menace. The blinding glare of strong sunlight became something he longed for; it meant he could rest.

While he was glad the skalen hadn't found Griff, he was anxious that the wherry would be close by, shadowing the column. Every time a scout came up to report to Watch Leader Rees, Taimin dreaded news that Griff had been found and killed. If Griff wasn't wise enough to stay clear, the wherry's soft skin might form a skalen's new boots.

As Taimin marched, he looked from side to side. The guards assigned to watch him and Lars didn't appear to care if the two men spoke, provided they kept their voices low.

"You know about skalen," Taimin murmured to Lars. "Why would they want to attack the white city?"

"No idea," Lars grunted. "I'll tell you one thing, though. It's rare for so many skalen to leave their home. Almost as rare as skalen meeting with bax."

"We have to warn the Protector," Taimin said, speaking quietly as he glanced at his companion.

"Aye," Lars said. "But first we have to get away."

Taimin inspected the warriors surrounding them. He and Lars were close to the front of the column, and he peered over his shoulder to take in as many skalen as he could. "If this is a clan, where are their young?"

"Left behind? With another clan? How would I know?"

"Any thoughts on escap—"

Taimin was interrupted when a sibilant voice up ahead called for the column to halt. He peered past the skalen in front of him to scan the dry terrain, wondering why they had stopped—if it was to rest, they would have said so. The golden sun was only beginning to crest the horizon. It wasn't yet bright enough for a rest period.

He squinted and finally saw a tall, muscular figure approaching the column, silhouetted by the rising sun. The figure was too upright for a bax, and too tall and broad to be a skalen, or even a human. Taimin blinked, and realized that there was a much slighter, stick-like figure trailing behind. A cord trailed from the hand of the bigger figure, dragging the creature along by its neck.

The two shapes moved past the sun and now he could see them clearly. He heard Lars mutter under his breath.

"Just what we need. A trull."

"A trull with a captive mantorean?" Taimin frowned.

"It's not the first time I've seen it. The mantorean is a female, of course. He'll have her eggs."

Although he was alone, the trull approached the column without fear. He was more than six feet tall, but it was his frame that caught Taimin's attention. His body looked like it was entirely made of muscle, without an ounce of wasted flesh on him. His broad face was dominated by a snubbed nose, flattened against his face, and his upper jaw was larger than his lower, leaving long, yellowed incisors to curve halfway down his chin. His head was covered in lank hair that hung to his broad shoulders, and his dark eyes, while large, looked surprisingly human. He wore an animal-skin vest and frayed leather trousers.

The mantorean that the trull dragged behind him was clearly weak. The trull remorselessly yanked her along and occasionally turned his head to snarl something back at her. She was slighter than the mantorean that Taimin and Selena had rescued, but had the same triangular head, beady black eyes, and pair of antennae.

As Taimin continued to examine the approaching trull he remembered the things his father and Abi had told him. Trulls were aggressive. They didn't get along well with the other races, nor each other, and were rarely seen in groups. Most often they traveled the wasteland, stealing and raiding.

Taimin watched an old skalen leave the column to meet the trull and his captive. Her neckpiece was steel and similar to Rees's, but with an additional circle of tiny green shards around the perimeter. Where Rees had a handful of dark feathers sprouting from his scalp, the older skalen's feathers were white, and age had weathered her reptilian skin. Nonetheless, her clothing was well-made and she held her back straight.

"You've heard them mention Rees's mother, Group Leader Vail?" Lars glanced at Taimin. "My guess is that's her. She's the one in charge of this column."

"Group Leader," the trull said in a harsh, barking voice. "I claim trade rights."

"Why would I trade with you?" Group Leader Vail came to a halt and scowled. The trull looked strong enough to crush her neck with one hand, but she wasn't intimidated.

"I am in need," the trull growled. He held up a satchel. "I risked much to capture this mantorean. I have her eggs with me, but I have no food." He jerked his chin at the mantorean, who stood with her shoulders slumped just behind him. "She is a mystic."

Lars gave Taimin a worried look.

"What does it mean?" Taimin asked.

"Vail will trade for her," Lars said. "The mantorean will do anything to protect her eggs. She'll cast in any way the group leader wants her to."

Out in front of the column, Group Leader Vail shook her head. "I already have mystics."

The trull pointed at the mantorean. "She has cast a firestorm ahead. You skalen are heading straight for it." He lifted his chin. "Tell me, have your own mystics seen the danger?"

"A firestorm?" Vail rubbed her chin. "Where?"

The trull snarled. "She will never tell you, not unless I give you her eggs."

Group Leader Vail addressed the insect-like creature. "Is this true?" she asked.

The mantorean gave a weary nod. Taimin saw that she had a gash as long as his finger on the side of her face. "There is a firestorm. I do not have permission to tell you anything more."

Vail frowned. "If you have her eggs, why drag her by a cord?" she asked the trull.

"She is weak," the trull grunted, "but I am sure you can remedy that."

"How much food do you want?"

"I want skins too," the trull said.

As the bargaining began, Taimin turned to Lars. "What does this mean for us?"

Lars's lips thinned. "It can't be anything good. Selena is not as useful as she once was."

———

The column had halted without explanation. Selena tried to see through the lizard-like figures ahead of her but there were too many of them to see what was happening up front. She briefly caught sight of Taimin and Lars farther ahead, still bound, but with their lips moving as they murmured to each other. There was no way to make out what they were saying.

In her glimpses of Taimin on the march she had seen that he was struggling to keep up. She was worried about him. As she caught another look at his face, she noticed that his eyes were shadowed. He was leaning, placing his weight more on one side than the other.

She saw Rees coming her way, weaving through the column. He reached out with his reptilian hand and his inscrutable eyes met hers. She heard his soft voice.

"Mystic," he called, beckoning. "My mother has asked for you. Come."

Selena shook her head. "I want to talk to my friends first."

When she didn't move, he frowned and reached out to grab her hand, yanking her until she was at his side. She resisted, but he was strong, and the other skalen parted as Rees dragged her along.

Soon she was through the crowd and out in the open at the front, a stone's throw from the rest of the group.

Rees's mother waited. Proud and stern, with tilted eyes that were sharp despite her age, Group Leader Vail impatiently watched Selena approach.

"Mother, here she is," Rees said.

"Finally," Vail said. Her narrowed gaze told Selena that she was not to be crossed. "Remind me of your name, mystic."

"Selena." As she spoke, Selena saw Taimin and Lars standing behind some of the skalen warriors. They both looked worried.

"In case you do not know, I am Group Leader Vail. I command here."

Selena didn't reply. Her nostrils flared as her intuition told her that something bad was about to happen.

"Do you see that trull?" Vail pointed and Selena saw a muscular figure in the distance, striding away from the group. On his back the trull carried a bulging pack that looked heavy but barely slowed him down as he left the skalen behind.

"Yes."

"He had a captive mantorean that he traded to our group. She is a mystic, and I have her eggs. Do you know what that means? She will do whatever I ask of her—anything she can to save her eggs."

Selena's stomach churned. The skalen had another mystic, almost certainly a mystic with more skill than her. "I understand."

"I am not certain you do," Vail said, meeting her eyes. "This one may not have your power . . . but here, let me show you."

Group Leader Vail waved her arm, and Selena saw an insect-like mantorean herded toward her. The mantorean's shoulders were slumped but she was obviously agitated from the way her antennae twitched. She had a seeping wound on the side of her triangular face but wasn't bound, lending credence to Vail's explanation about her eggs.

"Rei-kika," Vail said to the mantorean. "You say we are marching directly into the path of a firestorm."

"Yes, Group Leader," the mantorean, Rei-kika, said in her clipped, clicking voice.

"Which way must we travel, to avoid the danger?"

Rei-kika hesitated. "It is too far for me to cast the best route. When we get closer I will be able to tell you."

Vail rested her ancient eyes on Selena. "Do you see my problem? I have a tame mystic who will do everything I ask of her. She has spotted a hazard ahead, something that you," Vail's ominous tone made Selena's skin crawl, "were supposed to be doing."

Selena swallowed. She had been wary of farcasting. If she had a seizure, the skalen might decide that she, Taimin, and Lars were more trouble than they were worth.

"My problem," Vail continued, "is that this mantorean does not have the strength of my untrained, unhelpful human mystic. What is to be done?"

Group Leader Vail glanced at Rei-kika, and then back at Selena. Coming to a conclusion, the old skalen turned again to the mantorean.

"Rei-kika," she said. "I want you to channel through this human female. Use her strength. Find me the firestorm, and tell me truly which way to go, or I will crack your eggs on the ground."

The mantorean made a sound of distress. "I must not. It is forbidden."

"I mean what I say," Vail said flatly. "Do I have to ask again?"

"No. No, please."

Selena's fear grew as she wondered what was about to happen. She could try to run, or fight, but Taimin and Lars would suffer. The rest of the column watched nearby. She was out in the open as the rising sun washed the rugged plain in bright light. A hot wind blew against her skin. Her mouth was dry.

Then Rei-kika moved, her decision made. The mantorean faced Selena and fixed her with an unreadable expression like stone. Multifaceted black eyes stared at her, boring into her skull.

Then, with a terrible, penetrating sensation, Selena's mind was invaded.

It began with a dull ache between her temples. Selena put her hands to her head. She wanted to do anything she could to run away and escape the black eyes that stared into her, but the pain grew until it was so strong she could do little more than grimace. Her consciousness screamed at her: something was trying to worm its way inside.

The foreign awareness touched her mind again and again. At first it was a subtle caress, a peeling back of layers, a touch that attempted to slip through her mind's natural barriers to get inside. Selena instinctively tried to push it away and the touch recoiled for a moment but returned even stronger. The pain became agonizing. It was like a gigantic hand was wrapped around her head, squeezing with terrible force.

The touch shifted. Instead of a caress, regular blows fell like a hammer striking a chisel, peeling back her defenses to expose what lay within. The barrier between Selena's mind and the foreign awareness shattered like thin clay. She cried out and fell to her knees while the pressure continued.

The multifaceted black eyes continued to bore into her. The sensation of squeezing was so strong that she had no choice but to seek refuge. She gasped, her mouth open in a soundless scream. Still the pressure increased. She had to escape the pain.

There was only one place she could go. She retreated deeper inside her mind.

There was something there, a radiance that she had never been aware of before. She sought out the radiance, taking herself away

122

from the pain. It was bright and beautiful. She surrounded herself with it.

But the walls were closing in, walls of pain that were brought closer and closer by the foreign presence. The radiance knew Selena wanted to be free. It showed her that she could escape the pain completely. It could free her of it. All she had to do was allow it to pull her away.

She accepted the offer; she had no other choice. She took hold of the radiance and experienced a sensation like being unfastened and gradually rising up, akin to waking from a deep sleep.

In an instant she was free.

Selena looked down at the ground and saw herself: a young woman, her hair as black as night, kneeling on the ground with her face raised to the sky. As she floated above her own body, she became filled with awe. There was no longer any pain. Here, she could do anything.

She swept her gaze around her and saw that Vail, Rees—everyone was watching her body. They didn't know she had escaped her physical form. She turned in all directions, taking in the golden sun Dex, the rust-colored wasteland, and the pale blue sky.

She instinctively knew she could travel in any direction. A simple thought directed her perception to rise upward. She floated higher and higher to climb the sky until she was well above the plain and the mass of skalen were tiny figures below. In the distance she could make out strewn gravel and misshapen stone formations, gullies, ridges, and a field of boulders.

Selena knew she was casting, but this was completely new. She was able to make out detail: color and depth, size and distance. Part of her wanted to test her limits and travel as far as she could.

But then her perception was diverted.

The sensation was horrific and violating. Someone was here with her. She wasn't in control; this thing was forcing her to cast where it wanted. The other awareness made her turn. She fought it but the presence took charge with smooth, calm decisiveness.

Soon Selena was soaring, flying over and above the land. The blue-tinged field of gravel approached with speed and then it was underneath her. In moments it was gone, and she was passing above a stone tower formed of boulders piled one on top of the other. For a time she followed a deep seam in the ground, and then she reached a place where jagged boulders littered the landscape.

She saw a firestorm.

It was as if a piece of the firewall had broken off and traveled into the wasteland. It was initially hard to see, which was the danger, for it carried little visible signature to make itself known. She focused on a place where the air was a subtle shade of red. The wind was twisting, fast and hot, scouring the land as it moved.

The foreign presence knew what to look for. The firestorm left a track on the field of rocks and boulders, a swathe burned black, where smoke rose from the ground.

Selena was made to watch it for a time, and then she felt that the presence had seen enough. She heard a clicking voice break the silence.

Follow your lifeline to your body.

She was forcibly turned in her casting, until she faced the direction she had come from. The group of skalen was so far away it couldn't be seen. But she saw a faint white line, cutting through the wasteland in a direct line past the tall rock formation. She sensed that the softly glowing cord connected her to her body. It took little effort to gently pull on it. Soon she was flying over the plain once more. The tower of boulders sped toward her, then the field of pale gravel, and finally she saw a multitude of lizard-like figures and a cluster standing around a mantorean and a young woman on her knees.

Selena dived back into her body and gasped.

Slowly her eyes refocused. After a few breaths, her vision returned to the way it had been before. With an effort she climbed to her feet. Rei-kika's body slumped; she looked both tired and regretful. Group Leader Vail stood watching. The golden sun beat down on the plain.

"Well?" Vail demanded.

"If we go this way, the firestorm will be on our left." Rei-kika pointed.

"Good," said Vail. She turned to her son, Watch Leader Rees. "We will march in daylight, with a short rest at midday, until we are past the firestorm. Gather our people." She scowled at Selena. "Do not fail me again."

The march continued, but this time Selena traveled up front. As the golden sun climbed ever higher and cast fierce rays onto the barren landscape, she recognized features from her casting and directed the group, keeping the column clear of the firestorm's path.

She was still shaken by what had happened. Every time she remembered what it had felt like to have another awareness in control of her casting, she felt sick. Rei-kika had seen her as no one else had. Her very identity had been violated. She was glad that the mantorean was traveling with Rees, rather than with her and Group Leader Vail. She would do anything to avoid her mind being penetrated again.

But at the same time, when she managed to bring herself back to that moment of joy, before the mantorean took charge, she knew she had been free. Her casting was no longer hazy. It had been as sharp as what she could see with her own eyes.

She began to see the scars of destruction that the firestorm had left behind as it moved across the terrain. Being caught in its heart would lead to a fiery death, and even the smoking rock would burn anyone foolish enough to walk on it.

It was only when they were drawing closer to the small range of mountains and were well clear of the firestorm's path of travel that Group Leader Vail called a halt.

Two hours into the midday rest, with the skalen taking shelter below a low cliff, a pair of guards took Selena on another journey. They prodded her to keep her moving as she wondered where they were taking her in the blazing heat; the skalen usually conserved their energy. She looked everywhere for Taimin or Lars, scanning the mass of figures as she walked through the group, but couldn't see them. Her anxiety grew, working its way through her body until her jaw was clenched.

"You should never displease Group Leader Vail," said one of the guards. "But you are fortunate. Watch Leader Rees convinced her to give you another chance to fulfil the bargain you made."

Sweat beaded on Selena's forehead. A hill grew in her vision, dotted with sentinel cactuses twice the height of a man. She was brought to a halt.

"There, mystic," one of the skalen said. "Look."

Selena's eyes shot wide open. The hill was exposed to direct sunlight but the man-like shapes of the cactuses had confused her. Horror was a heavy, sinking weight in her chest.

She saw Taimin, recognizable by his brown hair and stubbled cheeks, bound to a thorny cactus's two broad arms. Lars, burly and bearded, was lashed to another cactus nearby. Their heads were slumped as they stared at the ground. Selena feared the worst, but then she saw Taimin make a weak movement of his head.

"They will be given water when the rest period is over."

"Why?" Selena rounded on the two guards. "Why are you doing this?"

"To them? We are not doing anything to them. Group Leader Vail is angry that you did not see the firestorm earlier. It is you who does this."

"Free them. Let them go. I'll do whatever you want."

The skalen both laughed as they dragged her away.

13

The golden sun slowly passed the midpoint of the sky before Taimin heard a distant cry: the call to march. A few moments later he felt his arms being moved as a skalen untied him from the sentinel cactus. He collapsed to the ground, sprawling onto his stomach, and then heard another thump as Lars crashed to the blood-red dirt nearby.

A skalen laughed and Taimin felt the point of a javelin pressed against the back of his neck. "Get up, human."

Too weak to move, Taimin struggled to follow the command but then the pressure on the back of his neck eased. Someone lifted his head. The touch was surprisingly tender and he looked up with bleary eyes to see Selena holding a flask. She turned his head to dribble water onto his lips. The liquid moistened his bone-dry mouth and then slid down the back of his throat. He gulped, trying not to cough.

He pushed himself up until he was leaning back on his hands. "Lars," he began, and then tried again. "Lars."

Selena gave the big man water until he was sitting up like Taimin. As he saw Lars's red, dirt-covered face, Taimin knew he must look the same.

"Hurry up, humans," one of the skalen called. "Mystic, the Group Leader said you must be quick."

Selena scowled at the guard, who was watching them from a distance. "Just remember what a mystic can do," she said in an ominous tone.

The guard's eyes widened, and he took a step back. Taimin heard Lars speak.

The skinner was looking away, and Taimin could only see the back of his bald head, but he spoke in a voice that was audible if Taimin strained. "I have a plan."

"Tell me," Selena murmured.

"Skalen burn more easily than we do. They won't follow us where the firestorm has been."

Taimin met Selena's eyes and felt a kindling of hope.

"I can probably guide us closer," she said. She returned to sit close beside Taimin, and made a show of passing him the water flask. "Also . . . Taimin, I saw something. It might have been Griff following us."

Taimin knew that unless he was reunited with Griff, he wouldn't be able to travel quickly. "Running won't be easy," he said, worried about slowing everyone down.

"What choice do we have?" Lars's voice was hoarse.

Taimin knew that Lars was right. They needed to escape. These skalen, and the bax they were traveling to meet, planned to attack the white city. The Protector had to be warned.

"I'll get us close enough to get away," Selena said. "Once we're at the right place, I'll tell them I want to check on you. Be ready." She glanced at Taimin. "Are you up to it?"

"With Lars's help," Taimin said. He turned to face her. She was pressed against him, close enough for him to stare into her eyes. "Are you sure you'll be able to get to us?"

"I'll do my best. But if something goes wrong, you'll have to leave me behind."

"That's not how this is going to go," he said firmly. As he gazed at her, for a moment he forgot everything: his exhaustion, Lars, the skalen . . . everything but her.

"Stay alive," Selena said.

Taimin felt a stab of fear, as if he might not see her again. "No matter what happens, this isn't goodbye—"

"Enough!" The guard came forward and grabbed Selena under her arm.

Both suns fell toward the horizon. The sky was a brilliant shade of blue. Boulders lay scattered across the plain, interspersed with thorn-covered cactuses, while the mountain range the skalen were heading for grew until the looming peaks cast monstrous shadows over the terrain.

Once more Taimin and Lars marched with their hands tied behind their backs. Every step for Taimin was agony, but he pushed through the pain, even as his crippled foot grew swollen and tight in his leather boot. A coat of dust covered his skin and clothing, and the fine grains even clung to his face, embedded in the stubble on his chin and in his dark hair. He had lost his pack as well as his sword and bow when they were captured. Even if they managed to escape, they wouldn't be past danger.

Nearby, Lars moved closer and Taimin heard the skinner whisper. "Look. To your right."

A hundred paces away there were no cactuses. Trails of smoke rose from the blackened ground and waves of heat shimmered as if the air was wet with moisture. Taimin was reminded of the time he had watched his parents' bodies burn beyond the firewall. The column of heat that caused this destruction had passed, but the land still showed the firestorm's effects. Swathes of dirt had become dark, forming crusts on top.

"It's the best place I've seen by far," Lars said. "A chance like this won't come again."

"We wait for Selena," Taimin insisted.

"She was supposed to get close to us. Where is she?"

"We wait," Taimin insisted.

"What if she can't get to us?"

"We won't leave her."

Each step forward brought them closer to the scar of destruction the firestorm had left behind. Lars's posture was tense as he walked, and Taimin could feel the older man's eyes on him. Taimin peered through the clustered figures of the marching skalen and wondered where Selena was.

Taimin and Lars had drifted to the edge of the column without being challenged. But soon they would be leaving the blackened ground behind.

Lars moved to speak into Taimin's ear, his voice filled with urgency. "You heard her. What if she can't get away? We're bound. There's no way we can fight our way to her. Think about it. She's gone to all this effort to get us here, risking her life. The group leader might be angry that Selena's taken us so near to the firestorm's path. Vail's not going to let Selena come and see her friends in that case, is she?"

"Blast it," Taimin swore. "Where is she?"

"It's now or never," Lars said.

In another dozen strides the chance would be gone.

"You go," Taimin said. "Leave me behind."

"We go together," Lars said flatly. "When we leave, we'll have no weapons, no food, no water. I need your wherry to help us find water. You need me to help you run."

"What about Selena?"

"We'll help her once we're free. If we lose this chance, then what? How does that help her?"

Taimin's heart was racing. His jaw was tightly clenched. He didn't know what to do.

"Taimin, we'll come back for her," Lars said. "She has to do whatever they say or they'll hurt us. She'll feel better if we're free. Here we're no good to anyone. Once we've escaped, we can go about helping her."

Taimin knew that Lars made sense. "We'll come back for her as soon as we're free," he said firmly.

"Of course we will."

He made a difficult decision. "Are you ready?"

"The glare will hurt their aim, but try to weave as you run."

Taimin took a deep breath and then hissed. "Go."

Immediately he broke away and ran as fast as he could, moving a shuffling gait. The nearest guards called out a challenge and hurried after him. It was then that Lars sped forward and crashed into the chasing skalen from behind, knocking them aside with his bigger frame.

Taimin's back itched as he hobbled toward the blackened ground. With his hands bound behind his back, his run was awkward, making the scorched area seem impossibly far away. He glanced over his shoulder and saw Lars catching up to him. Their actions had taken everyone by surprise. Some skalen up front were turning back, wondering what the commotion was. A few of their designated guards were still on the ground.

He was forced to slow when he reached the place where rocks still smoldered and heat punched into him like a fist; the risk was too great that he would stumble. Lars caught up with him, and then the javelins began to fall.

Where the aurelium-tipped weapons struck the ground, flame followed and sparks flew in all directions. Taimin leaned into Lars as he ran into the area that every sense told him to flee from. His skin was on fire. If he hadn't seen his aunt pass the firewall with his parents' bodies he would never have thought he could survive.

But where the land beyond the firewall was permanently scorched, this region had seen the firestorm pass some time ago. It was hot, nearly unbearable, but they could push through.

Taimin heard the sibilant shouts of the skalen behind him but didn't risk turning around again. He focused on his footing and avoided the bigger boulders. Both men were struggling with their hands bound. Taimin fell against Lars and the bigger man grunted to support him. They stumbled past smooth rock that had been turned to a glassy surface. Piles of ash showed where cactuses had once stood.

In the distance ahead, Taimin spied a tall hermit cactus that was green.

"This way," Lars panted as he saw it too.

The angry calls had faded away, and Taimin felt a surge of hope when they reached the hermit cactus and he thought they had reached safety. But it was just a clear area, and on all sides the terrain still cast off wisps of rising smoke. Without a word Lars turned his back to a hot rock and crouched down, resting the cord binding his hands against its surface. He winced but the leather parted, and Taimin immediately followed suit. The two men then pressed on, running more easily now, until finally they burst free into the usual colors of the wasteland.

Taimin now slowed to a walk, grimacing as his fear ebbed and the pain in his foot returned with force. Sucking in the fresh air, he continued until he had separated himself from the blackened ground by a few hundred paces, and then he stopped and put his hands on his hips while he gasped.

Nearby, Lars's chest was also heaving, but he was shading his eyes, his gaze moving as he watched something.

"Foolish creature," Lars muttered. "Like his master. No sense of danger."

A large four-legged animal crested a hill and Taimin heard a loud whine as Griff rushed straight at him. The wherry bounded forward and growled with pleasure, while he butted Taimin with his head and circled around him again and again. Some of the skin on his flanks looked a little singed, but other than that he had been swift enough to avoid injury.

Lars looked back past Taimin's shoulder. "We have to keep going."

Taimin turned to face the region of smoke and searing heat. "How are we going to go back for her?"

"We can't go the way we've just left. We both know it. And we can't circle round either. We'd be traveling where we've already been—where there's no shelter, no hunting, no water. We wouldn't catch up with the skalen. We'd be dead." Lars faced the mountains. "The only way is forward."

Taimin's mouth tightened. "Then what?"

"We're not out of danger yet. I need your help, just as you need mine. We need rest, food, and most of all water."

Taimin still didn't move as he stared in the direction of the shifting smoke. While he knew that now he was free he could do more to help Selena, he was worried about how much time it might take to find her again.

"We know where those skalen are going," Lars said. "You heard her. On the other side of the mountains there's a great canyon, the Rift Valley. Past the canyon there's a plain. On the other side of the plain, we'll find the white city. Selena's going that way."

Taimin made a decision. "You're going to have to go to the white city and warn the Protector. Lives are at stake."

"What about you?"

"Like you said, you and I need each other. But at some point we'll have to separate. Selena and I will meet you there."

Lars cleared his throat. "You'll find her, lad."

"I will," Taimin said firmly.

"She's important," Lars said. "They're not going to hurt her. And she's smart, you know that. She's a survivor." He clapped Taimin on the back. "Come on, this is no place to stop."

Taimin gave a sharp nod. He took a last glance toward the scar of the firestorm's path, before he set his jaw and focused on the mountains ahead.

14

Selena carefully chose the place where she, Taimin, and Lars would make their escape. As she traveled at the head of the column with Group Leader Vail, she casted the terrain up ahead. As always, her talent gave her impressions that were fuzzy and indistinct, but she was able to guide the skalen toward a place where the scorched earth left by the firestorm was thin enough to pass through swiftly, but wide enough that the skalen wouldn't follow.

She hoped that her tight expression wouldn't give away her tension. When she glanced back through the crowd of marching figures, she saw the skinny mantorean, Rei-kika, return her stare. She concentrated on her breathing. Soon she would be leaving behind the area. She had to act now.

"Group Leader," she said, pleased when she managed to keep her voice steady. "I think I can cast something up ahead but I'm not sure." She looked behind her. "Can I speak with Rei-kika?"

For a moment Vail didn't reply. Instead she watched Selena, her reptilian eyes narrowed and calculating. "What is it you can see, mystic?"

Selena was prepared for the question. "Tall figures in the shadow of a cliff . . ." She made a show of hesitating. "They might just be sentinel cactuses."

Selena's plan was to walk toward the mantorean, but rather than stop, she would pick up speed and keep going until she joined Taimin and Lars. By the time the nearby skalen realized what was happening, the three humans would already be making their escape.

As Vail considered, Selena tried to conceal her growing panic. She had expected the old skalen to agree; after all, Selena was only doing what was asked of her.

"How many can you see?" Vail asked. "Are they moving?"

Selena thought furiously. If she said there were a lot of them, Vail would question why she was finding it difficult to decide what they were. "Just three. They aren't moving at the moment."

Vail made a decision. "Then you stay with me."

"But—"

"I have enough warriors to deal with them, whatever they are. In case you have not realized for yourself, I want to see what you are capable of on your own."

Selena struggled to keep her face blank. Without Group Leader Vail's permission to leave her side, she would never get free. As time passed, Selena cast frequent glances to the right, toward the smoking terrain the firestorm had left behind. Her opportunity would soon be lost forever. She could only hope that Taimin and Lars had the sense to go without her.

Almost as soon as she had the thought, a commotion broke out farther back. As her heart began to beat rapidly, Selena couldn't stop herself from turning, but it didn't matter; she wasn't the only one.

She held her breath. The wait was excruciating. But then joy burst inside her. She saw two figures, Lars and Taimin, race away from the column and into the heat. The pursuing skalen faltered and then stopped.

Selena's relief was overwhelming. Taimin and Lars had made it. They were free.

At the same time, without any possessions, she knew they would find it difficult to survive. She had no doubt that Taimin would try to find her, but before he risked his life she had to do everything she could to escape her predicament herself.

Three days later, in a region where the tall mountains loomed over low hills, Vail's scouts returned with news that they had found a series of caves. The younger scouts told their leader with a breathless excitement, and for once Selena saw the skalen around her smile with relief, as if they had been given a gift.

"We will rest for a time and recover from the journey," Vail instructed those around her. "These suns are getting to all of us."

The skalen shook their weapons and gave something like a cheer, and with renewed vigor the group marched to follow the scouts who led from the front. There was a climb involved, an arduous ascent up the hills to a place where dark mouths indicated openings in one of the mighty peaks. Even Selena fixed her gaze on the caves with longing, and although she was breathless by the time she reached the heights, she plunged inside the largest entrance and sighed with pleasure as the cool interior enveloped her.

The skalen settled in, posting sentries, laying out blankets and mats, and sending out parties to search for water. Selena watched as two skalen hunched over a pyramid of sticks and set down some glowing green fragments at the base of the kindling. One of the pair used a rock to smash the bits of aurelium together, and immediately there was a puff of smoke, followed by long tendrils of flame that caught onto the tinder in moments.

With everyone busy Selena found a quiet place to be alone and sat with her back against the rock. For once she wasn't trudging through the dirt and dust, and no one appeared to expect anything from her. Of their own accord, her eyes began to drift closed, but then they snapped open when she heard shuffling and a strange clicking sound.

She turned her head and saw Rei-kika's stick-thin figure. The mantorean clearly had the same idea as Selena as she sat down and slumped against the wall ten feet away. Selena remembered the sensation of violation when Rei-kika channeled through her, but at the same time, she also felt sympathy for the mantorean's plight.

Rei-kika lifted her triangular head and noticed Selena's attention. She gave Selena a look of dejection before hanging her head once more. Selena wondered if the scar on the side of her face was painful. It probably didn't matter to her as much as the knowledge that Vail had her eggs.

A memory came to Selena; she again heard Taimin, telling her that her talent was a part of her. It had made her angry at the time. Taimin had said that what she really needed was to be taught.

Rei-kika was a trained mystic. In comparison, Selena had never learned control. People had always accused her of terrible things, but she didn't even know if they were possible.

Selena made a decision.

As Selena moved along the wall, the mantorean looked up and tilted her head. Rei-kika seemed puzzled, but she nonetheless rotated her body to face Selena, shifting posture with an unusual double-jointed motion.

"Your name is Rei-kika?" Selena asked softly. "Do I have it right?"

"You do," the mantorean said in a staccato voice. "And you are Selena."

"How do you know that?"

"I know many things about you," Rei-kika said. "I . . . I am very sorry for what I did to you. It is forbidden. But I still did it."

"It wasn't your fault," Selena said.

"The skalen have my eggs. I must do as they say. But what I did . . . the channeling . . . it was wrong. I know that."

"I can see why it's forbidden." Selena grimaced as she remembered the sense of violation and loss of free will. She didn't know what she would have done, though, if she were a mother and someone had her children. "How did your eggs get taken?"

Rei-kika made an odd sound, a swishing exclamation that echoed around the cave. Selena realized it was a sound of distress. Then Rei-kika settled and gave something like a sigh.

"I will explain," she said. "We are nomads, but laying eggs is a difficult time and a group must stay fixed in one position. If the female is a mystic, the time of laying also blocks her ability to farcast. Among my race, only females are trained to be mystics." She glanced around the cave, but no one was watching them. "The laying must be done in an exposed, sunny place. It is a time of terrible danger. Humans and trulls know this, and take advantage of it."

"What happened to your group?" Selena asked.

"All dead," Rei-kika said. "The trull killed the males protecting me."

"I'm sorry," Selena said.

Rei-kika gave a shrug of her shoulders. "Fate has not been kind to either of us." She gave Selena a considering look. "Did you know Group Leader Vail has another mystic?"

"What was his name . . . Aris?"

Rei-kika nodded. "His power is not great, but he will know when you are casting. Aris is not skilled enough to actually know *where* you are casting, but there are those who can. Me, I can see what you see. Your thoughts are so loud it is impossible not to. As long as the Group Leader believes you are casting on her behalf, you are not under suspicion. But be warned, if you cast for your own reasons, you may be found out."

Selena reflected on the time when she had been searching for a good place to escape. She realized she had to be more careful in future. The fact that there was so much she didn't know only served to strengthen her resolve.

"Rei-kika . . ." She hesitated, but then her voice firmed. "Will you teach me?"

"What is it you wish to learn?" Rei-kika stared directly into her eyes.

"I didn't even know I could cast like I did with you. I want to learn to control it."

Rei-kika took a few moments to reply. "Are you certain that is what you want?"

Selena knew what Taimin would say. "I can't spend my life being afraid." But as soon as she finished speaking, she put her hands to her temples when she felt the familiar onset of a headache. She inwardly cursed; she might not have an opportunity to talk to Rei-kika again.

Rei-kika watched her. "There is much you do not know. Your abilities are completely untrained. I can help you."

The mantorean shifted closer. Selena was fascinated by her bone-like carapace, so hard, like stone, yet somehow Rei-kika had a face that could be expressive.

"If you train your mind, the pain will lessen," Rei-kika said. "The more powerful the mystic, the worse the pain can be. Among my race, the pain is a sign that one must be taught control."

"You can make it go away?" Selena asked.

Rei-kika took Selena's hands in her insect-like claws so that they faced each other cross-legged. "Concentrate on my voice," the mantorean said. "Try to clear your mind."

"I can't. It hurts too much."

"Think of a symbol. Something you consider pure, unchange-able . . . solid."

An image appeared in Selena's mind: a pale sphere on a field of black. She remembered a time when she had been on her back with a padded blanket underneath her and a warm body beside her, staring up at the glowing disc in the sky.

"Like the moon?" she asked.

"The moon is good," Rei-kika said. "Create an image of the moon in your mind, but rather than picture it in the sky, put it in your mind. Make your mind large enough to have space for the moon inside of it, and at the same time make the moon small enough to contain."

Selena tried to do as Rei-kika instructed. The moon she pictured had no craters, but it still glowed, a white orb shining in her mind's eye. Rather than being seen against a haze of sky and a backdrop of twinkling stars, this moon sat against pure black.

"How do you feel?" Rei-kika asked.

"Fine," Selena said. "I'm having difficulty thinking of the moon as both small and large, though."

"Is that all?"

Only then did Selena realize. "My headache. It's gone."

"Good. Do you wish to continue?"

"Is that all I need to do? Picture a moon and the headaches will go?"

"No, I am afraid it is not that simple. Your ability is yearning to be used, so it pushes through to the forefront of your mind. However, even as you access it, you will have to work harder to find the source of your power. Do you understand what I am saying?"

"I'm not sure I do."

"It will not always be so easy. The headaches will persist until you learn control."

Selena examined the moon inside her mind. She imagined herself rubbing it, cupping it with tendrils like fingers, and all of a sudden it sparkled, shining for a moment as bright as the golden sun.

"What was that?" she asked.

"I felt it. You were touching your power. Try something for me. How big is the moon?"

"Big."

"Is it bigger than you?"

"Yes."

"Make it smaller, until it is the size of your hand, and then smaller still."

Against the darkness of her mind's eye, the moon changed, shifting until it was no bigger than a child's fist. "What then?"

"Hold your symbol in your palm."

It didn't make sense, yet somehow Selena knew exactly what to do. She picked up the glowing orb and inspected it, mesmerized by its radiance.

"Now imagine that the symbol is light, so light that it wants to float into the air. The only thing preventing it from rising is you. It is pulling you even so, and you are feeling yourself lifted up."

Selena felt a great change.

Something became unstuck, freed from confinement. She experienced a sensation like floating, and giddiness nearly overwhelmed her. Whatever had happened, she was no longer connected to her body. She rose up, apart from it, and looked down.

For the second time she saw herself, a young woman with long black hair, from above. Yet she was somehow separate from the woman who sat opposite a mantorean, their knees touching, neither of them speaking. She was in a cave, and she was worried she would hit the ceiling if she kept floating upward. What would happen when she drifted into the solid rock?

Be calm, a voice said beside her. She was aware of Rei-kika's soothing presence. *There are two forms of casting, and you are only familiar with the first. Mystics with little power or those without training only know they can sense things out of view. Your great power has*

143

enabled you to gain impressions from very far away, much farther than I could see. But with the exception of the time when I forced it upon you, you have never known the clarity of true farcasting.

Is this really happening? Am I looking down at myself?

You are.

Selena became filled with a pleasure she had never known before. Always she had seen her ability as a curse, something that drove people away and caused them to fear and hate her. For the first time she felt excitement at being truly free. No one could keep her prisoner now. Even if the skalen tied her down, she could rise above them and travel the world. What if there were other things she could do?

I can sense your pleasure, but be careful, there is danger in what we do, Rei-kika's voice sounded inside Selena's mind.

This is wonderful.

It comes naturally to you, Rei-kika said. *Now, let us travel a short distance together.*

Selena turned and saw a hazy figure nearby: a transparent, insect-like silhouette that could only be the mantorean. Rei-kika drifted away from where they sat with their knees touching and Selena floated over to join her.

Look back at our bodies. What do you see?

Selena was now a dozen paces from their two cross-legged forms. *It's faint . . . but I can see a white line connecting me to my body.*

This is your lifeline. Your lifeline links you to your body at all times. The more powerful the mystic, the longer the lifeline can stretch. If you go too far or stay out of your body too long, your lifeline will bring you back. But be careful. The connection gets weaker the farther you are from your physical form. If you panic and pull too hard, it can break completely. With no connection at all, your body will stop breathing. You would have very little time to find your way back.

As Selena looked around the cave, she tilted to peer up at the ceiling. *What happens if I fly up into the rock?*

You might find the sensation unpleasant, but it brings no immediate danger. Your lifeline will still be with you.

What else can I do?

The mantorean hesitated. *I think that is enough for today.*

Selena turned to watch the skalen moving about the cave. She could stare into the eyes of any one of them, and they wouldn't even know she was watching.

Selena, return to your body. Rei-kika's tone became alarmed. *Selena? Concentrate. Where is your focus?*

My focus?

Your symbol. Your moon. Your source of power. Where is it now?

Selena realized that the sphere of radiant light was gone. She suddenly felt lost; where was her body? What if she could never return? Fear shivered through her.

Steady! Rei-kika called in her mind. *Look for your lifeline.*

Selena was drowning, starved of air, her chest filled with nothingness. With a jolt she experienced a snap as she was abruptly pulled. With a strange sensation of reconnection, she opened her eyes and took a gasp of real air. She panted as the sound of her own ragged breathing dominated her hearing. Skalen sitting against the opposite wall of the cave looked curiously at her, while Rei-kika tilted her triangular head and gazed at Selena inquisitively.

Then pain struck Selena's temples. She cried out and put her hands to her head. Her heart pounded like a drum, far too loud in her ears as she rolled onto her back and the seizure struck her with force. She could see Rei-kika frantically moving her small mouth, but the words vanished down a distant hole.

A skalen arrived and prodded Rei-kika with his spear. Another came, and Selena recognized Watch Leader Rees. Rei-kika was hauled to her feet and marched away. Skalen guards watched Selena

145

and stood over her, their javelins held at the ready as if she were going to leap up and attack them.

The pain faded after a while, leaving Selena breathless and exhausted. She slept, a slumber of utter tiredness, her mind needing rest and recovery like never before.

Selena dreamed of a distant moon; she was floating toward it, and a man floated beside her. She turned to look at him and saw Taimin.

How do you know where we're going? Taimin asked. *What aren't you telling me?*

Selena wanted to tell him that she was trying to learn control, but when she moved her lips, no sound would come out.

———

Selena pressed forward to reach the front of the mass of skalen. Her recovery meant she had been one of the last to depart and she was worried about Rei-kika. She saw Group Leader Vail up ahead, conferring with her son Rees. It was early morning and Dex hung just above the peaks of the nearby mountains, which they were already leaving behind. The terrain was undulating but the ground was hard and clear of debris. She caught sight of the mantorean through the crowd of marching skalen.

"I see you are feeling better," Rei-kika said when Selena joined her.

Selena spoke softly so no one could hear them. "I'm sorry if I got you into trouble."

"I had some difficult questions to answer."

"What did you say?"

"I told the truth," Rei-kika said, glancing at the skalen walking around them. "You saw a group of bax approaching and were trying to gauge their intentions. That is why I left early. I explained that I cannot cast so far without your help. They decided to take me closer."

Selena felt her mind caressed. An image was passed to her, a frozen vision of a dozen bax seen from above. Selena's eyes widened. She hadn't known mystics could do this.

"You said there were twelve?" Watch Leader Rees asked as he came over, directing his query at Rei-kika.

Taking her cue, Selena spoke. "Definitely twelve. The leader carries a big axe at his side and wears a strip of cloth tied around his upper arm."

"How far?"

The image Selena had been passed hadn't given her an idea of how far away they were. Selena panicked for a moment until Rei-kika spoke. "They have covered more ground since Selena saw them. If we continue as we are, we will meet them within the hour."

"Good. I will tell my mother," Rees said.

Rei-kika waited until Rees was gone before addressing Selena in her low, clicking voice. "You need further instruction. Vail will make me channel through you again if you cannot show that you can control your ability."

"Is it true that you can read someone's mind? What about controlling their thoughts?"

Rei-kika made a croaking sound that Selena realized was laughter. "Let us concern ourselves with farcasting." Her voice became serious once more. "One day your power will kill you if you are not more careful. You cannot stop yourself from using it. It will give you pain until you develop skill."

"Will you teach me more?"

"Teaching quickly is dangerous."

"I don't care. I'm ready."

Rei-kika gave Selena an impenetrable stare. "We shall see if you still think so when the day is done."

15

"How do you know where we're going?" Taimin asked Lars. "What aren't you telling me?"

"Just a little farther," Lars said.

"What's gotten into you?"

"Nothing. Come on."

"If we don't find some more water soon we'll die."

Taimin glared at the big man. His bald head looked like a wyvern's egg as he strode purposefully ahead, almost too fast for Taimin to keep up. Griff trudged along at the rear, panting constantly. The wherry was as tired and thirsty as the two men.

All of a sudden Lars stopped in his tracks. His expression became puzzled and his head tilted to the side. They had been traveling underneath a rocky overhang, using its shade to give them some relief from the two suns. The foothills below the mountains were filled with deep gorges, bounded by tall walls.

Without warning Lars walked over to a huge pricklethorn bush, much bigger than he was, and grabbed hold of some of the spiky twigs in his meaty hands.

"What are you doing?" Taimin asked incredulously as he rushed forward. "You'll hurt yourself."

Lars pulled and the pricklethorn bush easily came away from a cavity. He soon held the entire plant mass in the air, away from the cliff, before planting it down on the ground. Taimin realized the bush was dead, with no roots embedded at all. He now saw a man-sized gap in the rock wall.

"How did you know?" Taimin asked. His eyes narrowed. "You've been here before."

"Never in my life," Lars said.

"Then how did you know?"

Lars hesitated. "I heard a voice," he said reluctantly. As Taimin frowned, puzzled, Lars tapped the side of his head.

"Someone's guiding you?" Taimin demanded. "Who?"

"He said he can help us. And the fact is, lad, we need help. You coming?" Lars indicated the opening.

"But why you and not me . . . ?" The truth dawned on Taimin. "It can't be . . ."

"What?"

"You're a mystic?"

Lars scowled at Taimin, and then his expression softened. He looked abashed. "Only a little."

The skinner entered the passage before Taimin could challenge him further. Shaking his head, Taimin waved Griff through. He then followed and replaced the pricklethorn bush behind him, pulling it in tightly so that it covered the hidden entrance. There was no need to duck his head, and soon the passage came to an end. He stepped out to find himself in a narrow gorge. He looked up; high above he saw a thin strip of sky. While Griff sniffed at the air, Taimin scanned the area cautiously.

"The gorge keeps going," Lars said when Taimin had caught up to him. "He said he lives alone. This way."

"So why did you need Selena?" Taimin asked.

Lars snorted. "Lad, you still don't realize, do you? That girl is infinitely more powerful than me. Her casting shines like Dex—I can see it, and it's beautiful to behold—while my talent is more like a shard of glass. With my eyes closed, I can sense that you're nearby . . . sometimes. That's about it."

"Yet everywhere Selena has gone people have feared her," Taimin said. "If she's so powerful, why didn't she do something?"

"Because she's wild . . . untrained and undisciplined. And because people have always tried to keep her potential from her. If you had a caged wyvern, and could convince the wyvern it's a lizard, you'd do it, wouldn't you?"

"What is it she's capable of?"

"By the rains, it's not like I know myself. But I'll tell you this: she's valuable to those skalen. And one more thing . . . if she ever gets instruction, I won't go within a thousand leagues of her without protecting my mind."

Lars glanced at Taimin and noticed his furrowed brow.

"Mystics have their abilities confused by aurelium," the skinner explained. "Sometimes people with wealth wear a circle of aurelium shards around their neck. Remember that skalen—the group leader, Vail? They say it protects a mind from intrusion."

The walls of the gorge soon parted to reveal a far wider area, with high cliffs on all sides. Taimin saw signs of habitation. The rows in the groves of lifegiver cactuses were too regular to be natural, and as he and Lars trudged between fields of razorgrass, he saw a workbench and some rough planks of blackwood. A cluster of basalt trees grew near a fire pit.

"Whoever lives here knows what he's doing," Taimin said. He conjured up an image of a tough, solitary settler; a male version of Abi.

"Still, one raid and it's all gone," Lars said.

"Which might never come."

"Or might come tomorrow," Lars said.

A squat house similar to the one Taimin grew up in dominated the center of the small valley, fenced on all sides at a height of twelve feet. Caves at the base of the cliffs gave the impression they were carved by an intelligent hand rather than nature.

Taimin's gaze moved from one area to the next. A mystic had spoken to Lars, in the same way that the trapped mantorean had sought help from Selena. Lars was right: they needed help. But what if it was a trap? He sought comfort by reminding himself that he and Lars had nothing to take.

Spying movement, Taimin tensed. He saw a figure walking toward them, a smile on his face and his arms wide in welcome.

"Lars . . ." Taimin said uncertainly.

The mystic who had guided Lars was a skalen.

Far older than Vail, he had a bald head, stooped back, and walked with slow steps. Most skalen were toothsome, but his broad smile showed missing teeth. Nonetheless, he bore scars on his hands and a hunting knife at his waist; to have lived so long, he was clearly a survivor. In comparison to the skalen traveling with Vail, his leather trousers and vest were surprisingly close to what a human might wear.

Lars gave Taimin a stunned expression. "It was just a voice . . . I had no idea."

"Please, you have nothing to fear," the old skalen said. "My name is Syrus. Welcome to my homestead."

"Why didn't you say you were a skalen?" Lars asked.

"Would you have come?" Syrus asked. "You are two travelers in need, and you might have stayed away."

Taimin's shoulders began to relax, but he was still wary. Not so long ago, he had been held captive by skalen, and here he was, seeking help from another.

Syrus glanced from face to face. His almond eyes had depth and conveyed the wisdom of many years. "There was a time when I feared helping others, afraid I would be murdered in the night for what I have." He chuckled. "But what I have is not much, and

I miss conversation. Perhaps a sword would be a better way to go than to die alone in my sleep. Time will tell."

"Skalen are supposed to live in mines and caves," Taimin said cautiously.

"So we are." Syrus smiled. He glanced over his shoulder. "I did not build my home. My adoptive parents did, and they were human. They found me when I was a youngling and raised me. My story is an unusual one, but not unique."

"Where are they now?" Lars asked.

"They were believers, so I like to think that they have gone to Earth."

Other than the occasional bedtime story, Taimin had never heard his parents talk much about the afterlife. Abi certainly wasn't the type to push the idea of Earth, and it was strange to now hear a skalen talk about it.

"As I said to Lars, I am all alone," Syrus said. "I can help you," he gave a wry smile, "if you can trust a skalen."

Taimin realized that he and Lars would be foolish to spurn Syrus's offer. "We will honor your trust," he said.

The old skalen gave Taimin a close inspection. "You're a young one, aren't you?"

"I'm Taimin."

"Yes, yes, I know. Lars here told me."

Taimin glanced at Lars, still struck by the ability the skinner had kept hidden.

"And this here is Griff," Syrus said.

Griff gave a curious whine. The wherry looked questioningly at Taimin, and when Taimin nodded, he came forward to nudge the skalen's waist, hoping for a scratch. But Syrus backed away. "Wherries make me sneeze." He gave Taimin an apologetic smile. "Apologies, but he will have to stay outside the fence."

"That's fine," Taimin said. "We don't want to be any trouble."

"I'm sure you don't," Syrus said, amused, "but trouble clearly found you." He cast his eyes over them. "No weapons. No water."

"We escaped from a group of skalen," Lars said. He cleared his throat. "Let's just say they didn't treat us well."

"Ah," Syrus said. Mirth creased the corners of his mouth. "I think you can be forgiven for your reaction when you saw me then."

Taimin hesitated, but he knew he had to ask. "Our friend is still with them. Have you seen them? Can you farcast to find them?"

"Sorry, but I can't cast farther than these hills. If Lars here didn't have some talent of his own, I doubt I would have found you at all. I just keep an eye out for prey to hunt, or anything that might hunt me. Now, both of you, come with me."

Taimin and Lars approached the homestead by the old skalen's side. When Griff reached the ditch and the fence behind it, Taimin made sure the wherry knew to stay where he was.

"You are safe for a time," Syrus said. "Once you have rested, then I'll help you get to Zorn." When Taimin threw him a puzzled look, Syrus met Taimin's gaze. "That is where Lars said you're traveling to. Zorn is the white city's name, and it is unlike any place you have seen before."

⁓

Syrus was generous with his hospitality, and soon Taimin and Lars had taken care of their first priority: survival. Water washed away their fatigue. Nettle soup, lizard eggs, and stewed raptor revitalized their spirits.

Taimin was anxious to keep moving, but he knew that they had to take advantage of the opportunity to gather their strength and also supplies for the journey ahead. The better he and Lars prepared themselves, the swifter they would be able to travel.

He pulled thorns out of Griff's paws and dug mites from under his drooping ears. He then searched for Lars and found him with Syrus. He was surprised to see Lars and the old skalen seated on armchairs on the homestead's porch, deep in conversation, and so proposed he go hunting with Griff. He was determined to repay Syrus's kindness and wanted to fill the skalen's larder as well as gather some meat for his own journey.

"Wait a moment," Syrus said. His reptilian eyes became unfocused and then he nodded. "Can't see any big hazards. That doesn't mean it's safe, mind, but there's nothing I can sense. Follow me."

The old skalen led Taimin into the wooden shack, which inevitably stirred memories as Taimin saw the water collector and nursery. Syrus continued into a small storage room at the back of the house. Shelves lined the walls and hooks hung everywhere, with an array of tools ready to grab at short notice. Syrus reached up to a hook and brought something down. As Syrus turned, Taimin saw a worn composite bow in his hands.

"Here, take this," Syrus said. Surprised, Taimin took the bow while Syrus fetched something else; soon a bundle of obsidian-tipped arrows followed the bow. "They're yours."

"I . . . Thank you," Taimin said. "I'll return them when I . . ."

The skalen's eyes narrowed. "I said they're yours."

"Thank you," Taimin said again to Syrus's departing back as the old skalen returned to the porch.

"You need it more than I," Syrus grumbled and sat down again beside Lars. "Now go catch supper. Come home before dark. And Taimin?"

"What?"

"If you forget to put the pricklethorn bush back in its place, I'll cut your heart out and feed it to your wherry for dinner."

Taimin smiled as he left the porch to walk through the fence and over the planks that crossed the spiked ditch. He saw Griff waiting for him and put his hand on the wherry's back. Soon he was leaving the homestead behind.

———～———

Taimin returned as Dex plunged toward the horizon, leaving the landscape tinged red in the light of the crimson sun. The area around Syrus's homestead teemed with game. Raptors, lizards, and even a scrub rat lay piled across the wherry's saddle.

As he rode Griff's broad back and traveled the narrow canyon, Taimin was again struck by the sense of returning home. At the same time, he wondered about the lives of the people who lived in Zorn. He didn't want to go to the white city alone, not without Selena. When she had been given a chance to wall off her power, she hadn't taken it. The Protector might still be able to help her. Taimin held on to the deep hope that his injury might be healed.

Taimin found Lars outside the homestead's fence, hauling dried cactus to a growing fire while sweat poured from his bald head in rivulets. Taimin marveled that Lars could have such a thick beard in the heat. He couldn't imagine the big man without it. With Taimin still riding, the swiftness of his arrival took Lars by surprise.

"By the rains, lad. You've only got two speeds, don't you? Slow and fast."

Taimin slipped off the wherry's back. "Here," he said as he untied the strung-up rat from Griff's rump. "I've got dinner."

"Scrub rat? Not for me, thanks."

"That's for Griff." The fat rat fell to the ground with a thump. The wherry whimpered in anticipation. "Just a moment," Taimin murmured, patting his side. "This is for us," he said to Lars.

Taimin unstrapped the raptors and carried them to Lars two at a time, laying them down on a flat rock nearby. Then he fetched the dead lizards, while Lars looked on hungrily.

"I'll take care of these," Lars said.

Spying movement, Taimin saw Syrus standing high on the cliff above. The old skalen gave a beckoning wave. Taimin shielded his eyes and waved back.

"What does he want?" he asked.

"Knowing him, you're in for a deep talk." Lars gave a jerk of his chin. "There's a path leading up there behind the house."

Taimin headed for the back of the shack, leaving Lars skinning the lizards while Griff bit into the scrub rat with stomach-churning crunching sounds. He soon found the path and climbed up, surprised at the old skalen's agility when he saw how precarious the trail was. He was panting by the time he made it to the top of the cliff; the day's hunting had taken its toll, but if Syrus could make it up, then so could he.

Syrus stood close to the cliff's edge and was gazing out over the landscape. As Taimin approached the old skalen, he realized that from his new vantage point he could see past the other cliffs and over the surrounding area. Most of the terrain was made up of varying shades of red and brown, but green spots marked out cactuses, and even a few gnarled trees fought for survival.

Taimin came to a halt beside the skalen, but as time passed Syrus remained quiet. Taimin opened his mouth and then closed it, before deciding to break the silence.

"You must know this land well," he said.

Syrus didn't stop looking at the expanse. "I suppose I do."

"When I was small, we lived near some cliffs and I used to stare out at the land below," Taimin said. "I wondered if what I could see was the entire world, or whether the world was a thousand times bigger. I wondered if I'd ever know."

"Good questions," Syrus said. He turned to face Taimin, but rather than smile, his flat, lizard-like face was unusually sober. "Worth asking."

"What is it you think about?" Taimin asked.

"I like to think about water," Syrus said seriously.

Taimin frowned, puzzled.

"Once there was water in the wasteland, out in the open," Syrus continued. "Rivers of it, and lakes, and even oceans."

Taimin wondered how old Syrus was. "You've seen it?"

Syrus laughed, a hearty sound given his ancient voice. "No, of course not. I only know because of the evidence of my eyes. Look." He pointed. "Do you see, in the distance? That snaking line is a dried riverbed." He glanced at Taimin. "I've been to places where what was once ocean left smooth ripples in the land and the salt still shining white."

"Where did the water go?"

"I don't know. This is a burning land. We have two suns and unbearable heat surrounds us. We call the boundary the firewall, but there is no wall, just a region beyond it where nothing can live. Perhaps once our world was a more hospitable place than it is now. Perhaps once there was no firewall at all."

Taimin felt hemmed in, surrounded by death on all sides. Syrus's talk of a small area enclosed by fire made him wonder if the wall could close in.

"Will the wasteland shrink? What if it gets worse?"

"We all die someday. But to reassure you, it seems clear to me that the time when water flowed is many, many years ago, beyond several lifetimes. There is just as great a chance that one day the rains might return."

As he gazed out from the summit, Taimin tried to imagine the rust-colored wasteland moistened by rivers but couldn't. It sounded like a pleasant dream.

"If these ideas confuse you," Syrus said, "then think on this. How do you know what a lake is? Or an ocean, for that matter? Neither you nor I have seen one."

157

"Stories of Earth, of course."

Syrus nodded. "A place with no firewall and a single, yellow sun. A land filled with green forests, rivers, and oceans. A world where white clouds drift through the sky."

"It's where we go when we die," Taimin said. "My father believed in it . . . I think. I'm not sure if my mother did."

"Let me tell you something," Syrus said. "Some mantoreans and skalen I've spoken to say they have their own Earth. But the mantoreans' paradise is dry, like the land we're seeing now, with vegetation that floats on the sea. My fellow skalen have a blue sun in theirs. Why such strong differences? I can only think of one answer. Perhaps rather than places we go to when we die, these might be the worlds where we were born. Perhaps rather than dreaming, we are remembering."

Taimin's brow furrowed. "But if we once lived somewhere else, how are we here?"

"I don't know." Syrus smiled. "We may never know."

Taimin thought for a moment. "You said the water dried up," he said. "Maybe Earth was here. If there was no firewall, the world would be a much bigger place."

"Ah." Syrus's strange eyes gleamed. "So, you are a thinker. There are too few of us, Taimin. The wasteland is a harsh place to spend much time on intelligent thought. It is a struggle, but do not stop."

Taimin had a question he had been burning to ask. "You know about the white city. Is it everything it's supposed to be?"

Syrus considered for a moment. "That depends on what you think it is. For you, a human, it may be."

Taimin thought about all the dreams he had shared with Selena and Lars on their journey. "It's supposed to be a haven. The Protector rules wisely and looks after his people. Fields of crops grow enough food for all. There's plenty of water. It's somewhere everyone is safe—"

"Everyone human," Syrus interjected.

Taimin paused and then frowned. If bax or skalen were threatening Zorn, of course the Protector would defend his city. "It's true, then?" he asked. "It's real?"

"Of course Zorn is real. I have never been there, but I would assume the Protector is certainly intelligent, to have remained in his position for many years. Yes, there are fields. And any large population requires a source of water to survive." Syrus's ancient voice became grim. "Remember, however, that the threat from the Rift Valley is a real one."

Taimin thought immediately about Selena and felt a chill. Vail and her group of skalen had been heading to the Rift Valley. Selena was a valuable mystic, but soon she would be put into a position where she would be forced to aid Zorn's enemies. If she helped, people would die. If she refused, either the skalen or bax would kill her.

He knew it was time to go.

16

After the dozen bax joined the hundred skalen, everything was different. The skalen drew themselves up and became sterner, more aggressive, as if mindful about the way they portrayed themselves to their soon-to-be allies. In turn, the bax made a point of traveling at the head of the column; it was their territory the skalen were entering. The two groups might be united in purpose, but even Selena could see that members of both races found it strange to be working together. The tension between them wasn't simply going to disappear.

The white city had a name: Zorn. Selena had overheard it on the journey, but now the place that her captors planned to conquer came up more often. Mugrak, the senior bax envoy—a stocky, wart-covered creature with ropy arms and a voice like gravel—spoke about the Protector with obvious hatred.

Meanwhile, as the large group left the mountains behind and entered the Rift Valley, Vail kept both Selena and Rei-kika close. Vail was pleased when Selena was able to accurately farcast without the ability being drawn from her like water squeezed from a stone. But Mugrak was often nearby when Selena made her reports, and she felt his deep-set eyes on her.

Selena and Rei-kika spent time together every night. The mantorean's instruction gave Selena a level of control she had never had before. Her headaches stopped altogether. Rei-kika kept telling her to slow down but she wanted to learn as much as she could. When she was casting, she was free.

Group Leader Vail called a halt.

The immense canyon had sucked the column into its depths. Caves, chimneys, and broad splits in the rock faces created openings that beckoned on both sides. Walls of imposing cliff rose to a towering height, blotting out the suns. For a long time they had been traveling in shade as they followed the canyon's floor, much to the relief of the darkness-loving skalen. Even in daylight, a multitude could hide in the Rift Valley.

Selena took the opportunity to sip from her water flask as she stood with Rei-kika near the front of the group. Her gaze roved. She was always alert for an opportunity to get away, but so far Vail was keeping her under close guard. Taimin and Lars would be out there, somewhere, but Selena knew she would be difficult to find.

She watched as Group Leader Vail testily discussed their route with Mugrak. The bax envoy was taller than Vail and the grooves above his eyes gave him a menacing scowl. Selena wasn't close enough to hear Mugrak's words, but his guttural voice didn't sound pleased.

"Why are they joining forces?" Selena asked as Vail lifted her finger and prodded it into Mugrak's chest. She had tried to get Vail talking, without success. Rei-kika, however, sometimes spent time with Vail's son Rees.

Rei-kika spoke softly as she replied. "The Protector's soldiers have been fighting the bax for years, but it is only recently that they began to raid the mines where skalen live."

Selena's brow furrowed. "If the Protector is under attack, he's going to fight back."

"Be that as it may, these skalen are not from this area. Vail's clan leader, Rathis, was captured by the humans while he was visiting another clan. Vail received news not long ago: Rathis is still alive. Vail has brought her warriors to the Rift Valley in order to see him freed."

The situation was more complicated than Selena had realized. "Can Zorn survive?"

"Have you seen it up close?" Rei-kika asked.

Selena shook her head.

"Zorn has a tall wall," Rei-kika said. "Who can say? With an alliance, the Rift Valley may finally have the power to conquer the city. Rees says that the Warden of the Rift Valley, a bax named Blixen, is a strong and capable leader."

Selena's worry grew when she remembered the bax they kept encountering, all traveling in the same direction. "I suppose it depends on the numbers Blixen can summon."

Rei-kika nodded. "One thing that is clear is that the bax traveling here are those most willing to risk their lives for plunder and status."

"Why are the skalen so afraid of the bax?" Selena asked as she watched Vail argue with Mugrak; the bax's ugly, knobbed head bobbed up and down while he spoke. She frowned. It looked like they were discussing more than just their route.

"Look at the difference in their size," Rei-kika said. "The bax are stronger and more numerous than the skalen. The skalen have superior weaponry, but a bax is an intimidating creature."

Vail and Mugrak stopped talking, and the old skalen gave a resigned nod. Selena was relieved to see that their argument appeared to have been settled, but then she felt a chill when Mugrak's dark gaze focused on her. Vail left Mugrak's side to walk toward Selena and Rei-kika. As the group leader approached, Selena was surprised to see that her tilted eyes looked troubled.

Vail came to a halt. She stood directly in front of Selena and waited a moment before speaking. Selena felt her heart rate increase. Her intuition told her something bad was about to happen.

"Mugrak and his followers are going to take you to cast for them, Selena," Vail said without preamble. "Rei-kika, you will stay with me."

Selena drew in a sharp breath. She glanced at Mugrak, who was watching the exchange with a satisfied look on his wart-covered face. Vail had been less than kind to her, but Selena feared the bax more. She remembered standing on the hill with Lars, certain she was about to die. Her thoughts turned to the idea of running, but she was surrounded by skalen and in Mugrak's home territory.

"Why?" she asked Vail. She shook her head. "No. I won't go."

"I am not giving you a choice," Vail hissed. "We have struck a bargain. When the fighting starts, Mugrak will help ensure our clan leader, Rathis, makes it out alive. In return, Mugrak plans to offer you as a gift to Blixen, Warden of the Rift Valley. We have Rei-kika to cast for us. You are the price he demanded."

"Group Leader, don't do this," Selena said.

Rei-kika made a clicking sound of concern.

"Listen to me," Vail said firmly. "Mugrak wishes to travel ahead, but our forces are to merge with the main host when we arrive. I will still be near, young mystic. Remember, you are valuable. No harm will come to you."

Mugrak and another bax came over. Selena's nostrils flared when she saw that Mugrak's companion held a length of leather cord in his hands.

"We will take the payment now, Group Leader," Mugrak grunted. "Borg, bind the girl."

The bax called Borg grabbed Selena and turned her roughly. She threw her body forward to pull free, but with a growl Borg grabbed her again, this time twisting her wrists behind her back. She struggled, but the stocky bax wrapped the cord around her wrists, tying them hard. When it was done, she stood with her heart pounding.

"Her talent is wild," Vail said to Mugrak. "I have learned to get the most out of her, but without your own mystics you may have difficulty."

"That is no concern of yours," Mugrak said. "We have ways to make her do our bidding."

———

Mugrak gathered the rest of his dozen warriors, and without a word of farewell he ordered the march to begin. In moments Selena had left the skalen behind, with Mugrak setting a far brisker pace to head deeper into the immense canyon. The maze of side passages was confusing but he obviously knew where they were going.

Selena fought to control her apprehension. She had never been this close to a bax before, and now she was alone with a dozen of them. She smelled their musty odor as Borg herded her along, and when she stumbled or made an involuntary sound of pain, a sharp jab silenced her. There was more variety in their appearance than there was with skalen. Mugrak's face was wart-covered and mottled with a fungus-like pigmentation, while Borg had the thickest neck she had ever seen. As she glanced at the other marching warriors she sensed there was no gentleness in their nature. Some had colorful blotches on their faces and necks, and they wore armor rather than clothing. Their weapons had all seen heavy use. Mugrak's harsh grunts kept them in line.

The forced march continued for hours. Selena wondered about her fate. She had to find a way to get free. Only then could she warn the Protector of Zorn about the growing threat on his doorstep.

But as the light began to fade and fatigue dragged at her limbs, her thoughts turned to a more immediate fear. She knew that if she didn't get a chance to rest, she wouldn't be able to think, let alone cast. Her dread grew every time one of the bax looked her way.

The ravine narrowed, and they followed a chasm with steep walls of rock on both sides. Mugrak evidently knew where he was going and turned when the path forked. Selena glanced up. The sky overhead was shifting in hue from blue to dark purple. The first stars appeared, one by one.

At last Mugrak called a halt. They had come to a place where the walls closed in to encircle a wide area of red dirt. Mugrak set Selena down and gave her some water from a leather bladder, along with a few strips of dried meat. Meanwhile the rest of the contingent erected tents made of animal skins stretched over frames of thin sticks.

Slumped with exhaustion, Selena sat on the dirt and ate to keep up her strength. Around her bax started fires and set off to forage and hunt. As soon as she finished eating, her eyelids dragged, but then snapped open when she had a sudden thought. She anxiously counted the tents. There were seven of them, so the bax must sleep two to a tent. She could only hope that the last might be set aside for her alone.

"Get up," Borg said. He reached down and hauled her to her feet. As soon as she was up, he then forced her over to one of the tents. "Get in." He gave her a push and she stumbled as she entered.

Falling onto her hands and knees, she glared back at him. "Stay where you are until Mugrak returns. He has a task to complete but will be back soon."

Borg disappeared, but everywhere Selena heard the grunts of the bax around her, mingling with the crackle of campfires. Despite her exhaustion, sleep was a long time coming.

17

"Mystic." A voice like sandpaper jolted Selena awake.

Bright daylight shone through the tent's opening. Mugrak loomed over her, but the tent was tall and he was only hunching because of the natural stoop of his back. He stared down at her with his menacing, deep-set eyes.

"You humans can certainly sleep. It is late in the day. Stir yourself."

The cobwebs lifted from Selena's mind. Sitting up, she warily looked at Mugrak as she wondered what was coming.

"I traded for you and now I own you, until I gift you to mighty Blixen," Mugrak said. "Unlike humans, we honor our trades. It will not be easy to find this Rathis when we conquer Zorn, but find him I will. Do you understand? I will get my value." With his last words spittle flecked from Mugrak's mouth. "Wait here," he grunted.

The powerfully built bax backed away and left the tent. As soon as he vanished from view, Selena saw his companion, Borg, watching her silently. Her pulse began to quicken.

Mugrak's thick body appeared at the tent's opening, and then something hit her, thrown with force. Selena barely caught the tangle of limbs and blonde hair. She managed to take one arm, then another, until she found herself holding a small, human girl. The girl was terrified, staring at Selena with wide eyes. Tear-marks streaked the grime on her cheeks and her nose ran while she trembled.

"Disgusting things," Mugrak grunted, wiping his hands on his leather trousers. "There is simply no good place to hold them."

"The hair," said Borg.

Mugrak came over to Selena and took the girl's hair in a gnarled fist. He lifted her high, holding her easily, the strands of hair as taught as a bowstring. The girl emitted a long, piercing scream.

"Stop!" Selena cried.

She lunged forward but Mugrak was bigger and stronger, and kicked her back. As the girl's shriek continued, Selena wanted more than anything to stop what was happening and take the child far, far away. For the first time she thought of using her ability to harm another. Was there something wrong in that? She decided there wasn't.

But even as she pictured the moon it vanished from her mind's eye. Her thoughts were in turmoil; she had no idea what to do. Rei-kika had never shown her anything about using her power as a weapon. The symbol in her mind faded before it was formed.

She tried again to throw herself at Mugrak, but he only lifted the girl higher. The girl's scream went on and on.

"How do I make her stop?" Mugrak asked Borg. "This noise jars my nerves."

"Stop hurting her!" Selena clenched her fists. "She's in pain!"

"From what?" Mugrak frowned.

"Her hair! Put her down!"

Mugrak set the girl down and she instantly folded into a heap. He turned to Borg. "Less mess on my hands, yes, but far too much noise," he said. "Take her away."

Borg grabbed the girl, lifting her up in his arms and throwing her over his shoulder. He left the tent, and Selena found herself alone with Mugrak.

"Why is she here?" Selena's eyes narrowed. Righteous anger coursed through her veins.

"You humans are sentimental creatures. I traded for her. She was being kept as a pet, but her owners were tired of her. She did not cost me much."

"Don't hurt her." Selena's fists were still clenched as she glared at him.

"Her fate is in your hands. You must do my bidding and, most of all," his expression darkened, "do not embarrass me when I present you to the warden."

Selena was so filled with rage that her jaw felt tight and sore. The child might still be with her family if it weren't for these creatures, who wanted Selena to spy for them, to guide them through dangers and search the city for weaknesses, so they could kill and capture more children, and end the lives of more humans. "Where are her parents?" she asked in a low voice.

"They were settlers. I joined in the raid. They are all dead."

"You killed them."

"Yes," Mugrak grunted. He turned as Borg re-entered the tent, this time without the girl. "Good. Now we can begin."

Mugrak crouched next to Selena, his breath hot and fast as he stared into her eyes. "I want you to tell me about Zorn, the city that protects the humans while they drive us from these lands. Describe it to me in detail. I have seen it up close, and risked my life to escape the city guard, so I will know if you are lying. If you are as strong as the skalen say, you will do this for me. My only reason to camp here was to give you this test, and I will give you one chance only. A dead human girl-child means nothing to me."

"No," Selena said, staring into his eyes. "I won't do it."

Mugrak turned to his companion. "Cut the girl's hand off and bring it to me. Do it quickly. Those weak skalen might catch up to us soon."

"Which one?"

Mugrak's face curled up. "What?"

"Which hand?"

"I don't care," Mugrak snapped. "Just get it done."

As Borg turned to leave the tent, Selena knew she had to act. Her mind worked furiously. Thoughts surfaced and arguments opposed them. She gritted her teeth.

If she helped Mugrak, she would be putting an entire city at risk.

If she didn't, she would be dooming a child to certain death.

"No, stop," Selena said, loud enough to catch Borg at the entrance. The look Selena gave Mugrak was venomous, but she reminded herself that all she had to do was describe a place to the bax that he already knew. "Don't hurt her. I will do it."

"Excellent," Mugrak said. "Describe the city. Farcast Zorn."

Selena drew in a deep, shaking breath. She tried to ignore Mugrak's glare and the sour stench of her surroundings.

Her vision became unfocused.

She again pictured the moon, round and indomitable, high in the sky, far away and massive. Remembering Rei-kika's lessons, she made the moon pure and featureless, a sphere of golden light without craters or flaws.

She continued to slow her breathing to calm herself. She fought the surging emotions and tried to bury thoughts of the little girl deep where they couldn't intrude. After all her practice, she was usually able to contain her symbol without difficulty, but now she struggled to make its mass something manageable. She attempted to touch the radiance inside her, but her concentration faltered, and then it was gone. She lifted her head.

"Why are you not casting?" Mugrak demanded.

"I'm trying," Selena protested.

"Would some of the girl's blood help you focus?"

Selena met the bax's dark gaze, hating him even as she pleaded with him. "Give me some time."

"You test my patience."

She concentrated on calming herself first. She took several more deep, even breaths, her chest rising and falling, and achieved a steady rhythm before she began. As she fought her fear, rage, and frustration, she recalled a time when she had been at peace. Once again she was on a hillside, looking up at the night sky while she spoke to Taimin about other worlds. She remembered the sense of safety he gave her.

She pictured the way the moon had looked that night, round and ethereal, yet so clear it seemed she could reach up and touch it. She focused on that thought: reaching up and grasping the moon. It wasn't big; it was small, the size of a bowl.

Then she had it. The glowing sphere was inside her mind and although it was fiery, she could grasp it. She tried not to think too hard about what she was doing; instead she maintained her breathing, and the feeling that Taimin was with her.

In an instant the orb in her mind flared brightly. She placed imaginary hands around it, and let it lift her up.

With a surge of pleasure, she floated free.

She looked down at her body and saw her straight back and even breathing; Rei-kika would be proud of her. But Mugrak's scowling face reminded her of the little girl.

Keeping careful control of her emotions, allowing no fear to surface, she imagined herself rising higher. In moments she was above the tent and climbing the sky. She soon looked down at a ravine that was just one seam in a canyon, and then she was ascending higher than the Rift Valley in its entirety. She saw a connected series of gullies and tiny dots that marked the mouths of caves. The golden sun Dex shone over the landscape, highlighting the wrinkles of the great canyon and revealing the nearby plain.

Continuing to rise, Selena climbed until she was higher than the tallest mountain. She then set her sights on the plain.

She headed away from the Rift Valley until she was soaring over the landscape. The flat terrain spread out below her, decorated by the occasional cactus and misshapen boulder. The sense of freedom was exhilarating. Even though she was casting for Mugrak, her excitement grew at the thought that she would be seeing the city of Zorn up close for the first time.

A small white circle appeared on the horizon.

"What is happening?"

Selena heard Mugrak's throaty voice, both distant and directly by her side. She started to speak, but then realized she had to direct some of her attention to her body in order for her lips to move.

"I'm nearly at the city," Selena murmured, instructing her body to speak.

She could see it in the distance, rising up out of the sunburned plain: a glistening white city shaped like a mountain and encircled by a tall wall. As she flew toward it, the city became larger.

"Good, good," Mugrak said. "Get as close as you can."

The city's color was brilliant against the rusted hue of the surrounding landscape. Selena saw rows of green outside the wall, fields of cultivated plants: cactuses, spindly vegetables, graceful whitewood, hardy basalt, and hedges of nutbush.

"I can see the fields outside the city," Selena said.

"I don't care about the fields," Mugrak said. "Get closer to the wall."

The white wall grew in her vision but it was the tower at the city's midpoint that drew her attention. The tall, graceful structure shot up into the sky; imposing, but also beautiful. She approached until she was level with the top of the tower but still a mile or so outside the wall. Streets framed structures that were the same pale color as the tower. The houses were all matched in height, giving the city a uniform character. The wall enclosed everything, far taller than the houses, but still well below the height of the tower.

"Can you see the wall?"

"Yes, I can see it."

"How high is it?"

"About thirty feet."

"How tall is the gate?"

"About twenty feet."

"Is it the only gate?"

"I don't know. It's the only gate I can see."

"It is. I was testing you," Mugrak said. "How thick is the wall?"

"I can't see."

"Then find out," Mugrak growled.

Selena sent herself forward. She was desperate to travel into the city and see the people in the streets, but she was also filled with guilt that they were the very people she was betraying.

"It looks like the wall is about six feet thick," she said, glancing down.

"Now look inside the city," Mugrak instructed.

Selena moved closer, eager to explore such an incredible place. Her attention was drawn to a massive oval-shaped structure on one side of the city.

"I can see a huge round building. It's—"

"That is the arena, where the humans watch fights. What else can you see?"

Selena's gaze inadvertently returned to the tower's summit. She felt a strange sensation of foreboding. There was a presence in the tower, and it wasn't friendly.

Then, before she had passed the wall, a wavering shape appeared directly in front of her. Shock coursed through her when the figure's penetrating black eyes stared into her. Pain sizzled through her mind.

Who are you? the figure asked. *Tell me now!*

Selena caught an impression of a triangular head and stick-thin body. Without knowing how she did it, she projected a force from her consciousness, pushing the figure away. She launched herself backward, whirling to fly far and high, until the city was distant again, a white-walled dream on the horizon that became smaller and smaller.

Wanting nothing more than to be back in her body, she searched for her lifeline and saw the glowing white cord connecting her to a place in the distant canyon. She pulled on the cord. Immediately she flew back toward the canyon, down to the ravine, and sped directly to the small collection of tents where Mugrak had made his camp.

A moment later her eyes refocused.

"What happened?" Mugrak asked.

"Something . . . someone . . . was keeping guard. I swear it's true."

Mugrak grunted. "Never fear, I believe you. You met the Protector's mystic sentinel. The Protector has a mantorean up in that tower. I was hoping you might escape her notice." Mugrak shook his head. "To cast so far . . . I am impressed." He met her eyes. "Blixen will have more questions for you. The next time you cast, it will be for him."

18

"Fare you well," Syrus said. The skalen's voice became grave as he stood with Taimin and Lars near the hidden entrance to his home. "And be careful. War is coming to Zorn. Be in no doubt. You are heading into danger."

"It'll be worth it in the end," Lars said. "No matter the risk."

Taimin knew that Selena was right: individuals should be judged on merit, and Syrus was one of the good ones. "Thank you," he said. "I mean that." He patted the bow on his shoulder. "I'm in your debt."

Syrus shook his head. "I have told you, young human, there is no debt."

As Lars said his goodbyes, Taimin was tense. All he could think about was Selena. She had put herself forward, offering her ability to the skalen so that the three of them wouldn't be killed. By now she was almost certainly at the Rift Valley, where she would have to make a choice, and he knew what she would do. If she refused to help the Protector of Zorn's enemies, she wouldn't be useful anymore. She would die.

Syrus and Lars were still talking. "You remember my directions to Zorn?" the skalen asked.

"Seared into my mind."

"Once again," Syrus said, "be careful of the Rift Valley. I don't have to tell you that the bax don't like humans at all."

"That's where I'll be going," Taimin said.

"Not me," said Lars. "As soon as I get to Zorn, I'll tell them about the things we've learned, but I'll leave the soldiers to do the fighting. I'm getting old. Give me a job butchering meat or tanning leather and I'll happily take it."

"The route I've given you will take you straight to the plain," Syrus said. He glanced at Taimin. "If you want to go to the Rift Valley from there, that's your choice. I know your reasons. Just keep your wits about you."

———

Three days after leaving Syrus's homestead, Taimin and Lars emerged on the far side of a narrow pass and stopped to gaze over the landscape. Tall mountains loomed behind them. A cool breeze blew from the heights, but Taimin knew that the air would become hotter as they descended. The bright blue sky contrasted with the colors of brown and rust below.

The two men were silent as they stood together on the slope, where the high ground gave them a sweeping view of the broad plain and the immense canyon on their distant left. The plain spread across the land until the Rift Valley at its edge fell away in a long, broken escarpment, as if some monstrous creature had plunged from the sky to devour mouthfuls of dirt and rock, leaving behind the impression of gigantic teeth. Deep and wide, the canyon splintered into countless smaller ravines.

Taimin glanced at Lars. The skinner scowled as he stared at the horizon. "Can't see it," he muttered.

"Still wondering if the white city is real?" Taimin asked.

"Zorn is real," Lars said. "But there's a difference between knowing it and seeing it for myself."

Taimin returned to his inspection of the great canyon. "She's down there, somewhere," he murmured, more to himself than the older man beside him.

Lars clapped him on the shoulder. "You'll find her, lad. I'm sure of it."

Taimin didn't reply. Instead he patted Griff's flank and, now that they were on open ground, pulled himself onto the wherry's back. Griff whined, excited. He hadn't had a chance to stretch his legs in a long time.

"All right," Lars said. "You're in a hurry, lad. I can see that."

The two suns beat down from overhead. Lizards clung to the sides of broad cactuses. A strong wind swept dust across the ground but did nothing to relieve the heat. Scavenger birds wheeled overhead, shrieking to one another as they tracked the two humans below in hope that they would falter.

Taimin and Lars walked side by side, with Taimin resting a hand on Griff's back. It was their third day on the plain. There was little conversation other than to remind each other to conserve their water. Their footsteps took them in a direction that would eventually fork and cause them to part ways. Veering left would lead to the Rift Valley; turning right to the city of Zorn.

Out in the open, the creeping tension that always accompanied travel in the wasteland had grown until Taimin was on edge. He knew that they were exposed, in a region inhabited by enemies.

Taimin didn't say it, but he was glad for Lars's company. Lars seemed to feel the same way about him. But despite knowing they would soon separate, Taimin didn't slow. As he traveled, his mind conjured up images of Selena coming to harm at the hands of the skalen or their bax allies. He became more and more impatient.

The suns' rays were still fierce when they came across the refugees.

The wavering figures ahead were too upright to be bax, too numerous to be trulls, too big to be mantoreans, and their gait was nothing like the sinuous movements of skalen. As Taimin and Lars caught up to them, Taimin saw that they were humans: old and young, male and female, entire families burdened with packs filled to bursting. Taimin waved and called out; one of them gave a desultory wave back. The rest offered the newcomers scant attention.

There were perhaps a hundred of them, settlers from different homesteads, banded together for protection as they headed for the safety of the city. Hardy people, they were survivors who had learned to keep their heads down and homes secure. They let Taimin and Lars join their group without question, perhaps too weary to care. An old woman told the newcomers that bax had ravaged their homes; all bore the stone faces of sorrow caused by hardship.

It was a somber bunch who walked together, hour after hour, helping the weakest among them but focused above all else on their destination. Everyone knew that they were in constant danger.

As part of a far larger group, Taimin and Lars continued to cross the plain, and Taimin knew that he would soon be as close as he would come to the Rift Valley before each step began to take him farther away.

The group had stopped to rest. As Dex sank into the horizon, the golden sun cast a warm light over the landscape that transformed the plain into an amber sea. It was time to say goodbye. Taimin set his jaw and walked over to Lars. With Griff following just behind him, he thought about what he would say.

Then Taimin realized why Lars, and all of the refugees, had come to a halt. It wasn't to rest. People were murmuring. All eyes were staring ahead.

A pyramid-shaped silhouette glistened on the horizon: a white city tinted rose by the setting sun. A tiny spike—a tower—shot up from the city's middle. The city of Zorn was small and distant, but even so it beckoned, and it was beautiful, putting out a call for weary travelers.

Taimin glanced at Lars. The old skinner had an expression of awe on his face. Lars had followed his dream, and despite all the obstacles in his way, here he was.

"There it is," Lars breathed. He glanced at Taimin. "Zorn." He said the name with relish.

Lars was right. There was a difference between knowing the white city was real and seeing it revealed on the plain. Taimin only wished that Selena was beside him. They were supposed to reach the city together. Of the three of them, each with their own reason for making the journey, it was Lars who would get there first.

As he stared at the distant city, Taimin was taken back to the time when, rifling through the remains of his home, he had found the drawing in Abi's clothing chest. He had lost the piece of paper when they were captured by the skalen, but the drawing had undoubtedly been made by someone who had seen Zorn firsthand.

It was a strange thing for his aunt to have in her possession.

He remembered her scowling. *There is no city, boy.*

At the very least Abi knew of the possibility that Zorn existed.

"Why?" Taimin whispered, so low that Lars couldn't hear. Why had she kept Zorn's existence from him?

Lars saw his expression. "Taimin? Lad? What is it?"

Taimin didn't take his eyes off the white-walled city on the horizon. He still couldn't believe it was real. In the emptiness of the wasteland, how had it come to be?

"Who built it?" he asked. "Did humans build Zorn? Was it us?"

"I . . ." Lars scratched his thick black beard. "I assume we did."

Griff snorted, reminding Taimin that it was time to go. He would say farewell to Lars and make his own way to the Rift Valley. Zorn would have to wait. When he saw it again, Selena would be with him. He opened his mouth, but then stopped.

Still looking in the direction of the city, he spied something else, something that made him frown. Several shapes in the sky, like tiny birds, were flying from the direction of Zorn. The shapes swiftly grew larger, traveling with speed to head straight for the people on the plain. They were far too large to be raptors.

Griff made a sound Taimin had never heard before: a low growl in his throat, trailing off into a whine.

The refugees began to mutter, and as their mutters became louder, they all exchanged glances.

The birdlike shapes flew in a tight formation. Moving as one, they descended directly toward the people on the ground.

19

The wart-faced bax, Mugrak, herded Selena between campfires and past tents. Selena's jaw was clenched tightly as she moved between hundreds of bax. They carried cactuses on their shoulders, practiced combat, sharpened spears, and turned skewered lizards over fire pits.

Selena's hands were bound in front of her. Her wrists burned from the tight leather, and dread was like an empty pit in her chest. She wore a collar around her neck, fixed to a cord that led to Mugrak's hand. He was taking her to Blixen, the Warden of the Rift Valley, who commanded every one of these warriors.

The encampment was located in a long, wide gorge. Tents filled the area between the two tall cliffs. But despite there being so many bax gathered in one place, the encampment felt far from permanent. For a start, there were no females or young: Selena had heard from her captors that Blixen was keeping them out of sight, dispersed throughout the Rift Valley to avoid the city's patrols. What she was seeing was the core of his army: hundreds of male warriors.

Coarse voices filled the air, along with the smell of wood smoke and roasting meat. The toad-like creatures watched her curiously as she passed, nudging one another and casting her malevolent smiles.

Surrounded by so many, Selena avoided the dark eyes watching her. As she instead looked into the distance, she saw that a large group of skalen had made camp in a place farther along the gorge, separate from the bax. If Group Leader Vail was here, then Rei-kika would be too. Selena tried to see Rei-kika's thin frame among the skalen, but couldn't.

Mugrak yanked on the cord and she stumbled. She fell down, hitting the ground heavily with her knees. The collar tightened around her neck, choking off her air.

Arms went around her, and she heard laughter nearby while Mugrak hauled her back to her feet. Air rushed into her lungs as her chest heaved.

"Careful," Mugrak growled.

He scowled at her as she struggled to catch her breath, but now that she had his attention, she saw a chance to ask the question she was desperate to have answered. She coughed one last time and then met Mugrak's deep-set eyes. "The girl," she wheezed. "Where is she?"

Mugrak snarled and held up the leather cord, shaking it meaningfully. "Keep moving."

Selena was forced to focus on her footing as he yanked her along again. It didn't matter if she quickened her footsteps; he seemed to take pleasure in her discomfort. Soon Mugrak took her past a cluster of fire pits toward a rise in the ground. She found herself walking uphill toward an alcove, a cleft in the rock that created a space separate from the main camp. Proud-looking bax warriors stood guard outside a broad pavilion, with skins laid out like a mat leading up to the entrance.

Selena gritted her teeth and brought herself to a halt. This time she was expecting the pressure on her collar. She wrapped her tied hands around the cord at her neck and stood her ground.

"Mystic . . ." Mugrak's eyes narrowed.

"I want to know where she is," Selena said.

"If Blixen is displeased—"

"I don't care. I might suffer, but so will you. The girl. Where is she?"

Mugrak's lip curled. He tried once more to pull on the cord, but Selena wouldn't be moved. As she continued to glare at him, he gave a shrug. "She was cold. Or hot. Or sick. It is hard to know with you humans. She died. Borg burned her body."

The blood drained from Selena's face. Her nostrils flared. "You killed her."

"I killed her parents, but she died of her own accord." He gave a malicious grin. "If I were you, I would worry about my own fate. Make me look bad in front of Blixen and I will roast you alive." He brought his mouth close to her ear. "Remember," he hissed, "it is you humans that started this."

He pulled on the leather and dragged her into the pavilion.

Selena blinked as her eyes adjusted to the dark interior. Blixen sat on a broad rock, legs apart and hands on his knees. Even among so many warriors outside, he was easily the biggest bax she had seen: tall and broad-chested, with muscled shoulders and fierce grooves above his eyes. A circle of bones decorated his neck and thorns studded his leather armor. He scowled impatiently while he waited for Mugrak's approach.

Selena's whirling thoughts took focus. Her shock was steadily shifting to anger. Her mouth tightened and she glanced at Mugrak. She wanted him to suffer for what he had done.

Mugrak brought her to a halt in front of Blixen. Selena was forced to return her attention to the huge bax in front of her.

Her eyes widened.

She hadn't initially seen the thin mantorean in the low light. Rei-kika stood at Blixen's side, waiting in the shadows. The scar on Rei-kika's face was now joined by a second, bigger scar on her forehead. Selena's anger grew. Blood roared in her ears.

"Rei-kika?"

"Silence," a bax behind her growled.

"Great Blixen," Mugrak said. "This human female can cast farther than any other. I offer her to you as a gift."

"Ah . . ." Blixen said as he regarded her. His size gave his rough voice a booming quality. "This is the wild one Group Leader Vail spoke of. You are Mugrak, are you not?"

"Yes, Warden."

"And what is your rank, Mugrak?"

"I am second file."

"You are now first file," Blixen said.

Mugrak puffed himself up, and then, while Mugrak and Blixen continued to speak, something snapped inside Selena.

She looked at the scars on Rei-kika's face. She remembered Mugrak holding the little girl up by her hair. The child had witnessed the death of her parents and then spent her last days in terror. How many children lived in Zorn? The rage grew until Selena's vision shrank to a narrow focus.

Fire sparked inside her.

Before she knew what she was doing Selena was holding the radiant symbol of her power pent up inside her mind. She fed it her anger, and with her gaze fixed on Blixen she concentrated on the idea of giving him pain. If she made the pain strong enough, she might be able to kill him.

What are you doing? Selena heard a voice inside her mind. She saw Rei-kika staring at her, the only one present who was mindful of Selena gathering her power.

I'm going to end this.

They will kill you.

I don't care.

They will kill me too!

Selena imagined the glowing symbol pulling her out of her body and she burst free of the bounds of her physical form. In an instant she could sense the mood of every creature around her. She felt Rei-kika's terrible anxiety, and Mugrak's cringing desire to please. Blixen carried an indomitable determination that was startling to behold.

Gathering her strength, Selena prepared to travel, but this time rather than journey to see things far away, she would tunnel inside Blixen's skull.

No! Rei-kika cried inside her mind. *Not like that.*

I'm going to hurt him, Selena replied. Her resolve was strong. Nothing would stop her.

He is not what you think he is.

He rewards his warriors for butchery.

Selena sensed Rei-kika relent. *Look. Like this. Let me show you.*

All of a sudden Rei-kika's ethereal consciousness was beside Selena's. While Blixen and Mugrak spoke, Rei-kika and Selena descended toward Blixen's skull and entered.

Selena found herself confronted with flashing thoughts and images. At first it was confusing, but then Rei-kika did something. She lifted a layer of Blixen's outer self, holding it up, and showed it to Selena before she wormed her way underneath. The mantorean did it with the gentlest of touches, sliding over rather than through Blixen's thoughts without disrupting them in the slightest.

It is similar to what they made me do to you, but softer, Rei-kika said.

Selena followed suit, touching another part of the warden's mind, feeling her own consciousness merge with his. Rei-kika helped her through until they were both within the outer layer and could see his thoughts even as they occurred to him. Selena gained an impression that Rei-kika's awareness was bobbing up and down like ripples on a bowl of water, becoming almost transparent before solidifying. She realized that where Rei-kika struggled to maintain her own sense of identity while merged with Blixen, she had little difficulty herself.

Thousands of potential thoughts whirled through Blixen's mind, but only some became actualized as he decided to form them, and only some were in the form of words; most were baser desires. Unable to help herself, Selena looked deeper, and burrowed down to reach his memories, the next layer within the bax's mind.

You learn fast, Rei-kika sent. *Some would say too fast. Wait. This is what I have to show you. Look.*

Selena experienced the memory as if it were happening to herself.

———

Blixen was angry. Surrounded by his personal guard, the strongest and most skilled of all his warriors, he took determined strides toward the place where the skalen under Group Leader Vail had made their camp.

The altercation was still underway. Vail's reptilian eyes blazed. A dozen skalen flanked her, javelins poised above their shoulders. Facing them were Kyrax, a second-file commander, and an equal number of bax under his command.

Blixen scowled as he approached, his attention on the ongoing scuffle between the two groups. Vail's son, Watch Leader Rees, held a pair of pale eggs in his arms. The young skalen was attempting to put his back to Kyrax, who lunged from one side to the other, trying to snatch the eggs. Rees's expression was desperate.

"Stop, you fool," Group Leader Vail hissed at Kyrax. "You will break her eggs, and then what?"

The mantorean trembled with agitation as her eggs threatened to tumble onto the hard ground. She tried to dart in to take the eggs herself, but one of Kyrax's underlings grabbed her from behind and threw her down. Her stick-thin limbs fell in a tangle. She lifted her head. A seeping wound had opened up above her eyes.

"Just give us the eggs," Kyrax grunted as he reached around again, with Rees narrowly evading him.

Blixen's powerful, booming voice cut through the commotion. "All of you. Stop this at once."

Heads whirled as both bax and skalen saw Blixen approaching with six menacing warriors in leather armor. Fear struck face after face.

"Warden . . ." Kyrax said. He stopped snatching at the young skalen. The eggs almost fell before Vail's son brought them close to his chest.

"Kyrax. Explain yourself," Blixen snapped.

"We wanted to borrow the mystic—"

"Borrow? Just for a few hours, or days, and you were going to give her back?" Blixen spoke in a low growl. "The skalen are our allies. I have made that very clear." He glared while Kyrax stood apprehensively. "Kyrax, you are demoted to third file. Now get out of here before I decide to punish you further."

Kyrax bobbed his head and rushed away, taking his warriors with him.

Group Leader Vail opened her mouth. "Thank you, Warden—"

Blixen lifted a finger and thrust it toward the old skalen. "I am not pleased with you either, Group Leader." He indicated the mantorean on the ground. "She is innocent in this struggle. We are fighting the humans. Are they not enough? Here." Blixen put out his hands. "Give the eggs to me."

Watch Leader Rees looked to his mother for orders. Vail hesitated and then gave a reluctant nod. Blixen took the two eggs; they were surprisingly heavy for their size. The mantorean's eyes followed her eggs as she climbed to her feet. Her antennae waved back and forth.

"Mantorean, what is your name?"

"Rei-kika."

"I need mystics, Rei-kika, more than you can know. If I help you care for your eggs, and promise to keep both you and your hatchlings safe, will you cast for me?"

Rei-kika replied in a croaking voice. "I will."

The memory drifted away.

Do you see? Rei-kika asked. *I have my eggs back.*

He is still using you, Selena replied. *And the things you do for him will cause humans to suffer.*

Have you not realized that everyone in this canyon is in hiding? Rei-kika replied.

Of her own accord, Selena examined another memory.

Blixen stood beside the burned-out remains of a tiny village. The stench of char was in his nostrils. His mouth tasted of ash.

"Humans did this," a voice said.

Blixen seethed with anger. He knelt down and stroked the cheek of the infant bax. "Why do they hate us so much?" he asked.

"It's their way," came the response.

Blixen spoke again. "But why burn them alive?"

Selena shuddered; the outpouring of emotion that accompanied the memory was overwhelming. There were countless experiences around her, a lifetime to behold, but there was one remembrance that stood out above all others.

* * *

Blixen, the Warden of the Rift Valley, stared in futility at the city of Zorn.

"She is in there," a voice said. "Your wife was only taken three days ago. We will do everything we can to get her back for you."

Blixen's response was slow in coming. "You know she is gone. I will soon be fighting humans wearing her skin as armor."

* * *

For a moment Selena didn't know where or who she was. Blixen's pain and rage still filled her. The grief that accompanied the loss of his wife was overwhelming.

His wife is the true reason that he is gathering an army to attack the city, Rei-kika said.

I'm sorry, Selena replied, *but it has nothing to do with me. If I can get away, will you come with me?*

The danger is too great. My eggs are safe here.

Selena wondered what she could do. She turned away from the memories and focused on the whirl of thoughts. She knew from Blixen's mind that the conversation with Mugrak was coming to a close.

Rei-kika sighed. *Try this.*

The mantorean formed a thought of her own and tossed it into the maelstrom. Selena looked on as it joined the other potential thoughts, spinning around with them, able to be formed yet not something Blixen would choose to think on his own.

Something else bubbled up instead. *Time to test this new mystic*, Blixen mused.

Quick, Selena, Rei-kika said. *I don't have the power, but if you are going to do something, you need to do it now.*

In desperation, Selena wondered what to do. She discarded one plan after another, until she had an idea.

Copying what Rei-kika had done, she formed a thought and tossed it into the storm inside Blixen's mind. It began to disappear, but she concentrated, pouring all her effort into keeping track of the one thought she wanted Blixen to bring to the surface and make his own. It was something close to his own heart.

"Well, mystic? Answer!" Mugrak was shaking Selena's arm.

With a sickening lurch Selena re-entered her body and looked around. Mugrak was glaring at her while Blixen leaned forward. All eyes were on her.

"The warden has asked you a question," Mugrak said through gritted teeth.

"Yes, I am ready to cast for you," Selena said, meeting Blixen's gaze.

"Good," Blixen said. He rubbed his wrinkled chin. "I am giving you a challenge. Two months ago someone close to me was captured by the humans, who took her, along with others, to the city of Zorn. I accept that in all likelihood she is dead, but perhaps I should not be so certain. I want you to cast for me, mystic. Dead or alive, I want you to find my wife."

Mugrak opened his mouth to protest. "Great Blixen, even for her, to search inside the city . . ."

Selena held her breath. She had encouraged Blixen's natural desire to discover his wife's fate, but the next part . . .

"She will need to be closer to Zorn, yes," Blixen said. "Which is why, Mugrak, you are to take her to where she needs to go. Be wary of the city guard. Your gift is appreciated. Use it to give me that which I want most."

Mugrak scowled, but he nodded. "Your will, Warden."

"And, Mugrak? I heard a rumor, something about a human girl-child. I trust it is not true." Blixen's voice became a low, ominous rumble. "The humans may murder our young, but we will not descend to their level."

A brief look of fear crossed Mugrak's face. "Of course." He dipped his head and gave something close to a bow.

Selena experienced a surge of triumph. She had found a way to get herself far from the canyon, and the army of bax.

Once she was close to the city, she just needed to once again find the mystic in the tower.

This time, she would ask for help.

20

"It's the city guard!" one of the refugees cried. "By the rains, we're saved!"

The men, women, and children watching the sky cheered, although there were some in the crowd who looked less ready to celebrate.

Taimin watched the huge, birdlike creatures descend. He swiftly counted twelve of them. The creatures circled as they lost height, wings spread and legs visible underneath their lean, rust-colored bodies. They had narrow heads that tapered to jaws filled with sharp teeth. Dark eyes remained fixed on the plain below.

Griff growled again, emitting the strange, low sound that ended each time with a whimper.

"They're riding wyverns," Lars said in astonishment.

Taimin had plenty of experience with wyverns. Despite his relief at finally making contact with someone from Zorn, part of him was unable to shake the thought that there was something menacing about the city guard, as if they were predators and the people on the plain were prey.

Griff's urgent growls became louder. Taimin glanced at the wherry and then returned to gazing up at the sky. The wyverns had been wherries at some point in their past, and had since transformed. It wasn't impossible that Griff might make his own metamorphosis one day. But as it was, he was clearly afraid of his bigger, stronger cousins.

As the wyverns circled overhead, Taimin saw people on their backs, dressed in crimson uniforms. The riders made sure they took a good look at the people approaching their city. Then they made a final approach, each peeling off from the group before descending. Wings tucked in as the wyverns plummeted, spreading out to brake at the end. Soon the riders had landed on the plain, one beside the other, a stone's throw from the refugees. Their coordination was impressive.

"Have you ever seen humans riding wyverns?" Taimin asked Lars.

"No. Never. You?"

"No."

Now that he had seen the city guard, Taimin could understand how the Protector controlled the plain. His worry about the city falling to invaders began to fade. Lars and Selena had been right all along. In a wasteland full of dangers, Zorn was a place of safety.

"We've done it," someone called. "With the protection of the city guard, we're going to make it."

The closest soldier, a tall man in uniform, slid off the back of his wyvern, leaving the winged creature to snort and claw at the ground. The wyvern looked similar to Griff but its transformation had changed more than its front legs, which were much smaller than a wherry's. Its ears were pricked rather than floppy, and its hide was redder and darker. The sharp teeth were as long as human fingers and its body was big, close to twice Griff's size.

Taimin examined the men of the city guard as they dismounted. The soldiers wore crimson tabards over their leather armor, the material supple and made of a shining fiber. A white tower surrounded by a circular wall formed an insignia in the center of their chest.

Having dismounted, the tall soldier, evidently the commander, came forward with long strides, his face hard and unsmiling. He waved an arm, and his men spread out to flank him.

Lars left Taimin's side. The bald, bearded skinner's expression was earnest as he approached the soldiers. "Well met," he said. "We can make our own way, but your protection is welcome. You need to hear what we have to say. There are bax in the canyon. A group of skalen—"

"We know," the commander interrupted, his face like stone.

A second soldier came up to stand beside the commander. Now formed up in a line, the rest of the city guard waited in disciplined silence. Some of the soldiers rested their hands on the hilts of the swords they wore at their waists.

Lars glanced over his shoulder at the refugees. "These people have lost their homes. They have nothing to go back to. We need food and water."

The tall commander exchanged glances with the soldier beside him and then returned his attention to Lars. His lips thinned. "We are accepting no one. The city is full."

"Full?" Lars scratched his thick black beard, perplexed. Color rose in his cheeks. "What do you mean, full?"

"Turn back from Zorn and do not encroach on our farmland."

"What are you talking about?" Lars scowled. "You're the ones fighting the Rift Valley. Everyone here was just caught in the middle."

"Leave now," the commander said curtly. His dark eyes narrowed. "I will not ask again."

"No, we won't leave," one of the older men said, coming forward. "I know you, Galen. You led the raid on the mine near our homestead. We traded with those skalen. There was friendship between us, but you slaughtered them."

The commander, Galen, gave a cold-faced reply. "The mine was Zorn's for the taking."

The soldier beside Galen spat on the ground. "I don't know how any human can call skalen 'friends'."

A skinny woman came forward. More of the refugees followed her to stand in front of the line of soldiers. "You started this war. Now you're saying you won't let us in?"

Galen put a hand on the hilt of his sword. The tall commander drew the weapon in a single, smooth motion. Immediately, every soldier in the line followed suit. But where the soldiers held swords of glossy basalt wood, Galen's blade was made of shining steel.

"You're implying that I care about you settler scum," Galen said. "You can take your chances with the bax and your skalen friends." He smiled without mirth. "I hear Blixen uses human skin to keep warm at night."

For the refugees, the commander's words were a call to violence.

The men and women surged forward until they were massed in front of the row of men in uniform. They screamed and yelled obscenities, fists held out in front of them. A few raised weapons—clubs, spears, and wooden swords.

Lars began a hasty retreat. He glanced at Taimin, his expression distraught. Zorn was supposed to be a place where everyone was welcome. His dream of a better life was rapidly fading.

As he stood transfixed, Taimin knew how the skinner felt.

The instant he had seen Galen, the commander with the shining sword, Taimin's world had crashed around him. Despite his desperate hope, the fabled white city and the real city of Zorn were not the same thing.

The soldier next to Galen looked similar enough to be his brother. In fact, Taimin knew that they were brothers.

Both had pale hair, although Galen's was more white than blond, close-cropped while his brother's was long. Both had dark

195

eyes and hard, angular features, although Galen was the taller and older of the pair. Galen's manner was assertive; he was accustomed to making decisions and giving orders.

Taimin knew that they were brothers because he had met them once before. He remembered a time when two rovers pretended to have peaceful intentions until everything changed. He saw his parents taking step after step backward, while the two rovers moved menacingly toward them. An arrow had suddenly sprouted from his mother's skull, while his father shoved him toward the cliff. As he ran, Taimin had looked back and seen Galen's sword—the same sword he was holding now—enter his father's chest.

The memory was so strong that Taimin felt sick. It was as if he had seen his parents die just moments ago. Everything in his vision became washed with the color red.

"I've had enough of this, Kurt," Galen said to his brother. "What do you say?"

"They need a demonstration," the long-haired soldier said grimly.

"Advance!" Galen called out. Then, without waiting for his men, he took action.

Fast as a snake, Galen brought the point of his sword toward the neck of the old man facing him and then flicked his wrist. The sharp steel entered the old man's throat and opened up a gaping wound. Galen continued moving, so smoothly it was almost a dance, carrying the sword through the strike and into his next target, a heavyset woman.

Before Galen's two victims had hit the ground, the other soldiers began to hack indiscriminately at the crowd. Screams rose in a chorus. While some of the refugees turned and ran, many tried to fight. But the soldiers were trained warriors, wielding swords and wearing armor. The refugees fell one after the other. In seconds, everything was chaos.

Taimin was barely conscious of moving.

As he ran, he left behind his bow, which was still fixed to his pack on Griff's back. He was unarmed, but he didn't even notice.

He first reached Galen's brother, Kurt. The blond soldier finished striking down a youth and then whirled toward Taimin and lifted his sword. The hardwood blade came sweeping down.

Taimin ducked under the sword and threw his weight forward. Time slowed. He sensed the sword whistling past his head as he put everything he could into striking his opponent's unprotected throat. He punched forward with the heel of his hand, twisting his body through the motion, pulling his left shoulder back as his right came forward. He shouted with primal rage.

Muscles expanded and contracted. Taimin struck with his entire body, honed by his training, hunting, and years of hard, physical work. With a sudden jolt, he made contact and with savage satisfaction he felt something break inside his enemy. The blond-haired soldier's long hair flew around his face and his eyes shot wide open. Kurt flew backward, his face bright red as he choked.

Galen looked over, only to see his brother go down.

Taimin's eyes met Galen's. He set his sights on the man who had been the first to act, thrusting his sword into Taimin's father's chest.

Taimin dropped to retrieve Kurt's sword. Filled with bloodlust, he was barely aware that most of the refugees had either run or fallen. Galen slashed his sword along the torso of a middle-aged man with a club. He immediately turned toward Taimin.

"Taimin!" Lars's voice cut through the red haze. "We have to go—now!"

Taimin pointed his sword at Galen. The other soldiers were still occupied with the crowd, and Taimin stood in his own space. Galen's face was filled with a fiery anger that equaled Taimin's own.

"You killed my parents," Taimin called.

"The wherry can't carry us both. You'd best go, lad." Lars sounded like he was speaking from a distant mountain, but the emotion in his voice cut through. Taimin glanced over at him, surprised to see that Lars was standing right beside him.

"Find the girl," Lars said in a hoarse voice. "Build a life together."

Without warning Lars pushed Taimin with force. Taimin fell onto his hands and knees. The sword tumbled to the ground, but as Taimin grabbed at the weapon he was nearly bowled over again. This time it was Griff, growling at him, leaning into him, pushing him with his head. "Stop it, burn you!" Taimin cried.

Griff shoved at him; the wherry was small compared to a wyvern, but that didn't make him weak. Taimin again spied Kurt's sword and lunged to retrieve it. But as soon as his hand gripped the hilt, strong arms plucked him up to throw him onto Griff's back. He caught a brief glimpse of Lars as the skinner slapped the wherry's flank. Before Taimin knew what was happening, Griff was bounding away.

He tried to rein the wherry in, but nothing could stop Griff once he had started. Glancing over his shoulder, he saw Lars facing the soldiers. His arms were spread; he looked like he was trying to talk. A soldier struck him and he went down. As soon as he was on the ground, more soldiers kicked his body.

Taimin knew he had to help, but as he looked back again dread sank into his chest. The skinner was dead. He had to be. No one could take such a beating and survive.

He didn't understand why Lars had done what he had, but he knew one thing: if he didn't get away, Lars's sacrifice would be in vain.

Lars, the aging skinner who had at last caught sight of the city he had dreamed of, was nothing more than a motionless lump on the ground.

Taimin's eyes burned. He rode as fast as he could, away from Zorn.

He headed directly for the Rift Valley.

———

The refugees were gone. They had learned their lesson and wouldn't be back. But the price had been high. Much, much too high.

Galen walked slowly to his brother's body. He knelt down beside him and kept his face hard, despite the painful grip on his heart. He let out his breath slowly, otherwise he knew it would come with deep, gulping heaves.

His men stood back, giving him space to grieve, but he was aware that they were watching. He reached out to close Kurt's eyelids and brushed a few long strands of blond hair away from his face.

"Sleep well, little brother," he murmured.

As Galen gazed at his brother's body, he felt a catch at the back of his throat. Kurt was gone. After all their travels together, this journey would be one he would make alone.

For most of Galen's life, it had just been the two of them. Their parents were killed in front of their eyes. He had been seven and Kurt just four. The trull had hunted their family while they were crossing the wasteland, on their way to the promise of a new settlement. Galen and Kurt hid behind some rocks while their parents fought the despicable creature that cut them to pieces, all for what they had: food, water, leather, and a few old tools and weapons.

Galen had always been the strong one. Kurt had his own strength, but he was quieter, more introspective. As rovers, sometimes they worked with others but theirs was a bond that couldn't be broken. Galen had lost track of how many homesteads they had raided as they roamed the wasteland together. At first it was just stealing, but sometimes people got in the way. With every kill, it became easier to kill again.

Galen knew that the world was a harsh place. If people invested their energy in supporting the weak—children, the elderly, the sick and injured—that was their problem. Settlers chose to make their group only as strong as the most feeble member. Galen and Kurt had always laughed at how foolish they were, trying to scratch a life out of the dirt. The life of a rover was the only one that made sense.

But then they heard about the white city, a place where two strong fighters might be able to make a mark for themselves. The brothers had begun to search for it. Sometimes they raided homesteads when they didn't need to, in order to question men, women, and children. Each piece of information brought them closer.

When Galen reached Zorn, and joined the city guard, his life changed.

He had always been his own man, but as he rose in the ranks he knew that in the Protector of Zorn he had met a leader he could follow. Kurt had thrived at his side. They were together as always, but a part of something greater.

As Galen stared at his younger brother's body, it wasn't just loss that burned inside him like an inferno. The rage grew stronger, and he fed the flames. Anger made his pain easier to bear.

At first he hadn't recognized the boy, now a man, from the failed raid near the firewall. Galen's life as a rover was a long time ago. It was only when Kurt's killer roared something about his parents that Galen remembered a settler and his wife, and a boy who tumbled off the side of the cliff. Once Galen had wondered, the man's limp had confirmed it.

In that one moment, when Galen hadn't been there to protect his little brother, this haunting from the past had struck, and he had struck hard.

Galen bent down to kiss his brother's forehead. "I will make him suffer, little brother. I promise you. Wherever you are right now, I want you to watch as I make him pay."

21

Taimin's despair fought with his anxiety. If a man like Galen was in command of the city guard, what did that say about Zorn? Galen and his men had butchered the refugees. They had beaten Lars to death.

Life had taught Taimin a harsh lesson, but he vowed to learn, and to keep going. He would search the Rift Valley for Selena. If she refused to help Zorn's enemies in the Rift Valley, she would die, and for what? She had to know the truth.

The next days were difficult. Taimin traveled by night, knowing that Galen and his men would be searching for him and that in daylight he could easily be seen from the sky. He crept through the darkness. There was danger in both directions. He had to be wary of both the city guard and the army of bax and skalen in the Rift Valley.

He knew that the wyvern riders were scouting. Again and again he saw the big flying creatures speeding overhead as they scoured the landscape below. Galen might even have mystics searching the plains. Taimin only stirred from the gullies he chose as hiding places when Dex and Lux were both well below the horizon.

It was so dark that Taimin could barely make out the range of mountains. Now that he was approaching the Rift Valley, the terrain was more broken, with hidden obstructions and fields of gravel that made his footing treacherous. With Griff at his side, he scampered from rock to rock, wincing as he heard stones roll from the passage of his feet. He worried that at any moment he and Griff might tumble into an unseen ravine.

When he saw the ground fall away ahead, he had no choice but to follow the cliff edge. The lip of the canyon formed a long, jagged line in both directions. Soon he would be descending into the canyon's depths. He moved as quietly as he could and kept his ears tuned to any sounds other than those he made himself. Tension formed knots in his shoulders. Griff picked up on the mood and cast him reproachful looks every time he unwittingly caused rocks to slip and tumble. From his position, there appeared to be one main route down. The chance of an encounter was high.

Taimin froze.

He could hear something: voices that broke the stillness of the night. The gruff tones and grunts weren't human. He ducked down and huddled against a boulder, using its bulk to disguise his body. Meanwhile Griff had the sense to sprawl out flat on the ground, sinking to his haunches and panting quietly. The voices grew louder before passing by and gradually becoming distant. Whoever it was, they were no longer coming toward him.

Taimin pulled his head out from behind the boulder and peered into the darkness. Ears pricked, he opened his eyes wide, turning his head as he tried to make out moving figures. He wanted to see who it was he was sharing the night with. If it was a large group exiting the canyon, it would be best if he fled the area altogether.

The voices had definitely belonged to bax. He warily left the protection of the boulder and crept forward, in the same direction he had been traveling. He knew from Abi that bax didn't see as well in the dark as humans and wondered why they were traveling at night.

He scanned in all directions, and then he saw them.

The hunched figures were walking in the far distance, barely more than black shadows. They were leaving the canyon and heading in the direction of the city. The bax were trying to stay hidden from the city guard, just like him.

Taimin thought about how he would find Selena. His current plan was to capture and question a bax or a skalen, but he knew it would be difficult to find one alone.

He watched the departing figures and wondered how many there were. At least ten, he decided. Too many for his purposes, but at least they were away from the others. They might split up at some stage.

He decided to trail them for a time.

He left his hiding place and patted Griff on the flank to indicate he should follow. "But stay back, understand?"

He moved from one piece of scant protection to the next as he crept closer. Using a gnarled tree for cover, he focused on the bax he was following and left the tree's protection. He scurried across the uneven ground. It was difficult to keep up while staying hidden and quiet. Ducking from gully to gully, slinking from boulder to boulder, he kept the bax in sight even as they drew away. He tossed up one plan and then another, unable to settle on any. He wondered if he should try riding Griff, but the terrain was treacherous and it would be difficult to stay silent on the wherry's back.

The crimson sun crept over the horizon. Lux was rising, making it a false dawn, but it would be hours before Dex fully lit the plain. The bax kept moving, faster now. Time passed, and Taimin struggled to equal their speed. He took more risks, and spent less time hidden. When he tried to run from a stone formation to a tall hermit cactus, his foot gave out. He slipped and then fell to his knees. Stones clattered together, but fortunately the bax kept moving. They hadn't heard him.

He pushed on. Meanwhile Lux shone brighter and washed the landscape a crimson shade. The group he was following came to a halt. He peered at them from behind a boulder on a hill. His position was high and, as far away as they were, in the red light he could make out the figures' stooped frames as they conferred. The distant red sun peeled above the horizon to rise higher in the sky.

Taimin's heart beat out of time.

The bax had a human with them, a slender woman with long dark hair and a length of cord traveling from her neck to a bax's gnarled fist.

He knew without doubt that he was looking at Selena. For a moment he was too stunned to think. She was so close that he felt he could reach out and touch her, but at the same time it would have taken a loud shout to catch the attention of her group, something he definitely didn't want to do.

The bax finished their discussion and set off again. With the golden sun soon to rise they appeared to be searching for a place to hide. The individual members of the group were already small in Taimin's vision. Now they were moving so swiftly that he knew he would lose them.

He turned and gave a low whistle.

Griff came bounding forward. Taimin threw himself onto the wherry's back. Knowing he was taking a great risk, but that above all he couldn't lose sight of Selena, he decided to head for a low crest, halfway between himself and the bax. It wouldn't provide much cover, but he would risk being seen in order to get close.

He dug in his heels. Griff raced along, his claws digging into the ground. The crest grew closer and closer. As he reached the top, Taimin brought Griff to a halt. He slid off the wherry's back to lie on his stomach on the waist-high boulder's slope. Griff sank to his haunches. Taimin scanned the area and strained his ears, anxious to know if he had been spotted.

At that moment Dex burst into the sky. The golden sun cast a brilliant glare over the plain. Taimin's heart sank. The bax with Selena must have taken cover. He couldn't see them anywhere.

He cursed and wondered what he should do. He couldn't just ride around in circles. Still on his stomach, he decided he would need to stay where he was and never take his eyes off the plain. It wasn't a good place to hide from the city guard, but he didn't have a choice.

A steady breeze came up, blowing hot air against his face as it sent dead bushes rolling along in its wake. Taimin gnawed at his lip, knowing he was in a bad position. He couldn't leave, but he knew he shouldn't stay.

Then he heard Griff growl, emitting a long, low rumble followed by a whine.

A shiver of fear crept up and down Taimin's spine. He recognized the sound. He frantically searched the landscape to find somewhere else to hide.

He was too late.

Griff looked up and give another fearful whine. A cold hand of dread squeezed Taimin's chest when he followed the wherry's eyes.

Dark winged shapes wheeled in the sky.

The wyverns were already circling toward the ridge. With Dex lighting up the plain, and the men of the city guard looking down from above, Taimin knew he had already been seen. There were more of the wyverns this time, at least twice as many. The winged creatures began to give piercing cries. Each shriek made Griff cringe.

Taimin climbed to his feet. He drew the sword he had taken from Galen's brother and moved away from the crest to stand in a cleared patch of ground.

He turned to Griff. "Go," he said. "They'll kill you."

Griff growled and then whimpered. His expression was distressed. His long lashes framed his gentle eyes as he moved closer to Taimin and nudged him with his head.

As Dex rose ever higher, chasing the smaller sun, the reddened plain shifted to gold. Taimin tilted his head back and held the sword high in the sky. He watched the sweeping wings of the wyverns as the creatures lost height. They were close enough for him to see Galen, the rider at the head of the group. His short white hair framed an angular face marred by hatred.

The wyverns circled one last time before commencing a swift descent.

"Go!" Taimin shouted at Griff. "Don't you realize they'll kill you?"

Griff took some steps away, but then whined and looked back.

Taimin crouched down and picked up a stone. Hating himself, he threw it at the wherry, and the stone bounced off Griff's sand-colored hide. He followed it with another. "Go! Get out of here!"

Griff shied. Taimin threw yet another stone. He kept his face cold, even as the wherry watched him in despair.

At last Griff scampered off, sprinting at speed and vanishing into the distance as the wyverns made their final approach. Taimin sighed and turned away. It didn't matter if Griff never forgave him; at least the wherry would survive. Taimin clenched his jaw as he waited in the open, sword in hand. His own life was almost certainly about to be cut short.

One rider landed, then another, until they were all on the ground in a circle with Taimin in the center. Taimin turned his gaze from one soldier to the next. He stood with legs apart. He waited, but the soldiers didn't dismount.

Taimin focused on Galen. The tall, white-haired commander's features were stiff, but his fierce eyes and the lines in his forehead revealed his loathing. Suddenly, however, he smiled; he was enjoying his moment. He had Taimin exactly where he wanted him.

"Chase the beast?" one of the soldiers asked.

"Let it go," Galen said. "We have what we want."

Taimin pointed his sword at his enemy. He knew he could never beat them all. He was going to die, but he was determined to take this one man with him.

Galen looked at Taimin. He still sat astride his mount. "You killed my brother." His lip curled. "You're going to die." He gave another cold smile. "But not today."

The commander gave his men an order. Four of the wyverns lifted into the sky, their wings pounding at the air with strong movements. Taimin followed them with his eyes, wondering what was about to happen. Their actions were coordinated; whatever they were doing, they had done it before.

The four wyverns continued to climb until they were high above Taimin's position. Then a rider flung out his arm. A net opened up, forming a neat circle. The net fell swiftly, weighted at the ends and expertly thrown. Taimin knew he would never outrun it. Instead he dived to the side and rolled, narrowly avoiding the tangle of webbed cord. A second net opened up above him and he threw his body again, wincing when his bad foot sent pain shooting up his leg.

A third net fell, and this time when Taimin leaped to the side his leg gave out completely. He involuntarily cried out and then the net was over him. Small hooks in the strands grabbed hold of his skin and clothing. He tried to pull it off but only made matters worse. Every tug caused another hook to grip onto his body. Spikes of pain accompanied each movement. The net drew blood in a dozen places.

He stopped when he sensed movement.

Galen towered over him. Taimin looked up to meet his eyes, while the commander stared down at him. Galen rubbed his sharp chin. He appraised Taimin for a long time before speaking.

"So, young warrior, I killed your parents," he said. "I remember you. You went over a cliff. What are you, a cripple? Is that how it happened?"

"Face me like a man," Taimin said hoarsely. Despite the hooks in his skin, he strained at the net, desperate to free himself. He had taken Galen's measure during the encounter with the refugees. The commander of the city guard was skilled, but Taimin's aunt had trained him well. It would be a close match.

"I found my place in Zorn," Galen said, ignoring his challenge, "and now I am the Protector's right hand, commander of the city guard. I worked my way up the ranks, and I now lead the most lethal fighting force in the world. What can you say for yourself? Have you found a purpose, other than to search for me?"

Taimin heard a grunt and then a heavy boot struck his head; only the tangle of netting saved him from a more vicious blow. Even so, the strike made his entire world give a sickening lurch. A second kick landed in the pit of his stomach, robbing him of breath as he doubled up.

"You think I will give you a quick death, after you killed my brother?"

Taimin choked, struggling to get air into his lungs. Another kick smashed into his abdomen.

"Think again."

Taimin was trussed up like an animal, expertly tied until he could barely move a finger. Galen's men then wrapped another net tightly around him and tied it to a strap around a wyvern's lean body.

Clearly, this wasn't the first time the city guard had returned to Zorn with a prisoner.

He felt himself lifted into the air and gasped as the hooked net pressed into his body. The wyverns climbed the sky and formed a wide triangular formation. Taimin swung back and forth in the air, his stomach clenching with every change of direction. He shifted his position to look down. For a long time he watched the dry plain far below, and then he saw fields of cactus and razorgrass. A moment later he caught sight of a tall, thick wall of white stone. Then he was flying over streets and rooftops. High as he was, he had an all-encompassing view as he sped past row after row of houses. Humans walked the streets below, dressed in a variety of styles of clothing. Few looked up. The other races were conspicuously absent.

The wyverns' path drew close to the central tower and Taimin saw oval-shaped windows at intervals. At the very top he caught a glimpse of a room open on all sides, with tall columns supporting the peaked roof.

Then Taimin began to lose height. He was heading toward a long, rectangular space with a stone floor and enclosing walls—evidently the soldiers' base. Circling toward the ground, the soldiers took turns to descend. Taimin's rider waited, and Taimin watched from above as the soldiers led their wyverns to a series of outer buildings that framed the central floor.

When it was Taimin's turn, the wyvern plummeted and then pulled up sharply to bring him down with a heavy thump. Taimin's chin cracked into his knees, rocking his senses. He was still dazed as the soldier came and cut the cord before leading the wyvern away.

Wrapped in netting, all he could move was his head as he looked around with bleary eyes. He had to think, to understand, if he was ever going to get out of his situation. Everything was so strange and foreign. But he had to try.

He knew immediately that humans hadn't built the city: for a start, everything was too big, too out of proportion to the human form. Even the place he was thinking of as a barracks didn't appear to have been designed for the purpose. The archways that the soldiers led their wyverns through were tall enough to dwarf the men, but too narrow for the wyverns to enter easily. Perhaps this place was once a storage area, with the individual compartments designed to hold supplies. But who would need such large doorways?

"Free his legs." Taimin heard Galen's voice. "Haul him up."

Knots were untied, cords were cut, and Taimin soon stood, held up by two soldiers on either side of him. With tiny cuts all over his body, he weaved on his feet. If he hadn't been supported, he would have fallen.

Galen regarded him for a moment, then brought his face close. "You are going to walk to the place where you will die. March!"

Taimin concentrated on placing one foot in front of the other as Galen and the pair of soldiers led him through a guarded entrance and out onto the street. All of his strength became consumed by the struggle to stay upright.

The city's thoroughfares were paved with white stone. Houses and other buildings with oversized entrances filled every vacant space and provided shade from the two suns. People walked with purpose. Some cast Taimin swift glances but seemed wary of showing too much interest. A burly man pushed a handcart filled with dried cactuses; he gave the soldiers a wide berth despite his heavy load. Some of the passersby wore bright linen clothing, but most were dressed in dirty laborer's smocks, and these people were skinny, with gaunt faces and limbs like sticks. Their faces were downcast. The only laughter came from the children who followed Taimin for a time, daring each other to get close.

Taimin's march was a blur of stone facades and guarded faces. Thoughts darted through his mind as he wondered where he was being taken. At first, as he was led toward the city's center, he thought he might be going to the tower, but then Galen's path took him away from the huge wooden door at its base.

A plaza surrounded the base of the circular tower. Market stalls stood in rows. Galen stopped to exchange a greeting with a plump man in a garish robe. Taimin was able to rest for a moment and stood with chest heaving as he struggled to fight the pain. He looked at the nearby market and a commotion drew his attention. Locals dressed in rags were pushing past each other to get to one of the vendors. They cried out while they held up flasks, and they were all saying the same word. "Water!"

He tore his eyes away when he realized that Galen was talking about him.

". . . the man who killed Kurt, and here he is," Galen said. "You will soon see him die in the arena."

"I will watch with pleasure, commander."

Taimin was shoved along once more to follow another wide street. He turned into another avenue, and then followed a series of turns as he was taken deeper into the city.

Gazing ahead, he found himself looking at a great stadium, a structure so big he could hardly believe it was real. Most of its bulk was obscured by the buildings around it, yet just the part he could see told him of its size. A series of grand archways formed the main entrances, but Taimin was marched toward the back.

Galen came to a halt at a sturdy grid of stout wooden bars. A burly guard, grubbier than the uniformed soldiers, emerged from the darkness behind the gate and jangled some keys. The gate creaked open.

"Welcome to the arena," Galen said.

Taimin felt a shove in the middle of his back. He fell forward and onto the hard ground. The guard, a big man who would have dwarfed Lars, easily took him in hand, and then a second, lankier guard came to help.

Taimin struggled weakly as he was led down a series of stone-walled passages, and through another barred gate. He tried to pay attention to where he was going but it all looked the same, and after the beating and the march he was barely able to stumble along, forcing the guards to do all the work.

Yet another barred gate opened onto a large room with stone walls. The room was filled with rows of bed pallets, and Taimin was aware of many eyes watching him.

The guards threw him to the floor.

22

Hope stirred for the briefest moment, but then Selena's shoulders slumped when the wyvern riders continued to pass overhead, leaving her behind as they flew over the plain.

Mugrak made a wheezing sound, the bax equivalent to a sigh of relief. "The city guard has not seen us. Even so, we should wait out the day. This may be the last protection we find for some time. We depart at nightfall."

Selena and the dozen bax were in a narrow gully. The base was made of loose stones, and there was nowhere comfortable to sit, but she had done her best to wedge her body against the wall. She wanted to sleep if she could. She knew she needed to keep up her strength if she was going to seek help in the city and escape.

Mugrak gave her a dark look. "This is a foolish plan," he muttered. "Mystic, how close must we be to the city to do as the warden asks?"

"I need to be close to the wall," she said.

"His wife is dead." Mugrak spoke more to himself than anyone else. "Why can he not see it?"

Selena felt vaguely guilty for using Blixen's grief at the loss of his wife. Looking at Borg, who was snoring loudly despite his uncomfortable position a short distance away, she steeled her resolve. She remembered the little girl Borg had held up by her hair.

Selena would contact the mystic in the tower. The city guard would come to help her. Soon she would be free.

———

"This is as close as we can get you," Mugrak said. "The danger is great."

It was just before midday. They were in the midst of the fields surrounding the city, hidden within a grove of tall lifegiver cactuses. The bax grunted to each other nervously until Mugrak silenced them with a glare and a slashing motion of his hand.

"Hurry," Mugrak grunted. "Do what it is you need to do."

Selena nodded and took a deep breath. She scanned the area. The suns were both up; she had told Mugrak she needed to see clearly in order to search for Blixen's wife in the city. Clamping down on her fear, she moved away from the dozen bax and settled herself on the dirt.

She visualized her symbol and felt her consciousness expand to surround it. She fought to calm her emotions, containing her trepidation as she forced her breath to slow until it was steady and even. Soon she was touching the radiant orb in her mind. She let it pull her up and out of her body.

As her awareness became unfastened, she looked down at herself, sitting cross-legged on the ground. She then turned to the hiding bax, who were all watching the body she had left behind with a combination of fear and impatience. Focusing her attention on the city, she climbed the sky until she was gazing down at the rooftops, and then she flew forward and sped across the fields, heading for the white wall.

She traveled directly to the tower, but even as she approached she was again struck with awe as the city revealed itself in more detail. Wide streets stretched out in all directions. All of the

215

buildings were of a uniform height with the exception of a few large structures. In the distance she again saw the massive, oval-shaped arena.

Zorn was beautiful and alien. Everything was walled with brilliant stone, and there were stairways and arches, stout columns and smooth paths. She watched from above, unseen, as a man in a bright red tunic led a long file of laborers in rough smocks, each burdened with the lopped off limbs of cactuses. Two girls played a game with rolled stones, under the supervision of a pair of richly dressed women seated nearby. Another group of workers carried heavy sacks as they were hectored by a barking overseer.

This was the most Selena had seen of Zorn, and she knew immediately that it wasn't built by human hands. It was too big, in every way. The doorways were too tall, the steps too far apart.

Yet no matter who had built it, humans lived in it now.

Selena had never seen such numbers of people before. Some of Zorn's citizens walked at a leisurely pace but most were purposeful. Everyone she watched was unarmed. She longed to be among them.

Even as she had the thought, she knew that back in the cactus grove Mugrak would be increasingly impatient. She only had this one chance to ask for help and secure her freedom. It was time to make contact.

From just outside the city wall she rose higher, until she was level with the open-sided chamber at the tower's summit. Focusing on her symbol, she drew on her power until it was shining brightly, glowing like the golden sun.

Who is there? A wavering shadow suddenly appeared in front of her. She once again had an impression of a triangular head and multifaceted eyes. *Who are you?*

I have to be quick. I'm outside the city wall, here. Remembering the trick Rei-kika had shown her, Selena sent an image of where she was in the grove of lifegiver cactuses, pleased by how quickly she could do something once it was shown to her. *I need your help. Some bax are holding me captive.*

The hazy figure turned back to look at the tower. *I will tell the Protector.*

The figure vanished a moment later.

Selena's eyes refocused and she looked around her. She was still sitting cross-legged on the ground. Tall, spiky cactuses flanked her on both sides. Mugrak hovered over her with his hand out, evidently about to shake her.

"Well?" he demanded. "What news do you have for Blixen? Did you find her?" He waved Borg and the other bax over to hear her reply.

Selena supposed it was possible that Blixen's wife was in a cell somewhere, but Mugrak was right; it was far more likely she was dead. "I searched the city," she lied. "Every building except the tower."

"And?"

"There are no bax in the city—"

Mugrak grabbed Selena's arm and peered into her eyes. "Of course there are. We all know what happens at the arena." His voice became a low, menacing growl. "How do I know you haven't just sat there for a time?"

Selena's panic grew. "What would be the purpose? Why wouldn't I want Blixen to know?"

Beastly cries sounded overhead. The chorus of piercing shrieks became louder.

Mugrak's eyes widened. "You?"

He snarled as he grabbed her arm. He pulled her toward him and his strong hand grasped at her throat.

—⁓—

Galen gazed down as his wyvern shot over the city wall. Arrayed around him were dozens of his men, astride their own winged creatures. The wyverns formed the shape of an arrow. Soldiers' heads turned as they searched the ground below.

Galen caught movement and his head jerked to the side. He saw a young woman with coal-black hair at the edge of one of the cactus groves. She was struggling in the grip of an ugly, wart-covered bax. The bax wrestled with her, trying to grab her neck, but she shoved her elbow into his face and knocked him back.

The young woman burst free and sprinted away until she was in the cleared space between the groves. She gazed up at the sky and waved her arms.

Galen felt a surge of admiration. Most of the women he knew from the city wouldn't have the courage to fight back in the way she had. He had no doubt she was the mystic he was trying to rescue. He wondered how she had convinced the bax to travel so close to the city wall. She wasn't just brave, she was also resourceful.

As soon as he saw her, Galen shouted at his men and pointed. Wyvern after wyvern swooped toward her. Galen's men lifted their bows and fitted arrows to the strings as they began to circle. The black-haired woman glanced back at the area of the cactuses.

The stocky, wart-covered bax she had fought with stood at the edge of the grove. He had spread out his arms to hold his subordinates back. He glared at the woman and snarled, but as he looked up at the circling wyverns, he knew that if he tried to reach her, arrows would pepper his body. He shrank back into the tall green plants surrounding him. Clearly he was hoping that if he could hide from the threat in the sky, he still might get away alive.

The young woman had stopped waving her arms, but she still alternated her attention between the wyverns above her and the grove she had just come from. Galen focused on the bax. Their squat bodies were crouched lower under the cactuses and their mottled hides blended with the spikes and broad limbs. For the time being Galen ignored the mystic. He inspected the groves he was now traveling over. Some of the other wyverns circled even lower. Soon Galen was directly above the area where the bax were hiding.

As soon as it was clear that the city guard knew exactly where they were, the bax bolted. Loping along with their strange but swift gait, they kept to the groves and moved between the cactuses.

But all Galen and his men had to do was follow from overhead. When the first bax left the fields altogether, arrows rained down from the sky. A pair of sprinting bax died next. Another fell with three shafts in his back. Some of the group had second thoughts and tried to hide, but Galen's men saw them and they fell like the rest.

Soon there was only one ugly creature left. Galen recognized the wart-covered bax that the woman had broken free from. He was ducking and weaving while he ran, narrowly avoiding arrow after arrow.

Galen made a circling motion with his arm. His wyvern flew forward while the rest of his men gathered behind him. Just above the ground, Galen pulled up, and the following wyverns drew together in a ring around the bax.

The wart-covered bax came to a halt. Galen turned his head to scan his men, seeing that they all had their bow strings drawn to their cheeks. Panting, the bax opened his mouth to bellow something up at the sky.

Galen lifted his arm, making sure all his men could see it, then he swept his arm down.

Arrows flew from every bow. They flashed down from the sky to pummel the bax's body. He jerked with every strike. When it was done, the bax collapsed onto the dust.

Galen then indicated for his men to gather. His wyvern wheeled, turning hard. With strong sweeps of their wings, the wyverns gathered behind him and followed him toward the mystic. She gazed up at the circle of winged creatures that soon surrounded her from above.

Her face was flushed with pleasure and relief. She had been held captive, and now she was free, just outside the safety of the city's tall white wall.

As the rest of the wyverns hovered, Galen indicated to his men that he would be the only one to land. Watching the black-haired woman, he left his position to fly down at her. The mystic bravely stood her ground, even as Galen headed straight toward her. He slowed only at the last moment, feeling the saddle below press hard against his body. His wyvern settled its limbs to the ground.

Galen climbed off his mount. He gave the mystic a more detailed inspection as he walked toward her.

She was slender, with sharp features and long hair as black as night. He already knew that she wasn't as delicate as she looked, and as he approached he saw strong lines of resolve in her mouth and intelligence in her eyes. She was pretty, something he hadn't been expecting when he set out for her. He realized her eyes were odd-colored, one brown and the other green.

He kept his manner businesslike. "You're the mystic?"

"Yes." She met his gaze directly and her voice was like her: soft but strong. She glanced over her shoulder. "Are they all . . . ?"

He kept his face cold. "Every one of them. I know my business."

"Thank you." She turned and looked toward the city. Emotion worked its way across her face. "I'm here. I almost can't believe it." A smile brightened her face. "I've made it to the white city."

"Its name is Zorn."

She was still smiling. "I know that." As the moments dragged out, she gave him a curious look. "What now?"

"You can start by giving me your name."

"Selena."

"My name is Galen. I am the commander of Zorn's city guard." He indicated his wyvern. "The Protector wants to see you."

"He can help me?" Selena asked.

Galen nodded. "Of course he can," he said. "Follow me."

23

The Protector of Zorn enjoyed a sense of height, of looking down upon others. When he stood face to face with one of his citizens he knew the effect that his tall frame, stern manner, and intense blue eyes had upon the subject of his attention. Whether in public or with his aides, he made sure to maintain an imposing appearance. He wore tailored clothing in dark shades. He kept his gray hair neatly combed. Like his father, he had once had a name, but names belonged to children, not to the ruler of a powerful city. He had renounced his old name the day his father died.

The soaring tower at Zorn's heart, where the Protector lived along with his key advisors, also gave him a pleasant feeling of height. No other place had a view like the one from the open-sided chamber at the highest level. From this observation room, the Protector saw all. He could watch the citizens scurrying in the streets and gauge the city's mood. He could monitor anyone crossing the plain to approach his city. This large, circular space, from where he looked down at the rest of the world, was where he spent most of his time.

As he gazed out at the city's white rooftops and the rust-colored plain beyond, the Protector frowned. There was something he tried not to think about, but he was reminded almost every day. His father had been a strong mystic. The same had been true of every ruler of Zorn before him.

The Protector may have a commanding view from the place where he was standing, but, because he had not been born with the talent, he was less than what a Protector of Zorn was supposed to be.

He often imagined the things he could do if he had the power. What need was there for a lofty view if he could free his awareness and roam anywhere he wished? If there was dissent in the city, he would be there, unseen, watching and listening. His citizens would hold him in awe, like they had his father.

Nonetheless, he was an intelligent man, and he had made the best of his situation.

Once he became Protector, he had searched for others with the talent and recruited two men to his service. Turning away from the vista of rooftops and streets, he faced them now.

Arren and Merin were childhood friends. They weren't powerful mystics, but what they lacked in strength they made up for in skill. When they had first offered their services, the Protector had initially been dubious, but over the years they had proved themselves time and again. While they weren't able to farcast a great distance, what they could do was work together to channel through another mystic—whether that mystic wanted it to happen or not. Then they could do anything.

Arren—a wiry, narrow-faced man with lank dark hair—sat on a stool close to the center of the observation room. Nearby, straddling another stool, was Merin, who was stockier and plumper with close-cropped hair. The attention of both men was focused intently on the mantorean, Tika-rin, who occupied a hard-backed wooden chair in front of them.

The Protector examined the mantorean. "Arren, how far can Tika-rin cast?"

Arren's stare didn't leave Tika-rin. The Protector was well-accustomed to the scene; when Tika-rin was working, the mystics had to give her almost all of their concentration.

"She keeps her casting to the plain," Arren slowly replied. "She saw those refugees that Galen stopped."

"Have you tried pushing her harder? There must be a way to get her to farcast the Rift Valley."

Arren's nostrils flared slightly, but he still kept his focus on the mantorean in the chair. "Of course we've pushed her. Look at the state of her."

Tika-rin's bone-colored carapace was scarred with ugly marks. Her antennae drooped and her frame was so thin it was almost skeletal. The Protector's lips thinned. Even given Tika-rin's poor health, he needed her too much to let her rest for more than a short period. He couldn't let her die, and he would never let her go.

Along with the high-backed chair in the observation room's center, the area was sparsely furnished with a desk, table, and a few divans. The Protector turned to face his desk, where an egg rested on a stand.

"So even if I tell Tika-rin I will destroy her egg, she still would not be able to cast any farther?" The Protector left unsaid that as far as he could tell, the egg might already have decayed.

"No, Protector," Arren said. "Her lifeline can only stretch so far."

"Hmm," the Protector mused. "And this new girl?"

The human mystic, someone almost certainly not from Zorn, had contacted Tika-rin, who had consulted the Protector and then passed the message to Galen to rescue her from outside the wall and bring her to the tower.

"We won't know until we meet her," Arren said.

The Protector nodded. He had thought as much. Turning away from Arren and Merin, he resumed his contemplation of the view and pondered.

In times of crisis, people needed a strong leader. Over his years as Protector, he had always shown resolve, and while the current crisis would test him like nothing before, he was a determined man, born to rule, and he had already found a way through.

Zorn was unique. There was no other place like it in the wasteland, and he was well aware of the lure of his city to distant rovers and settlers. With a multitude of stone houses, everyone had a roof overhead to protect them from the elements and a home in which to raise a family. The fields just outside the wall grew tubers, nuts, berries, and razorgrass for bread. In a world full of predators and hostile enemies, the city's soldiers—not to mention the Protector's decisive leadership—meant it was the only settlement where safety could be guaranteed.

And until recently, the city could also boast that there was a reliable supply of water.

Even now, strident cries drifted up from the markets that surrounded the tower. "Water! Water!"

The Protector cast his two mystic aides a sharp glance. "Arren. Merin. Check the city for me."

He waited impatiently while Arren and Merin used Tika-rin's ability to farcast as if it were their own. The silence dragged out, before Arren met the Protector's gaze.

"Nothing serious," Merin said. "No more riots, Protector."

The Protector clenched his jaw. Here was the cause of his crisis. The idea of plentiful water was a lie. There was a well at the bottom of the tower, below ground. Over recent years the well's level had diminished until it was now as dry as the winds that blew across the wasteland.

The only people who knew the truth were the Protector's confidants, those allowed inside the tower, which was guarded night and day. Without doubt, the people could never know. The Protector was feared, but he knew he wasn't loved. His control of the well was the source of his power. His fate would be sealed. His head would roll.

But he had a plan. It was the manner of his father's death that had given him the idea. His father had been butchered near the Rift Valley while away from Zorn's protection. At the time, the bax had said it wasn't them, but they would say that. The Protector had never believed them.

The Protector's calculating thoughts had turned to the Rift Valley. A large number of bax had lived there for a long time. Clearly, they had their own dependable water source.

His plan was to drive the bax from their territory. He had always maintained power by pitting humans against non-humans, but he would take the situation further, and seize the Rift Valley before Zorn's citizens found out the truth about the city's well.

He needed the citizens' support, even as he began to ration the water he had. As he instructed his city guard to burn bax villages, killing and capturing as they went, he whipped up hatred. He pointed out all the things that made the other races different, and scorned any talk of similarities. Bax were ugly and murderous, skalen cold and slippery, trulls monstrous, and mantoreans scuttling vermin. At public gatherings, he spoke to his citizens' emotions and heightened those that were most keenly felt: fear, anger, and a sense of kinship for their friends and neighbors.

It didn't work on everyone, but all the Protector needed was a core of vocal supporters. As his remaining barrels emptied and the price of water went up, he blamed his enemies. If Blixen laid siege to the city, the water sourced from the lifegiver cactuses in the fields would no longer be accessible. The citizens believed that the Protector was doing the responsible thing and building up a reserve. He had diverted their attention. No one wondered if there was a problem with the well.

Once the city had a defined enemy, the Protector discovered that he had more power than ever before. He always had a reason to deal harshly with the malcontents and subversives who questioned his rule. There were rebels in the city, people who didn't want a war, but once identified they didn't live long. Galen rounded them up and sent them either to the fields or the arena. Few spoke out now.

The Protector's city guard only had a hundred wyverns, but they were a decisive force, able to shoot arrows from the sky. Slowly, surely, the Protector would destroy anything that moved in the Rift Valley, until Blixen fell, and the last bax fled and never came back.

The plan was working . . . except that there was one minor, but growing issue.

The Rift Valley was a maze of ravines. The bax who lived there, and the warriors Blixen was forming into an army, were able to hide from the city guard.

A mystic could search a larger area than a thousand wyverns, and in a fraction of the time. Unfortunately, Tika-rin couldn't cast as far as the Rift Valley.

But the Protector had a newfound hope. He might soon have two mystics. If the girl had power, he would use her to find his enemies no matter how they tried to hide. If she served willingly, he would treat her well enough.

If not, she was going to serve anyway.

24

Selena was free.

As she walked the streets of the white city, she had to keep telling herself that she wasn't dreaming; this was real. Her plan had worked. Mugrak and Borg were both dead. Her actions had finally brought her to the place she had dreamed about for so long.

Her head turned from side to side; she had never been more excited. Zorn was beautiful, everything she had wanted it to be. The streets were clad in smooth paving stones that gleamed in the bright daylight. Tall white houses stood proudly side by side. Soaring over the rooftops, the tower ahead of her was a grand, noble structure that announced to the world that this city was a haven from the precariousness of life outside the wall.

Selena wished more than anything that Taimin was walking beside her, rather than the commander of the city guard. Lars should be with her too. Yet even thinking about the two companions she had become separated from couldn't banish the pleasure she was feeling.

"I take it this is your first time in Zorn?" Galen asked.

"Yes," Selena said with a smile.

He nodded, as if confirming something to himself. Other than that, his face was carefully blank as he guided her through the streets and toward the tower.

"Why does the Protector want to see me?" Selena asked as she watched the commander's face.

"He takes an interest in all newcomers," Galen said, and then paused. "Particularly mystics."

Selena remembered when she had wanted more than anything to remove her curse. She realized that she had changed. She no longer had seizures or headaches. Her talent had brought her to where she was now.

She returned her attention to the streets. At first everything she was seeing was overwhelming, but as she began to make sense of the place, she was able to focus on more of her surroundings. The broad avenue she and the commander were following thronged with city folk. Rather than gaze in awe at the structures on all sides and wonder at the city's sheer size, she began to look at the citizens.

At first, the figures blurred together. But as she inspected people individually, she experienced a strange feeling.

A slight sense of unease began to grow in her chest.

Dusty laborers with gaunt faces trudged. Scrawny women carried sloshing water sacks and glared at anyone who strayed too close. The faces Selena saw were careworn. Several of the laborers had thin scars on their shoulders . . . the lines left behind by a whip.

Selena was now close to the tower, where a plaza and bustling market surrounded the broad, circular base. Her misgivings grew. Hearing shouts, her attention was drawn to a crowd that surged around the nearest stall. Men and women held up a variety of flasks, gourds, and clay jars. There were few among them dressed in the fine clothing that some of the citizens wore. Young or old, they all cried out the same word. "Water! Water!"

The vendor, a skinny man with a wispy beard, struggled to keep up as desperate people reached out to him. He took containers and filled them from a barrel on a stand behind him. He then exchanged them for money until, with nothing more to give, he began to turn customers away.

Other stalls displayed wares Selena was familiar with: lizard and wherry skins, treated leather, lengths of woven plant fiber, tools, weapons, and dried meat. Yet water was clearly the most popular commodity, and the crowds only appeared to be growing.

Selena cast a swift look at the man walking beside her. Galen's features were hard and angular. His eyes were dark, as if warmth never touched his heart. His white, close-cropped hair made him striking, easily picked out in a group.

"Is there a shortage?" she asked.

Galen glanced at her sidelong. "Only for the time being."

Selena's mind was spinning. She had told herself she would be safe in Zorn . . . she had done the right thing, and the commander had gone out of his way to help her. She was going to see the Protector, which was what she had always wanted.

At the same time, another part of her knew that it wasn't supposed to be like this. She should be here with Taimin, instead of the cold-faced commander of the city guard. Rather than help her, she sensed that the Protector wanted something from her.

All she knew for certain about Zorn was what she had learned from Blixen's memories. She had believed that Blixen's experiences must be the result of a few overzealous soldiers, and that in turn the bax had committed their own atrocities. Humans were her own kind.

No. Something wasn't right.

Selena brought herself to a halt. As the commander stopped alongside her, his expression changed. He didn't look pleased.

"Well?" Galen asked impatiently. "What is it?"

"I don't want to go with you," Selena said firmly. She lifted her chin and held his eyes for a moment, and then made to turn.

Quick as a snake, Galen's hand wrapped around Selena's upper arm and he yanked her toward him. She tried to fend him off, but his grip was unrelenting. Her struggles made him growl at her to stop, and then she froze as the sharp point of a dagger pressed into her side.

Galen barely tried to hide his movement. Passersby shied away and pretended to look elsewhere. "You may be a mystic, but my mind is protected," he hissed into her ear. He tapped his collar meaningfully, and Selena saw a metal necklace that sparkled with tiny green pieces of aurelium. "My instructions are to take you to the Protector."

"Why?" Selena demanded.

"Because of what you are."

Selena tried to pull away again, harder this time, but Galen held her tightly and used his dagger to keep her moving toward the tall doorway at the tower's base. A soldier wearing a crimson uniform made way at the entrance and opened the heavy door.

She scanned people as she passed them. Surely a young woman being dragged toward the tower wasn't something that happened every day?

With a horrific, sinking sensation in her stomach, Selena knew that everything she had thought Zorn to be was false. This was a place where laborers were whipped. The poorer citizens were skinny and desperate for water. The faces she saw were afraid. No one was going to help her.

Selena stumbled into the tower, where an immense circular chamber opened up in front of her. A series of oval windows let in the sun, but the air was cooler than outside. A curling stairway disappeared into the ceiling high above.

"Keep moving," Galen grunted. "Up the steps."

With Galen behind her, Selena began to climb. Each step was spaced strangely far apart, which meant she had to lift her legs more than felt natural. The first level she came to was as wide and open as the one below but far less empty. A multitude of storage crates filled the space.

As her thoughts whirled, she glanced back at Galen. For a brief moment she wondered if she could push him, but he was watching her every move. As she continued to climb, with the commander following behind, she soon realized that what she had seen was just one storeroom of many. Several doorways on the next level were open and she glimpsed sacks and ceramic jugs. It was the same on the levels above.

Soon she reached levels that were more functional. She saw corridors lined with linen mats and guessed they might lead to sleeping quarters. Rooms off to the side were sealed with sturdy doors. The plain furnishings were obviously human in origin: woven rugs, tapestries, barrels, wooden tables, and chairs. There was a strong contrast between the graceful, oversized beauty of the tower and the furnishings within its walls. The occasional window gave her an incredible view of the city from above.

She still hadn't encountered any other people; the Protector evidently kept himself separate from his citizens. Passing a level, she glanced into an open archway. Beyond was a large, high-ceilinged room with wide windows that let the light inside.

Selena was expecting to see another storeroom, but the sight that greeted her was something else altogether. She gasped.

A snub-nosed trull stood next to a pair of skalen, a male and a female. Farther away, three mantoreans had their heads together in a pose that suggested they were conferring. She saw bax of both genders, and even some bax young. The adults held the weapons typical of each race: javelins for the skalen, bows for the mantoreans, and clubs or spears for the bax. Every creature was utterly motionless, supported by sharp poles embedded in their bodies from below.

The corpses had been preserved and put on display.

The sight was so shocking that Selena came to a sudden halt. She stood frozen in place as a chill raced along her spine. Her gaze darted from one corpse to the next. Each creature made her stomach churn.

Any remaining belief that the Protector might be a wise, good man, vanished in that moment.

"Keep moving," Galen said sharply. "The Protector is waiting."

Selena felt a burning desire to run, but her fear grew stronger when she realized that she wouldn't make it far. What kind of man was the Protector, to have such a display? She tried to find a rational explanation. Her mind drew a blank.

With no option but to keep walking, she was short of breath by the time she reached the top of the stairway. A shorter, narrower set of steps lay ahead of her, and she could sense from the change in the commander's manner that she was close to the Protector.

"If you need to rest, here is a good place," Galen said.

She stared into his dark eyes. The commander was fit and strong, and she had never climbed so many steps, but she wasn't going to show him any weakness. "The Protector wants to see me. Why wait?"

Galen gave her a cold smile. "You have a strong spirit," he said, "but be mindful of who you are about to meet. Go on, then."

As Selena climbed, she looked up and ahead. She saw that the steps terminated at the floor of the level above. She had no doubt that she was entering the room at the tower's summit.

When she made it up and emerged from the stairway, she stepped into a place unlike anything she had seen before.

The chamber was open on all sides, with a roof supported by columns. The lack of a rail created a terrible sensation of exposure—all she had to do was walk off the edge and she would fall to her death. Whoever had built this tower had no fear of heights.

Divans sprawled on one side of the chamber and faced a table and a brooding desk. A warm breeze blew. The stairway was located at the back of what Selena was already thinking of as an observation room, given the sweeping views.

Selena inspected the room's occupants. Near the desk, a tall, older man in black trousers and a snug vest was frowning as he sipped from a cup of steaming liquid and gazed out at the city. His skin was weathered and his hair was neatly combed. When he turned, his blue eyes widened slightly before they became narrow and appraising.

Her gaze moved to the center of the space, where a straight-backed wooden chair had been given special importance. Two men in white tunics sat on stools and faced the chair. Surprisingly, upon Selena's arrival, the two men on the stools didn't look up at all. Instead they never stopped staring at the chair's occupant.

Selena couldn't take her eyes off the mantorean in the chair. She was a pitiful creature. Her carapace was marred with ugly patches and her antennae drooped. The men facing her were both dark-haired and a decade or so older than Selena. One was stocky and round-faced, the other thin and wiry.

As Selena sensed Galen emerge from the stairway behind her, the mantorean turned her triangular head and looked at Selena with sad eyes.

"I am sorry you came," the mantorean said in a weak voice. "I would have warned you if I could."

"Enough!" the thinner of the two men snapped. Like his companion, he never took his gaze off the mantorean.

Selena's head jerked to the side when the older man set his cup down on a table and approached. Dread sank into her chest as she saw the man's eyes, which were an intense shade of pale blue. He

234

was a tall man, imposing despite his gray hair and craggy skin. His forehead was creased, lending him a stern expression.

He regarded her with a look of assessment. When he spoke, his voice was smooth and confident. "What is your name, girl?"

"Selena."

"You are a wastelander?" he asked. When she didn't answer immediately, he nodded. "Of course you are. And you are alone. No one knows you are here." He cleared his throat. "Selena, I am the Protector of Zorn. I command this city and keep my people safe from our many enemies." He glanced past her to Galen. "You did well. Perhaps she will prove easier to manage than Tika-rin."

As Selena looked at the mantorean, the forlorn creature spoke again. "If you can get out of here, leave," she said in a voice without hope.

Meanwhile Galen had moved to stand with his legs apart and fingers hooked into his belt, where he could watch the proceedings while also blocking the stairs—the only exit from the room.

"Our friend exaggerates," the Protector said. "You will be valuable to Zorn, and I mean you no harm." He tapped a silver neckpiece he wore around his throat. "I also do not fear you. My mind is safe." The Protector continued to examine her. "Well, Merin?" he finally spoke. "How powerful is she?"

One of the two men in the chairs, the stocky one, stopped watching the mantorean. As Merin focused on Selena, she felt a touch, a slight probing of her mind. An expression of surprise crossed his round face. "Powerful."

"More powerful than Tika-rin?"

"Yes."

Then something strange happened. As soon as only one of the two men on the stools was watching the mantorean, Selena heard a voice in her mind. *Please, help me.* She recognized the voice, even though the mantorean wasn't looking her way. *I need to know if my egg is safe.*

Perplexed, Selena scanned the room until she saw a small stand on the desk, supporting a pale egg the size of a big man's fist. The desk was only a few steps from where Selena was standing.

Just rap it with your fist. It can survive a much more powerful blow. I need to hear the sound it makes. Please. I am desperate.

Feeling nothing but pity for the wretched creature, Selena wondered what to do. She frowned at the Protector. "What is it you want from me?" She made a show of looking around. "What is this place?"

As she examined the chamber, she moved closer to the desk. She heard a voice and glanced at the two men in white. She knew they had to be mystics.

"Arren," Merin said to the thin man beside him. "I think they're communicating."

As soon as Selena was close, she turned and gave a firm but gentle knock on the egg. She expected to hear a thud, which would tell the mantorean something about the state of her egg. But the moment Selena touched it, the top of the egg caved in as the shell crumbled to dust. Any life inside the egg had been extinguished for a long time.

The mantorean cried out. Despite her clicking, croaking voice, it was a loud sound, a cry of utter anguish. Without warning, she shot up out of the chair, startling the two mystics. She burst into a run, heading directly for the void.

Arren and Merin both shouted. Merin lunged but his fingers closed on empty air and he was unable to prevent the mantorean's mad dash. The pitiful creature reached the edge of the floor and, without pause, threw herself from the tower.

It was over in moments.

Selena gasped, shocked to her core. With a sharp jolt, the knowledge of what the mantorean had been driven to do made her feel sick. The Protector's eyes flashed with anger as cries came from the streets below.

"You fools," the Protector snapped at the two mystics.

"It's the girl's fault," Merin said, scowling at Selena. "What did she say to you?"

Selena's chest was heaving. "She only wanted to know if her egg was safe. How was I to know it wasn't?"

"We shouldn't have had two strong mystics here in the first place," Arren said. He glared at Galen. "The commander should know that."

Galen returned the thin mystic's stare and put a hand on the hilt of the sword he wore at his side.

"Enough!" the Protector said curtly. He stared directly into Selena's eyes. "Girl, I have brought you here to serve. My men rescued you, at no small cost, and serve me you will, whether you wish to or not. I could have made this pleasant for you, but it appears you have already made your choice. Arren and Merin have skill in abundance, but what they do not have is strength. That means I need you."

"You don't need me. I can barely farcast." Selena willed him to accept the truth of what she was saying.

Merin snorted. "Her ability is untrained, Protector, but that won't stop us."

"Let us hope you are correct," the Protector said. He turned to the commander. "Galen, instruct some of your men to deal with Tika-rin's body."

With a look of disdain at Arren, Galen turned and exited down the stairs. Selena watched him go. Her heart was racing. The tower had one set of stairs, and one door at its base, which was guarded. The Protector was now standing uncomfortably close to her.

"What is done is done," the Protector said. "Tika-rin is no more. Arren, Merin, it is imperative that you harness our new mystic's talents. I expect results and soon. A long delay in our casting could be fatal."

"Understood, Protector," Arren said.

"As for you, Selena," the Protector said to her, "you will help to ensure our survival. You have a unique talent, as you are no doubt aware, and fate has marked you as a tool for this city to wield. We will keep you safe, here in this tower, and in return you will farcast for us. You will track the movements of our enemies and guide our patrols. Do you understand me?"

Selena made no reply. Instead she was thinking about the multitude of steps down to the door at the bottom of the tower. The Protector's previous mystic had been exploited and was now dead. Despite her spinning thoughts, Selena had to focus. There was no way she planned to suffer the same fate.

The Protector indicated the two men in white. "Arren and Merin here are mystics like yourself," he said. "They may not have your power, but they know how to channel through someone like you. You will only cast when and how they let you. They know how to hurt you, mind and body. I suggest you obey them in all things."

Selena felt the eyes of the two mystics boring into her, but, worse, she experienced another, stronger touch on her mind. She tried to find her symbol. Something was preventing her from reaching it. Her nostrils flared. Even the freedom she had discovered with Rei-kika's help was gone.

"It will not all be bad," the Protector said. "You will have some comforts. You will be allowed to sleep, although when you do our city will be exposed, so we cannot let you sleep for long."

Selena wanted nothing more than to get away from the two mystics and the tall man standing far too close to her. She lifted her chin. "I need to sleep now," she said.

The Protector frowned and then he looked at Arren, who nodded. Selena heard a sound and saw that Galen had returned to the room at the tower's summit.

"You can cast for us when you wake," the Protector said. He turned. "Galen, take her to Tika-rin's bedchamber. I'll have Ruth clean it up."

Galen indicated for Selena to start walking. The Protector returned to his desk, while Galen led her from the room and back down the stairs.

He took her two floors down, guiding her away from the stairway and crossing the floor to open a heavy door. After following a long passage, Selena came to another door, which was ajar.

Selena entered a tiny windowless room, where the only furniture was a rumpled bed pallet and a chest in the corner.

"While you are in your quarters the door will be locked," Galen said from the doorway. "But if you serve the Protector well, you will earn more liberties. I suggest you do your best to please him."

Selena stared into the commander's eyes. "I came to you for help."

"You will be safe here. You are with humans, and you are alive." His face remained cold. "It could be much worse."

Galen turned away and Selena heard a new voice, this time belonging to a woman.

"Excuse me, Commander."

With a grunt, Galen stepped aside to allow the newcomer into the room. A woman a few years older than Selena carried a bundle of coarse linen in her arms and a rag over her shoulder. She was pretty, with brown eyes, a wide mouth, and short wavy hair that was a mixture of red and brown. Tight leather trousers and a matching vest were snug on her curvy figure. Selena guessed she must be Ruth, the servant the Protector had mentioned.

Selena waited for the woman to say something, but she barely gave her a glance. The young woman set the clean linen down on the floor, then swept the old away from the bed pallet. It took her no time at all to set the bed back up again. A few swipes with the rag cleaned up some grubby patches on the floor and walls. When she was done, the woman picked up the dirty linen. She still didn't say anything as she left.

Galen checked that the short-haired woman was gone and then turned back to Selena. "As I said, do what we ask and you will be well-treated. There's no reason you can't have a decent life. Get some rest, mystic. You're going to need it."

The door closed, and Selena heard the sound of a bolt being thrown.

25

Taimin opened his eyes and winced at the throbbing pain in his head.

"Looks like you've rejoined the land of the living," a voice said.

He tried to lift his head but it was a heavy, great weight. He heard a scuffle and then a face came into his vision. The man was perhaps a couple of years older than him, with light-brown hair and a neatly trimmed moustache and beard covering his sharp chin. He had twinkling eyes, as if prone to mischief.

"Careful now," the man said. "You've taken quite a beating. Here, drink this."

Taimin drank as a wooden cup was brought to his lips, tasting water and the metallic note of blood from his own loose teeth.

"Where am I?"

"You're in the arena, the blood temple of the city of Zorn. Here people come to worship the god of death and revel in their place among the living. In case you hadn't already guessed, like me, you're a prisoner."

Taimin closed his eyes and it all came back: Selena traveling with the bax toward the city; following them and then being caught out in the open; his capture by Galen and march through the city streets. Remembering Lars's sacrifice, he felt a sinking feeling in his stomach. Lars's death had been in vain. The big, bearded skinner, who cared for no one, had sacrificed himself so that Taimin could be free. All for nothing.

With a supreme effort Taimin sat up. He put a hand to his forehead as his vision swam. He fought down a bout of nausea and tried to distract himself from his churning stomach by examining his surroundings.

He lay on a hard pallet bed, one of many lined up against the perimeter of a huge stone-walled chamber. It was a dim space, without windows, and barred gates stood at both ends of the room. Rows of tables filled the center, along with wooden stools. Taimin started when he saw the other prisoners sitting in small groups and talking amongst themselves. There were skinny humans, twenty or more, but there was also a skalen, the faded patterns on his skin showing his age. A handful of grunting bax sat apart from the humans, and there were even two trulls toward the back, given a wide berth by everyone else.

He turned his attention to the trulls. They were taller and broader than humans, with snubbed noses flattened against their faces and long upper incisors that protruded from their mouths. Most of all, they looked strong, with muscles defined on their bare arms. Almost everyone, trulls included, wore trousers of coarse cloth and sleeveless vests.

Two of the bax glanced over at Taimin. A middle-aged man with thinning hair also looked his way.

"They're curious about you," the man with the beard and moustache said. "We heard the commander brought you to the arena himself." He grinned. "Quite an honor. Whatever you did to him, all I can say is: well done."

"I killed his brother," Taimin said flatly.

The man's eyes widened. "Kurt? Oh," he said. "I see." He let out a breath. "There you have it then. You won't be living long now. No one leaves the arena in one piece."

"What should I call you?" Taimin asked. "Or is there no point finding out . . ."

"It's always good to know a man's name, even if it's just for a short while. I'm Vance."

"Taimin."

Vance nodded at the other occupants. "The skalen over there is Rathis. He's some kind of leader, so the Protector considers him quite a prize. He's also the only skalen so he gets along with everyone. Stay clear of the trulls, especially Sarg—the one missing half an ear. There are a few thieves among the humans, but most are all right."

"And the bax?" Taimin's eyes were on the stocky bax, who watched him back.

"The different groups pretty much keep to themselves. You're safe for the moment. If we don't get along in here, they stop giving us food." He gave Taimin a meaningful look. "No one wants to fight on an empty stomach."

"They make us fight each other?"

"Sometimes," Vance said. "As a rule, humans never fight humans. Most often we fight creatures from the waste."

"How does it work?" Taimin asked, still watching the bax. "Knowing that you might have to kill someone you're in here with?"

"The odds aren't high I'll fight any particular prisoner. And one thing about the bax over there: they hate the Protector even more than we do. It's not their fault they're here. In a strange way, we're all on the same side."

"They plan to attack Zorn," Taimin said.

Vance raised an eyebrow. "Perhaps. But if you think they started the fighting, you're wrong."

Taimin tilted his head. "What do you mean?"

"Everyone in Zorn who isn't a fool knows the truth, they're just too afraid to say it out loud. Bax . . . skalen . . . they all just want to be left alone. It's the Protector who started stirring things up—raiding, burning settlements. It's almost like he's provoking all-out war. He says that anyone who isn't human doesn't deserve to live."

Taimin stared into the distance. The skalen, Syrus, had told him war was coming. Vance now said it was the Protector who was to blame. Of course the bax who lived in the Rift Valley would fight back. He glanced at the bax in the prisoners' quarters. If the Protector was the aggressor, then perhaps they were victims as much as the refugees on the plain.

"Why are you here?" Taimin asked.

Vance shrugged. "I stole something from the Protector. Here, have some bread."

Taimin's stomach heaved, but he forced down the hunk of pink razorgrass bread, following it with more water. "Is that what you did, before you came here?"

"Steal things?" Vance gave a short laugh. "No, not me. Although I can't say the same for some of the others. I was a weapons trader." He held up a hand. "Before you ask, it's a long story. They're going to make you fight soon, you know. They might give you a day or two but not much more than that. Are you up to it?"

"Why doesn't Galen just kill me?"

"Where's the sport in that? By now the whole city will know you killed the commander's brother. Seeing you publicly carved up satisfies his reputation in some strange way. No doubt he will enjoy your struggles."

"So he's going to bring me out and his soldiers will overwhelm me, but in front of everyone?"

Vance snorted. "No, you don't have it right at all. They'll certainly give you a fight you can't win, but the odds can't be too skewed or the crowd will feel cheated."

"How long have you been here?"

"A lot longer than you. So far I've won my fights. Still, they've taken my measure now and I won't last much longer. A word of advice: when the assessors come, highlight your weaknesses and hide your strengths."

Taimin reflected for a moment. His situation was dire, but he had to find a way to survive. "Thank you, Vance. For the food, and for the information."

"The guards called you a wastelander. I know my way around a sword but I can't say the same for the others. I don't plan to die in here, so it makes sense for those of us who can fight to band together." Vance gave a wry smile. "It also increases the chance that it's worth getting to know you at all."

As Vance had predicted, the assessors came the next day. Taimin did the only thing he could. He removed his boot and sat on his pallet as they approached, neither looking up nor standing. He tried to tell himself that he was feigning weakness, but the fact was, while his strength had improved, he was far from his fighting best.

The trio of older men moved throughout the prisoners' quarters and gave each and every fighter a short examination. They spoke to each other in low tones, clearly knowing that ears would be pricked as everyone tried to hear what judgments were made.

Taimin glanced down at his crippled right foot. It twisted slightly outwards and the shape was wrong, nothing like the other. The toes were squashed together and one bone overlapped its companion.

Soon the assessors were standing over him as they conferred. When Taimin stayed seated, shoulders slumped and head down, a skinny arm reached out and he felt a hand grip his chin and tilt his head back so they could look into his eyes. He heard them discuss

245

the state of his body and take note of the bruises of his face. His foot interested them the most, and the same skinny man crouched and lifted it up while they talked about it. Without warning, the assessor squeezed hard. Taimin drew in a sharp breath. It wasn't an act. The assessors spoke some more and then left.

Vance came over and whistled when he saw Taimin's foot. "I hope you believe in the afterlife. It's Earth for you. You're not going to last two minutes in the arena."

Taimin wondered if Vance was right as he struggled to squeeze his foot back into his boot. "I was taught by the toughest woman I ever knew."

"A woman?" Vance spluttered, his eyes crinkling with mirth. "You'd better hope she was Abigail."

Taimin froze.

He looked up to meet Vance's eyes. Vance's laugh faded when he saw Taimin's expression.

Taimin spoke slowly. "What did you just say?"

"Abigail. You really do know nothing about Zorn. She was an arena fighter, the best of them all. The story is she led the city guard. Something happened out in the waste and she snapped, refused to serve. The Protector—the current one's father—sent her to the arena, but she survived battle after battle. Eventually the crowd cheered her on and the Protector risked a riot if he let her die. He gave Abigail her freedom and she vanished, never to return."

"Did you ever see her?"

"Not personally, no. Before my time. But they say she had wild red hair."

A vision came to Taimin of his aunt, returning from the fire-wall after carrying the bodies of his parents into the heat. He again saw her burned skin, matching the color of her hair.

Wild red hair.

"Did she have a scar?" Taimin asked Vance. "On her face?"

He frowned. "Not that I know of . . . I don't think so."

Taimin remembered his aunt's story about the origin of her scar. *Your father did this.* She had held off the firehounds alone while Taimin's mother gave birth.

In Taimin's memory, she had never called Gareth her brother. *Wild red hair.*

Taimin's mother, Tess, had dark brown hair. Gareth's was a mixture of black and gray. In fact, there was no resemblance between Gareth and Abigail at all.

An image came to Taimin. He was holding up the drawing he had found in Abi's clothing chest. The sour stench of char wrinkled his nose. In his mind's eye he saw the image of the city of Zorn. Taimin's parents had always held Abi's abilities as a fighter in awe.

The pieces fit together.

When she was younger, Abigail had spent time in the city. Perhaps she had even grown up in Zorn. She must have been a skilled fighter, even then, for she had risen in the ranks of the city guard. Something had happened that caused her to turn against the Protector. She had been imprisoned in the arena and fought her way to freedom. She had met Gareth and Tess, two people in need of her protection. Calling her Taimin's aunt had been a convenient fiction.

It didn't mean Taimin cared for her any less.

There is no city, boy, Aunt Abi had said.

Yet here he was.

Taimin drew in a breath. "It was her," he said, meeting Vance's eyes.

"What are you talking about?"

"It was her. The woman who raised me and taught me how to fight. Her name was Abigail and she said she was my aunt. I realize now that wasn't true. She was from Zorn."

Vance was incredulous. "Abigail? You were taught by Abigail?"

Taimin gave a slow nod.

Vance tilted his head back and laughed. "What a story! I can't wait to tell the others. A cripple who was taught to fight by Abigail herself. Whatever you do, don't tell the guards. With Galen eager for your blood, survival is going to be hard enough. Whatever skills she taught you, you're going to need."

As Vance left, Taimin pondered all the things he had learned.

He remembered his journey with Selena and Lars: encountering bax who were heading to join the struggle in the Rift Valley, and trading with mantoreans who gave him arrows while asking for nothing in return. Skalen had captured them, but Syrus, another skalen, had given Taimin and Lars food and shelter.

His thoughts then moved onto the confrontation between the refugees, who had been driven from their homes, and Zorn's city guard, under the command of Galen, who was responsible for the death of Taimin's parents as well as his current plight.

Along with Selena and Lars, Taimin's initial instinct had been to warn the city and help the Protector. They were wrong.

He knew what he had to do.

He had seen Selena for the briefest moment, but she was alive. Her talent made her valuable to whoever kept her captive. But more lives would be lost, and Selena's might be among them, as long as the fighting continued.

His goal steadily took focus.

Men like Galen, who were responsible for death and suffering, only had as much power as the people gave them. Abigail had won over the crowd. She had done it by surviving against the odds.

So would he.

26

Taimin tried to ignore the heavy thumping from above. As the people in the crowd stamped their feet, each beat echoed his pounding heart. Even their shouts penetrated through to the prisoners' quarters.

He was about to fight for his life.

He stretched his muscles, conscious of his fellow prisoners' eyes on him as he leaned into one position and then the next. Like them, he wore a leather vest and coarse trousers, along with the boots he had made himself what felt like an age ago. As he worked each limb in turn, he made sure to flex all of the places where he needed to be limber. He took deep breaths to flood his lungs with air in preparation for the battle to come.

It was a struggle to keep his mind clear as he prepared himself. The knowledge that he was likely to meet his end bubbled up again and again. Vance hadn't been able to find out who or what he would be fighting, and Taimin hated not being able to form any kind of plan.

Galen wanted to make him suffer, he knew that much. He stared down at the ground. His chest heaved. He did everything he could to focus on his body, his hands, his breathing.

He looked up. Vance stood in front of him.

"It's time," Vance said.

Rathis stood by Vance's side. He was nearly as old as Syrus, with all the feathers on his scalp long gone and his diamond-patterned skin so faded it was hard to tell where one segment started and the other finished.

"We are here to see you off," the skalen said. His tone was grave. "No one should walk through the gate alone."

Taimin knew from Vance that the gate led from the room filled with prisoners, along a corridor, up a sloped path, and to the sandy floor of the arena. As the pounding of boots on stone benches continued, Taimin glanced up at the ceiling, Vance scratched his neat beard and spoke again. "I might have some bad news."

Taimin's head jerked. He focused on the man in front of him and wondered how his situation could get any worse.

"Look," Vance said, nodding toward the far end of the room. "Sarg is gone."

Taimin turned and his heart sank. Sarg was the arena champion. The biggest of the trulls, he had survived longer than anyone else.

Rathis's voice was cautioning. "It is not certain you will be up against Sarg."

"Just concentrate on the fight," Vance said. "Focus on survival."

"What will I fight with?"

"You'll get a sword. Cheap and basic, but serviceable," Vance said. "Don't expect steel."

"Wastelander!" a rough voice called from the far side of the room.

Taimin's gaze shot to the gate and he saw the guard on the other side scowling at him.

"He means you," Vance said.

"I realize that," Taimin said dryly.

"Are you ready?"

Taimin drew in a deep breath and let it out slowly. "As ready as I'll ever be."

He began to walk toward the gate while Vance and Rathis flanked him. He understood without being told that this was part of the ritual of the arena: being given the comfort of companionship as he walked to what would likely be his death. As his heart beat faster and faster, he continued the heavy breathing, and flexed his shoulders and arms to prepare himself for combat.

A pair of the prison guards—a rougher kind than the Protector's uniformed soldiers—stood on the other side of the gate, watching Taimin approach. They hauled the gate open and the three companions passed through. The gate slammed closed a moment later.

Taimin turned a corner and looked up a sloped path. The bright light of day shone through an archway at the end of the corridor, where a portcullis was already open. The archway, twice the height of a man, led directly to the fighting pit.

The light was temporarily blinding. Taimin clamped down on his fear, knowing it could weaken him. He heard a roar as thousands of voices bellowed, a burst of sound that jangled his already taut nerves.

Vance and Rathis stayed with him until he was just a dozen paces from the archway.

"That's far enough, you two," one of the guards called out to them. "As for you," he glared at Taimin and patted the heavy club that dangled from his waist, "keep moving."

"By the rains," Vance muttered when he saw what awaited Taimin in the pit.

Taimin came to a sudden halt. Fear made him freeze when he saw what he was about to face on the sand. The black shape was as big as a wyvern but insectile, with a coiled tail and twin pincers as dark and shining as obsidian. Three bent legs on each side supported the creature's lean body. Four eyes jutted out on stalks, above a gaping maw filled with rows of sharp black teeth.

"It's a hellstinger scorpion," Vance said. His face was pale.

Abi spoke in Taimin's mind.

I don't need to tell you to avoid scorpions. They range from no larger than your finger to the size of a wyvern. The biggest are the hellstingers. If you find yourself facing one, the only way to survive is to cut off its tail. You'll ruin its balance and remove the threat of the sting. Its other weapons are its claws, which are razor sharp and can take off a limb as easily as you can pick a cactus flower, and its spit, which is a painful acid. Just avoid them, Taimin. Avoid them at all costs.

"Listen, Taimin," Vance said. "If it stings you, and I get a chance, do you want me to end it?"

Taimin knew what Vance was asking. The poison in the hellstinger's tail was said to be unlike anything else: lingering and excruciating, leading to hours of mindless screaming followed by certain death.

"You won't get a chance. Galen wants to see me suffer. But if you do . . . then yes. And, Vance?"

"Yes?"

"Thank you."

"Move!" the prison guard growled at Taimin.

Vance squeezed Taimin's shoulder and Rathis gave a nod. Leaving Vance and Rathis behind, Taimin forced himself to keep walking toward another pair of guards at the end of the corridor. He could feel his companions' eyes on his back.

One of the guards below the portcullis passed him a short hardwood sword. Taimin swiftly examined the blade. It was chipped in places, but at least it looked sharp. When the fight was done, either way, the sword would be taken from him. He left this last pair of guards behind. Light poured from the archway. He tested the balance of the sword, gripping the hilt in his right hand, trying to hold it firmly but not too tightly, the way Abi had shown him. To drop it would be to die.

He stepped out into the open. A roar greeted his appearance.

Behind him, the raised portcullis dropped down. He was now trapped. Dex's glare was blinding and Lux shone angrily from a higher place in the sky. On all sides he saw tiered benches, protected from the sandy floor by a tall wooden fence. People called out from all directions, their faces flushed. Laborers in ragged clothing made up the majority of the crowd, but there were also well-dressed citizens on the tiers at the back. Youths jumped up and down in excitement. Fathers held up their children so they could see.

As he took it all in, despite his situation, Taimin was surprised. From the thumping he had heard down below, he had thought the crowd must be in a frenzy. It was true that many of the onlookers were leaning forward in eager anticipation, but others, particularly from the poorer sections at the front, looked like they wished they were anywhere else.

He knew in any case that he had to ignore them. Returning his attention to the pit, he walked in a slow circle around the hellstinger, swinging his arms and preparing himself. The immense scorpion lashed its tail but appeared to be confused by its surroundings. Meanwhile, Taimin blotted out the sights and sounds above. He resisted the temptation to look for Galen. Of course the commander of the city guard would be watching, but Taimin couldn't think about him now. He had to survive.

The hellstinger's attention was now entirely focused on Taimin. Aware that one human was closer than any other, the creature made a hissing sound.

Taimin decided he was ready and came to a halt. He faced the hellstinger and turned his body to the side to present a smaller target. He lifted the tip of his sword and watched the hellstinger warily.

He almost jumped when he heard a strident horn blast and the crowd went silent. A prison guard opened a gate in the wooden fence to allow a herald to enter the fighting pit. Even though both Taimin and the hellstinger were on the far side of the floor, the herald walked only a short distance from the fence before he came to a halt, his nervous eyes on the huge black scorpion. He was a plump man in expensive clothing, with a wobbling chin and a crown of curly hair.

The herald opened his arms. "Citizens of Zorn!" he bellowed. "Welcome once more to the arena! I bring you these words from our exalted Protector, which I will convey to you now."

As the herald paused to clear his throat, Taimin wondered what it was that the Protector intended to communicate to the crowd.

"Today, my people, I, the Protector of Zorn, gazed out from the Great Tower. As I searched the lands around our fair city, I watched raptors fight over the carcass of a firehound. I saw skalen gnaw at the bones of a child. I heard bax as they laughed over the ruins of a human homestead. I witnessed the efforts of our valiant soldiers as they killed those same bax where they stood. Zorn is safe! Your Protector sees all."

The words had the pattern of something the crowd had heard before. No one appeared to be surprised at the horrific scenes that the herald described, and he moved on as soon as he had finished.

"Now, without further ado," the herald cried, "I bring you one whose heinous crimes have brought him to do battle here today. This man, a wastelander without a shred of civilized custom, came to Zorn to steal our wealth and plot against our Protector. In cold blood he murdered the soldier Kurt, a proud member of the city guard and the blood of our commander, Galen. He then fled into the waste like the coward he is. With relentless courage our commander hunted this man down and captured him alive so that we may witness his death today. He is to fight a hellstinger scorpion, and if, by chance, he is victorious, he is to then fight the mighty Sarg, most vicious of the trulls. Justice will be done."

When the herald mentioned Sarg, Taimin drew in a sharp breath. He saw the snub-nosed trull standing in an enclosure behind the protection of the wooden fence. Sarg looked at Taimin and grinned, showing off his long teeth.

Then Taimin inadvertently raised his gaze. He scanned the sea of faces until he saw him.

Galen sat at a high tier where he had a clear view of the fighting pit. He was leaning forward, and although his face was as cold as ever, his gleaming eyes betrayed his anticipation.

"Let the battle begin!"

No sooner were the words out of the herald's mouth than he fled back through the gate. The horn blasted again, louder this time, and the hellstinger reared back at the noise, claws clicking together as its eyes on stalks twitched one way and then another. Taimin continued to wait. If he was a nimbler man, he might try to take the hellstinger by surprise, but with his bad foot he knew it would be better to save his strength and let the creature come for him.

"Fight!" someone from the crowd jeered. "Coward!"

With his sword gripped in both hands, Taimin continued to wait.

More people called out and hissed. Above and behind them, Galen smiled with thin lips.

Taimin saw Sarg gesturing as he said something to one of the guards. The guard nodded, and Sarg left the enclosure to enter the fighting pit. Moving slowly, the trull crept up close to the hellstinger. Even Sarg was clearly afraid as he gripped his spiked club and stretched his arm. As swiftly as he could, he swung his weapon at the hellstinger's tail. It was a rap more than a hard blow, yet it clearly enraged the creature. Sarg leaped away as the tail lashed the air. He darted back, before exiting the fighting pit once more.

As soon as its tail stopped swishing, the hellstinger sped forward on scuttling legs.

Taimin's senses became heightened as fear surged through his veins. A snapping claw thrust at his head and he ducked. The fight had begun.

He knew the hellstinger would spin to bring its tail forward and he watched for the movement, even as he ducked another swipe from a claw. He came in close and slashed his sword at the hellstinger's eye stalks, but missed. He was forced to dive and roll when a claw grabbed at his abdomen. The moment he shot back up again, the hellstinger whirled to face him and spat.

White fluid shot from the scorpion's maw and splashed onto Taimin's shoulder. The leather vest barely protected him. Pain seared across his neck and upper arm. But he knew how to fight pain and pushed it down.

The hellstinger had closed in to spit and Taimin saw an opportunity. He swung his sword at one of the four eye stalks. The pale wooden blade sliced clean through and sent the eye it was attached to flying. Even as Taimin cut, he leaped backward, and then the hellstinger spun its body.

The tail uncurled and came forward, where its path would take it into Taimin's torso.

The crowd roared.

Taimin fell flat onto his back. He saw the black tail cleave the air in front of his nose and heard the whistle of its passage. He tried to raise himself fast enough to swing the sword at the tail. His blow struck the sand.

The hellstinger's motion took it in a complete rotation. Taimin again faced the enraged creature as it spat a second time. He lunged to the side and the white spray missed him by inches. When he returned to a standing position, he found himself panting heavily as he fought the pain in his shoulder and the crunch of bones in his foot.

The hellstinger now began a flurry of blows from its claws, pushing Taimin back and forcing him to give ground. Taimin thrust with his sword but the blade was too short and the creature too fast. He knew he would have to come in close if he wanted to halt his retreat and prevent himself from being pushed back against the fence.

He initiated a series of attacks at the eye stalks, but every time he tried to land a blow it was blocked by the scorpion's claws. Then his intuition told him that the hellstinger was going to spin again.

This time he crouched down, and as the tail came around he jumped into the air. Even with most of his weight on his good leg his jump was weak, and the tail struck his foot, knocking him down.

The back of his head hit the sand. He blindly swung.

He felt the sharp blade make contact. As his sword sliced through the tail at its midpoint, he swiftly rolled to avoid the severed section, desperate to keep it away from his skin.

The hellstinger gave a terrible, piercing shriek and reared back onto its stump, but there was no tail to give it balance. The crowd bellowed approval.

Taimin pushed himself back to his feet. His chest heaved as he gathered himself and waited for his opportunity. The hellstinger lurched from side to side. The creature's claws snapped together and its three remaining eye stalks twitched.

Taimin tried to circle around it, his stride hobbled whenever he put his weight on his bad leg. The hellstinger kept turning to face him so he launched into a shuffling sideways run to force it to constantly change position. He knew that he often fell when he attempted to run, but he pushed the thought from his mind.

Spying an opening, he darted forward while the scorpion's eyes faced the wrong direction. He plunged his sword into the hell-stinger's carapace and withdrew it immediately. He then slashed at the three stalks, taking them off with a single blow. The creature's six legs trembled and then it collapsed as the life went out of it. Taimin waited for its death throes to finish while he gathered his breath.

He had forgotten the crowd, and once more he heard their cries. He lifted his gaze. Some of the loudest people were calling encouragement, telling him to do the same to the trull; others jeered, shouting that he was about to meet his match.

The horn blasted. The herald entered the pit, again as far as possible from Taimin.

"We at the arena promise to always give you a fight to remember, and today we have delivered on that promise!" the plump herald cried, his chin jiggling with every word. "Now let this man of dark deeds fight the arena champion, the one you have come here to see, the strongest in a race known for its strength. Give a warm welcome to Sarg!"

The trull lifted his snout and raised his club into the air as he entered the fighting pit. He had half an ear and his brow was wrinkled in a perpetual scowl, but it was clear that he took pride in his title of champion. His supporters in the crowd cheered him on. He walked toward Taimin with purposeful strides. The gate in the fence slammed closed behind the herald.

There was no chance for Taimin to rest as he watched his opponent advance. The trull was much taller than him, with a thick body that rippled with muscle. Taimin knew he wasn't strong enough to fight again, let alone take on a trull. Sarg met his eyes and grinned.

"Come, human," Sarg said in a throaty voice. "What are you afraid of?"

Taimin shifted his position, but then he came to a halt on the sand. His shoulders slumped. Fatigue washed over him as the sharp pain on his shoulder returned with intensity. A trull's weakness was lack of speed, but there was no way he could outmaneuver a skilled fighter in his current state.

He did the only thing he could. He held up his sword and then threw it past his opponent, to the far side of the fighting pit. He spread his hands to show he was unarmed.

Some of the onlookers cried out in despair.

Sarg smiled as he closed in. The trull was confident and held his club overhead, ready to bring it down. People yelled at Taimin to fight, but he just stood and waited, panting with exhaustion. There was only one option available to him. It might be the last move he ever made. He watched his opponent approach until he was ten paces away, and then eight.

Taimin's eyes rested on the ground between them. When Sarg was six paces away, Taimin took a deep breath and then dived forward.

He landed heavily on one knee, but at least the churned-up sand cushioned the impact. Even as pain shot up his leg, he took hold of a moist, slippery stump: the hellstinger's severed tail. The thick end of the tail was wet with the hellstinger's blood and Taimin thought he felt a stinging sensation. Regardless, his was an act of desperation.

He held on tight with both hands and twisted his body at the same time to swing the tail with all his strength.

The sharp end of the black tail left a red gash across the trull's cheek. As Sarg's eyes shot wide open, he screamed.

Taimin threw the tail away from him. He brought his body into a crouch, watching his opponent. He slowly straightened.

Sarg was roaring with agonizing, terrible pain. The trull clasped his hand against his face and then fell to his knees. He tumbled backward and started to roll. His body twitched while he continued to howl.

Taimin waited, but there was no fight left in his opponent. His plan had worked. Someone else might have realized what he was doing, but trulls weren't known for their quick thinking.

Breathing heavily, covered in sweat, he realized that the crowd was in shock; every mouth was open and every voice utterly silent. Taimin walked over to his sword and picked it up. He then returned to the trull and looked up at Galen.

The commander's stony expression was gone; he could barely contain his rage. Galen watched as Taimin thrust the point of his sword into the writhing trull's neck, and then the arena champion was dead.

The crowd roared.

Taimin heard a grinding sound and saw that the portcullis had been raised. Ignoring the cacophony, he walked out of the fighting pit, and the portcullis closed behind him.

27

Selena sat in the hard-backed wooden chair while the eyes of the two mystics, Arren and Merin, bored into her. She hadn't been seated for long but already she felt her back ache and calf muscles twitch, as if in anticipation of how she would feel after she was stuck in place for hour after hour. When the thin-faced mystic, Arren, pulled his stool a little closer, she remembered Tika-rin, the mantorean who threw herself off the tower. After that experience, the Protector and his followers wouldn't take any chances with her.

Nearby, the gray-haired Protector waited impatiently as the short-haired servant entered the observation room, carrying a tray bearing three ceramic cups filled with steaming liquid. As the auburn-haired woman set the tray down on a table, Selena watched her carefully.

"Thank you, Ruth," the Protector said curtly. "That will be all."

Selena saw Ruth cast a quick glance her way. Their eyes met. But then Ruth broke the contact and departed down the steps set into the back of the floor.

The Protector picked up a cup and brought it to his lips to blow across the top. Selena guessed it was some kind of tea as he took a careful sip. The other two cups would be for Arren and Merin.

Selena again wondered about Ruth. At the very least, Ruth wasn't under guard like her. Something had passed between them.

Returning her attention to the two mystics, Selena decided to try something. She focused on Merin's thick neck and brought up memories that made her feel revulsion. Imagining a black, eight-legged insect climbing Merin's sleeve, moving toward his collar, ready to bite, she formed a clear thought.

That is the biggest spider I have ever seen.

Nothing happened. Neither Arren nor Merin reacted in any way. Whatever the two mystics were doing now and planned to do soon, they weren't reading her thoughts. Her experiences with Rei-kika told her that if they did, she would be aware of the touch.

Her mind was always working. She had been in difficult positions before and had always managed to find a way out of her predicament. Galen had said that she would be granted more liberty as time went by. She would search for an opportunity, and, in the meantime, lull her captors into believing she was more passive than she truly was.

The Protector wanted her to keep his city safe. She had yet to find out what that meant, but his plans for her must relate to the conflict between Zorn and the Rift Valley. Perhaps she could use her talent to save lives, on both sides.

As she waited in the hard-backed chair, her mouth went dry when the Protector approached. Tall and stern, he stood over her, between the mystics seated on stools on either side.

A stiff, dry breeze blew against the tower. The observation room possessed an unparalleled view of the city and the barren plain, but Selena couldn't take the sight in. She didn't know where to look. On her left, there was Arren's pinched face and small eyes, staring holes into her skull. If she turned to the right, Merin's round face would be waiting. Directly in front of her, the Protector's pale blue gaze was the worst of all.

"Tell me, Selena, what do you know of our great city?" the Protector asked.

Selena fixed her gaze on the Protector's gray vest. "Nothing," she said. "In the vastness of the wasteland, no one knows you exist."

The Protector snorted. "I am surprised there are humans still living out there. So, let me tell you of Zorn. Long ago, my great-grandfather founded this city."

"Found, you mean, not founded," Selena said. "You can't tell me humans built this place."

As the Protector gave her a thin-lipped smile, Selena bit down on her tongue.

"You are, of course, correct," he said. "My great-grandfather discovered this city. It was mostly abandoned, occupied only by a few trulls and bax, despicable creatures who lived in their own filth."

While the Protector spoke, Selena looked down at her hands, resting on the arms of the chair. She was free to move them, but what could she do? Even if she made it from the observation room, at the top of a tower guarded by the Protector's soldiers, where could she go? She couldn't even farcast and leave her body. As a test, she tried to touch her power, but the two staring mystics prevented her; they had put up some kind of wall.

"My ancestor gathered followers and freed the city," the Protector continued. "Humans finally had a place where we could live free from the dangers of the waste. His name was Zorn, but he gave his name to the city and instead took the title of Protector. After he died, my grandfather became Protector, then my father, and now it is my turn to defend this haven from those who would seize it for themselves. I will do whatever it takes to keep Zorn safe. I hope you understand me, Selena. I will stop at nothing. No one life is more important than this city, and that includes yours."

While the Protector was not a young man, he was still young to be without his father. It didn't take him long to answer her unspoken question.

"My father—" His piercing blue eyes narrowed. "My father taught me about the dark nature of the other races. Ten years ago he traveled to the Rift Valley to trade with the bax who live there. He left his group for just a moment." He paused and Selena heard a catch in his throat. "His men discovered his headless corpse, sliced neatly above his shoulders, but his head . . . that was never found." He cleared his throat and recovered his composure. "Despite all my father taught me, even he never understood the true savagery he was confronting. Zorn will only be safe when those outside the city wall are destroyed." The Protector bit his next words off. "Every last one of them."

Selena had to say something. "You can't judge everyone who isn't human the same way."

"On the contrary, they all mean us harm. If Blixen and those like him are allowed to thrive, we put the entire human race in peril. Surely you, as a wastelander, understand the constant threat that humans face outside this city? Blixen wants to grind us into the dust and seize Zorn for himself. Other races are joining his cause. We must defeat him."

"Have you tried talking?"

The Protector scowled. "Talk would get us nowhere. Our conflict will only end when it is humans, rather than bax, who occupy the Rift Valley. Your role, Selena, is to help our struggle, willingly or not. You may earn my trust, but until then, you have little choice in the matter."

Selena swallowed. Arren and Merin didn't move at all and continued to stare. Still trying not to meet their eyes, or the intense blue gaze of the Protector, she looked directly ahead.

"I can always refuse," she said.

"I disagree," the Protector said. "Arren and Merin will see that you perform." He turned his gaze toward the plain that surrounded the city, before focusing on Selena once more. "Our enemies are in the Rift Valley, but we do not know how many there are, and we do not know where to find them. Blixen is clever, and no doubt his warriors are scattered throughout the canyon. I realize this makes our task difficult. Yet we also have an advantage. The soldiers of the city guard are swift on their wyverns. My plan is to destroy one band after another until there is no threat remaining." The Protector gave a sharp nod. "Now begin." With a last glance, he left his mystics to their work.

The Protector had only just left when Selena felt a growing pressure in her head. It was a penetrating sensation she had experienced once before, out in the wasteland when Group Leader Vail had ordered Rei-kika to invade her mind. Arren and Merin were trying to channel through her.

She gritted her teeth. She wished more than anything that she knew how to stop what was happening. People had always been afraid of her. They thought that a mystic like her could hurt them. It was something she had never done, but now, she wished that she might be the one to cause her captors pain.

As the pressure increased, the ache between her temples became stronger. Invisible fingers peeled away layers, trying to worm their way inside. The touch was far from gentle as it tried to tunnel its way in. She grimaced and tried to push it away, but then the touch became a hard blow that drove into her skull with the force of a hammer. She looked down at her hands but couldn't move them; the pressure in her head was too great. Her lips parted. Her breath caught in her throat. If the chair hadn't been supporting her, she

265

would have fallen. The eyes of the two mystics continued to bore into her.

She had no choice. She had to escape the pain. As she sought refuge, there it was: the glowing sphere inside her, the source of her power. She surrounded herself with the radiance. For a time she felt peace. But the pain was closing in. The pressure was unstoppable.

The radiance knew that she wanted to escape the agony, but when it tried to take her free there was a barrier. The wall that the mystics had erected was still there. But even as the barrier frustrated her, it melted away. Caught between the pressure and freedom, there was only one option available. She grabbed hold of her power and used it to pull herself free of her body. She experienced the familiar sensation of being unfastened as she left her physical form.

Selena found herself floating, but rather than relief she felt panic. She looked down at her body, which was still and unresponsive in the chair. She tried to return.

She couldn't. The wall was back up, barring her from entry. As her panic grew, she sensed two entities with her, hovering in the air above her body.

One of the mystics spoke. *We can force you from your body, just as we can prevent you from returning. We can make you stay here forever, conscious but unable to interact with the world, watching yourself waste away until you die. Or we can give you sustenance, so that you never know when it will end. We can do terrible things to you physically and make you see us do them, knowing you won't feel the pain until you are whole. We can do all of these things, and more.*

Why? Selena said, unable to take her eyes off the young woman with the coal-black hair, so close yet so distant. *Why would you do this to me?*

To break your will, of course. She recognized Arren's voice. *We cannot have you fighting our control. You are an important tool. You are going to find our enemies in the Rift Valley.*

Why can't you find them yourselves?

We don't have your power, Merin replied, *so we must leverage yours. Arren, are you ready?*

I am.

Selena's perception was diverted. As with the first time this had happened to her, she felt violated not to be in control of her own casting. She was forced to look out from the height of the tower, past the fields, and across the plain, in the direction of the immense canyon that lay at the foot of the mountains.

She was made to fly forward. Only vaguely was she aware of the bright sunlight that lit up the white stone buildings below. People scurried about, but their figures were indistinct; the mystics were uninterested in them. The two men were like parasites, traveling with her as she soared over the city and then left it behind altogether. Her speed increased. She tried to fight what was happening to her but the two mystics beat her down easily, causing pain to stab at her mind.

What I wouldn't give for her power, Arren murmured from somewhere nearby.

She isn't close to reaching her limit, Merin replied.

The plain sped past until the red dirt and scattered boulders became a blur. The mountains grew in size until they dominated the landscape. The first hint of the gorges and ravines that made up the Rift Valley were soon visible.

Selena was forced to rise into the air and hover. The vista spread out below, a great expanse of thin seams, wide valleys, deep gullies, and towering cliffs.

Selena, we are going to wear you out, Arren said matter-of-factly. *Look back.* She turned and saw a faint white line that traveled as straight as an arrow over the plain, heading directly toward the city. *If you become weak, your lifeline will return you to your body.*

Such length, Merin murmured. *Much longer than Tika-rin could manage. The Protector will be pleased.*

Don't be too hasty, Arren said. *Let's find our enemies first.*

With her power at our disposal, we will find them, have no doubt of that, Merin said.

The sooner we start, the better, Arren said.

Agreed.

The two mystics directed Selena to investigate the immense canyon, pushing her to explore the network of ravines, one after the other. They were looking for tents, fires, and piles of animal bones. Most of all, they became excited when she saw anything that moved or had arms and legs, even if the first few times it was just the silhouette of a sentinel cactus.

Time trickled by as Selena swiftly explored, darting along one winding passage after another. She knew that back in the tower her body would be aching, but it was the state of her mind that troubled her more. The two mystics were using her ability with no regard to what it was doing to her. She was fatigued after two hours and exhausted after a third. Still they maintained their pressure on her, sending her along the seams of the Rift Valley.

After a time she saw a place she remembered. She was following a thin ravine that began to open up and she recognized the narrow gorge between two opposing walls of rock. She sensed Arren and Merin's excitement when dozens of tents came into view, along with rising smoke from several campfires and an expanse of dirt scuffed by the passage of many feet. Close to a hundred bax busied themselves with one task or another. Warriors sat on rocks sharpening their weapons, fletching arrows, or grilling meat on skewers. Discarded bones lay scattered along the base of the cliffs. A returning hunting party weaved through the camp, carrying a dead firehound on a pole.

Selena scanned the area. She saw the slight hill where she had met Blixen, but the pavilion was gone, and there was only a third as many tents as there had been before. Blixen was wise enough to keep his warriors scattered throughout the caves and hidden ravines. The skalen under Vail were also nowhere to be seen.

Excellent, Arren said.

There was once a greater number here, Merin mused. *Where are they now?*

We will find them. Mark the place.

Selena flew higher, rising at a constant speed until she was above the ravine. The two mystics took a bearing from some of the oddly shaped rocks and a withered tree that clung tenaciously to the top of the cliff.

That's enough for today, Arren said. *She's nearly done in.*

Relief flooded through her at the thought that she could return and rest.

Wait, Merin said. *There's something moving in that gully, the one between the two bigger ones. Do you see?*

Selena was forced to travel farther until she was floating above the area. She peered down and saw that Merin wasn't wrong. There was definitely movement at the base of the gully: small figures that darted back and forth. The two mystics made her descend, taking her to the cluster of figures. Once more, walls of rock enclosed her on both sides. She plummeted until she saw that there were just four little shapes.

Her heart sank. They were bax young, playing in the red dirt near the base of the cliff. An older female watched from the mouth of a cave while she sat on a rock and skinned a lizard. As Selena looked on, three other females and half a dozen more infants exited the cave. The excited younglings ran past their mothers to join the others.

The pain in Selena's head increased. She was exhausted. She couldn't keep going.

We've seen what we need to see, Arren said. *If we want to use her again today, she'll need rest.*

Take note of the location.

Got it.

Selena? Selena! Return to the tower.

Selena heard the voice from a distance. She turned and there was her pale lifeline, fainter than before, begging her to return to her body. She took hold of it and pulled with the last of her strength.

"And the second group?" A strong male voice jolted Selena awake. She was still in the hard-backed wooden chair. She didn't know how long she had been unconscious.

Galen was nearby, speaking with Arren and Merin. From their manner, the pattern of their conversation was familiar. Arren and Merin found anything that moved beyond the city wall, and the commander was the one who did something about it.

"Bax females," Arren said in answer to Galen's question. "There's a patch of blue rock on a cliff, above a gully. At the base of the gully you'll find some caves. I counted at least four females, along with their young."

The fog finally cleared from Selena's sluggish mind. With a growing sense of horror, she realized what Arren had said.

"We'll fly out immediately," Galen said.

Selena stared up at the commander as outrage washed away her fatigue. "I thought you were after enemies. Why go after the females? It's the warriors you want."

"Females breed warriors. It's not a complicated concept," Galen said.

Selena felt sick. "I won't be a part of this."

Galen raised an eyebrow. "Do you care more about bax than your own race? Surely you have more sense than that."

Selena thought about Blixen and his warriors, dispersed throughout the Rift Valley. What chance did they have? The city guard rode wyverns. Galen and his men could shoot arrows from the sky, picking off enemies below until there was no one to stand against them. She finally understood Rei-kika's words: *Have you not realized that everyone in this canyon is in hiding?*

What, then, was Blixen's plan? He must be biding his time, waiting until he had the numbers to rush the city. But with Galen hunting down every bax in the Rift Valley, Blixen's army would break up and flee.

Arren's next words filled her with dread. "Come, Selena. Find us some more."

When Selena found a group of six bax hunters, the city guard flew out to make the kill. The two mystics made her travel to the mountains, and, when she came across some skalen, Galen rode forth with his men.

Arren and Merin forced Selena to watch as Galen butchered mantoreans in the foothills. The city guard toyed with some bax infants, carrying them into the air on their wyverns before dropping them from a height to the rocks below. The two mystics controlled Selena's casting for hour after hour, and sometimes the city guard brought home prisoners for the arena.

Galen never showed any emotion. The cold-faced commander butchered every non-human he and his men came across.

Blood flowed in the Rift Valley and beyond.

***

Selena was given a bigger room, with an oval window that at least let in some fresh air. The Protector even provided fresh clothing and a bone comb. He gave her water to wash the dirt from her hair and face.

She often saw Ruth, cleaning, carrying linen, or serving tea. Ruth was in the tower at all times of day and Selena guessed that, like her, she must have quarters inside. But every time Selena tried to catch her eye, Ruth's mouth tightened and she gave a barely noticeable shake of her head. Once, when Arren and Merin were talking in the corridor, Selena tried to take the opportunity to speak with her, but Ruth looked panicked and rushed away.

Meanwhile, the things Selena had seen and done gave her nightmares. She knew that there were many more bax in the Rift Valley and hoped that they had the sense to flee.

The Protector was pleased. He made no secret of his hope that Blixen himself would soon fall under the commander's sword.

28

Taimin glanced at the slim man seated across from him at the long wooden table. There hadn't been much conversation over the midday meal. Usually Vance was talkative, making expansive gestures while he told stories from his time as a weapons trader in the city. But today his face was pale and he had barely opened his mouth to speak or eat. As the other prisoners finished and left the table, Vance stayed where he was, staring down at his untouched plate.

As soon as he and Vance were alone at their section, Taimin leaned forward. "It's just you and me. Out with it."

Vance looked up at him, and Taimin saw more than worry in the man's eyes. His jaw was tight. He could barely hide his fear. "The guards told me I'm going to be fighting a wyvern." He let out a breath. "I knew my luck couldn't last forever."

Taimin knew there must be more to it. "You've survived this long."

Vance shook his head. "It's got blood madness. One scratch and I'll have blood madness too. You'll have to put me down like an animal while I try to gouge out your eyes."

Taimin became truly concerned. Fear was the greatest enemy of all. It was a heavy weight to bear and dragged at the limbs, causing hesitation when decisiveness was needed. He realized that it wasn't just death that Vance feared; it was the manner of his passing. Vance needed to face down his fear or he would die.

He met Vance's gaze and spoke firmly. "You're not going to go mad. I know about these things. Humans can get blood madness from a firehound's bite, but not from a wyvern."

Vance raised his gaze. "Really?" He frowned, puzzled. "Why not?"

"I don't know, but it's something Abigail told me."

"I can't catch it?"

Taimin hesitated for the briefest instant. "No."

Some of the tightness left Vance's face.

"Like you said to me, just focus on the fight," Taimin said. "You'll still have to work hard. Even with clipped wings a wyvern can still bite and scratch. It'll be angry, without doubt. I can give you some advice, if you like."

"Anything."

Taimin wondered if this was what it had felt like for his aunt when she taught him to fight the creatures of the wasteland. "First, wyverns are flyers, so they're used to looking down. Use your height, and try to get above it and strike down. Also, their skin is soft under the wing. It's a good place to strike."

Vance gave Taimin a weak smile and returned to something like his usual self. "Thanks."

"Do you think they'd let you have a spear?"

Vance snorted. "I'd have just as much luck getting a bow and half a dozen aurelium-tipped arrows. Or a steel sword made by Manis the blacksmith."

"Don't forget," Taimin said, "it's just a wyvern."

"Just a wyvern," Vance repeated. "Unfortunately for me, I wasn't trained by Abigail."

Taimin pictured his aunt, pushing him hard, tending her garden, grumbling about Griff sleeping in the doorway. His thoughts then turned to Griff. He knew he had broken the wherry's heart by driving him away, and, although he didn't regret saving his life, he missed him. Now and then he pictured his bounding friend, panting and grinning as he hunted lizards. He had to believe that Griff was happy and free.

Vance shook his head as he continued. "I still can't believe you defeated a hellstinger and Sarg, all in the same fight. I wish I'd seen Galen's face."

Taimin lowered his voice. "Why am I still alive?" Enough time had passed for his wounds to heal after his last fight, and he had yet to be called up again.

Vance shrugged. "Be glad. It's the arena. They keep bringing in more prisoners every day. They're probably saving something special for you."

Taimin turned to scan the prisoners' quarters. Most of the newcomers scattered throughout the long room were human—a skinny and downcast bunch, imprisoned for stealing water or shirking work—but his gaze also took in some recently arrived bax from the Rift Valley. At least the two trulls weren't around anymore.

Returning his attention to Vance, Taimin glanced at the untouched plate of food in front of his friend. "Going to eat that?"

Vance picked up a hunk of pink razorgrass bread. But as soon as he put it to his mouth, his eyes shot wide open.

He could hear the guards calling his name.

Taimin and Rathis watched through the bars of the lowered portcullis as Vance fought the wyvern. Taimin's knuckles were white as he gripped the wooden bars and his stomach clenched every time Vance dodged the ferocious creature's teeth and claws.

"He fights well," Rathis said. "The overhead blows are effective."

"Look at it, though—it's mad," Taimin said. The wyvern's jaws snapped together, narrowly missing Vance's sword arm. "The wing!" he cried. "Strike under the wing!"

"Thank you for helping him overcome his fear," the old skalen said. "I was not aware that transmission of blood madness could not take place between wyverns and humans."

"I lied," Taimin said. "Look out!" he shouted as a swipe of the wyvern's foreleg carved the air between the two combatants.

"You lied?" Rathis's eyes widened.

"He was more afraid of blood madness than being killed. As scared as he was, he would have lost."

Rathis tilted his head back, and a hissing sound came from his throat that Taimin realized was laughter. "Well done, young warrior. You would make a fine leader."

Vance lunged forward and thrust his sword hard into the soft skin under the wyvern's clipped wing. He withdrew the sword and a burst of bright blood splashed out of the wound. The wyvern trembled and fell to the ground. The creature gave a shudder and then its eyes glazed over.

Vance raised his arm into the air. The crowd roared, and Taimin cheered along with them.

"I hear that's what you were," Taimin said to Rathis. "A leader." He decided that the skalen deserved to know. "I once met a skalen called Vail, a group leader in charge of a hundred warriors. Her plan was to join with Blixen and assault the city."

Rathis made a sound of surprise. His shoulders slumped. "I feared this may happen. I hoped Vail would have the sense to stay away." He paused as the crowd roared again. "The new arrivals among the bax say they are finding it harder to evade the city's patrols. Even hiding in small groups, the Protector somehow finds them. Blixen will surely attack before his army falls apart, and he will bring Vail with him."

"How do you feel about all this?" Taimin asked bluntly.

"What is it you are asking?"

"Zorn, the Protector, Blixen and his army . . . How do you see it working out?"

The old skalen pondered for a moment. "There is no way for it to end well, not unless every skalen, trull, mantorean, and bax within range of the city guard leaves this area to search for another home. I know, however, that this is something Blixen will never do. I once met him and took his measure. The Protector captured his wife. He still knows nothing of her fate. More bax are taking up his cause every day. A battle is coming. If the city falls, many humans will die. If it does not, Zorn will remain supreme, and," Rathis indicated the arena, "this will continue."

Taimin returned his attention to the fighting pit. He saw Vance walking toward the portcullis, which made a grating sound as it lifted.

"And you? What is it you want?" Rathis asked.

"I want to survive," Taimin said. "I once had some friends. We dreamed of a new life in Zorn. One of them is dead, but the other . . . I'm going to find her, and I'm going to do something about Galen. When I grew up, I didn't know any bax," he met Rathis's gaze, "or skalen. But here we are. This city needs to change."

"A worthy ambition," Rathis said.

Vance approached, breathless but smiling. Taimin and Rathis came forward to clap him on the back.

"It's easy when you know how," Vance said with a grin and a shrug.

"Stay quiet and follow me," Vance said.

He glanced at Taimin as he walked. It was late in the evening, and Vance had been full of boundless energy after his victory.

Taimin followed, perplexed, as Vance went straight to the barred gate that Taimin hadn't passed through since he first came to the arena. Taimin waited as Vance said something to the heavyset guard on the other side. He saw Vance pass the guard a small chip of something shiny. The guard vanished.

"How did you get that in here?" Taimin asked, surprised.

Vance gave a quick shake of his head.

The guard's bulk appeared again a few minutes later. He spoke with Vance in hushed tones, and then Taimin heard a creak and the gate opened. The guard gestured for them to go through.

Taimin's eyes widened, but he kept his lips sealed. He followed just behind Vance, aware that he was walking corridors that might one day lead to freedom. He passed a junction and inhaled deeply to see which direction the freshest air came from. He peered along the tunnels to see where the light was brighter. But as the guard continued in front of them and he realized just how many doors and gates there were, his heart sank. If escape were easy, the guard would never have let them out.

The fat guard waddled along until he stopped outside a door, opening it wide to reveal a storeroom filled with wooden barrels of all shapes and sizes, as well as crates and boxes. He then held out a meaty hand.

"Now give me the rest," the guard said flatly.

"The rest?" Vance scowled. "I told you, that's all there is."

"I said the rest. Or do you want me to call out I've found two prisoners in hiding?"

Vance's eyes narrowed. "You'd get in trouble yourself."

The fat guard shrugged. "Then let's go back."

Vance's nostrils flared. He took out another metal chip and gave it to the guard, who shoved it into a pocket in his trousers.

"I'll come and get you in a while," the fat guard said. "The wine's hidden in the usual spot. Don't do anything stupid. If someone else opens the door, you don't know me."

The guard waited for Taimin and Vance to enter and then closed the door behind them. Taimin heard a clunk as a bolt was thrown. They were now alone in the storeroom.

"I've been saving my iron bits for a good time, and now seems as good as any," Vance said, sitting down on a barrel. "I probably wouldn't be alive without your advice. I always pay my debts."

"You're a resourceful man," Taimin said. He looked around and found a seat for himself. "Ever thought of turning those talents to escape?"

Vance rummaged around in a crate to pull out a small flask that he revealed with a flourish. He took a blunt wooden tool from the same crate and levered out the stopper. "Aha! Here, take the first sip."

Taimin sniffed the contents. Wrinkling his nose, he lifted the flask to his lips. Liquid fire touched the back of his throat and then spread throughout his chest. Sweat broke out on his forehead and he coughed at the sour taste. "Here," he choked, passing over the flask.

"That good? They ferment it from lifegiver cactus." Vance grinned. He took a mouthful, before giving a sigh of pleasure. "As I always say, all men are corruptible."

"You haven't answered my question," Taimin said.

"Of course I've thought about escape. I know Rathis has, and so has everyone else."

"What have you come up with?"

"Nothing," Vance said with a shrug. "The whole city comes to watch us fight. They know our faces—there's no doubt we'd stand out. And no one would hide us, they're all too afraid of the

Protector. The soldiers ride wyverns. Even if we could break out, they'd round us up in no time."

"Why are people so afraid of him?"

"The Protector? For a start, he forces everyone to come to the fights. They don't have a choice. Anyone who doesn't attend gets marked for observation, and that's not a good thing. The citizens know that if they speak out, they'll end up where we are. It's amazing what the frequent sight of blood can do."

"Some of them love the fights," Taimin said.

Vance laughed. "Ha! Yes, I know what you mean there." He took another sip and then sobered. "But in truth, most people are simply afraid."

"Why don't they do something?"

"Because the Protector controls the one thing no one can do without: water." Vance smoothed his moustache. "You've seen the groves of lifegiver cactuses? They take a lot of manpower to cultivate and harvest. Without the well at the bottom of the tower—which the Protector keeps guarded, of course—there wouldn't be enough water to go around. The Protector controls the well. He pays the laborers in the fields. He's the one who stores the water and sells it in the market."

Taimin pondered the situation as he took another draught; the cactus wine was starting to taste better. "You said you stole something from him. What was it?"

Vance sighed. He looked at the wall, seeing something else entirely. "A woman."

Taimin raised an eyebrow.

"One of the Protector's 'mistresses'," Vance explained. "He takes the occasional city girl up to that tower—they know that if they refuse him their family will suffer. I met Cora out in the street without knowing the full story." His voice became wistful. "She was different, Taimin. Beautiful and intelligent, with golden hair the color of Dex at noon. I charmed her, but she warned me away, and the more she told me I shouldn't be speaking to her, the more I wanted her. I thought she was married, but I didn't care. I could see that even if another man had claimed her, she didn't love him. When she told me she wasn't married, I saw no reason we couldn't be together. It was only later, when she was in my bed, that I learned the truth. By then it was too late. I was in love."

Taimin watched Vance take another swallow of the wine.

"It's not a long story. We took risks to be together and the Protector found out. I ended up here."

"What about her?"

Vance's face became grim. "I don't know. It's why I haven't given up. I have to find out what happened to her, and if she's still alive. I realize she's probably dead . . ."

When Vance faltered, Taimin leaned forward. "I'm sorry. This city is not the haven I thought it was."

Vance controlled his expression and brightened, though Taimin knew him well enough now to realize it was a façade. "Perhaps I set my sights a little too high in thieving the Protector's woman, eh?"

"Perhaps." Taimin gave a slight smile.

"How about you?" Vance suddenly asked. "You must have someone who keeps you going."

Taimin immediately thought about Selena. He always wondered where she was, and what she was doing. He constantly reminded himself that her talent meant she was valuable. She was still alive and well.

"There is someone," Taimin said. He explained about meeting Selena and searching for the city with her, only to become separated. "I finally saw her with some bax," he concluded. "But, before I could get to her, Galen found me."

Vance handed Taimin the flask. "Here," he said. "Your turn."

Taimin drank more of the wine. He and Vance didn't speak for some time, both lost in their thoughts, and they finished the bottle in silence. Soon after, the guard knocked on the door to escort them back to their quarters.

Taimin didn't have long to wait for his own name to be called.

He wondered why he wasn't following the usual route as he was taken along the stone-walled corridors. As the raised voices of the crowd grew louder in volume, his imagination conjured up one opponent after another. Perhaps he wouldn't be fighting at all. Perhaps Galen had lost his patience, and Taimin was about to be shot full of arrows as the citizens looked on.

Taimin kept his face like stone, even though his heart was racing in his chest. Dread made his stomach churn. He kept reminding himself that fear was the enemy, and that, right now, fear was the only thing in his power to control.

He climbed a set of stairs, taking each step slowly while he made himself go through his usual exercises. He sucked in deep breaths of air and swung his arms. At the top of the steps he saw another barred gate, and beyond it lay the sandy floor of the fighting pit. His eyes scanned the area, searching for his next opponent. But the pit was empty. Taimin would be the first to enter.

A lanky guard handed him a sword and then pulled the gate open.

Taimin walked through.

What had been a loud murmur swelled to a powerful roar. The sound of it was deafening; it struck him like a punch in the face. He continued until he was standing in the center of the fighting pit. With no opponent in sight, he turned slowly, taking in the faces of the people of Zorn.

It wasn't just those in the nearest tiers who were crying out. Rather than heckle him, people were shouting encouragement. He was surprised when he heard his name called from the crowd.

"Show us what Abigail taught you!"

"Taimin! Fight for your freedom like she did!"

Taimin raised an arm and the roar swelled even louder. He then tried to forget about the crowd as he swung his sword with wide strokes to loosen his muscles. As he stood under the burning rays of the golden sun, his head turned when he heard a scraping sound.

He faced the portcullis as it started to open, suggesting he would be fighting one of the other prisoners. He wondered who it would be, and why the guards had taken so many pains to ensure they entered the arena separately.

Rathis emerged into the sun.

Taimin's mouth dropped open. The crowd collectively gasped. They knew that Rathis was a leader among the skalen, a prized prisoner of the Protector. Now Rathis would face Taimin, and only one of them would leave the fighting pit alive.

Rathis walked toward Taimin until he came to a halt just a short distance away. He held three javelins bunched in his left hand, leaving his throwing arm unencumbered.

"So, young warrior," Rathis said, "it seems we are to face each other. The guards are cruel."

Thoughts whirled through Taimin's head. Looking up at the crowd, he scanned the faces on the upper tiers until his eyes rested on Galen. The commander's face was twisted in a wry smile.

Taimin turned back to Rathis. "It isn't the guards who are doing this. It's Galen."

"You are young," Rathis said. "If you can survive and find your woman, you have a life of promise ahead of you. I am old. I plan to let you defeat me. Make it quick."

Evidently trying to goad Taimin, Rathis swung one of his javelins like a club. The slap against the bare skin of Taimin's arm made him wince. But rather than respond, Taimin put distance between himself and the skalen. As he walked away from Rathis, he lifted his chin and faced the crowd.

He remembered the first time Selena had made him think about the other races differently. Taimin had come to know and even like Rathis. And confined together as they all were, it was impossible not to encounter bax in the prisoners' quarters. The bax knew of the enmity between Taimin and Galen, a man they all despised. Some of them had been almost friendly.

His head held high, Taimin directly addressed the crowd.

"This skalen," he called as he pointed, "is a clan leader. He is beloved. Can you tell me, any of you, why he is here?"

"Fight!" a red-faced man cried.

Taimin reminded himself about everything he had learned from Vance, Rathis, and the bax among the prisoners. "He is here because the Protector wants you to see him as an enemy. Not just him, but all of his race. The Protector wants you to fear those who live outside this city. He raids the Rift Valley and provokes conflict. The invasion he warns you about is part of his plan. As long as you are afraid, he remains in power."

"Give us blood!" a well-dressed older man shouted from the upper tiers.

But the roughly dressed laborers in the crowd, the poorer and skinnier people, weren't calling for blood. They were listening.

Taimin knew that any change in the city had to come from them. "When I first came here, I thought Zorn was a place of hatred. But looking at your faces, I can see that isn't true. You know as well as I do that humans can't survive as one race against all others." He thrust out an arm to point at Rathis. "He and his kind mean us no harm. I am not speaking to the commander up there,

284

I am speaking to you. Out in the wasteland, people tell stories of the incredible white city. A haven. A place of peace. You can make the stories true."

Meanwhile Rathis called out imploringly. "Fight me, Taimin," he hissed. "Live!"

Taimin spied movement and looked along the perimeter fence to see that in addition to the prison guards, dozens of Galen's uniformed soldiers stood on the other side.

One of the soldiers stepped up to the fence and called out, "Prisoner, you must fight."

"No!" Taimin pointed his sword at the soldier. "I will not."

He threw down his sword. The gesture was unmistakable.

As soon as he did it, the gate in the fence crashed open. The soldiers in crimson uniforms poured through. While the crowd watched in horror, the vicious beating began.

29

Selena explored the Rift Valley. Speeding from place to place, flying as fast as thought, she searched a landscape filled with wrinkles, like the palm of a hand held up for close inspection. She traveled over deep ravines and wide valleys, always casting with a power that wasn't hers to control.

She knew that back in the tower her body sat erect in the hard-backed wooden chair, and that the young woman's eyes were glazed and unfocused. Her consciousness was here, separated from the city by a journey that would take days on foot. Arren and Merin directed her attention. Their constant presence would be with her until fatigue meant she couldn't farcast anymore.

She scanned the terrain and looked for movement. Her vision swept over the rust-colored rock and paused as she focused on the occasional hardy cactus or spindly tree. No matter what she found—warriors or innocents, young or old—when Arren and Merin reported back, the city guard would venture into the wasteland, and bloodshed would follow.

The mountains loomed overhead. Areas that Selena had explored previously were becoming familiar. She was made to descend. What came next would be hours of searching the individual seams of the Rift Valley.

Arren and Merin had now become accustomed to their role. They even allowed her to communicate with them. But if she protested, they caused her pain, or prevented her from re-entering her body for a time as punishment.

As she descended into a wide gully with a dried riverbed along its base, she tried to think of a way to fight back. How did Arren and Merin know how to control her the way they did? Perhaps they had a teacher, someone with even more power.

Someone who might be able to help her.

She ventured a question. *Who taught you to do this?* She mentally held her breath but Merin seemed happy enough to answer.

Arren and I were lucky. We met as children and learned that what we lacked in other areas, we made up for with our shared talent. We have practiced on each other over many years. Everything that we do to you, we have also done to each other, many times over.

Enough, Arren said. *We have work to do.*

The search continued.

Hours passed as Selena explored the mazelike chasms of the Rift Valley. As always, Arren and Merin discussed places to search in dry, dispassionate tones.

Should we look closer to the mountains? Arren asked.

When Merin agreed, Selena was made to travel to the base of the peaks, where previously she had found both mantoreans and skalen.

Nothing here either. Where are they?

Back to the canyon?

Even as she was directed back to the Rift Valley, Selena felt fatigue like a crushing weight on her senses. She knew that her body in the tower would be tensed with hands formed into fists. When she returned, she would feel wretched.

Wily creatures, Arren said. They were following a passage between two tall cliffs. *Look, you can see signs of them everywhere.*

They are learning, Merin replied. *They know we can't see anything at night so they hide during the day.*

Galen thinks Blixen must have a mystic of his own. The bax often flee before he arrives. He says it's the only explanation.

Selena instantly thought of Rei-kika. She was glad that the mantorean was out there, working to prevent Galen's raids.

After another hour of fruitless searching, Selena was made to hover in the middle of a low valley, where scorched circles marked out past campfires. A piece of cloth had snagged on a pricklethorn bush and fluttered in the breeze. As with many of these places, splits in the sides of the cliff formed natural hiding places.

Arren sounded irritated. *There must be thousands of caves.*

And some are deep.

I suppose we're going to have to search them one by one.

Unless Blixen has finally fled the Rift Valley?

It's possible.

Selena was directed to travel into one of the larger caves, but could only penetrate a short distance before the darkness become absolute. The two mystics cursed, realizing it was impossible to see anything, and then she was turned back to the exit.

The caves can't be searched, Merin said.

The Protector isn't going to be pleased.

Not necessarily. If he wants them gone . . . well, it looks like they are.

Just because we can't find them doesn't mean they aren't here, Arren said.

Selena climbed the sky. She again swept her gaze over the entire Rift Valley. Arren and Merin were always with her, peering down into the bewildering complex of gullies and ravines.

While the two mystics formed plans, Selena thought about Blixen. She had seen inside his mind. She knew he would never give up the fight. And Group Leader Vail wouldn't stop until she had rescued her clan leader.

Unbidden, Taimin's face came to her. After a life spent with no one to look out for her, she had trusted him. She missed him. She wondered if she would ever see him again.

Meanwhile the two mystics discussed their options. They had no choice. They would have to return another time to find something for the commander.

While Arren and Merin conferred, Selena's fatigued mind continued to wander. It was then that she spied movement in the distance. Four tiny figures were walking on the plain, a few miles from the Rift Valley. They were too lean to be bax, and with both suns high in the sky it was too bright and hot for skalen to be traveling. They definitely didn't have the insect-like frames of mantoreans. Trulls had thicker bodies and broader shoulders.

Look, Merin said.

Humans, said Arren.

Selena's perception gave a sickening lurch as she was pushed beyond endurance to speed toward the four figures heading away from the Rift Valley. The humans on the plain grew in her vision. She now saw that there were two adults—a man and a woman—and a pair of children.

She hovered directly above them while Arren and Merin inspected the group. The adults—she assumed they were husband and wife—were burdened by heavy packs. Even the children, a boy and girl, clutched straps on their shoulders to carry water sacks made of stitched leather. The group looked tired and careworn, in the middle of a long journey.

Look at the markings on the water sacks, Arren said.

Selena turned her attention to the black symbols written with charcoal on the two sacks. The intersecting lines were sharp and aggressive.

Bax markings, Merin said. He came to a conclusion. *They've been trading with the enemy.*

Undoubtedly.

Selena couldn't help herself. She had to speak up. *You don't know that.*

Arren snorted. *Don't be a fool, girl. The water sacks are full. They've just left the Rift Valley. It's as clear as day.*

Well, at least we found something for the commander, Merin said.

Mark the location, Arren instructed.

Selena couldn't believe what she was hearing. *Why?*

Use your eyes. They're traitors, Merin said, speaking as if she were a child.

You can't— she began.

Arren interrupted curtly. *Silence. No one asked your opinion.*

Selena experienced a sharp jolt of pain. The two mystics could hurt her mind at will. But when she saw the two children struggling under the weight of the water, and the bowed shoulders of the man and woman, she knew she had to do something. The girl was about the same age as the girl that Borg had held up by her hair.

It's time to go back to the tower, Arren continued. *The commander won't have any difficulty finding them. Selena, we will deal with you when we return.*

Selena began to panic. The family she was looking at didn't deserve to die. In desperation she turned to look back at her lifeline, the connection between her awareness and her body in the tower. The white line was fainter than ever before; she had been casting for a long time.

She remembered sitting in a cave full of skalen, across from Rei-kika. She again heard Rei-kika's clicking voice. *If you go too far or stay out of your body too long, your lifeline will bring you back. But be careful. The connection gets weaker the farther you are from your physical form. If you panic and pull too hard it can break completely. With no connection at all your body will stop breathing. You would have very little time to find your way back.*

Selena's fate was already sealed. She might not be able to save herself.

But she could save this family.

She focused on her lifeline and took hold of it, which was what the two mystics were expecting her to do. Their guard was down. They had control of her casting, but her lifeline was hers alone.

Summoning her courage, she pulled on her lifeline. Hard.

Part of her screamed at her, telling her that what she was doing was wrong. She felt like she was putting a knife to her own throat.

Stop! Merin cried.

You fool! Arren shouted.

Selena's lifeline pulled back. It wanted her to return to her body. The tension increased. She fixed herself with one clear goal. She was going to break it. The already weak connection pulsed and wavered. She put all of her strength into her objective and heaved.

The lifeline snapped. The white line vanished immediately.

We have to get back! Arren shouted. *Now!*

She saw the two wavering figures fly away, making all speed across the plain as they headed for their bodies. She prayed that they wouldn't make it back to the tower before the lack of air killed them. If Arren and Merin died, the family below would live.

Meanwhile, Selena could no longer sense any connection with her body at all. The experience was unlike anything she had felt before. She knew that something was badly, terribly wrong.

But she had tried to do what was right. Forgetting the city, forgetting her body in the tower, she watched the family, who continued their journey utterly unaware of the sacrifice she had made.

The mother turned her head to say something to her daughter. The little girl laughed.

Despite Selena's plight, the sight made her happy.

All of a sudden, Rei-kika was directly in front of her.

The shadowy silhouette of the mantorean appeared so swiftly that Selena almost cried out. Rei-kika's body was ethereal but her triangular head was tilted as she regarded Selena with her black, multifaceted eyes. Her antennae twitched in agitation.

I have told you before, Rei-kika said. *Your casting announces itself to the world.*

It's you, Selena said. *You're the one helping Blixen avoid the city guard.*

I know what those two humans are doing to you, but you must return to your body or you will die.

My death will save lives. Selena looked at the mother, father, and their two children as they walked away from the Rift Valley. *If not today, then tomorrow.*

I heard them call you a fool. Is that what you wish to be?

I have no other option.

Look, Rei-kika said. *Come quickly. You don't have long.*

Rei-kika climbed the sky and Selena traveled with her. The mantorean's hazy form flew swiftly, urgently, until she was at the height of the tallest mountains, gazing far beyond where Selena usually searched.

Look between the peaks. Do you see?

Fixing her sight between two of the triangular summits, Selena saw the region where Taimin and Lars had escaped the skalen. There was something there . . . dark shapes swarming across the land.

She realized she was looking at a multitude of figures, tiny as ants, heading toward the mountains and the Rift Valley beyond. Despite how far away they were, the hunched posture of bax was unmistakable.

Blixen will soon have the numbers he needs, Rei-kika said. *I tried to warn you about Zorn. You have now experienced the Protector's evil, as we all have.*

Selena knew that so many bax warriors could change the fate of the entire city. The soldiers of the city guard were deadly, but there were fewer than a hundred of them. *But the people of Zorn . . .*

Blixen is not a butcher. Live, Selena. We will come. Your suffering will not last forever.

Selena turned away from the mountains and stared in the opposite direction, toward the city.

Fly. Fly faster than you ever have before.

30

Selena gasped. She took in a series of deep breaths while stars sparkled in her vision. As she tasted bile in the back of her throat, she coughed and tears formed in her eyes. One by one, the stars faded.

Her vision was blurred but gradually her eyes refocused. The first thing she saw was Arren and Merin, seated across from her, both red-faced and panting as if they had run a race. Arren stood and reached down to his waist. A moment later a knife was in his hand.

"You almost killed us," he snarled. "You would have killed yourself too. And for what? Some traitors." He shook his head. "Look at you. You've come back. You didn't even have the courage to go through with it."

Round-faced Merin climbed to his feet and glared down at her. "She must suffer."

"I agree."

Selena was still weakened from her ordeal. There was nothing she could do as Arren clamped his palm over her wrist, holding her hand flat against the arm of the chair. Fear shot up her spine.

Merin grabbed hold of her shoulder to pin her in place. Arren then pressed the blade of the knife to her wrist. Sweat broke out on her brow. The wiry mystic grimaced as he began to bear down.

The sharp knife edge broke skin. The first drops of red blood burst free. Selena cried out.

Loud footsteps made a clatter on the stone floor. "What's happening here?" A strong male voice spoke curtly.

Selena's head jerked round. Arren and Merin were both startled to see Galen approaching. The commander's angular face was stern and unyielding. Tall and athletic, wearing a crimson uniform emblazoned with a white tower on the breast, he looked every inch the soldier.

"Let her go," Galen said. "She's valuable."

"You don't know what you're talking about," Arren snapped. "She's a traitor. She's working against us."

"I won't tell you again," the commander said in a low voice. "Take your knife away."

Arren still didn't remove the blade from Selena's wrist. "Losing a hand is the least she deserves. You don't know what she did."

"Tell me then."

"She severed her connection with her body," Arren said. "Tried to kill herself."

"Could have killed us too," Merin added.

"She can do that?" Galen frowned, and then his eyes narrowed. "I thought you could control her casting."

"We can," Arren said. "But now she knows that we can't stop her ending her own life."

"And you think taking her hand is going to make a difference? She could bleed to death. For two intelligent men, you can both be quite stupid."

"We found humans in the wasteland. They were trading with the bax," Merin said.

"She is more important," Galen said. "Without her we can't protect the city."

"She must be punished," Arren insisted.

Galen moved uncomfortably close to the mystics. As he loomed over them, the two men exchanged glances, and when Galen spoke they clearly knew better than to challenge him. "I'm taking her to her quarters. If you two can't control her, I will. I'll have her casting again by tomorrow."

No one mentioned the human family. Even as she worried about Galen's plans for her, Selena felt relief that they would live.

———

At last Selena had something she had been without ever since her arrival at the tower.

Time.

Until now, she had either been casting or numb with exhaustion, but the two mystics were wary that she would break her lifeline again. No matter what, she wasn't going to stay in her room and wait for whatever Galen had planned for her. The commander had said he had some plan to get her casting again. No one was going to help her escape. She had to do it herself.

As she waited for darkness, she stripped her bed of linen and then tipped the pallet up on its side, just below the high oval-shaped window. She tested climbing up to the window a few times, and, once she was satisfied, she yanked and twisted at the bed's wooden frame until she had broken off a plank the length of her arm. Hours passed, and as midnight approached she fashioned her bed linen into a makeshift rope. Her final task was to fasten the cord to the rectangular piece of wood.

The silver moon glowed against a backdrop of stars as Selena perched precariously on the upright bed frame and leaned out of the window. A vista of stone structures filled her vision, but the city was quiet so late at night. Far below, the plaza that surrounded the tower was too distant to make out individual paving stones.

If Selena fell, she would meet the same fate as the mantorean, Tika-rin.

The tower's tapered exterior stretched both up and down, with far more of the tower below her than above. Selena peered up at the oval window on the next level. She had to throw the plank into the opening above until it wedged tightly.

The linen cord was in her hands. The plank swung at the end, outside the tower. She watched the plank. Her heart pounded. She felt giddy with vertigo.

This would be her fifth attempt, and the more she tried and failed, the greater the chance she would slip and fall to her death.

She leaned out farther. As she perched on the windowsill, gripping the wall with one hand and the linen with the other, she reminded herself that Galen had some sinister plan for her. Her only hope lay in escape.

She swung the plank from side to side, judging carefully. At the right moment, she grunted and twisted her shoulder to throw the plank up and over her head.

The plank disappeared inside the oval window above. A muffled clatter reached her ears. With no idea who or what was in the room on the upper level, she froze and counted her heartbeats. She held on to the linen cord and listened carefully. The silence dragged out.

Nothing.

Now came the final test.

"Please," she muttered as she pulled on the cord. When it became taut, her hopes rose. She peered up and realized that she could see the plank wedged soundly within the window above.

She wasn't satisfied until she had pulled on the linen with both hands, using as much force as she could. The next part would be the most difficult of all. She swung her legs out of the window. Keeping the cord tight, she stood on the window ledge. She was now outside the tower. She told herself not to glance down at the paving stones far below.

Reminding herself that she had always been a good climber, she began to pull herself up.

———

With a heart-wrenching sensation of falling, Selena tumbled into the room above her own. The plank came with her, along with the twisted length of linen, and as she crashed onto the floor everything became tangled. The sound she made was far too loud, but there was nothing she could do about it.

She brought herself into a crouch and scanned in all directions.

The room had the same layout as her own but was mostly bare. Broken furniture sprawled against a wall. She glanced toward the door, which was wide open. Someone could have heard her and might come to investigate.

Selena knew she had to move quickly, but first she hurried over to an old wooden chair and grabbed a leg before yanking it back and forth. Twisting hard, grimacing with effort, she finally pulled the chair leg free.

Now she had a weapon.

She left the room and crept along the corridor, ears pricked for the sound of footsteps. It was dark inside the tower. She reached the stairway that curled along the inside of the tower's perimeter.

All she had to do was get to the ground level.

———

Selena descended the last step and found herself at the bottom of the tower. She entered the wide-open space, as circular as the tower itself, framed by a series of oval windows that allowed pale moonlight to pour inside. A second stairway at the back of the room descended deeper, indicating a level below ground. She glanced at the windows, but they were too high, and there was nothing that could help her reach them. She began to creep toward the huge, heavy door. Beyond the door lay freedom.

Her heart raced as she hefted the chair leg. One of Galen's soldiers would be standing guard outside. Her only advantage was surprise. If she threw the door open and attacked, the guard would be momentarily stunned. She would then be able to flee.

She was a dozen paces from the door when the sound of foot-steps brought her to a sudden halt. Her gaze shot toward the stair-way that vanished into the ceiling above. A green glow grew steadily brighter. The Protector had enough wealth to use aurelium lamps. The approaching patter of feet became louder.

Selena stood frozen in place. She couldn't reach the door before whoever was approaching saw her. They would shout. The soldier on the other side would hear.

As she searched desperately in all directions, she made a quick decision and raced to the back of the room. Coming to the steps that led below ground, she climbed down them as quickly and qui-etly as she could. As she descended, she knew she had to hide until the newcomer was gone. The stairway finished. There was just the one level below the tower. A closed door greeted her.

Pulling the door open, Selena stared into a vast, dark space. With no windows, and faint light at her back, she had no idea what was in the room she was facing.

She glanced back up the way she had come. The glow of green light made sweat break out on her brow. Whoever was holding the lamp—perhaps the Protector or one of his men—was now on ground level.

With no other choice, she entered the huge, dark room. Shutting the door behind her, she winced when it made a soft clunk. The darkness was now absolute, but the person behind her held a guiding light. She had to find somewhere to hide.

She warily placed each foot in front of the other and kept her hands stretched out in case she encountered an obstruction. She took ten steps, then fifteen.

Her knees bumped into something. She reached down. Her fingers discovered stones, formed into a low, curved wall. Moving faster now, she soon learned that the wall was formed into a circle.

She leaned over the wall, searching for the ground. On its own, the wall wasn't big enough to hide behind, but it appeared to enclose a round hole. How deep was it? She used her chair leg to probe, but still couldn't find the bottom.

Sweat coated her forehead. More than anything, she wished she could see.

She needed to know if the hole would hide her. Attempting to climb inside would be too risky; the hole might be so deep she would die. She tried to think. The chair leg was her only weapon. But should she drop it into the hole? There must be something else she could try.

Her hands searched the ground.

She found something with a familiar shape. A bucket. Fumbling, she discovered a rope attached to the bucket's handle.

She held the rope as she leaned over the wall and dropped the bucket into the hole.

It took a few moments before the rope went taut, and the bucket hadn't even found the ground. Selena's heart sank. The hole was deep. Far too deep.

A sound made her head whirl. Her breath caught. The door behind her was beginning to open.

She let go of the rope and a clatter echoed throughout the room as the bucket struck the hole's bottom. With no other option, she turned and brandished the chair leg. Panting hard, she first saw a bright green rod in the hand of an approaching figure. Then, as the rod was lowered, Selena found herself looking at a young woman with short, wavy, auburn hair, dressed in a brown linen vest and snug leather trousers.

"You?" Selena asked incredulously.

Ruth scowled. "You're lucky that I'm the one who heard you and not someone else. What did you think you would do? Open the door and fight off a bunch of armed soldiers with a chair leg?"

Selena realized she was still brandishing her makeshift club. "How many soldiers?" she asked as she lowered the chair leg.

"The Protector put a ring of guards outside the tower after you came."

Selena was shaken. If she had tried her surprise attack, she might have been killed.

Ruth's expression softened. When she spoke, her voice wasn't unkind. "I know your name, Selena, and I know why you want to leave. Come on. I'll take you back to your room." She tilted her head. "I have no idea how you got out, but do you think we can make it so they won't know?"

Selena's thoughts were still spinning. As Ruth continued to stare at her, she shook herself and nodded. But as relief caused her heart rate to approach something close to normal, she scanned the room, at last able to see where she was by the green light that filled the vast space. She first noticed the enclosing walls, where big barrels were stacked in rows, one on top of the other, almost all the way to the ceiling. A few more empty barrels lay on their sides.

As she took it all in, Selena turned back toward the low circular wall that surrounded the hole in the room's center. The rope spilled over the wall and into the hole. She walked over to the rope and began to pull, taking length after length until she retrieved the bucket.

Selena looked back at Ruth. "What is this place?"

"It's the well room," Ruth said matter-of-factly.

"And this is the well?"

"It is," Ruth said. "The only well in the city."

Selena looked at the bucket in her hands. "But it's dry."

Ruth came over to stand beside her. Together, they stared down into the well. Even with Ruth's aurelium rod, they couldn't see all the way to the bottom.

"I know," Ruth said. "That's why I'm like you. I also can't leave the tower." She glanced at Selena and then returned her attention to the hole below. "The people think that the Protector controls the only reliable source of water. But as you can see, the well's completely dry. That's why he's trying to drive the bax from the Rift Valley. He wants their water supply."

Selena's mouth dropped open. It all made a terrible kind of sense. "I thought it was because he hates the other races."

"That's part of it, and it's what he wants everyone to think. No matter what, he can't tell them the truth."

Everything became clear in Selena's mind. She had always gained the impression from both bax and skalen that the current hostilities were a relatively new thing. Rei-kika's words and Blixen's memories had led her to wonder who was truly to blame. Now she knew.

Selena gazed into the deep hole in front of her. "We have to tell the people the truth."

"About the well?" Ruth was startled. She shook her head vigorously. "There would be riots. The price of water is already high enough as it is, but at least everyone thinks the Protector's just building up a reserve."

"The people should know," Selena said firmly.

"Think about what you're saying," Ruth said. "If there's chaos, no one would work in the fields. And if there's water in the Rift Valley—"

"Have you been there?" Selena interrupted.

"No . . ."

"I have," Selena said, staring directly into Ruth's eyes. "I've met Blixen. Zorn could trade for the water it needs. Blixen doesn't want war. He just wants the raids to stop." As Selena's thoughts took focus, she put determination into her voice. "Listen to me. If we tell the people the truth, then the Protector will fall. We can stop the fighting, on all sides. You don't want to be trapped in this tower forever, do you?"

Ruth looked uncertain. "I don't have anywhere else. Or anyone."

"You know it's the right thing to do. If you had seen the things I have . . ." Selena grimaced. "Galen and his men are butchers. And it's all done in this city's name."

"Even if I agreed with you . . ." Ruth hesitated. ". . . how would we tell the people?"

"The chance will come. We'll find a way."

"I'm not promising anything," Ruth said. "But one thing I do know is that we don't want them to catch us here."

Selena and Ruth crept back up to the higher levels. Working together, speaking only in whispers, they gathered the plank and linen from the room above and headed back to Selena's bedchamber.

On the way, Selena continued to think. She wondered what Galen had meant when he said he knew of a way to control her. She pondered what Rei-kika had shown her. Blixen would soon have the numbers he needed to make an assault on the city. Whatever Selena was going to do, she had to do it soon.

Selena opened the bolt holding her door fastened. As she entered, she turned when she realized that Ruth had stopped in the doorway.

"You should come in," Selena said quietly. They were both speaking in low murmurs, but there was less chance of being heard with the door closed.

Ruth shook her head. "I shouldn't be here."

"Please," Selena said as she stared into Ruth's brown eyes. "We might not get this chance again."

Ruth cast a swift glance down the corridor. Her body was tense, but reluctantly she entered. Selena gently closed the door as soon as Ruth was inside.

When she saw the bed frame leaning up against the wall, Ruth shook her head. "All right," she said. "I can see you need my help."

Together they started to set the room to rights. As they put the pallet bed back into its original position, Selena glanced at Ruth, her only potential ally in this place.

"You said you don't have anyone," Selena asked. "What happened to your family?"

"We were settlers," Ruth said. "One day my father went hunting and never came back. My mother was a healer, and when she couldn't feed us on her own, she thought her skills might be needed in Zorn. She was right, and she entered the Protector's service. Then my mother went out into the wasteland to find herbs . . ." She trailed off.

"What happened?"

"Thirst," Ruth said plainly. "The city guard found her body. She ran out of water."

With their work done, Selena faced Ruth directly. "Why didn't you leave?"

"Where would I go? What would I do? This is the only home I have. I'm not allowed out into the city. I know too much." Ruth stared into the distance. "I helped the Protector once. When he was sick. I have some of my mother's skill. I know he's not a good man, but I still did it. Was I wrong?"

"It's what a healer does."

"And you're a mystic."

"Yes," Selena said flatly. "You heal. I kill. They make me find anyone who isn't human. It doesn't matter if they're warriors or not, they all die."

"But they're just bax . . ."

Selena shook her head. "If you could look into a bax's mind, see his thoughts, his memories . . . They care for their young. They love. They marry. They try to keep their families safe."

Ruth was pensive for a moment. "I have an idea . . ." she said slowly. "I've been thinking about what you said. I once heard the commander mention some dissidents he was trying to track down. Rebels. There might be someone out there we could talk to."

Selena felt a stirring of hope. "Do you have any names?"

"No."

"How can we find out where they are?"

Ruth sighed. "I don't know."

Selena spoke firmly. "Then we'll just have to see what else we can find out."

There was silence for a time, before Ruth changed the subject. "Where are you from?"

"Nowhere, really."

Ruth raised an eyebrow. "Nowhere?" She waited for Selena to elaborate but then shrugged. "Fair enough. Life in the wasteland is never easy." She paused. "Do you have anyone?"

Without meaning to, Selena conjured up an image of Taimin's face. "I . . ." She trailed off.

Ruth tilted her head. "Who did you think of, just now?"

"There is someone. A man."

"This man," Ruth said, giving a slight smile, "is he . . . handsome?"

"Why do you ask that?"

"Selena, it's the way you said it. What's his name?"

"I'll probably never see him again."

"So how can it hurt to tell me his name?" Ruth's smile broadened.

"Taimin," Selena said. "His name is Taimin. Satisfied?"

"No, I'm not satisfied," Ruth said. She sat down on the bed. "Go on. I want to hear all about Taimin."

31

Blixen paced the length of the subterranean cavern. His stride was angry and he muttered to himself as he walked. He was desperate to go outside for some fresh air, but he knew that leaving was the last thing he could do.

This was the largest of the caves, yet it was stifling, and he could only imagine how it felt in the others. The walls were made of a crumbling, dusty rock, and somehow everything continually became covered in yellow grit. Any fires had to be contained to the deepest sections, far from the open air. The smoke made everyone cough and stung their eyes, so most meals were cold and it was dark for much of the time. The movements of hunting parties and scout patrols were restricted to the night. Getting through the periods of daylight tested everyone's endurance. Only when darkness came could they go outside, in small groups, to take deep breaths and stretch cramped limbs.

Blixen and his followers had taken refuge ever since the dramatic increase in the Protector's raids. If any bax moved during the daytime, the wyverns would soon come. There was only one explanation: the Protector had a new mystic, perhaps even the human female Blixen had asked to search for his wife.

Not for the first time, he wondered why he had sent the young mystic so close to the city. He knew his wife was dead—how could she not be? The mantorean, Rei-kika, was useful, and saved many when her casting brought news of the wyverns' approach, but she didn't have the human girl's power. Rei-kika's warnings only came when a raid was imminent.

Blixen had lost weight, and was now as wide as any other bax, although his height still singled him out—his height, his powerful frame, and the circle of finger bones around his neck.

He halted his pacing. "Blast it!" he growled.

Around him, the younger bax huddled against the walls looked up fearfully. They filled the cave; only Blixen was given some space to himself. He was keeping his army together, but for how long? He was surprised that the skalen under Vail hadn't given up and left long ago. Instead, Vail and her warriors were hidden in another cave nearby. Their sense of duty to their clan leader must be strong.

He wondered how it had come to this.

Zorn and the Rift Valley had never been on the best terms, but there was occasional trade between bax and humans, and each had recognized the other's territory. He was aware that the Protector blamed everyone who wasn't human for his father's death. Blixen knew nothing about how the man had died, and every trull, skalen, or mantorean he had questioned on the matter had been just as ignorant as he was. Why would anyone kill Zorn's leader, knowing that his death would incur the city's wrath? And who would take his head as a trophy? It wasn't something any bax would do. The same could be said of the other races.

Yet after the ruler of Zorn's death, as the years passed, the new Protector had made his intentions clear. He had slaughtered both bax and skalen. The last few remaining mantoreans in the Rift Valley had fled. The Protector now presented all non-humans in the Rift Valley with a choice: leave or die.

There was a time when Blixen had considered evacuation, despite the difficulty. He and the bax he led would have to survive a difficult journey, with no promise that they would find a new home as good as the Rift Valley. It wouldn't be easy, not at all. But the Protector made a powerful enemy, and, yes, Blixen had considered flight.

That was before they took his wife.

He had made his decision. Rather than flee, he would wage war. He had sent out word and entreated more warriors to join his cause. Many had come, seeking plunder, glory, and Blixen's commendation to their wardens back home.

But while Blixen was desperate to discover the fate of his wife—and if she was dead, to make the Protector suffer—he was also a pragmatist. If revenge had been his only motive in the war against the humans, he would have had few followers. What he also desired was safety for his people. Bax had lived in these lands for generations, where there was a steady supply of water and good hunting. If the Rift Valley fell to Zorn's control, the humans would continue the slaughter. Even the skalen had been driven from their mines. All looked to him for guidance.

Blixen's army had taken shape, but now, here he was, holed up in hiding. Soon the newcomers would begin to leave. When they did, he couldn't blame them. He had been waiting until he had greater numbers, but he knew that the time had come. He had to attack the city now. If he didn't, the opportunity would never come again.

He continued to pace as he pondered. He reached the wall and sighed, before sinking to a crouch. It wasn't just his warriors who had been watching him. A wherry had entered the cave a while ago, and Blixen had decided to keep him. The wherry seemed devoted to him, and even brought in lizards to supplement their diet. No one complained.

Blixen put out his hand and began to stroke the wherry's floppy ears, while the creature regarded him with gentle eyes framed by long lashes.

"What do you think?" Blixen murmured. "I don't have a choice, do I? It must be now."

The wherry panted softly and whined.

Lost in thought, Blixen heard the sounds of a whispered argument and straightened. Two of the young bax warriors sitting with their backs against the wall were having a heated conversation. One of them was gesturing with his hands. Blixen could tell that whatever was being discussed, it was something to do with him.

"You two," Blixen said. He straightened and strode over to the two warriors. "What is it?" he demanded as he glared down at them.

They both fell silent. In an instant all eyes were on them. The cavern became quiet, broken only by the sound of Blixen's heavy breathing.

"Speak," Blixen growled. "I am the warden. You will do as I command."

One of the pair opened his mouth. "It's the wherry, Warden."

Blixen tilted his head and turned to glance back at the creature, before returning his attention to the young warriors. "What of it?"

"He is about to change. That's why he is here, underground."

"Change? What are you talking about?"

"I . . ." the warrior glanced at his companion, "that is, *we* thought you should know."

The other warrior spoke up. "It's the ears. That's the first sign. They're straightening. And see the ridges behind his shoulders? They are bigger than they should be. He is about to transform."

"That wherry is about to become a wyvern," the first warrior said.

Blixen looked at the wherry again. Suddenly he didn't seem so harmless. He was big, after all. Not as big as others he'd seen, but he had a powerful frame and probably weighed five times what Blixen did himself. Now that Blixen was looking for it, he could see that the wherry's skin was becoming red in patches. The once-floppy ears were slightly pricked. Above the wherry's eyes were defined brow ridges. And were its front legs shrinking?

"Fine," Blixen said. "I'll send him away."

Despite the fact that his warriors were only worried about his safety, Blixen felt vaguely irritated that he would soon be parted from his new companion. He resumed his pacing. This time he occasionally glanced askance at the wherry.

He heard a clicking sound.

Turning toward the cavern's entrance, he recognized the mantorean, Rei-kika. She moved with that odd gait that all mantoreans had and fixed him with her unsettling black eyes. The scars on her face had faded to thin white lines.

"What is it?" Blixen asked. He knew that Rei-kika had been in another part of the Rift Valley. The range of her casting wasn't great, so she often remained closer to where the canyon opened onto the plain. "You have been moving in daylight?"

"I had to," she said. "I have important news. You said to be on the lookout for your brother. He now approaches."

Blixen froze. "Alone?"

"He brings warriors. Many of them."

Hope kindled in his heart. "You are certain?"

"I saw them from a distance, but who else could it be?"

Blixen punched his fist into the palm of his hand. "How many?"

"Perhaps equal to our current number."

"How far away?" Blixen's mind worked furiously.

"More than two days' journey. Less than three."

Blixen stared into the distance while he muttered to himself. "The city's mystics may not have seen him yet. But if he keeps heading this way, they undoubtedly will."

One of the young warriors spoke up. "What if we guide him here, to these caves?"

Blixen shook his head. "From what she says he brings more warriors than we can easily hide." He looked again at Rei-kika. "How long has it been since you farcasted my brother?"

"Close to a day."

"I need you to cast again. My brother has a small amount of your ability. You must contact him." Blixen scratched at his chin. "This is important. Tell him that if he continues to march in daylight he will be seen. He needs to hide from the suns and travel only in deepest darkness. Tell him to meet us on the plain, near the stone formation in the shape of a pyramid, at midnight, five nights from now."

Blixen waited impatiently as the mantorean withdrew into herself; he knew better than to interrupt her casting. Time dragged on and his tension grew. If Rei-kika couldn't reach his brother, the city might become aware of his arrival. He resumed his pacing.

At last Rei-kika shook herself.

"Well?" Blixen demanded.

"I spoke with him. He will do as you say."

"Did you hear that everyone?" Blixen called out. He swept his gaze over the warriors in the cavern. "Spread the word. We leave as soon as it gets dark."

"We will fight?" a young bax warrior asked.

"We will," Blixen said. "My brother will join us on the way." His voice firmed. "We will not stop until we have taken the city."

The warriors all shot to their feet. The din of conversation filled the cavern. Blixen glanced once more at the wherry and realized that the creature was like him. The beast had retreated underground. He was gathering his strength.

He would emerge twice as strong.

32

Taimin could finally sit up. His bruised ribs would take a long time to heal, and he still spent most of his time in bed, but at least his head was no longer pounding.

Rathis, the old skalen liked by both bax and humans, was still alive. Taimin had no regrets, and he had gained the respect of the bax in the prisoners' quarters when he had called for peace between the races. He knew that he had to do what he could, while the crowd looked on, to bring about a change in the city and stop the fighting.

But there was a price to pay. Taimin's refusal to fight Rathis hadn't been taken lightly. After his savage beating, Taimin had hovered in and out of consciousness for days.

He saw Vance approaching his bedside, but then his heart sank. Vance's usually twinkling eyes were solemn and his bearded mouth was tight set.

"I have bad news," Vance said bluntly.

Taimin tensed. "Just tell me."

"You've been called up to fight."

Taimin steeled himself. He had been expecting this. "When?" As Vance hesitated, Taimin's stomach churned. "Now?"

Vance nodded. "That's not all. The Protector is in the arena." He met Taimin's gaze. "People are talking about you everywhere in the city. Abigail too. You defy the soldiers they all fear. Galen can't let you survive any longer. If the Protector is here, you're going to be given an enemy you can't beat. The odds will be against you, even at the risk of angering the crowd."

Taimin tried to summon his courage. "I understand." He sat up higher in the bed, wincing as he felt the tightness in his ribs. "How long do I have?"

"They'll call us forward any moment."

Vance said it with such finality that Taimin felt dread closing in on him, like a heavy weight pressing down on his body. He was going to die. Yet even through his fear, he heard a catch in Vance's voice. When he tried to meet his friend's eyes, Vance looked away.

"There's something else you're not telling me," Taimin said. He started. "Wait." His eyes widened. "You said they're calling *us* forward."

Vance's face was pale. "I'm to fight by your side."

Taimin's breath came out of him. "Brother, I'm sorry I brought you into this."

Vance shrugged. "My time had to come eventually. The Protector wants to see my blood, just as Galen wants to see yours." He gave a weak smile. "We'll give the crowd a fight to remember."

Taimin saw Rathis approach. The skalen's tilted eyes were troubled.

"You told him?" Rathis asked Vance.

"I did," Vance said.

"I know what you are fighting."

Taimin leaned forward. "Tell us. Anything that can help us plan."

"Trulls," Rathis said. "Three of them. The city guard captured them from the waste, along with their firehounds. I am sorry."

"Three trulls, each with a firehound," Vance muttered. "By the rains . . ."

314

"It's time!" a voice called from the far end of the room.

Taimin set his jaw and straightened. He threw his legs over the side of the bed, then turned and glanced at the ground where his boots rested on the floor. It took him a few moments to yank them on, before he left the bed in one swift motion. As he stood beside his two companions, he tried not to wobble.

He looked down at himself. He was wearing a leather vest and coarse linen trousers. His sturdy boots were on his feet. This was what he would be wearing when he died.

He glanced at Vance. His friend wore similar clothing, but his face looked clean and his moustache and beard were newly trimmed.

"You cut a fine figure," Taimin said.

Vance's tone was grave. "It's you the crowd will be watching."

The first beats of a heavy, regular thumping came from above. Already the people were making themselves heard. The sound thudded along with Taimin's heartbeat. Vance looked shaken.

"Prisoners, move!" a deep voice bellowed from the far end of the room.

Taimin turned to Vance; the slim man nodded but his face was grim. Together they walked through the prisoners' quarters and headed for the barred gate at the end. Taimin was surprised to see that the other prisoners stood in two files along the approach to the wooden gate. He felt their eyes on him and heard their voices as he and Vance walked past.

"Fight well."

"Survive."

"Don't let Galen win."

Taimin's feet felt heavy as he and Vance walked through the gate. The crowd stamped above. Dust fell from the ceiling. A pair of burly prison guards waited on the other side of the gate, and when Rathis tried to follow they barred his way. With only each other for company, Taimin and Vance followed the stone-walled corridor. The sloped floor climbed. The tall archway beckoned, and, as ever, the light that poured through the opening was bright and dazzling. The portcullis groaned as it was raised. Taimin heard the roar of a great number of people, louder than ever before.

"Prisoners, go forth!" a guard called, shouting to be heard above the din.

Taimin and Vance exchanged glances. Taimin tried to remember everything Abi had taught him about trulls and firehounds. As he clamped down on the pain from his broken ribs and bruised body, he and his companion were given hardwood swords.

On his final approach to the archway, he gave a few swings of the sword to loosen his muscles.

Taimin and Vance walked out to a mighty cacophony of sound.

Selena felt sick and the fight hadn't even begun. She glanced left and right, overwhelmed by the sight of so many people crowded together in one place. They filled every tier surrounding the fighting pit, separated by nothing more than a tall wooden fence from the place where blood was spilled. Those closest to the fence were the most roughly dressed: the field workers, haulers, laborers, and water gatherers. But everyone was shouting. Even the people at the back, in their bright, garish clothing, leaned forward in their seats and raised their arms to cheer. There were so many loud voices that Selena couldn't hear individual words. A cluster of people started to stamp their feet and it was taken up by the rest of the crowd. The noise was thunderous.

Selena had learned from Ruth that the citizens were forced to attend, yet some of the onlookers looked far more involved than she had been expecting. She wondered if this reaction was normal, or if the fight she was about to see was special in some way. All she knew was that two men—one an enemy of the Protector, and the other the killer of Galen's brother—were both about to die in front of her eyes.

Beside Selena, Galen leaned forward on his stone bench, the veins in his throat betraying his tension. The Protector, dressed in a black tunic and with his gray hair parted, sat next to Galen. Behind Selena were Arren and Merin, the two mystics, on a higher tier.

Galen looked Selena's way. As ever, his angular features and stony expression were cold. "We have noticed you and Ruth speaking. First it will be her down there," he said, throwing a meaningful glance at the fighting pit. "The Protector has agreed to it; we can always find another servant. Then it will be someone else—perhaps a young girl or boy. Today you will see what happens here. If you ever fail us, someone close to you will die, whether you are around to see it or not."

Selena's stomach churned. She finally knew Galen's plan to control her.

She kept her face blank. "Do what you want," she said. "Why would I care what happens to your servant?"

Now it was the Protector who fixed his piercing blue eyes on her. "We shall see," was all he said.

Selena could feel Arren and Merin's wards clamped tightly on her mind. Their ever-present wall separated her from her ability to summon her power. She wouldn't be able to escape what was about to take place in front of her.

The sense of anticipation grew. The fight would soon begin. The crowd became even more raucous, far too loud for Selena to hear her own shallow breathing. She was all alone, despite being surrounded by people.

"Please, let it be quick," she whispered under her breath.

But she knew it wouldn't be. The Protector wanted her to see this demonstration. She would witness every moment.

The crowd gave a collective gasp, although Selena couldn't see what had caused it. Then Galen turned and spoke to the Protector, nodding toward the fighting pit. "Three trulls. Each with a tame firehound."

The Protector peered down to make his appraisal.

Selena followed their eyes and saw an enclosure built alongside the wooden fence. The three trulls who waited inside were thick and muscled, over six feet tall, with upturned snouts and long incisors protruding from their mouths. Two held thorn-studded clubs while a third hefted the biggest hardwood sword she had ever seen. Each had a loop of leather around his left hand, connected to the collars of slavering beasts.

Selena had never seen firehounds in captivity before. She looked down in morbid fascination. As she watched, one of the creatures darted forward before its master reined it in. The firehound's skin was red and it was lithe—a sinewy creature, built for speed. Its hind legs were powerful, but it was the oversized head that drew her gaze. Two curling horns sprouted from the firehound's crown and its jaws looked large enough to crush a man's skull with a single bite.

"Here he comes," Galen said.

"At last," the Protector said. He glanced at Galen. "I trust nothing will go wrong this time. Your enemy is becoming too popular."

The crowd roared as the portcullis on the far side of the arena ponderously rose.

Two men walked forward to a deafening chorus of howls and screams. Galen clenched his fists.

The Protector's voice was incredulous. "That is the man who killed your brother? He doesn't look like much. Is he limping?"

Selena couldn't believe what she was seeing.

The warrior with the limp was Taimin.

Selena wanted to cry out. Taimin's face was bruised. He looked terrible. Thoughts whirled through her mind. How had he come to be here? She could hardly breathe as she realized that Taimin was going to be killed, and she would be forced to watch it happen.

Despite Selena's horror, she had to know the truth. "Why did he kill your brother?" Her voice was shaking as she leaned forward to stare at Galen.

Distracted, he cast her a quick look. "Eh?"

"The man down there. You never said why he did it."

It was the Protector who spoke. "In days long past, our commander was a rover. He and that man have a history."

Selena gasped. It was Galen. Taimin's parents had been killed by rovers—two brothers—when he was young. His injury came from the same event.

Now he was about to die.

Down in the fighting pit, Taimin's head turned. He lifted his gaze, searching, until he stared directly toward Galen. Then a change came over his face.

There was some distance between them, but it shrank to nothing. Selena felt as if she was right in front of him. He met her eyes as he saw her.

33

Selena.

It couldn't be.

Her eyes were wide, and Taimin's vision shrank to a narrow focus so that he could see the irises and the whites around them. He saw her parted lips, furrowed brow, and long coal-black hair.

Hope soared in his heart. She was alive. He had found her. After all his searching, here she was, so close he felt like he could reach out and touch her.

Then his emotions swiftly changed. How could she be sitting beside his greatest enemy? He had last seen her with a group of bax, who had also been hiding from the city guard on their wyverns. Galen must have freed her.

Surely she couldn't be working with the Protector? As soon as they came, his doubts vanished. Selena was pale. He knew her too well. She would never assist Galen in his raids unless it was against her will.

The trumpeter gave a strident blast of his horn, forcing Taimin's attention back to the fighting pit. He clenched his jaw. He had to survive.

When the crowd continued to cheer, another series of blares rang through the arena until the citizens at last fell silent. The plump herald, dressed in a bright-blue tunic, entered through a gate in the fence and opened his arms. He cast a beatific smile on the people above him.

"Citizens of Zorn!" he bellowed. "Welcome once again to the arena! I bring you these words from our exalted Protector, which I will convey to you now." He indicated the Protector, seated near Selena, who stood and waved. After showing himself, the Protector sat down once more and the herald continued. "Today, my people, I, the Protector of Zorn, gazed out from the Great Tower. As I searched the lands around our fair city, I watched mantoreans fight over the stinking carcass of a wherry . . ."

With no time to lose, Taimin put his head close to Vance's. "The trulls aren't quick, so it's the firehounds we'll need to worry about first." The herald was making an elaborate speech, but if Taimin was being insulted, the man's words were wasted. "At some point we'll have to engage the trulls, but for now, whatever you do, stay away from them."

Taimin and Vance stood side by side, near the middle of the sandy floor. Both men watched the enclosure on the pit's far side. The three trulls were new; Taimin had never seen them before. Trulls were never known to back down, and, even as he watched, the firehounds were sensing the growing tension. The red-skinned creatures snarled and threw themselves against the fence.

"By the rains, look at those monsters," Vance muttered. "Have you ever seen jaws that big?"

"Listen to me," Taimin said sharply. "They crunch bones in their jaws, that's why their heads are so big. Worry about the horns before anything else."

"So what's the plan?" Vance asked. He cast Taimin a fearful look.

"We need to stay clear of the trulls and wait until the firehounds lower their heads to charge. Right before they make contact, their heads are down and they can't see. So you have to stand firm. Wait until they're on you and then dodge at the last possible instant. That's your opportunity."

Vance swallowed. "You've fought them before?"

"No," Taimin said grimly. "Never."

"That's comforting."

"Remember: don't go near the trulls. Run if you have to, but don't get tied up in a swordfight until the firehounds are dead."

"Taimin?"

"Yes?"

"You can't run, can you?"

"No, I can't."

"We're dead, aren't we?"

Taimin let out a breath. "Our chances aren't good."

The herald left the floor and then a strident blare of the horn signaled the start of the fight. The crowd gave a shout when the enclosure gate crashed open. Taimin moved to the side, circling around so he and Vance would present two separate targets.

Immediately two of the trulls released their firehounds.

The creatures' lean red bodies were a blur as they sped forward. Taimin cursed when he saw that both had gone for Vance, with one just ahead of the other.

The nearest firehound to Vance lowered its head to charge. Taimin tensed; the creature was big enough to place its horns at the height of Vance's waist. Vance deftly jumped to the side and cut down with his sword. Taimin saw his friend's blade bite deep into the firehound's flank, opening up a terrible wound. It was a death blow, and the best start Taimin could have hoped for. The firehound gave a yelp and collapsed.

Then, as Vance's lunge took him off-balance, the second firehound struck. The creature barreled into Vance's upper leg, striking more with its head than its horns. Vance went down, and a trull snarled as he lumbered forward to follow up and attack the prone man. The trull raised his spiked club.

The crowd roared.

Although Vance was in trouble, Taimin was forced to tear his eyes away—the two remaining trulls, one with a firehound, were both nearly on him. Taimin knew he had to keep them both in front of him and backed away. A swift glance told him that Vance was fighting the third trull. His and Vance's strategy had fallen apart in the first moments of the fight.

Retreating slowly, Taimin was keenly aware of the wooden fence behind him. He came to a halt and watched carefully as the two trulls closed in. One gripped an immense sword. The second held a studded club as well as the leash of his snarling firehound.

Taimin glanced left and right, desperate to find some new plan or advantage he could use. He decided to do the last thing his enemies expected.

Before the trull could release the firehound, Taimin charged.

He focused on his footing and struggled to control the jarring pain as he ran. After the trulls' initial surprise, the one with the leash did what Taimin expected him to do. He released his firehound.

Taimin knew he was making a gamble, but this fight wouldn't be won by conventional tactics. He planned to use his momentum, and that of the firehound, to best advantage.

Even as he lumbered forward, he judged his moment carefully. The firehound raced toward him. The distance shrank. Taimin sank to one knee. He held his sword in front of him with both hands gripping the hilt. He didn't plan on stabbing the animal. He only wanted to create a threatening barrier.

The sharp point of the sword startled the animal and it reared. Taimin saw his chance. He grunted and stabbed. The firehound howled when the sharp sword plunged into its chest. Taimin withdrew the blade and immediately launched his body into a forward roll that would take him between his two snub-nosed opponents. He left the dead firehound and kept rolling, until he was past the trulls. When he shot back to his feet, he was behind them.

He took swift stock of his situation. He had startled his two opponents, but Vance's expression was desperate as he fought his own enemy. Taimin's movements had taken him closer to his friend and he knew he had to come to his aid. Taimin moved again into the awkward run that was the best he could manage. While Vance held the attention of the trull facing him, Taimin moved to approach from behind. He raised his weapon above his head. With a savage cry he slashed at the exposed back of Vance's opponent. The basalt wood cut through the trull's thick skin, biting deep.

The crowd gasped. As the trull twisted in pain, trying to combat the new threat, Vance lunged and the point of his sword thrust into the trull's chest. Taimin and Vance moved to stand side by side as the trull's body fell heavily to the sand.

Taimin and Vance exchanged glances. Vance was pale; he had escaped being gored, but the firehound's charge had injured his leg. Meanwhile Taimin was panting and his bruised ribs hurt with every breath. He had been weak when the fight began, and already he felt light-headed. Despite the pain, he knew it was the fatigue that would kill him. As he weaved on his feet, Vance reached out a steadying hand.

But then Taimin realized that the firehound that had struck Vance was far from dead. The red-skinned creature had lurked near the barrier fence, awaiting its opportunity, and now it raced forward. Taimin only saw the blur of its passage as it struck.

"Look out!" Taimin cried.

Vance tried to turn but he was too late, and the firehound's horns struck him hard in his side. For a moment Taimin couldn't make sense of what was happening as the firehound tossed its head and Vance tried to evade the snarling creature. When Vance fell to one knee, Taimin made a desperate lunge and the point of his sword dug into the firehound's side. Striking ribs, he pushed as hard as he could before the blade slipped through.

In an instant the last of the three firehounds was dead. Vance was on the ground, grimacing as he pressed his hands against the wound in his side. Blood welled between his fingers. He looked at Taimin and shook his head, and then fell back to stare up at the sky.

There was nothing Taimin could do for Vance other than put some distance between himself and his stricken friend. As the two trulls closed in, working together, Taimin's gaze shifted from one to the other. The trull with the sword was tall and powerfully built. Taimin's other opponent had a missing eye, yet he swung his spiked club with short, chopping motions, as if the heavy basalt wood was as light as a feather.

Taimin knew he could never defeat them both. If he was at his full strength, there was a small possibility he might survive. But his thoughts were dull and part of him just wanted to sleep. As hope fled, a growing weariness came over him. His short hardwood sword felt impossibly heavy.

The raised voices of the crowd came from all directions. There were no jeers or heckles; people in the front were standing and shouting, calling out words of encouragement. The two trulls approached slowly, still wary and taking their time. The bigger one glanced at Vance, lying in the sand, but knew he was no threat.

A man from the crowd yelled. "Come on, Taimin!"

A youth cupped his hands around his mouth. "Fight, Taimin! Fight!"

More shouts came from every direction.

"We're with you, Taimin!"

"Don't let them win!"

"If Abigail can do it, so can you!"

Taimin glanced at Vance again. His friend's face was pale and his eyes were closed. Blood soaked the sand around him. Vance needed urgent help.

Desperation brought strength back to Taimin's limbs. As the two trulls closed in to attack, Taimin's hardwood blade immediately barred the air in front of his face to block a blow from the spiked club. The one-eyed trull snarled, and then Taimin's intuition told him to duck. The bigger trull's huge sword whistled over his head.

Taimin weaved and struck into the big trull's backswing, scoring a shallow hit near the collarbone. Remembering Abi's advice, he moved to place the one-eyed trull in the way of his bigger ally. For an instant they were both confused.

But Taimin had only bought himself a few moments. He faced his opponents and took steps backward, breathing hard as his lungs fought for air. He knew he couldn't last long. He was simply too weak.

The big trull with the sword touched his fingers to the wound just below his neck and scowled when he saw his own red blood. Both trulls sensed victory and came in fast. If they could pin Taimin against the fence, he would die.

Taimin had to attack before it was too late. He singled out the trull with the sword and tried to rush forward, but his leg wasn't up to the task. The big trull swung his sword and Taimin leaned to the side as the blade whistled past his ear. Off balance, Taimin fell and was forced to roll to evade a second sword blow. The agony in his foot gave him an idea, and while he was on the ground he chopped at his opponent's ankle. The big trull bellowed and looked down to find the source of the pain, which gave Taimin the opportunity to thrust upward through his torso. Another roll took Taimin away from the trull as he collapsed.

Taimin's chest heaved as he climbed to his feet. He now faced the one-eyed trull with the club. The trull came at him with a strong overhead swing, and with all of his weight on his good leg Taimin knew that if he tried to weave, he would fall. He raised his hardwood sword and felt the force of mountains strike the blade. The muscles in his arms screamed.

Taimin gritted his teeth and pushed. He put all of his strength into throwing his bigger opponent back. But as he glanced at the blade of pale basalt wood, he saw a long crack appear. The crack widened.

Wood splintered and the blade broke off at the midpoint. Taimin found himself holding nothing more than a shard of wood. The trull raised his club over his head.

With a gasp, Taimin fell to one knee.

He knew it was over.

———

Selena felt the blood drain from her face.

Taimin's sword had shattered. With just a wide splinter of basalt wood in his hands, he was on one knee with his opponent looming over him. The trull lifted his spiked club over his head. When it struck Taimin's skull, nothing would save him.

Unable to restrain himself, Galen stood, eager to see the blood of the man who had killed his brother. The Protector chuckled and tapped his fingers on his knee.

The people of Zorn shouted until all their words mingled together, their pleas for Taimin to survive merging to become one. Every member of the crowd gazed down at the man below. Tight faces betrayed tension as the onlookers waited for what would happen next. The golden sun Dex was directly overhead, bathing the arena in a furious brilliance.

Looking up at the golden orb, Selena felt something terrible rise within her.

She could sense her power, trapped by the wall that the two mystics had built, confined by the pressure they exerted. Although they were behind her, she knew that Arren and Merin would be focused on the fight—as distracted as they would ever be. They weren't aware that Selena and Taimin knew each other. They would be consumed by the prospect of death, excited that blood was about to be spilled.

Selena reached for her symbol, and as the savage emotion inside her spurred her to greater efforts she felt her ability swell. She fed her desperation to her power, and like dry tinder given to a fire, the radiance inside her blazed.

She couldn't have calmed herself no matter how hard she tried, so she poured all of her fears into the raging inferno inside her mind. She fed it until it was too bright for her to contemplate, too huge to stay small for a second longer.

Then Selena realized what it was she had built. Rather than a moon, she had created a sun. Her sphere of fiery energy pulsed and glowed. The sphere was still confined, but inside her mind she had taken hold of more power than she ever had before.

Rei-kika had taught her to control her emotion, to be calm and at peace as she imagined the soft light of a moon pulling her out of the shell that was her body. Instead, Selena fed more power to the sun she had made. It grew as if exploding, incredibly swiftly, far too big and powerful to be confined by the wall around it.

The wall burst to nothingness, and then Selena was out of her body.

Behind her, part of her was aware of the two mystics crying out a warning, but their shouts were lost in the roar of the crowd.

Selena ignored them and concentrated on the events unfolding in the fighting pit. The trull's club was in mid-swing.

Selena left the area above her body to dive toward the trull's snarling face. She peeled apart the layers of the creature's mind and then plunged inside. She sensed the maelstrom of the trull's thoughts and sent one command louder than anything else. She focused on it and brought it to the forefront, shocking him into obeying.

Stop.

Taimin's expression shifted to wonder as the club froze. The trull's eyes widened. Seeing a brief window of opportunity, Taimin seized it. He straightened from his position on one knee to thrust the remnant of his weapon deep into the trull's neck, withdrawing the shard a moment later.

The crowd gave a collective gasp.

Selena's power was exhausted. The radiant sun was gone. She felt a jolt as her lifeline drew her back into her body. As her eyes refocused, she knew that the people in the crowd would assume Taimin had pretended to be weak in order to lull the trull into a false sense of confidence. The trull's hesitation might be remarked on, but stranger things would have happened in the arena.

But when she blinked, she realized that Galen was gripping her arm. He was staring directly at her. Arren and Merin's startled voices had finally reached him. Galen knew.

Down in the fighting pit, the last of Taimin's opponents crashed to the ground and toppled over. For a moment Taimin looked confused. He dropped his broken sword. His head turned, and his gaze went to Selena.

Then he shook himself and ran over to the man who lay bleeding on the sand. Taimin crouched by his fallen companion's side.

The crowd began to chant. It began as a rumble and then rose to fill the arena. It was one man's name, shouted again and again.

"Tai-min!"

"Tai-min!"

The Protector scowled at Galen. "Let's get out of here."

Selena was hauled to her feet. The roar of the crowd was so loud that anything else Galen or the Protector said was lost.

"Tai-min!"

34

The crowd continued to cheer. Raised voices chanted Taimin's name over and over as he carried Vance through the open portcullis.

Taimin ignored everything but the injured man in his arms. Grimacing, he concentrated on the groaning muscles in his back and shoulders. As he took step after laborious step, with Vance's weight trying to bow his knees, he walked through the archway and down the sloped corridor until he came to the gate. He was surprised when the prison guards holding the gate looked at him with something approaching admiration.

The other prisoners were ready and waiting. Taimin had done the impossible. He had made it out alive. Two men helped Taimin to rest Vance on the closest bed. Others ran to fetch water and cloth. Vance groaned while they maneuvered his legs. The firehound's horns had torn his vest and trousers below his waist and opened a messy wound. The gash steadily seeped blood.

Vance opened his eyes and smiled weakly. "If this is Earth, your looks haven't improved, and the afterlife seems a lot like the arena."

"Where do you keep your money?" Taimin asked. "Quickly."

"Rathis has it."

"Good. Now be quiet." Taimin swiftly scanned the room. "Rathis!" He saw the old skalen hurrying forward with strips of torn cloth in his hand. He grabbed Rathis's shoulder and pulled him forward to whisper into his ear. "I need Vance's money."

While Rathis disappeared, Taimin wadded up the rags and pressed the bunched cloth against the wound in Vance's side. Vance's eyes were closed and his face was pale, but at least he was breathing. Rathis hurried back with a small pouch.

"Here," Taimin said to Rathis. "Hold this against the wound."

Taking the pouch, Taimin then strode to the far end of the room and shook the barred gate that only opened when new prisoners came or food was provided. "Guards!"

A heavyset man approached. Taimin breathed a sigh of relief when he recognized the guard who had procured the wine.

"What is it?"

"Here." Taimin shook the pouch so the guard could hear the jingle. "I need a needle and gut as well as the strongest cactus spirit you can find. Bandages too."

"All right." The guard held out his palm.

"Wait," Taimin said, holding the pouch back. "You can get the things I need and keep whatever's left, or you can betray me." His voice was low and deadly. "Do not betray me."

"Yes, yes," the fat guard muttered. As Taimin handed the pouch over, the guard immediately upended it onto his palm and began to count the metal chips.

"Hurry!" Taimin growled.

Closing his fist over the metal bits, the guard walked away.

Taimin returned to Vance. Rathis still held the wad of bloody cloth and lifted it up to look underneath.

"How bad is it?" Taimin asked.

"How would I know?" Rathis frowned at the wound. "My body isn't made the same way." He stared into Taimin's eyes. "You will have to treat him."

Taimin swallowed. Aunt Abi may have been a tough fighter, but she didn't know much about healing; the way she had treated his foot had proved that. He knew he had no choice. His friend needed him. He took the stained cloth from Rathis while the skalen backed away.

"Go to the gate and wait for the guard to bring the things I'll need," Taimin said to Rathis. He then inspected the wound.

The firehound's horn had gored Vance's upper thigh, near his hip, but missed any important veins—otherwise Vance would already be dead. At the same time, the firehound had twisted its head as it struck, leaving behind the mess that Taimin was looking at. As he lifted a flask of water and spilled it over the gash to clear the blood away, Taimin's hopes rose when he saw that there was only one wound deep enough to require stitches.

Once he was sure he had inspected all the damage, he tore more strips of fabric and wadded fresh cloth. He wrapped the strips around the rough bandage and tied everything up while he looked into Vance's pale face. He listened to Vance's shallow breathing and waited impatiently.

At last Rathis returned. Taimin sighed with relief when he saw that the old skalen held a flask, clean linen bandages, and a needle and gut.

Taimin removed the already soaked rags. He pressed wadded cloth to the deep part of the wound that still bled freely. Vance groaned when Taimin splashed spirit over every gash. Then, with a shaking hand, Taimin threaded the needle.

He leaned forward, blinked sweat out of his eyes, and began to sew. Some of his fellow prisoners watched him while he worked, bax and humans standing side by side.

When he was done, Taimin splashed more spirit over the stitches. He applied fresh bandages, and then sat on the ground by Vance's bedside.

As Taimin watched his friend, he thought about all that had happened.

Selena had saved his life. He knew without doubt. The trull about to kill him had simply . . . stopped. When Taimin had seized his opportunity, and survived, he had looked her way. One glance had been enough to know. Galen's expression had been vicious as he held her.

Even exhausted as he was, Taimin's heart soared to know she was alive.

Then his shoulders slumped, and his eyes slowly closed.

It was four days after the fight with the trulls and Vance's color had begun to return. Taimin sat at Vance's side while Rathis leaned against the bed opposite. Their voices were low as they shared their thoughts.

Vance's tone was sober. "If she hadn't saved you, I would be dead too."

"You say that she is a powerful mystic," Rathis said to Taimin. "My guess is the Protector is using you to ensure she does what he wants. At any moment he can make you fight." He looked Taimin up and down. "In your current state, if you fight, you will die. Whatever she is doing, she is keeping you alive."

Taimin understood something of the city from the other prisoners, and he knew that Selena was almost certainly being held in the tower. "We have to get out of here," he said.

"How?" Vance asked. "We can overwhelm the prison guards, and maybe we'd get as far as the lower gate. But out in the streets we'd still have the city guard to deal with."

"I know," Taimin said. "We need help from outside."

"Who would help us?"

Taimin met Vance's eyes. "The people."

"New prisoner!" A bellow came from the end of the room. "Stand back!"

Taimin glanced over, curious. It had been a while since there had been any newcomers. On the other side of the barred gate that led to freedom rather than the fighting pit, he saw some of the guards. They waited until the other prisoners had cleared the area before the gate crashed open. Two guards dragged in a big man, supporting his weight between them.

Without ceremony the guards let go and the newcomer fell heavily. The prison guards departed the room and the gate closed. Soon the clatter of their footsteps became distant as they left the new prisoner to his fate.

The big man had obviously been beaten, but that wasn't what caused Taimin's mouth to drop open. He shot to his feet.

"What is it?" Rathis asked.

Taimin didn't answer. He walked toward the newcomer, unable to believe his eyes.

"Taimin?" Vance called after him.

Taimin's footsteps quickened. The newcomer groaned. With a great effort, the big man brought himself into a sitting position.

Hairs poked out from the big man's vest, the same black color as his thick black beard, but his head was completely bald. His eyes were dark and his shoulders had fresh diagonal lines across them: the marks left by a whip. But despite his situation, he had a wry expression on his face.

"Well, lad," Lars said. He cast his eyes over the fading bruises on Taimin's face. "I would say it's good to see you again, but it appears we've both seen better days."

Taimin and Lars sat together at one of the tables. The other prisoners cast them curious glances, but gave them some space so they could talk.

"They took me to the city and threw me into a cell. I was hurt but I recovered eventually." Lars looked into the distance. "They picked me out because of my size. Got me working in the fields. Forced labor. Guess who got to cut off cactus spines? But there was food, bad as it was, and a place to sleep at night." He gave Taimin a rueful look. "I guess we both know by now that the white city isn't what we thought it was."

"Then what happened?" Taimin asked.

"You did," Lars said bluntly.

Taimin frowned, confused.

Lars waved his hand. "I don't expect you to know what I'm talking about. Lad, you may not realize it, but you're famous in the city. You've been given fights you can't win, but here you stand—even after the beating you took when you wouldn't kill the skalen. Everyone knows who you are. They remember the speech you gave."

As Taimin's bemusement grew, Lars continued. "When I was working in the fields, I heard rumors. Not every laborer was a slave like me, but they might as well be. Without money, they can't buy water, and their wages are pitiful. I heard some of them talking about a resistance. I thought I might have a chance to change my circumstances, so I kept asking round. Soon I was talking to someone who wasn't full of mud. He didn't want to open up until I said I knew you. Then he became very interested indeed."

"I don't understand."

"The rebels needed someone to get a message to you. I volunteered. It's not like it was hard—I just refused to work anymore, and when that wasn't enough I picked a fight with a guard. Next thing you know, here I am."

Taimin felt a stirring of hope. He had always known in his heart that of all the faces he saw in the crowd, some must have listened to his words and thought in the same way. "Tell me," he said urgently.

"A woman, Elsa, wants to meet with you. I think she might be the rebels' leader. If you're interested, you have to send her a message through the prison guards. Their pay is as bad as the field workers and a few are supporters." Lars glanced over his shoulder toward the end of the room. "Wait at the gate when the guards bring food in the morning. Don't cause trouble. Just make sure you're seen. She'll do the rest."

Taimin stood up from the bench. "Come with me."

Lars gave Taimin a wary look. "Where are we going?"

"To meet some friends of mine. They're going to want to hear this." Taimin hesitated. "Also, Lars . . . I have to thank you. When—"

"Lad, whatever you're about to say, I don't want to hear it. I lost my head for a moment. Don't expect it to happen again. I'm not here out of any desire to help you. I don't want to be a slave, and I don't want to be a prisoner. I want this city to become the place it was supposed to be."

35

For the second time, Taimin followed the stone-walled corridors toward the storeroom where he had shared cactus wine with Vance. The guard who led the way had a long face and mournful eyes and had quietly introduced himself as Lewin. As they walked, Taimin inspected him, curious now he knew that Lewin belonged to the secret group Lars had described. Lewin glanced back at Taimin and Rathis when they came to the wooden door.

"When I knock, you leave," Lewin said.

"Understood," said Rathis.

Lewin opened the door and pushed it wide. Taimin went in first with Rathis close behind him. The door closed as soon as they were in the storeroom.

A woman was already waiting for them. She was perhaps fifty years old, with weathered skin and piercing green eyes that rested on the two newcomers. Her arms were thin and streaks of gray threaded her brown hair, but her slight frame was athletic rather than frail, and if anything she gave off an aura of impatient energy. Her tunic was well-made and cinched at the waist and she wore sturdy leather boots.

"I assume you're Elsa?" Taimin asked.

A flash of irritation crossed Elsa's face when she saw Rathis. "What's he doing here?"

"His name is Rathis—"

"I know who he is," she said, scowling at the skalen. "I asked what he's doing here."

"Whatever is happening in the city, it's linked to what's going on outside," Taimin said, holding Elsa's stare. "He knows Blixen's mind. Most of all, I trust him."

Elsa took a deep breath. "Fine." She swept her arm over a few of the crates. "Sit down, and we can talk."

Taimin and Rathis both found places to seat themselves but Elsa remained standing. As small as the storeroom was, she nonetheless paced while she spoke.

"The people are ready to rise up."

"Why now?" Rathis interjected. "From here it looks like the Protector has his citizens firmly in his power."

"From here you don't know a thing," Elsa snapped. "The common folk hate the Protector. He controls the water and keeps them in line, but the time has come for change."

Taimin glanced at Rathis. "The question still stands. Why wait until now?"

"The Protector has thrown this entire region into chaos. Outside trade has dried up completely. The cactuses are being harvested faster than we can grow them and the price of water has nearly doubled in the last month." Elsa continued to pace with a quiet fury. "Until now the Protector promised safety and used fear of his soldiers to keep people in line. He guards the one reliable water source, the city's only well. He says that he's stockpiling in case there's a siege. Well, guess what?" Her voice lowered. "Blixen's army is on the plain. Soon the only water left will be whatever the Protector has stored up in that tower."

Rathis drew in a sharp breath. "Are there skalen with Blixen?"

Elsa frowned. "How would I know? Does it matter? The Protector has his city guard and nothing can beat them in the sky, but there are only a hundred soldiers, and Blixen comes with many more than that."

"How long until the army reaches the city?" Taimin asked.

"Four days at most. Soon everyone will know."

"What is it you want?" Rathis asked.

"Isn't it obvious?" Elsa threw up her hands. "I want to stop this madness. I want to come to terms. The bax can have their Rift Valley, the skalen can have their mines, and we can have peace here in Zorn. No more arena fights. No more raids. But it won't end, it can't end, as long as the Protector rules."

"I want the same thing," Taimin said seriously. "What can I do?"

"We have numbers, but most of us aren't fighters. Even if we overthrow the Protector, there is no guarantee we can make peace with Blixen." Her expression was grim. "I'm a pragmatist. If it all goes badly, we'll need someone to lead the city's defense. People will be scared. Your story is known, Taimin, everywhere in the city. They remember Abigail."

Taimin considered Elsa's words. "What are you going to do about Galen and his men?"

"We're working on it," Elsa said flatly. When Taimin raised an eyebrow, she grimaced. "We can probably get you out—"

"We can probably get ourselves out," Rathis interrupted. "It is once we are out that things become a problem."

"Tell us clearly," Taimin said to Elsa. "If you can defeat Galen and his men, and bring down the Protector, what then?"

"We release all the prisoners, here and elsewhere. Then we meet with Blixen and broker peace." A shadow crossed her face. "If that's even possible. Terrible things have been done in this city's name."

Elsa had struck an area of Taimin's own concern. It was Rathis who spoke to fill the silence.

"Neither of you know Blixen," Rathis said. "I do. I have also learned much from the bax held prisoner. More than anything,

Blixen wants to discover the fate of his wife, and for his people to live in peace in the place they call home."

"I hope you're right," Elsa said. "In any case, whatever we do, we must do it quickly. If Blixen reaches the city while the Protector rules, the people will react with fear. Frightened people are easily controlled."

"And there's no doubt the Protector will make them defend the city," Taimin said grimly, "with their lives."

Rathis nodded. "The Protector must be overthrown before Blixen attacks and the opportunity for peace closes forever."

While Elsa and Rathis spoke, Taimin's mind was working. He had the seed of an idea, a seed that grew and blossomed. It was risky, and could see him killed, but he had to do something to get out of the arena, to help in the struggle and free Selena.

"You said you have supporters," Taimin said to Elsa. "How many are willing to fight?"

"They're all willing to fight," Elsa said. "Most would give their lives rather than see their children die of thirst or fall in battle. It's the wyverns that pose the problem." Her brow furrowed. "One got loose recently, but I don't see how we could free the others. Even the one that escaped still flies over the city sometimes. The rest are guarded, night and day."

"I have a better idea," Taimin said. "What if I can find a way to get all of Galen's men in one place at the same time, without their wyverns? Could your supporters do what needs to be done?"

"Go on."

Taimin made sure he had the attention of his two companions. "Here's my plan . . ."

"You can fight," Vance said to Lars in admiration.

Lars sat down wearily on his pallet and scowled at the younger man, whose bed was right beside his. "What made you think I couldn't? I'm old, but I'm not that old."

"Hey," Vance put out his hands in a placating gesture, "that was meant to be a compliment."

Taimin's lips tugged up at the corners as the two men bickered. He couldn't tell if Vance and Lars genuinely disliked each other or were connecting in their own way. "You survived, that's the important thing," Taimin said.

"Bah," Lars growled. "The assessors probably thought my heart would give out. It won't be as easy next time round." He glared at Vance. "It's true. I'm old."

"I never said a word!" Vance protested.

"I probably wouldn't even be here if it weren't for that wyvern circling overhead." Lars grunted. "Kept distracting the sand lizard."

Vance frowned. "I wonder how it escaped its cage."

"Who cares?" Lars glanced at Taimin. "What's got your attention?"

Taimin was tense, watching something past Lars's shoulder. He saw Rathis talking with the guards on the other side of the gate.

"It's going to be soon," he murmured.

The following day, Rathis was called up to fight. The guards didn't bother hiding anything from the old skalen. He would be battling a firehound. He wouldn't even be given a javelin, the weapon favored by his race; instead he would be fighting with a sword. Rathis had never held a sword in his life.

Vance was now on his feet and hobbled while he and Taimin walked Rathis toward the gate that led to the fighting pit. The pair of prison guards on the other side put their hands on the clubs at their waists when they saw that Taimin and Vance intended to join Rathis on his walk to the portcullis.

"That's far enough." One of the guards allowed the skalen through the gate, but stepped forward to block Taimin and Vance.

"Do you think he will survive?" Taimin demanded. "No, you don't, and neither do we. We're walking him to the next gate."

The two guards exchanged glances. They were both armed, and Taimin had no weapon, but Taimin had built a reputation as someone who could fight, and he wasn't asking for much. There were many more guards surrounding the pit.

"All right," the guard said. "We'll be close behind." He nodded at Rathis. "He enters the pit alone."

"Understood," Vance said.

Escorted by the pair of guards, Taimin, Vance, and Rathis climbed the path and headed toward the archway and the closed portcullis. Voices from the crowd echoed down the corridor. Another two guards waited up ahead. A horn blared, and the portcullis made a grating sound as it moved upward.

"Well?" one of the guards said to Rathis. "Get moving." He scowled at Taimin. "You two stay here."

Rathis didn't move. He had his gaze fixed on the circle of sand on the other side of the sliding portcullis. The snarl of a firehound cut through the rumbles of the crowd.

Taimin also cast a glance in the direction of the fighting pit. The portcullis was nearly all the way open. A second horn blast came from outside. The firehound bayed, excited by the noise around it. The two guards near the archway came down, and Taimin saw that they were preparing to force Rathis into the arena; it wasn't the first time a fighter had been reluctant to meet his end. One of the newly arrived guards shoved a sword into Rathis's hand. Vance intervened, pleading that Rathis just needed some time, doing his best to get in the way while appearing to be helpful.

The time was right. Rathis put his hand behind his back and passed Taimin the sword. Vance and Rathis both stepped in to block the group of guards, giving Taimin a clear approach to the fighting pit.

Taimin burst into a run.

He lumbered toward the open portcullis. He heard shouts behind him as the guards realized what he was doing.

The crowd had been somewhat subdued, but as soon as they saw Taimin everything changed. A powerful roar rose up to fill the entire arena. People shouted and cheered, waving their arms.

"Tai-min! Tai-min!" The chant began immediately.

Taimin walked to the middle of the floor and raised his sword above his head. He turned slowly to meet as many eyes as he could. The roar came up again, overwhelming the chant.

Taking his eyes off the crowd, Taimin turned his attention to the enclosure on the arena's far side and saw that it was open. The red-skinned firehound inside leaped and snarled, eager to charge. Looking back the way he had come, Taimin saw two of the angry guards he had evaded reach the edge of the fighting pit. One of them made a decision. Rather than approach, the guard waved an arm toward his fellows on the arena's other side.

Taimin heard a command, and the man holding the leash released the firehound.

The firehound came forward almost too fast for the eye to follow, legs digging into the sand as it sprinted. Long and lean, with a muscular body, oversized head, and curved crimson horns, the creature lowered its head when it was close to the end of its charge. Taimin knew the damage those horns could do. He turned his body, legs apart in combat stance. He waited until the last possible instant and then he stepped to the side, letting the horns spear the empty air as he thrust deep with the sword.

The firehound collapsed and skittered along the sand until it came to a complete rest. Barely any time had passed. The firehound was dead.

It was over so quickly that the crowd was momentarily stunned. Then the shouts began anew, a chorus of cheers that must have been heard throughout the city.

Taimin raised his sword into the air. He had a plan. This was his moment. "Quiet!"

He was almost surprised when the onlookers stilled as soon as they realized he planned to address them directly. He waited until the crowd was completely silent before sucking in his breath. He wanted everyone to hear what he had to say.

Taimin called out in a voice that he knew would carry throughout the arena. "I challenge the man Galen to a duel. Let the commander of the city guard defend his honor himself. I give him his choice of weapons, and I seek a battle to the death. Let the commander face me here in the arena. Let us all see how brave he is."

Taimin threw his sword so that the point slammed into the sand. He then turned and left the fighting pit, leaving the weapon where it was.

36

The Protector stood and gazed out from the observation room at the top of the tower. He sipped on the fragrant tea that Ruth made and stared past the rooftops and the wall, toward the rust-colored plain and the hazy outlines of the mountains. The low light of early evening began to settle on the landscape. Darkness was on its way.

A voice came from behind him. "Soon that plain is going to be full of bax," Galen muttered. "I hope you planned for this."

The Protector gave his commander a piercing stare. "Of course I did."

He frowned. Galen should know better than to question him. The Protector was an intelligent man, and knew that while he couldn't control all events, he could anticipate them.

Selena had just returned to her bedchamber, escorted by Arren and Merin. Galen's plan to give her a demonstration at the arena had worked out better than they could have hoped. They no longer had to worry about her willingness to serve, not when they could force Taimin—a man she clearly cared about—to fight for his life at any time. Although, this talk of a duel did complicate things . . .

Exhausted from farcasting, Selena had struggled to walk, but Arren and Merin had revealed critical information and that was the important thing.

Blixen was crossing the plain much faster than the Protector had been expecting. An army of bax and skalen would be at Zorn's gates in a number of days.

As Galen came up to stand beside him, the Protector glanced at his commander. "We were always going to face one of two outcomes," he said, taking another sip of tea. "Either Blixen would flee, or he would gather his warriors and attack Zorn. Remember, our goal has always been to seize the Rift Valley while maintaining the support of the people. We have kept our secret. No one knows about the well. If we had not made an enemy of Blixen, there would already be riots. A decisive outcome is what we want. True, we have not driven the bax away. But Blixen is coming to us."

Galen's face was cold. "And you think that's a good thing? I have a hundred men. Blixen isn't even trying to hide his presence. He knows we can't attack. Small groups are no trouble, but a sky full of arrows is something my men and I can't defend ourselves from." The commander's eyes narrowed. "Blixen's army is coming to this city, and there is nothing we can do to stop it."

The Protector turned away to set down his empty teacup. "Stop it? Why would we wish to do that? You asked if I had a plan, and I told you that I do. We have a population of thousands. Our wall is strong. The people are already afraid of Blixen. How will they react when we say his army is on its way?"

"With fear."

"Exactly." The Protector nodded. "With fear. As panic spreads, we can tighten our grip. No one will be asking about the well below this tower, not when we are sending every able-bodied male over the age of fourteen to the wall." He gave Galen a slight smile. "Under your leadership, of course."

"These people are city dwellers. Most of them can't fight."

"And therefore many will die," the Protector said.

"Yes," Galen said flatly.

"But all we need to know is: will the city survive?"

As the Protector had intended, his question forced Galen to think. "Blixen has hundreds of bax in his army," he said. "Skalen too. But the city's wall is strong. If we put every man and boy up there, even if it's just with a wooden spear . . ." He nodded slowly. "Yes, we can win."

"They will be fighting for their homes," the Protector said, "with nowhere to fall back to. Once we have broken Blixen's army, the Rift Valley will be ours."

As the Protector returned his attention to the darkening plain, Galen remained pensive. He finally spoke up. "I will agree to your plan, on one condition."

"Not this again," the Protector muttered.

"My honor is at stake." Galen's nostrils flared.

"I know you wish to see your enemy dead, Galen, but we need him alive," the Protector said. "Selena has been much more cooperative lately."

"I must face him," Galen insisted. "You want me to lead the city's defense? He issued a public challenge. I have no choice but to accept. The people know he killed my brother. Let me deal with him, Protector. I'll kill him myself and then no one will question my right to command, from the stubborn old men to the mothers of the boys we'll be rounding up."

The Protector realized his commander might have a point. It was important for Galen to be both feared and respected. He was silent for a moment as he pondered. "Give me another mystic, one with Selena's power, and I will allow it."

"You think you need Taimin to control her?" Galen shook his head. "It isn't true. Ruth would serve the same purpose. Selena is sentimental—ask Arren and Merin. Even toward our enemies."

The Protector smoothed his neatly combed gray hair. As always, he thought about all the difficulties that would have been avoided if he had the power to farcast himself.

One thing he knew was that Taimin was a distraction. Once the man was out of the picture, Galen would be able to focus on his duties. "Consider this a favor. I will grant your request, commander. You may have your duel. But, my friend, I need you too much for you to be killed. Make sure it is Taimin's blood, not yours, that soaks the sand of the fighting pit."

"Gladly," Galen said. His eyes gleamed. "It will appear to be a fair fight, but it will be nothing of the sort."

As she slept, Selena's dreams were dark and ugly. She was kneeling on the ground. A pool of blood surrounded her body, but she was frozen in place and unable to move her limbs. As the red liquid grew deeper, covering her legs and still rising, she kept telling herself to move but she couldn't. Everything began to shake and tremble. Her body rocked from side to side. A sharp, pinching sensation developed in her shoulder. Her breath quickened. All of a sudden her world shattered into a million pieces as pain struck her cheek.

She woke with a gasp. For an instant she had no idea where she was. She threw her body violently forward so that she was sitting up, and at the same time put a hand against her cheek, which still stung.

As her vision took focus, she saw Ruth crouched beside her bed. The short-haired woman had clearly just slapped her across the face.

"I'm sorry," Ruth said quickly. Her expression was grim. "I couldn't wake you. I don't have long. If they catch me here, they'll kill me."

Selena's thoughts were sluggish. "What's happened?"

"Taimin has challenged Galen to a duel. Galen's accepted."

Now Selena was truly awake. Her mind worked furiously. "Galen will make sure he wins."

"Of course he will."

Selena reflected on the fact that it was her farcasting that had been keeping Taimin alive. "They're going to make me watch," she said. "Then they'll find someone else to threaten."

"Probably." Ruth left unsaid that it might be her, but they both knew it.

"We have to do something." Selena held Ruth's gaze. "You wouldn't have come to tell me if you weren't willing to help."

A look of panic crossed Ruth's face. "I just thought you should know. What can I do?"

Selena remembered the last time she had watched Taimin fight. Galen would make sure he had an advantage. She needed to do something to even the odds in Taimin's favor. Yet this time wouldn't be like the last. Arren and Merin would both be guarding her closely.

She had an idea.

"You know herbs?" she asked.

Ruth frowned. "Of course."

"And you make their tea."

Ruth stood and backed away. "I don't like where this is going. And anyway, Galen never drinks the tea."

Selena persisted. "But I'll be at the arena, and Arren and Merin do . . ."

37

The mood was tense in the prisoners' quarters. In just a few hours, Taimin would fight Galen to the death. Conversations began and then faltered. Eyes drifted over to where Taimin sat on his pallet while he spoke quietly with Rathis.

After Taimin had issued his challenge to the commander, all other fights had been cancelled. Whether bax or human, Taimin's fellow prisoners knew they were still alive because of what he had done. They wanted him to win.

As Taimin and Rathis discussed their hopes and fears, Taimin no longer found it unusual to have a skalen so close beside him. In fact, he was thankful for the companionship. Hearing footsteps, he turned and saw Vance heading his way, carrying a plate piled high with bread and dried meat.

"Here, eat," Vance said. "You need your strength."

"How did you get so much food?" Taimin asked as he took the plate.

Vance shrugged. "Everyone pitched in."

"Wait." Rathis put out a warding hand, just as Taimin was about to pick up a hunk of pink razorgrass bread. He cast Vance an inquiring look. "Has someone tasted it?"

Vance snorted. "I'm no fool. I tried it myself."

Ever since Taimin's challenge had been accepted, his companions had insisted on tasting his food before he was allowed to eat. No one thought the coming fight would be a fair one. It just remained to be seen what Galen would do to tilt the odds in his favor.

While Taimin ate, he glanced at Lars, who was pacing the far side of the room. Occasionally the big skinner cast anxious looks Taimin's way.

"Your friend likes to keep his own company," Rathis said, noting Taimin's attention.

"He prefers not to rely on other people."

"You trust him?" Vance asked.

Taimin pondered while he chewed on a strip of dried meat. "I suppose I do."

Lars scowled when he saw the three companions watching. He hesitated and then made a decision to come over. Taimin could guess what he was about to say.

The skinner came to a halt and stood with his legs apart. "Are you sure this woman, Elsa, will come through for us? This plan has a lot of moving parts." Lars frowned at the gate that led to the fighting pit. On the other side, Taimin recognized Lewin, the sad-faced guard who had taken him to his meeting with Elsa in the storeroom. "I don't even know which of the guards are hers."

"It's probably best we don't know," Taimin said. "It might change the way we act around them." He tried not to look toward the gate. "Don't worry about the prison guards. They're not soldiers. They give us food and call us up to fight, but that's all."

"We can trust her," Vance spoke up. "I don't know her well, but I've spoken with her a few times. Not that she'd remember me." Taimin raised an eyebrow and Vance explained. "She runs a guild for the city's traders. They give her a tenth of their earnings and she makes sure they're looked after . . . helps if they're swindled, lose cargo, that sort of thing. She means what she says."

"We all have to keep to the plan," Taimin said. He met his companions' eyes, one at a time. He could understand their fear, for he could feel it himself: a gnawing sensation inside his chest that made him want to do anything except eat. Vance had given him food far better than the usual fare but it tasted like ash. He decided to change the subject and turned to Vance. "What are you going to do once you're free?"

Vance looked into the distance. "Find out what happened to Cora."

"Who?" Lars asked.

"The woman I loved," Vance said. "She was the Protector's mistress. I—"

"That's enough." Lars held up a hand. "I can piece the rest together."

Vance's face darkened. "What about you, rover?"

"When I'm free?"

"The city might become something else with new leadership," Taimin said, meeting Lars's gaze. "Perhaps you'll find a place here, after all."

"Perhaps," Lars said.

"Rathis?" Taimin asked the old skalen.

"I agree with Elsa. We need to prevent further conflict between Zorn and the Rift Valley. I do not want my clan to sacrifice their lives and I must do what I can to end this foolish war. Then . . . then I will go home."

Taimin nodded. He realized that all eyes were now on him.

"And you, my friend?" Rathis asked gently.

"The only reason I'm still alive is because of Selena."

"If you want to help her, you have to beat Galen," Vance said, "or this rebellion will be over before it's begun."

"And Taimin," said Lars, "be prepared for anything. Galen wants you dead, but he also wants to prove his skill in front of the city. I doubt he'll deploy something as blunt as poison, but it's almost certain he'll have some way to make sure he's the only man standing at the end."

Ruth's hands were shaking. She had carried her tray and its load of ceramic cups to the observation room too many times to remember, but this occasion was different. Steam rose from every cup. Liquid sloshed. The tea's floral aroma drifted into her nostrils. She would never hide the fact that she had made a completely different brew from usual.

As she crested the stone steps, she saw three familiar figures in the tower's highest room. The Protector and his two mystic aides faced in the direction of the arena. Ruth overheard their conversation as she approached with her tray held in both hands.

". . . commander will be putting his armor on right now," the Protector was saying. He moved some strands of carefully combed hair. "I suppose we should leave. The sooner this duel is over, the better."

"He shouldn't be risking himself," Merin said. "If he falls, who will lead the city's defense?"

"Did he tell you how he will ensure victory?" asked thin-faced Arren.

"No," the Protector said, still gazing at the arena. "He was evasive when I asked, but you know Galen: he is a resourceful man. He knows what he is doing." The Protector broke off when he saw Ruth. "Ruth?" He frowned. "I didn't ask for tea."

Ruth had her response prepared. When she spoke, she couldn't hide the fact that her voice was shaking. "Protector . . ." She

354

hesitated. "The mystic, Selena. She has been . . . giving me strange looks."

"Strange looks?" The Protector raised an eyebrow. He turned to focus his intense blue eyes on her.

Rather than disguise her fear, Ruth used it. "It's like she's afraid for me," she said. The cups trembled on the tray. She knew the Protector would notice. "If Taimin dies . . ."

"Ah." Realization dawned in the Protector's eyes. "You think I would use you to make Selena do what I want? Ruth, listen to me. Your fate here is secure. You have proved your value." He gave her a thin-lipped smile. "There is no need to bring tea in order to remind me."

He looked down at the tea and reached out, but then he noticed the color. Bringing his head down, he inhaled just above the cup he had been about to take.

Ruth's heart began to hammer in her chest. "It's a new tea," she said quickly. "I've made it sweeter, with different herbs."

Watching the exchange, Arren's lip curled. "None for me," he said. "In my view, tea should never be sweet."

Even as sweat broke out on her forehead, Ruth's heart sank. The Protector spoke in a voice that wasn't unkind. "I am afraid that, like Arren, I am in no mood for tea."

Ruth's gaze shot to Merin. The stocky mystic gave a shrug and came over. "I'll try it," he said.

She watched as he snatched a cup and brought it to his face. He inhaled, and Ruth's entire body tensed, but rather than set the cup back down, he made a sound of appreciation. She saw him take a tentative sip. Another followed.

Ruth glanced in the Protector's direction. He was staring at the arena once more, and had already forgotten about her.

"Enough," he said sharply. "Arren, Merin, it is time to go." He indicated the steps with his chin. "Ruth, leave us."

Merin hurriedly set the cup back down on the tray. Ruth turned away, but as she departed, she threw one last look toward the only tea that had been touched.

Round-faced Merin had drunk her concoction, but he had only finished half of it. He might become sleepy; he might become ill.

Or nothing might happen at all.

———

The steady thud reverberated throughout the prisoners' quarters. There was no way to escape the regular, pounding rhythm. The roar of the crowd filled the spaces in between, louder than ever before. Humans and bax alike looked up at the ceiling as if worried it would cave in.

Two guards came to the gate that connected the prisoners' quarters to the fighting pit. Resting as much as possible before the fight, Taimin recognized Lewin's lanky figure. He wondered if the heavyset guard beside Lewin was also part of Elsa's conspiracy.

"It's time!" Lewin called. He nearly had to shout to be heard above the din.

Taimin stood, stretched, and loosened his shoulders, rolling his head from side to side.

He was surprised to realize that the fear that had been gnawing at his stomach had vanished. What he now felt was determination. The anticipation had been the worst part. Now the wait was over. He would soon face his enemy.

All of the other prisoners had assembled near the gate. More than twenty humans and a smaller number of bax stood together. Rathis and Lars were at the front of the group.

Vance spoke from Taimin's side. "Rathis and I will walk with you. Lars too—"

"No," Taimin said, low enough that he wouldn't be overheard. His attention was on the two guards on the other side of the gate. "Everyone's on edge. The guards can probably sense it. It's better I walk alone."

Vance let out a breath and then nodded. "Fair enough. Just be careful out there."

"I will."

Taimin squeezed Vance's shoulder before he reached the other prisoners. He swept his gaze over them all. For the guards' benefit, he kept his face expressionless. He would do nothing to give away that those surrounding him might soon be fighting as well.

"Good luck," Lars said. His face was deadly serious. "Survive."

"Let fortune guide your blade," said Rathis.

"Strength to your sword arm," said one of the bax.

Taimin walked toward the gate, nodding to everyone he passed. The guards hauled the gate open and he strode through. He heard a loud clang behind him.

The din in the arena grew even louder as he followed the corridor. The sloped floor climbed upward, heading to the archway and the portcullis, which was already raised. Golden light poured down and made him squint. His boots crunched on the first grains of sand as he neared the archway. The crowd was so loud that he couldn't distinguish the voices. High-pitched and low-pitched cries mingled with the boots pounding on the tiers that formed the arena's seating.

As Taimin took the last few steps toward the archway, one of the last pair of guards handed out a sword. Taimin's fingers closed tightly on the hilt. He sliced at the air. It was early afternoon and the combined ferocity of the two suns seared his vision. As ready as he would ever be, he walked through the archway and stepped out into the open air.

The crowd saw him. He held his sword high. The roar was deafening.

Taimin blinked in the bright sunlight but soon his vision cleared. Countless faces surrounded him, watching his every move, but he banished the crowd from his awareness. He came to a halt on the sand of the fighting pit. Gradually the faces of the people faded away. The shouts became muted.

He forced himself to remember his parents' deaths.

An arrow had plunged into his mother's cheek. She had once pressed her cheek against his when he was a child. Galen's sword had entered Taimin's father's chest. Gareth had been a gentle man.

Taimin returned his attention to the fighting pit.

He fixed his gaze on the single, solitary man in the center of the sandy floor. Galen wore leather armor and held his shining steel sword in front of him. The sharp blade reflected the bright sunlight. Galen's angular face was like stone as he returned Taimin's stare.

Taimin wondered what trick Galen would employ to win. Or could Galen's honor, the reason he had accepted Taimin's challenge, lead him to make it a fair fight?

Whatever happened today would decide the fate of the city. Taimin glanced around the arena and took in the tall wooden fence that separated the fighting pit from the crowd. The prison guards who usually manned the fence were gone. Instead, Taimin saw Galen's uniformed soldiers on the fence's other side, watching carefully. They were all armed with bows.

He looked higher. Scanning past the wide exits located on both sides of the oval-shaped arena, his eyes roved over the crowd and then he saw them: the rest of Galen's men. As expected, every soldier was present to see his commander fight. They sat together, not far from one of the stairways. A wide gap separated the soldiers from the common folk nearby. In their crimson uniforms they were easily picked out from the people around them.

Taimin continued to scan the tiers of benches.

His heart thudded in his chest.

Selena was in the same place she had been last time. Her face was pale, framed by her black hair. She looked afraid.

Galen called out. "Ready to die, cripple?"

Taimin didn't reply. Instead, he inspected the terrain. His gaze traveled over the sand as he looked for small depressions and crests, taking note of where he might trip or gain an advantage.

"I can read the thoughts on your face," Galen said, speaking for him alone. "You are wondering if the fight is going to be fair." As Taimin focused on his enemy once more, Galen smiled. "As you can see, I have the protection of armor." He brandished his sword. "I have my steel and you have hardwood. There is some advantage, but that was always to be expected."

Galen took a step toward Taimin, who held his ground. Taimin's palms felt sweaty. He gripped the hilt of his sword, holding it warily in front of him.

Galen's lip curled. "The people don't want to see me defeat a man who has been poisoned or had his fingers broken. But I will kill you," he said. "Look at your woman, the mystic. Do you see her?"

Taimin glanced again at Selena. She was on one of the highest tiers, between two men, one with a pinched face, the other stocky. The Protector himself, a well-dressed older man with neatly combed hair, sat beside the stocky man and leaned forward as he watched. The Protector's group was located above Galen's soldiers, also separate from the rest of the crowd.

Galen continued, "What not even the Protector knows is that one of my men is seated behind the girl. Do you see him? The one with the scar on his face." Taimin spied him immediately. The tall soldier with the pale line on his cheek was on the tier behind Selena. He was a few feet from her, but it would be simple for him to move closer.

"I am sure you want to know what orders I have given him," Galen said. When Taimin didn't reply, Galen's eyes narrowed. "If my blood is drawn, he is to kill the girl with a knife in the back. He plans to retire with family, settlers far from here. If he has to do it, my men will help him escape." Galen spoke with ferocity. "You are going to let me win. Do you understand me? Fight badly. If you draw my blood, she dies."

Taimin tried not to show any emotion as thoughts whirled through his mind. He heard a trumpet blare as the herald entered the fighting pit to address the crowd.

"Today, my people, I, the Protector of Zorn, gazed out from the Great Tower. As I searched the lands around our fair city . . ."

The herald followed the same pattern he always did, but then, at the point where the Protector stood and waved at the citizens, Taimin looked up sharply.

Angry murmurs swelled up from the seating gallery. The Protector looked surprised before he sat back down. The soldiers on the tiers below him turned their heads to search for where the raised voices were coming from. The crowd became still once more.

Taimin returned to his predicament.

Tension filled every part of his body. Galen had set a neat trap. Taimin had thought that, whatever the commander did, it would be done to him. He hadn't expected Selena to be threatened. She was obviously important to the Protector. One thing he knew, though, was that Galen meant what he had said.

He considered the plan he had made with Elsa. If she lived up to her word, in the crowd were rebels who were willing and able to fight. Every member of the city guard was here, without their wyverns, and Elsa had promised that any isolated soldiers in the city would be dealt with.

This opportunity would never come again. When the bout between Taimin and Galen was at its peak, the guard Lewin would free the prisoners, and Vance, Rathis, and Lars would lead them into the fighting pit. When they saw their commander about to be overwhelmed, the soldiers of the city guard would come running to his aid. Then Elsa's supporters in the crowd would rise up. It was a good plan.

But what would happen to Selena? Taimin couldn't fight while she was in danger. He would barely be able to defend himself, fearful that he would draw Galen's blood and she would die.

He had to find a way to neutralize the threat.

The trumpet blared. The crowd roared. Taimin readied himself.

The fight had begun.

Galen came in, sword held out in front of him, and Taimin retreated. Galen hacked down with his blade but Taimin stepped to the side. The two men circled each other. People in the crowd shouted Taimin's name, calling encouragement, but he knew he couldn't allow himself to be distracted.

What could he do to help Selena?

A bow. He needed a bow. Abi had always said he was a fine shot.

He watched Galen and continued to move to the edge of the fighting pit; his goal was to bring himself closer to where Selena sat with the Protector's group. Casting a swift glance up, he gauged the distance to the tall man with the scar on his face. The scar-faced soldier looked impossibly far away.

Focus on one problem at a time, Abi had always said.

He needed a bow.

38

Selena never heard what Taimin and Galen said to each other, but she saw him look her way more than once. It was Galen who did the talking, despite the fact that Taimin had his own reasons for wanting to see his enemy fall at his feet.

For the first time in her life, Selena wanted a man to die. The sensation came from deep in her chest. She had seen Galen and his men ride out on their wyverns and slaughter anything that moved. If she hadn't broken her lifeline, the city guard would have slaughtered a human family, for nothing more than trading with the bax in the Rift Valley.

Now Galen was facing Taimin in a fight that would see only one of them leave the arena alive.

As the two men circled each other, Galen's movements were fluid, despite the fact that he was more than a decade older than Taimin. In comparison, Taimin's limp was pronounced.

Galen attacked and Taimin weaved. Quick as a snake, Galen thrust again and Taimin dodged to the side. The crowd bellowed at the two combatants. Selena heard Taimin's name from all quarters. It was clear that he had the support of the people. Taimin continued to retreat and evade his enemy. Why wasn't he fighting back?

Selena leaned forward in her seat. She pressed her fingernails into her palms. Her mouth was dry. She turned her head to glance first at Arren, and then Merin. If either of them had drunk Ruth's drugged tea, it wasn't evident in their faces.

The last time Selena had broken free of the wall that kept her power confined, she had been able to take the two mystics by surprise. They would be prepared if she tried to repeat the same feat. As a test, she tried to reach her symbol, but as soon as she took hold of it, the wall closed in, like a fist closing over a candle flame.

The crowd roared as Taimin kicked sand into Galen's eyes. It was skillfully done, stunning Galen for a short time, yet Taimin didn't follow it up with an attack.

Selena tried to access her power again. She gritted her teeth and poured her frustration into the radiance inside her mind. The symbol swelled. Arren glanced at her. His narrow face broke out in a dark smile.

There was nothing Selena could do but hope.

"You can do it, Taimin," she whispered under her breath. "You can beat him."

Taimin was desperate. Without a bow he would never remove the threat to Selena. The sand of the fighting pit had been churned up, yet there had barely been an exchange of blows. After evading Galen's successive attacks, Taimin had managed to draw his opponent close to the fence. He continued to back away, never taking his eyes off the older man with the close-cropped white hair.

Taimin's heel struck something hard with a jolt. He was at the fence and could go no farther. But he might now have a chance. On the other side of the barrier was a soldier with a bow. Yet Taimin was in an impossible position. Galen was a skilled warrior and watched him constantly, looking for an opportunity to strike. Taimin would never have time to climb the fence and throw himself over.

"What is your plan, cripple?" Galen sneered. "Hide from me until something comes up?"

As soon as he finished speaking, Galen slashed his sword at Taimin's face. Taimin ducked and tried to weave but Galen changed his approach and his next blow was a straight thrust at Taimin's stomach. Taimin dodged, but he was trying too hard to stay close to the fence and the promise of the bow on the other side. He felt a sharp sting as Galen's steel blade bit into his side.

He managed to create some space between them and gasped. He put a hand to his side and felt wetness, but didn't know how deep the wound was. Of the two of them, Galen was now closer to the fence. Taimin couldn't fight back unless he knew Selena was safe. The constant evasion was taking its toll, and the pain in his foot was already fiery, as if a hot poker was being pressed between his ruined toes. He had yet to even attempt to strike his opponent.

"Fight, Taimin, fight!" a voice roared from the crowd.

"You can do it!"

Taimin's desperation shifted to despair. His situation was impossible. He couldn't risk drawing Galen's blood; if he did Selena would die. Even if he had a bow, it was a difficult shot, and there was a chance that he might hit Selena, rather than the scar-faced soldier.

He knew he was letting down everyone, including Vance, Lars, Rathis, and all the other prisoners. The rebellion was supposed to begin when the duel was at its peak. He was expected to fight back.

Galen came forward with his sword held out in front of him. Taimin was forced to give up on his idea of somehow scaling the fence. There were gates, but he would never get through them before he was cut down from behind. Galen launched a flurry of blows, and Taimin had no choice but to raise his sword to block. Each time Galen swung at him, Taimin took a step back and the steel sword clashed against his own blade of hardwood. Fear was constantly with him. He was terrified that he would accidentally hurt Galen and Selena would be killed. He was thinking too hard about how to save her, and his lack of concentration made it easy for Galen to find holes in his defense.

Galen dropped low and cut at Taimin's leg. Remembering his training, Taimin leaped to the side but his crippled foot flared up, causing him to stumble.

He gasped with pain and rolled on the ground. Bringing himself to one knee, he had no choice but to raise his sword horizontally as Galen hacked at him with a strong overhead blow. Galen continued to press his advantage and, pinned on the sandy floor, Taimin saw the triumph in his opponent's eyes. Taimin blocked two more strikes. The last came within inches of his face. The muscles in his arms groaned; he couldn't hold his sword up forever. Galen had the advantage of a higher position and it was easier swinging from above.

Everything slowed down. Taimin was acutely aware of his surroundings. The two suns glared from high in the sky, silhouetting Galen's body. Taimin was forced to squint as sweat trickled down his forehead. The crowd roared, calling on him to do something. He wasn't just fighting for his life, or trying to destroy his enemy. He was fighting for the city's soul.

Elsa's followers would be watching. It wasn't the fight they had been expecting, but perhaps, when they saw Taimin die, they would realize that the time to take action had come. Perhaps Selena might escape in the chaos and confusion. There was nothing Taimin could do to save himself.

Despite his burning arms, Taimin held his sword high. His face was grim and his jaw was set. Galen's next strike would be a killing blow.

He heard a piercing shriek.

The sound was beastly, so out of place that it cut through the roar of the crowd. Taimin was looking into the light. The glare affected his vision, but he was sure he saw two broad wings that became larger and larger. Spread wide, the wings swept down at the air. The winged creature was directly behind Galen, approaching with formidable speed.

Galen's eyes went wide. He began to turn.

The wyvern struck him with force.

Taimin dived to the side at the same time that the creature and Galen tumbled together. The wyvern's grasping claws hit Galen's shoulders but scraped against his leather armor and lost purchase. Despite his shock, Galen was wise enough to roll again and again, taking himself away from his assailant.

The wyvern's wings slapped against the sand as it hovered. The creature's eyes narrowed as it faced the commander and gave another piercing shriek.

Taimin straightened. He was alive, and he still had his sword. He remembered that one of the city guard's wyverns had escaped. But why was it helping him?

The wyvern's gaze moved. The creature never stopped facing the armored soldier it had just knocked down, but brown eyes met Taimin's. The wyvern had a long, narrow face, pricked ears, and a rust-colored body. But Taimin knew those eyes.

"Griff?" Taimin asked in disbelief.

The wherry had transformed.

39

Despite his gratitude and joy at seeing Griff alive and well, Taimin knew he had to make Griff leave. He felt like he was failing his old friend, who had just saved his life once again. But if Galen was killed, Selena would die too.

Stunned to be facing an angry wyvern, Galen returned to his feet and held his steel sword in front of him. Griff snarled. The wyvern's wings stirred up the sand.

"No!" Taimin cried. Griff took his eyes off Galen to look at Taimin in confusion. "No," Taimin repeated. He made a pushing motion with his hands. "Go!"

Perplexed, Griff climbed into the air. A moment later a gate in the perimeter fence crashed open. Three of Galen's men rushed in. They were already fitting arrows to bowstrings.

"Go!" Taimin bellowed.

As Griff spread his wings and gave another piercing shriek, he gave Taimin a last look before swiftly gaining height. As arrows followed him, one struck his underside but bounced off his tough hide. The wyvern flew higher into the sky and swept his wings furiously until he was soaring above the city.

The crowd stirred. People exchanged stunned glances. A wyvern was loose in the city, and the creature was prepared to attack people. They no longer shouted; instead they began to look uncertain.

Meanwhile, Taimin realized that he and Galen were no longer alone in the fighting pit. His heart pounded as he focused on the three bowmen. He then glanced up at Selena. Galen wasn't close. This was his chance.

With the three archers' attention on Griff, Taimin started to run. Still holding his sword, he brought on every bit of speed he could and prayed his leg wouldn't give out. The distance narrowed to the nearest of the bowmen, a stocky soldier with thick black eyebrows. The soldier turned, too late. His eyes widened.

Taimin crashed into the soldier and brought him to the ground. As they rolled together, both trying to get the upper hand, Taimin caught brief flashes of his surroundings. He saw Galen racing toward him. The other two archers were preparing new arrows, but they couldn't shoot with Taimin so close to one of their own.

Taimin dropped his sword and wrapped his hand around the thickest section of his opponent's bow. He then brought his knee into the stocky man's stomach. Breath came out of the man in a whoosh. The soldier crumpled, and as he went down, Taimin yanked an arrow from the man's quiver.

Taimin's back itched as he straightened and fitted an arrow at the same time. He drew in a fluid motion and looked up at the tiered benches above the fighting pit. His focus narrowed on the tall soldier with the scar on his face, seated behind Selena. He knew he might kill her, but he couldn't think about what could go wrong.

He held his breath. His arms tensed for a heartbeat before he released.

The arrow flew faster than the eye could follow. An instant later the scar-faced soldier fell back and his hands went up to grip the shaft that sprouted from his neck. The arrow was swift and Selena's assassin tumbled backward without a cry. Only those nearby realized what had happened. Most people in the crowd would think that Taimin had fumbled and loosed a wild arrow.

As soon as he had shot the arrow, Taimin grabbed the stocky soldier and lifted him up. It gave him the protection he needed as two arrows plunged into the man's body. Taimin then reached for the quiver on the dead man's shoulder and took out a second arrow. While one of the soldiers frantically tried to prepare another shot, Taimin's arrow took him down.

A dive and roll took Taimin out of harm's way while another arrow sank into the sand. He had intentionally brought himself closer to his discarded sword. With no more arrows, he swiftly made the exchange. He charged the last archer and thrust his sword into the soldier's chest. The man fell with a cry.

Taimin whirled. He saw Galen racing toward him with his steel sword ready to strike. Taimin took a few steps to the side, moving away from the hazard of fallen bodies, and raised his own weapon.

The two swords crashed together. The crowd roared. They had just seen Taimin defeat three men in quick succession. Hundreds of people were on their feet.

Taimin and Galen circled each other, but there was a different mood now. The two men locked eyes, seeking weakness.

This time, it was Taimin who attacked. He cut at Galen's head, before shifting to thrust at the commander's body. Galen stepped to the side, but not before the sharp edge of the sword sliced through his leather armor and opened up a gash in his abdomen.

Both Taimin and Galen were out of breath. Sweat coated Taimin's forehead. But he wasn't about to falter. This was his chance. Selena was safe. He could end this.

Taimin moved forward, and now it was Galen backing away. A shift to the left made Galen's guard come up, but then Taimin lunged to the right and came in from a place where Galen wasn't expecting him to be.

Taimin found his opening. He thrust directly into his enemy's torso. Galen brushed his sword away but was awkward on his feet and exposed to a follow-up attack.

A series of cries and bellows came from the crowd. The sounds were out of place and mostly lost in the roar of the onlookers, but Galen's eyes widened as he looked past Taimin's shoulder.

Taimin risked a swift glance. In the heat of the moment, he had forgotten all about the plan he had made with Elsa.

———

In the prisoners' quarters, no one spoke. Everyone sat on a bed. All eyes were raised to look up at the ceiling.

Vance glanced at Lars, who shuffled restlessly on the pallet opposite. He and Lars exchanged grim expressions when the sound from above became deafening.

"By the rains," Lars said, breaking the silence. "I wish I could see what was happening out there." The crowd roared again. "He could be dead already for all we know."

Vance looked toward the gate that led to the fighting pit, but there was no one standing on the other side. Lewin must be watching the duel. He returned his attention to Lars. "You've seen him fight?"

Lars nodded. "Aye. I have. Still—"

"Have faith," Rathis called from across the room.

Vance almost jumped when the commotion outside became even greater. He heard a piercing shriek. The cry was beastly in nature.

"Burn me, what was that?" Lars's mouth dropped open.

Vance turned to gaze across the room. The prisoners who met his eyes shook their heads. "If you don't know, then neither do I," he said.

Lars's voice was incredulous. "If I didn't know better, I'd say it was a wyvern."

"Is it time? Should we go?" Vance asked. He could hear the worry in his own voice.

"How would I know?" Lars glared back at him. "You're in charge here."

"Rathis?" Vance called across the room. He extended his address to all of the prisoners watching him. "All of you? Is it time?"

No one replied. But then the crowd roared and the powerful sound made Vance's heart race. He took a deep breath as urgency pulsed through his veins. He realized that if he was in charge, he had to lead.

Vance climbed to his feet. All of the prisoners were now watching him, waiting for him to speak. Another breath steadied his nerves. He swept his gaze over everyone in the long room. "It's time!" he called.

They all stood as one. Hands reached under bed pallets to take out the motley assortment of weapons smuggled in the previous night. Vance retrieved a sword. Lars hefted an axe with a half-moon blade.

Vance hurried to the gate that led to the fighting pit. As the crowd bellowed in the arena, the prisoners fell in behind him, one after the other.

Someone approached the gate, and behind it Vance recognized the guard Lewin's lanky figure. Lewin headed right up to the gate. Vance held his breath, but then Lewin rattled the bolt holding the gate fastened and hauled it open.

Lewin stood to the side.

Vance lifted his sword, and then he started to run. Blood roared in his ears. He was terrified, but he had never felt so alive. With a cry he led his fellow prisoners through the gate and headed directly for the fighting pit.

Galen's eyes were wide open as he stared past Taimin's shoulder.

Taimin realized the time had come.

With a series of bellows, close to thirty arena fighters raced into the pit. Vance led from the front, waving his sword over his head like a madman. They knew the plan and spread out as soon as they entered. Taimin watched fighter after fighter rush over to join him. In moments he had a collection of allies arrayed around him, a large group that stood and faced the solitary commander of the city guard.

Taimin watched Galen carefully. He and the commander still held their swords in front of them, but there was a momentary lull. The crowd had fallen silent.

Galen looked uncertain. The white-haired soldier found himself up against an overwhelming number of fighters. The prisoners stood ready with their clubs, swords, axes, and daggers. The bax in the group glared at the commander of the city guard.

Galen took a step back.

Taimin could have overwhelmed his enemy. He wanted to, desperately. But he waited. The city's fate was more important than vengeance.

Now it was Taimin's turn to smile.

The crowd stirred. Murmurs became louder, and more than a few people began to leave their seats and stream toward the exits. Taimin watched them go; they were the wealthy citizens who fled; those in bright-colored clothes. No one would stop them.

As expected, Galen turned and called for help.

"Men!" Galen beckoned to the uniformed soldiers, calling them down to the fighting pit. The city guard would never let any prisoners escape. Galen's men would come to their commander's aid.

Dozens of uniformed figures were already running. Row after row emptied out. The gate in the barrier fence crashed open. Soon the soldiers were rushing to fill the sandy floor.

Still Taimin waited, even though it felt wrong to allow Galen's men to gather. There were more soldiers than there were prisoners, and despite the fact that many of the prisoners were skilled fighters, the soldiers were trained and better armed.

As the soldiers formed ranks, raised voices filled the air with panic. More citizens on the upper tiers left their seats and pushed against each other as they tried to reach the nearest way out.

But not everyone tried to flee. The Protector, Selena, and the two men who flanked her still remained seated. The soldiers had all left their places, which meant that Taimin could see the Protector clearly. The Protector's brow was furrowed in an angry glare. Evidently he could see that Taimin's group was outnumbered, and was waiting for Galen to take care of the situation.

Taimin turned his attention to the lower tiers. He braced himself. If Elsa's rebels decided to flee rather than fight, Taimin's group would be overwhelmed. He could see some of the poorer folk heading for the nearest exit. He gritted his teeth. They couldn't go. This was their time.

Galen had regained some of his confidence. The last of his men had entered the fighting pit. He rested his gaze on Taimin and opened his mouth, no doubt to order the attack.

Taimin knew he couldn't wait any longer.

He raised his sword and sucked in a deep lungful of air. His voice had to be loud enough to be heard above the cacophony. "People of Zorn! This is your time. Rise up and join us!"

As soon as Taimin finished, Galen cast him a look of dry humor.

Taimin turned his head to stare in all directions. Disappointment was like a heavy stone in his stomach.

No one was coming to his aid.

40

"I feel ill," Merin said in a weak voice.

Arren gave Merin a look of contempt. "Have some faith. Galen will sort this out."

As Taimin called on the citizens, all Selena knew was that she had to help him. The soldiers outnumbered the prisoners. The people in the crowd were afraid.

Selena used her rage to feed the power that was walled off in her mind. She thought about Galen, who had burned bax settlements, butchered their infants, and thrown prisoners into the arena to fight and die. The Protector's worst crimes were perpetrated against his own people. He had lied to them, and incited a war, simply so he could maintain power.

The fiery inferno that was her symbol grew larger and larger. With Merin weak, the wall that she pushed against wasn't as strong as it had been before. She clenched her jaw tightly as Taimin's desperate face searched the crowd. Stars sparkled in her vision. The wall tried to close in, but hers was a fire that could not be extinguished. Her symbol grew bigger and brighter, a great sun that overwhelmed her senses.

The wall burst into nothingness. Selena was free.

Arren cried out.

Outside her body, Selena flew toward the one man she cared about.

Taimin's eyes widened as Selena's voice spoke inside his mind. As soon as she had finished, he thrust out an arm to point at the Protector.

"The well is dry," he shouted. "There is no water in the tower at all." He continued to single out the Protector. "Ask him!"

Heads turned sharply to focus on the Protector. Even Galen faltered, and glanced over his shoulder to see what the Protector would say or do.

The Protector slowly stood. Tall, proud, and stern, he opened his arms to address his people directly.

But before he could begin, a man's voice cried from somewhere in the crowd. "We want to see!"

The shout was taken up again, until it came from all quarters. "We want to see!"

The Protector's hesitation was obvious. He raised his arms higher. Even as the prisoners and soldiers still faced each other across the fighting pit, everyone waited to hear his words.

"There is water in the Rift Valley—"

The Protector never finished what he was going to say. All around, the people closest to the fighting pit gave a loud roar. Suddenly they held weapons, ranging from cudgels to kitchen knives. Matching blue arm bands decorated every sleeve.

Taimin cast another swift look in the Protector's direction when he saw a commotion involving Selena. The flash of steel made his heart beat out of time.

Then Galen called to his men. "Attack!"

As soon as Selena had returned to her body, Arren tried to grab her, but she knocked him back. Determination fired through her veins. If she could get away, she would be free to join the uprising.

"Merin, help!" Arren grunted. But Merin had his hands at his temples. His eyes were confused.

With Arren off balance, Selena saw a dagger still held in the hand of the dead soldier Taimin had shot. She lunged to the tier behind her and fumbled for the hilt.

Arren wrapped his wiry arms around her and pulled her toward him.

All of a sudden, the narrow-faced mystic grunted. He looked down, toward his chest, at the dagger gripped in Selena's hand. He didn't make a sound, but his entire body relaxed, shoulders slumping as he crumpled.

Momentarily stunned by what she had done, Selena turned and saw a flash of the Protector's face. Something crashed into her head.

"Grab her." The Protector's voice sounded muffled. "Arren is dead. Leave him."

The prisoners rushed forward. More than twice their number of soldiers charged. The two groups collided.

Taimin tried to get to Galen but a soldier with broad shoulders attacked and he found himself engaged, parrying until he saw an opening and took his opponent down. Nearby, Vance roared and dispatched a scar-faced soldier with a feint and thrust. Bax smashed into the men who had slaughtered their friends and families. Lars swung a wicked-looking axe into a crimson-clad soldier's chest.

As Taimin tried to cut a path through to Galen, he reminded himself of the refugees on the plain, and the things the bax had told him. In his peripheral vision he saw bax hack and grunt as they battled their enemies. Fighters on both sides cried out in pain when blows struck home. Soldiers tripped on the uneven sand. Prisoners gasped as swords entered their chests.

Taimin defeated another opponent but after just a short time the superior number of soldiers began to tell. Around him his companions were being pushed back. Vance was under pressure, up against two soldiers at once. The bax fought together at the front, in a cluster that grew ever smaller. One bax fell, then another. Soon there was only one bax fighting. A sword plunged into his torso, and he fell too.

Then everything changed.

Taimin had forgotten the rebels.

People from the crowd reached the battle and immediately enveloped the soldiers. The prisoners took heart and renewed their efforts; soon it was the uniformed soldiers who were giving ground. The newcomers were a range of ages and their weapons were improvised. But they had numbers.

Taimin caught sight of Galen.

A patch of ground cleared between them. Everything else diminished in Taimin's perception. Galen thrust his sword into a youth's chest. He then turned and his eyes narrowed when he saw Taimin.

Taimin gripped the hilt of his hardwood sword in both hands. The point of Galen's steel blade went up.

Taimin reflected on his constant practice with Abi. She had drilled the moves into him over and over again. She taught him how to move in deft, unpredictable ways, despite his impediment.

He attacked.

He slashed with his sword. Galen's sword followed his movement, and the two weapons collided. The sharp steel bit into the wood but Taimin's blade held. The two men soon stood chest to chest, teeth gritted, eyes glaring.

Taimin put his weight onto his bad leg. The pain was excruciating, but he knew how to bear it. He freed up his other leg and smashed his boot into Galen's ankle. Galen gave a cry of pain but was too experienced to shift his posture. Instead, Galen pushed back in an attempt to throw Taimin from their locked position.

Taimin was expecting it. He rolled with the motion, but rather than fall back he dropped. Galen's sword arced down over his head, but Taimin was still moving and the steel blade struck the sand.

With the older man overextended, Taimin was now inside Galen's reach.

Taimin gripped the hilt of his sword with both hands and brought the point up as he straightened. The blade entered his enemy's chest, penetrated the leather armor, and continued. Abi had always taught Taimin to never falter, to stay committed until his enemy was down. Taimin kept pushing, and his sword slid through to emerge on the other side of Galen's body.

Galen gasped and staggered. The sword dropped out of his hands. He looked down at his chest and the blade buried in his body.

Taimin held fast. Galen took another step backward. As the hardwood blade left his body, he pressed his hands against the gaping wound in his chest.

Galen collapsed.

Taimin took a deep breath as he stared at the commander's lifeless body. His enemy was dead.

He swiftly took stock of his surroundings. Fighters surged back and forth. Bodies lay scattered across the sand. A final pocket of resistance held out, but it was clear that soon the last of the soldiers would fall. Now the most experienced arena fighters threw themselves at the last members of the city guard standing. Lars barreled into a stocky soldier and knocked him down before finishing him off with the axe. The big skinner stood with his chest heaving.

There was no one left to fight.

The two groups had now merged. Prisoners and rebels mingled together as they slowly lowered their weapons. Everyone exchanged glances, shaken by the experience.

"Well?" Lars called out to Taimin. "What now?"

Taimin was surprised when everyone turned to face him. It felt strange when he became the focus of attention, having them look to him for leadership. He didn't know them, but they expected him to know what to do.

The city guard was gone. Galen had fallen, but the Protector still lived. Taimin opened his mouth to call on everyone to head to the tower.

But then he heard a cry. He raised his gaze and saw a dark-haired youth on one of the stairways. The newcomer raced down the arena's empty seating gallery, heading directly for the fighting pit. As some of the rebels exchanged worried glances, Taimin saw that the youth wore a blue armband.

The boy pushed through the crowd. "Taimin . . ." he panted.

"What is it?" Taimin asked.

The youth was breathing so hard that he struggled to speak. "He's here."

"Who?" asked one of the rebels, an older man with a balding crown and a thick neck.

The youth spoke only one word: "Blixen."

41

Out in the streets people were screaming. When Taimin had first been led through the city it had been bustling but orderly. Now citizens raced in all directions, shouting to one another to flee. Parents burdened with their possessions herded children toward the gates.

"We have to leave!" a bearded man bellowed as he raced into a white-walled house.

"Joram? Where are you? Joram!" a matronly woman cried while she ran past.

Surrounded by rebels and former prisoners, Taimin took it all in. His large group was in the shadow of the looming arena and had come to a halt, stunned by what they were seeing.

Not everyone was looking to escape. Taimin saw an old laborer in dusty clothing grab hold of the people he passed, calling on them to help with the city's defense. A yellow-haired woman with a determined expression strode toward the gates with a bow in her hand and a quiver on her shoulder. Some of the people with weapons wore blue armbands, but many were common folk, frightened but prepared to fight for their homes. The number of citizens heading in the same direction increased by the moment. Taimin knew there would be even more panicked people in the main avenue connecting the tower and the gates. There was only one way in or out of the city.

Taimin turned and watched as a dozen men of all ages ran together, armed with clubs, swords, and spears. The burly man leading the group called out to everyone who could hear him. "Save our city!" He saw Taimin's group and waved his arm over his head. "Come on! You're needed at the wall!"

The man was right; Taimin had a large group of fighters with him. If Blixen attacked, they would undoubtedly be needed to help with the city's defense.

But any chance of peace with Blixen depended on ending the Protector's rule.

Taimin addressed Rathis. "Find Elsa," he said. "She'll be at the gates. This is what we were worried about. Blixen has come too soon." He moved his gaze to take in all of the rebels in blue armbands. "All of you, go with him."

"What do I tell Elsa?" Rathis asked.

"If the city was already under attack, we would know about it. Just try to keep the situation calm. I'll be there as soon as I can." Taimin indicated for Lars, Vance, and half a dozen former prisoners to follow him. "Come on," he said. "We're going to the tower."

As Taimin hurried along, flanked by his companions, he set his sights on the tall structure that dominated the city. Shouts continued to come from all directions. A sea of people streamed toward the gates.

The Protector hadn't waited to see the outcome of the battle between Taimin's group of prisoners and Galen's larger number of soldiers. He had left the arena and taken Selena with him. Taimin had to get to the tower before the Protector learned about the successful uprising.

Taimin kept his gaze fixed on the tower's summit. He and his companions turned into a side street, and the tower was perfectly framed by the rows of houses, distant but directly ahead of him. Desperation drove him on.

———————

The Protector threw Selena into the hard-backed wooden chair that was the focus of the observation room. Seeing that she was still groggy after he had cracked her over the head with the hilt of his dagger, he shook her shoulders, hard. She stirred, blinked several times, and then looked up sharply. From her expression, he knew that she had realized where she was.

"Use her," the Protector snapped at Merin. The round-faced, stocky mystic had already staggered over to the desk and leaned against it. Merin's face was pale. "Get her to convince the people that I am still in charge of this city."

Merin was breathing heavily. He shook his head. "It doesn't work like that. There are limits to what a mystic can do."

The Protector made a sound of disgust and walked away, leaving Selena where she was. He strode to the edge of the floor and watched the streets, before moving to get a different view. With his feet close to the drop, he held on to one of the columns supporting the ceiling and peered down at the plaza.

Four uniformed soldiers stood guard far below, outside the tower's entrance. The bodies of rebels and soldiers alike sprawled across the paving stones nearby. The attack had come while the Protector was at the arena, but his men still held the tower.

Then, as he raised his eyes, he saw something else that seized his attention.

He squinted past the wall to stare farther into the distance. The flat plain was tainted orange in the afternoon light. His breath caught as he saw a multitude of dark specks on the horizon. The specks were moving toward the city. Blixen's army would soon be at the gates.

"Protector, we should leave," Merin said.

The Protector glared at the round-faced mystic. "Galen will survive, you will see. When Blixen comes, the people will turn to me for help, and this uprising will be over."

Merin's expression was doubtful. The Protector's gaze moved to Selena when she spoke up.

"You know it's over," she said. She held his stare. "Let me go."

The Protector scowled. He returned to scanning the streets, wondering where Galen was, but then Merin cleared his throat.

"We might have to do what she says," Merin said.

"Eh?"

"I can't control her on my own. She has become too powerful. Without Arren . . ." Merin trailed off.

The Protector gave Selena a humorless smile. He indicated the empty void that the observation room opened onto. "If you want to leave, I have a suggestion for you."

A piercing shriek split the air. The Protector saw a flash of wings, and the outline of a lean creature with a tapered head, before it was gone from sight, curling around the other side of the tower.

"It's that wyvern," Merin said.

Selena stood.

The Protector watched, perplexed, as she walked to the edge of the floor. She stood on the verge of the precipice and her expression was thoughtful. While he looked on, the set of her jaw became more determined. For a time, she stood and stared down at the white city below.

The Protector and Merin exchanged glances.

"She might actually do it?" Merin asked incredulously.

The Protector began to walk toward her. "Selena," he said. "If you serve me, I will give you anything you want."

Selena turned back to him. "There is nothing you have that I want."

Her legs bunched. She tilted her body forward.

The Protector gasped as she gathered herself and dived.

⸻

Taimin had reached the city's main avenue and was watching the tower when it happened.

He saw a figure dive from the tower and recognized Selena. A tall, gray-haired man—the Protector—stood framed by the columns she had leaped between.

Taimin's entire world came crashing down around him. The Protector had pushed her. She had risked everything to give Taimin the information he needed to launch the uprising. She had paid the ultimate price.

Time slowed as Taimin stood in complete shock. Vance, Lars, and everyone around him disappeared from his perception. There were no people running, no stone buildings on the street he had been racing along. There was just a tower, and a woman falling to her death.

But even as Selena fell, a wyvern came up from underneath her.

Selena struck the wyvern's back. Between the wyvern's sweeping wings and Selena's scrabbling limbs, Taimin couldn't make out what was happening.

Then Griff steadied himself.

The setting sun was in Taimin's eyes, but there, above the white structures of Zorn, he was sure he could see Selena's silhouette as she rode on Griff's back. He shielded his gaze and stared intently. Griff's wings moved up and down. Taimin heard a piercing shriek.

The wyvern turned on the tip of his wing, tilting away from the orange sun.

Taimin saw Selena.

Relief flooded through him. She was alive. He hadn't been able to help her, but she had helped herself. Griff knew her and would take care of her.

She was free.

42

A swell of panicked voices seized Taimin's attention. As he stood in the middle of the broad avenue, the loud cries and shouts came from the city gates. He saw a great crowd pushed up against the wall. The pair of tall wooden gates, several inches thick, remained tightly closed and barred with stout timber.

Selena might be safe, but the city was still in danger.

Taimin had an idea, and immediately turned to Vance and Lars. "The Protector is in the tower." He directed his words to the entire group. "I need you to secure the entrance. Don't enter. Just make sure no one goes in or out."

Vance gave a puzzled nod. "Sure." He met Taimin's eyes. "Where are you going?"

"To do what I can."

Taimin burst into the fastest run he could manage. The cries of the crowd grew louder. He began to make out individual figures. People were shouting. The crowd surged back and forth. Soon he heard both men's and women's screams.

"Open the gates!"

"It's too late, Blixen's already here!"

"Let me out!"

Children wailed. Fear was on every face as Taimin plunged into the crowd. The frantic people pushed back and forth. He turned his body to the side as he worked his way through, heading toward the wall of white stone, and the diagonal stairway leading up to the wall's summit.

Taimin began to climb. He swiftly gained height as he lifted himself up one step after the other. With the shouts swelling below him, he moved onto the top of the wall. From his new position, thirty feet above the ground, he came to a halt and stood alone, a solitary figure framed against the sky. He looked down from his height at the city folk below.

People turned and saw him. A middle-aged man, holding a child in his arms, called out, "It's Taimin!"

The name bounced throughout the crowd until every head had turned and then tilted back to look up at him. Gradually, the panicked cries fell silent. The surging motion stopped.

Taimin saw a sea of faces; these were the same people who had watched him fight in the arena. Many held weapons; they were prepared to fight for their homes, but they were afraid. They knew his story, that he was taught by the famed fighter Abigail, who had raised him after rovers killed his parents, men who turned out to be Galen and his brother. Taimin had refused to fight a skalen he considered a friend. He had challenged the commander of the city guard to single combat. He had led his fellow prisoners to freedom.

Taimin called down to the crowd below the wall. "People of Zorn!" Their expressions were expectant as they waited to hear his words. "The Protector has used fear as his weapon. He has sought to create hatred for anyone different from ourselves. He wants to make us so afraid of everything outside this wall that we will agree to anything, even terrible deeds against those we share this world with, so long as we think we're safe."

He scanned the crowd and saw the gaunt faces of the field workers. "Why did he not tell you that the well was dry? You know the answer. Because his rule would be threatened. Rather than find a solution together, and share his authority, he has lied. Rather than trade with those outside, he has made enemies out of them. Rather than protect you, he has brought an army to this city's doorstep."

"But how can *you* protect us?" a man with a gray beard called up.

Taimin turned to look out from the wall, toward the plain. A long line of figures, a dark mass on the horizon, was growing bigger. Even as Taimin watched, Blixen's army marched inexorably toward the city. Bax after bax stood in long, frightening lines. Soon Taimin could make out bristling spears held upright.

He once more addressed the crowd. "We began this war, and we can end it. With the fall of the city guard, we have an opportunity for peace."

"How can we trust Blixen?" a dark-haired woman shouted. "If he knows we have no soldiers, what is to stop him killing us all?"

Taimin called down to her. "I will ask him that myself."

The stout wooden gates drew open, just wide enough to allow Taimin, Elsa, and Rathis to emerge from the city's protection. There was something final about the thunderous clatter the gates made as the timbers crashed together once more.

With his two companions on either side of him, Taimin started to walk.

As his group of three left the city behind, Taimin's hands were moist and his shoulders were tight with tension. He felt naked without a weapon, but he also knew that where he was going, a sword wouldn't do him any good. If Blixen wanted him dead, he soon would be.

Now that he was no longer looking out from a height, all he could see at first was a haze of dust ahead. It was late afternoon.

Soon night would descend on the wasteland. Softened rays lit up the landscape as the golden sun fell from the sky.

Blixen's army appeared out of the haze.

Taimin's heart rate increased. Unarmed and walking directly into danger, he wondered if what he was doing was the right thing. It was nerve-wracking to see a long row of armored bax warriors marching side by side. Squat figures held clubs, axes, swords, and long spears. Their eyes were dark and deep-set. Behind the first row of marching figures came another, and another. A group of skalen with patterned skins, armed with javelins, appeared on the right flank.

As the army neared, Taimin stopped walking. Beside him, Elsa and Rathis came to a halt. Taimin glanced at Elsa. Her usually stern expression was gone. Her face was pale.

He then looked back at the city. The wall was tall and the gates were closed. The citizens of Zorn were prepared to fight if they had to. The population was large enough that even without skilled soldiers, lives would be lost on both sides.

The army marched. Two humans and one old skalen waited to greet it. Taimin heard a bax bellow a command in a hoarse, throaty voice.

"Halt!"

The army came to a thunderous stop. A cloud of dust billowed around the area, obscuring the bax and skalen completely. For a moment everything was still.

Taimin waited and wondered what would happen next. Then a bax, taller than those around him, appeared out of the dust. He walked with the strange, hunched posture of all his kind, but was still big enough that his stride was long. Six warriors flanked him, spread out on both sides.

"Blixen," Elsa murmured.

Taimin's mouth was dry as he looked at the bax leader he had heard so much about. Blixen's torso was thick, dominated by a powerful chest and wide shoulders. The thin slits of his nostrils were his smallest feature, and his mouth was set in a grim expression, made even more menacing by the folds above his eyes. A circle of what appeared to be finger bones enclosed his thick neck. His studded leather vest was obviously made to fit. Far broader than Taimin, everything about him communicated size.

As Blixen and his escort approached, Taimin glanced at Rathis. The former prisoner was shielding his tilted eyes as he peered at the army's distant flank. As the dust began to settle, Rathis left Taimin and Elsa without a word.

Taimin stayed silent as he watched Rathis's departing back. The air continued to clear, revealing more and more figures, and he saw expressions of disbelief on several faces among the skalen. He heard a cry, and finally recognized Group Leader Vail and her son Rees. All of the skalen surged forward and surrounded Rathis. Taimin couldn't help but smile.

He heard Elsa speak and tore his eyes away.

"Come," she said.

Taimin and Elsa walked forward to meet Blixen and the six warriors with him.

"I am Blixen, Warden of the Rift Valley." His gruff voice had a booming quality. "If you want to say something, speak and be done with it." As soon as he had finished, Blixen looked past Taimin's shoulder. Taimin turned, following his gaze. A long row of city folk stood on top of the wall. They were being watched.

Taimin opened his mouth to speak, but then a series of what sounded like cheers came from the direction of the skalen. Blixen turned his attention to the commotion on his army's flank. His brow furrowed as he considered Rathis's newly won freedom.

"You may have satisfied the skalen, but nothing will stop me from assaulting your city." Blixen's dark eyes met Taimin's. "The Rift Valley is our home. We will be victims no more."

"I agree," Taimin said.

Blixen frowned. He tilted his head, surprised.

"We bring news," Taimin continued. "Every soldier who once bore arms against you is dead. The city guard is no more. I am sure you had your own score to settle with the commander, but he and his brother murdered my parents. I avenged their deaths."

Blixen was silent for a time as he inspected the city. "How can I believe you?"

Taimin nodded at Elsa. "There has been an uprising. This is Elsa. She is in command."

"We come to broker peace," Elsa said.

Blixen's frown deepened. He looked at the city wall while he considered their words. He turned his head to glance at his army. Even if the skalen no longer wished to join his cause, he still had a great number of warriors.

Taimin spoke up. "If you choose to fight, you may conquer Zorn, but you also may not. The people inside would be fighting for their homes and for their lives, just as you have been. The power to end this is yours."

"The city acknowledges your right to the Rift Valley," Elsa said. "We want peace restored. We want to trade and share knowledge."

"Let this end—today," Taimin said.

Blixen didn't speak again for a long while. When he chose his words, he spoke them slowly. "I need to verify the truth of what you are saying."

"I understand," Taimin said. "I would expect nothing less."

Blixen lifted his chin and scowled. "And there is one matter I can never let go. My wife. She was captured by the city guard close to three months ago." He clenched his hands into fists. "I want to enter the city to find her."

Elsa's mouth dropped open, but Taimin spoke first, forestalling her reply. "We agree to it. You may enter." When Elsa gave him an alarmed look, he continued before she could speak. "If you enter with your escort, we will keep the gates open, and that will remain the case. In turn," he now addressed Elsa, "the bax will not attack while we have their warden inside."

Elsa was pensive for a moment. She then nodded. "That can work."

Taimin had one more offer to make. It was the reason he had sent Vance to guard the tower. "And to demonstrate our desire for peace," he said to Blixen, "we offer you a gift. The Protector is in the tower. Do with him what you will."

While Elsa watched Taimin, her expression shifted to one of respect. She spread her hands. "Will that work for you?" she asked Blixen.

Blixen thumped his chest. There was something ceremonial in the gesture. "I am the warden and I can speak for all here. I agree to your terms. Now," he said, "I want to find my wife."

"How will you find her?" Elsa asked, puzzled. "I can promise you I don't know where she is."

Blixen called over his shoulder. "Rei-kika!"

Taimin was surprised to see a mantorean push through the ranks of bax warriors. Even more surprising was the realization that he had met her before. As she came forward with the unusual double-jointed walk that mantoreans employed, he recognized the shape of a healed scar on the side of her triangular face.

He remembered the trull trading the mantorean to Vail. Evidently Rei-kika had made her own unusual journey, and now accompanied Blixen. Her antennae swished from side to side as she approached. Her black, multifaceted eyes gave Taimin an unnerving stare.

"Rei-kika," Blixen said to the mantorean. "I want you to enter the city with me and use your abilities to find my wife. Do this, and I will free you from my service. You may take your eggs wherever you wish to go."

"I will help," Rei-kika said in a clicking voice.

As Blixen prepared to enter the city, Elsa raised an eyebrow at Taimin.

"Go," Taimin said to her. "Leave me here."

He stayed where he was as Blixen, Rei-kika, and the escort of six bax warriors followed Elsa toward the city gates. He then gazed up at the darkening sky, heedless of the fact he was standing between Blixen's army and the city gates.

Whatever happened next was out of Taimin's control. For the time being, war had been averted. Blixen had accepted his proposals.

Taimin was instead thinking about Selena. He had no idea where Griff might have taken her. She could even still be on the wyvern's back. All he knew was that he needed to search the sky, and it would be harder within the city wall.

Selena was the reason that the uprising had been successful.

He wouldn't rest until he found her.

⌣

Griff soared over the city, and Selena flew with him. The buildings below sped past, making her feel dizzy. Her heart beat faster with every strong movement. At the same time, her spirits soared. The experience was exhilarating.

Even as Griff's leathery wings swept up and down, his wedge-shaped head craned from side to side. Selena thought he might be searching; perhaps trying to find Taimin. A wyvern's eyes were far sharper than a human's, but, even so, to pick out one man in the streets below must be close to impossible, particularly with nightfall fast approaching.

All of a sudden Selena felt her whole world tilt. She leaned forward and gripped the ridges of Griff's shoulder blades, hugging the wyvern's body. Her knees tensed as she tried to prevent herself from falling. Griff was turning, banking sharply to head back toward the middle of the city. The tower approached, becoming steadily larger.

"No," Selena said sharply. "Not there."

Griff's wings gave another series of sweeps, and then in an instant the tower was behind Selena rather than ahead. From her height she saw a great crowd at the city gates. Farther away, past the wall, was a multitude of dark figures that could only be Blixen's army.

Griff began to swoop down toward one of the wider streets, but a handful of people saw him and cried out in fear. The wyvern's wings came down again to lift him up and away.

Selena leaned forward and brought her face as close as she could to a pointy ear. "Griff? Where are we going?"

Griff gave a piercing shriek, which she took as the only reply she would get.

As the wyvern's body leveled once more, Selena's eyes stung from the constant stream of air against her face. She tried to guess Griff's destination, and then she saw a huge, oval-shaped structure directly ahead.

Her breath caught as she realized where Griff was going. The arena was somewhere he knew, and was the last place he had seen Taimin.

Griff shot over the arena's perimeter and immediately Selena spied the sandy, blood-stained floor. Bodies lay strewn across the sand on one side of the fighting pit. While she took in the grim sight, Griff tucked in his wings and dived. Her stomach churned as the wyvern pulled up sharply, broad wings blowing up sand. Griff found a secluded place to land, away from the scene of recent fighting, where he probably thought she would be safe.

Selena slipped off Griff's back. With sand below her feet and her chest heaving, she turned to face the wyvern. Griff watched her for a moment, eyes filled with concern. His face was different, more tapered, but his gentle, sad eyes were the same.

"Griff . . ." Selena said. She stepped forward and reached out to stroke his face. He had changed, but she knew him, just as he knew her. "Thank you."

He moved his head slightly to nuzzle her hand. Then, giving another shriek, he startled her by launching himself once more into the sky. Selena followed him with her eyes until he was gone, and she was alone in the fighting pit. She guessed that Griff would continue to search the city for Taimin.

After the frantic pace of events, Selena took a slow, steadying breath. The bodies of so many uniformed soldiers told her that the uprising had been successful. She tried not to look at them, but then her gaze alighted on the corpse of a man she recognized.

Galen's body was on the far side of the fighting pit, but his close-cropped white hair singled him out. Taimin had done it; his enemy was dead.

Thinking about Taimin, Selena tore her gaze away and instead scanned the sky, wondering if Griff might soon appear with Taimin on his back. As she stood on the sand, in a cleared space that was hers alone, it was growing dark and, as blue shifted to black high above, stars began to shimmer across the expanse.

Wherever Taimin was, she was going to see him soon.

But even as she had the thought, a strange feeling of dread crept up unbidden. She couldn't explain it at first. Her talent was trying to tell her something. The sense of unease grew stronger. There was terrible danger behind her,

She whirled.

Arren stood facing her.

His pinched face looked haggard. He was wheezing, and a wide patch of crimson stained the material of his white tunic.

But the wiry mystic was wounded, not dead. He held something in his hand.

It was the dagger Selena had stabbed him with. Arren snarled as the dagger came forward.

Aware that she was unarmed, Selena freed herself from her body faster than thought. In an instant her ethereal consciousness was floating in the air. She shot toward Arren's skull and dived inside.

Stop. She sent the single, strong command, just like she had with the trull who had been about to kill Taimin.

But Arren was a skilled mystic. He didn't have her power, but he had his years of training with Merin.

The dagger in his hand kept moving.

43

Vance stood guard outside the white tower. With him were a handful of other fighters and the irritating rover, Lars.

The tall tower cast a broad, tapered shadow on the plaza. It was growing dark and, high above, the azure sky shifted hue, becoming deep blue and then black. Vance glanced up and saw the cratered moon, pale and glowing now that its brighter rivals had departed. The plaza was deserted, as was the broad avenue that led to the city gates. Everyone was either hiding in their homes or had joined the crowd at the wall.

As Vance paced, he kept looking askance at the tower's oversized door, wondering who was inside and what was happening within. He tilted his head back but couldn't make out the open-sided room at the tower's summit.

Lars stood nearby with his fingers hooked into his trousers. "Do you have to move so much? You're making me nervous." The bald, bearded skinner scowled. "I'm surprised you've got the energy."

Vance put his back to the skinner. He didn't know how Taimin had managed to put up with Lars when they had traveled the wasteland together.

Now that Vance had turned, he couldn't help looking at the corpses of several uniformed soldiers, sprawled out a dozen paces from the tower. The last of Galen's men were dead. Vance had killed two of the soldiers standing guard himself. In another life, when Cora had been caught in his bed, these were the same men who had thrown him into the arena.

"No one's going to miss them," Lars said, noticing Vance's attention.

Vance nodded but didn't reply. Instead he glanced again at the tower and wondered if Cora was still alive. She had been the Protector's mistress. How vengeful had the Protector been? Was she locked up inside? He was desperate to find out. He tried to clamp down on the faint hope that he still held on to. Over and over again, he kept telling himself that she was almost certainly dead.

A startled sound from one of his companions made Vance return his attention to the street. His eyes shot wide open. Even Lars had frozen and looked poised to run.

A huge bax, the biggest Vance had ever seen, was striding directly toward them. The insect-like form of a mantorean walked at his side. Half a dozen younger bax warriors followed, all carrying axes. Vance began to panic. If the city had fallen, why hadn't he heard anything?

Lars let out a breath. "It's all right, lad," he said.

As Vance saw that Elsa was part of the group, his heart rate slowed to something approaching normal. He had been so focused on the huge bax that he hadn't seen her. Elsa didn't seem afraid. Nonetheless, it didn't put Vance at ease to see the circle of bones around the bax's neck.

"Is that . . . is that Blixen?" asked one of the former prisoners.

Another glanced at Vance. "It must be."

"Be prepared for anything," Vance muttered in reply.

While Elsa continued walking toward them, the imposing bax stopped to crouch beside one of the bodies of the soldiers. He reached out and gripped the dead man's chin. He then tilted the soldier's head from side to side and stared into his glazed eyes. When he straightened, the folds above his dark eyes gave him a satisfied expression.

"Yes, you are looking at Blixen, Warden of the Rift Valley," Elsa said to Vance, coming to a halt. "Now I need you to stand aside."

"But Taimin said—" Vance began.

"Taimin is the one who brokered this arrangement," Elsa interrupted. Her eyes narrowed with impatience. "Do as I say."

Vance turned and nodded to the others. "Let them in."

His companions moved away from the tower's entrance and allowed Blixen and the mantorean to approach the door, with the six axe-wielding warriors flanking their leader.

Before he tried to enter, Blixen addressed the mantorean. "You may remain outside, Rei-kika. If you say you cannot find her, I believe you. No matter what happens next, I release you from my service." He turned his grim attention to the tower. "The only man who might give me some answers is inside."

The mantorean bowed her head.

Blixen then turned to Elsa. "I will consider our agreement broken if the Protector is not within."

Elsa gave Vance an inquiring look.

He spread his hands. "I came as soon as Taimin asked me to. No one has come in or out, not while I've been here."

Blixen swept his gaze over his warriors and beckoned them to follow. He then walked to the heavy door, but rather than open it he lifted his leg and, despite the door's size and thickness, he kicked hard. A sharp clatter split the air as the hinges broke. With a crash the door fell inward and tumbled to the ground. Vance jumped when it made a resounding boom. Blixen then entered the tower, and his escort followed.

It was the last thing Vance wanted to do, but all he could think of was Cora, and whether she was inside. He turned to Elsa and inclined his chin in the direction of the doorway.

Elsa thought for a moment and then nodded. "Go with him."

Vance took a deep breath. Then, without thinking too hard, he hurried to the tower and stepped over the splintered door.

A circular space confronted him, paved with stone. Moonlight shone through a row of high oval windows. Already Blixen and his escort were climbing a winding series of oversized steps that curved around the inside of the tower's perimeter.

As Vance began to climb, Blixen glanced over his shoulder and saw him.

Vance swallowed. "The Protector should be on the highest level," he said.

Blixen didn't reply but continued his ascent. Vance trailed behind the group, not wanting to follow too closely. He passed archways leading to storerooms filled with crates and saw corridors lined with linen mats that might lead to sleeping quarters.

Still thinking about Cora, he saw that Blixen's group had come to an abrupt halt.

The bax were several levels below the uppermost floor, but something had definitely attracted Blixen's attention. Vance climbed the steps to see what it was. A wide archway opened up near the stairs, where it was easy to see through while passing. Vance couldn't yet see what Blixen was looking at. A bax's thick body was blocking his view.

Vance instead watched Blixen.

Blixen's chest rose and fell but he stayed where he was and said nothing to his companions. They too remained silent. Vance hung back, waiting for them to move, and then they did. Blixen left the steps and walked with a heavy tread toward the archway. His breathing sounded labored.

Vance climbed higher. He gasped. From his new position, he finally understood what Blixen had seen.

Through the archway was a wide, open space. Vance's stomach churned when he saw corpses that had been stuffed, mounted, and arranged on display. Closest was a trull, powerfully muscled, with a bare chest and his jaws open to display his curved incisors. A pair of young skalen, a male and a female, stood together. The diamond pattern of their skin reflected the pale light that poured through the windows.

Vance walked slowly as Blixen and his escort entered the arched opening. Vance's hesitant footsteps finally faltered. He stopped at the room's entrance.

The Protector's macabre museum was fully revealed. Vance saw a pair of bax, one from each gender, standing above three bax young. A mantorean had his body arched, posed with a bowstring against his triangular face. All of the different races held weapons appropriate to their kind: a club for the trull, javelins for the skalen, and axes for the bax. Every creature was perfectly still, supported by sharp poles embedded in their bodies.

Vance didn't want to go on. He watched Blixen come to a halt in front of a female bax. As he reached out and touched her face, Blixen's body quivered with suppressed emotion.

Vance knew that it was time to leave. Keeping his head bowed, he retreated and waited. Soon he heard footsteps climbing the stairway once more.

Blixen was on his way to the top of the tower.

Darkness seeped into the observation room, banished only by the moonlight and the cool green glow of a handful of aurelium lamps.

At the end of a normal day, the Protector would be enjoying his dinner. But this wasn't a normal day.

"Galen didn't make it," he said softly.

He stood near the edge of the observation room's floor, where he had a direct view of the army outside the city. Strangely, the mass of distant figures remained half a mile from the wall. In the time since he had last looked, the gates had parted, and now stood wide open. He struggled to make sense of it.

The Protector's mind worked furiously. There had to be some way for him to salvage something from the wreckage of his reign. He was the city's rightful leader. His great-grandfather had given the city its name and made Zorn what it was.

He turned and glared at Merin, who was watching him, pale faced. "There must be a way out of this tower."

"It's secure." Merin's voice was shaking. "We made sure of it."

The Protector grimaced. The fact that there was only one way in or out was now working against him. Over the years, he had kept various mystics captive while Arren and Merin forced them to watch over the city and its surroundings. Now rebels stood guard outside the tower. And it was he who was their captive.

Why hadn't anyone come to seize him? Surely it was only a matter of time.

Even the arrival of Blixen's army hadn't caused the people to regret their revolt. He couldn't believe it: they had made peace. It was the only explanation.

The Protector considered plans and then discarded them as he tried to think of something he could do. He swallowed as he realized that his position might not be his primary concern. He now had to think about his own life.

"What now?" he asked. His eyes narrowed at Merin. "You think you're clever. Well? What are we going to do?"

"We could try to climb—" Merin ventured.

The Protector snorted. "You think they aren't watching?"

"We have to try, don't we?"

"There must be another way." He scowled impatiently at the stocky mystic. "Can't you do something with your talent? How do you plan to get me out of this?"

Merin's mouth dropped open. His skin went gray.

"Answer me," the Protector snapped. Merin's eyes were wide open, showing the whites. Something had taken hold of the mystic, and it wasn't fear of him. He was looking past the Protector's shoulder, toward the stairs sunken in the floor.

The Protector whirled.

Fear stabbed into his heart like a sharp, red hot poker.

Blixen, Warden of the Rift Valley, entered the observation room with six strong, axe-wielding warriors behind him. The Protector knew without doubt who he was; the huge bax had been described in detail by the captives he had questioned.

Blixen's face was murderous. He was shivering with barely contained rage. He turned and snatched an axe from one of his warriors.

The Protector stood paralyzed with terror.

Vance lost track of how many doors he had opened. He had discovered rooms where food was prepared and rooms filled with discarded furniture. Now his heart had started to beat more rapidly. This time he was excited.

He faced a nondescript door at the end of a stone-walled corridor. As with the other hallways leading to living quarters, a long, woven mat lined the floor. But this door was different. It was locked.

The latch was on the outside, which meant that it was designed to keep someone in. Vance told himself that he shouldn't believe that the kind, gentle, golden-haired woman he had loved would be inside.

With a shaking hand he reached out and unfastened the latch. He opened the door slowly.

"Hello?" he asked hesitantly.

He stepped through the doorway. The bedchamber he entered was well-ordered and clearly lived in, with a bed, desk, oval mirror, and clothing chest. Vance's vision blurred.

His gaze rested on the room's occupant.

She was standing on the bed to peer out the sole window at the city below, evidently trying to gauge what was happening outside. The woman turned when she heard Vance calling.

She wasn't Cora.

Disappointment struck him with force.

Instead of Cora, he was looking at a young woman with short, wavy hair a dark shade of red. She was pretty, with a wide mouth and full lips, and wore a vest and tight-fitting leather trousers.

She climbed off the bed. Her brown eyes narrowed. "Who are you?"

It took Vance a moment to speak. He told himself that hope remained. She might know where he could find Cora.

He found his voice. "I'm Vance. Who are you?"

"I'm Ruth." She regarded him seriously. "What's happening out there?"

"The Protector no longer rules Zorn." Vance left out the fact that, given Blixen's justified rage, the Protector was most likely dead. "There's been an uprising."

Ruth's eyes grew larger and larger. For a time she looked stunned.

"Your door was locked. How long have you been here?" Vance asked.

Ruth shook herself. "In this room? Not long. They locked me in here. If you mean in this tower . . ." She let out a breath. "Too long."

"Well, you're free to go."

Ruth thought for a moment, and then without a word she went to the corner and grabbed a cloth satchel. She crouched at the wooden chest and lifted the lid as she began to stuff items into her bag.

Vance was nonplussed. "Did you hear me? I said you're free."

She scowled at him. "Leave me here if you want to go. I'm a healer. I need my things."

"Fine." Vance let out a breath. "Do what you want. But I've helped you, so I want you to help me."

"What do you want?" she asked while she continued to fill her satchel.

"I'm looking for someone."

"Who?" Ruth asked absently. "I've been stuck in this tower. I don't see how I can help."

"Her name is Cora."

Ruth stopped what she was doing. She looked down, not meeting Vance's eyes, and then set her bag on the floor and straightened. She now gave him a sad, steadfast expression.

Vance paled when he saw her face.

"Vance," she said his name softly. "I remember now."

"Where is she?"

"She's dead. I'm sorry."

"How?" Vance whispered.

"There's no easy way to say this. The Protector beat her. I tried to help her, but I couldn't."

Vance was utterly still for a time. Ruth kept staring into his eyes; she looked surprisingly understanding. He wished she would return to her packing.

Cora was dead. He knew it had been an impossible hope that she might be alive. He had been thrown into the arena for the risk he had taken. But she had been beaten to death. She was gone.

He didn't know if Ruth called out anything when he raced from the room. He crossed the floor and launched himself at the stairway. In moments he was climbing as fast as he could. Level after level passed him by. He ascended a last set of steps and burst into the open-sided room at the top of the tower.

Wind blew throughout the observation room. The cool green light of aurelium lamps banished the darkness outside.

The bax were already gone. They had left behind two corpses. One was a round-faced, stocky man, who stared back at Vance with glazed eyes.

The other man's features were unrecognizable, but his expensive clothing marked him out. As always, his gray hair was neatly combed.

44

Selena had no idea how much time had passed. Her perception had shrunk to a narrow focus. There was only her, and the wiry man standing in front of her with a snarl on his face and a dagger in his hand. He had been poised in the same position for what felt like an eternity. Night had settled its dark curtain over the arena.

Selena was also frozen in place as she tried to burrow through Arren's defenses and the maelstrom of his thoughts to stop him from burying his dagger in her heart. If she tried to move physically, her concentration would be gone, and she would be dead in moments.

Arren's dagger came a little closer.

Anyone watching would have seen two figures facing each other, both grimacing, with barely any shift in their posture. Selena's fists were clenched at her sides. Fatigue washed over her. Her abilities were being tested like never before.

The bloodstain across Arren's chest had grown wider. Each breath came labored. But determination filled his narrowed eyes. He was going to kill her, even if it was his final act.

Selena's only hope was to break his will.

Every time she tried to thrust a thought into his mind, she could only hold on to it and make it strong enough to be a command for a short time before it vanished, forcing her to try again.

Arren's thoughts weren't like Blixen's: they were slippery. His skill was ensuring that even if Selena could slow him down, she couldn't stop him altogether.

The dagger moved forward, before Selena sent a sharp directive into the mystic's mind. *Stop.*

The dagger ceased moving, but Arren's lips curled in a smile of triumph. He knew he was winning. The sharp point of the steel dagger was now just three inches from Selena's heart.

⁓

Taimin walked swiftly, frantically, as he paced the plain and scanned the sky. As nightfall set in, his anxiety grew. It would be difficult, if not impossible, to see wings against the darkness. Perhaps Griff had landed? If so, where? Selena was the reason Taimin was alive. He was desperate to find her, to know that she was safe.

He made a decision and began to head toward the city gates. Then, as he approached, he saw movement. Several figures exited the city. Blixen was among them.

Even from a distance, Taimin couldn't help but notice the burden in the huge bax's arms. Some of the members of Blixen's escort were similarly weighed down by bulky loads. The mantorean, Rei-kika, trailed at the back of the group.

Taimin focused on Rei-kika.

As he hurried toward Blixen's group, soon Taimin was close enough to see more clearly in the moonlight. He drew in a sharp breath. Blixen was covered in blood and it wasn't his own. His face was grim and he carried the body of a bax female. Some of his warriors also carried bodies. Taimin could barely bring himself to look at them.

Blixen recognized Taimin and muttered something to his warriors, bringing the group to a halt. "I have what I came for," he said in a hoarse, rumbling voice. "The Protector is dead. We will camp here tonight, and tomorrow we will talk."

Blixen made to leave.

"May I speak with Rei-kika?" Taimin asked.

Blixen glanced back at the mantorean. "She has her freedom. She can do whatever she wants." He barked for his group to resume, leaving Taimin and Rei-kika to talk.

The mantorean faced Taimin with her head slightly tilted.

"I need to find someone," Taimin said. "A human. Will you help me? Her name is Selena."

Rei-kika made a swishing sound. "I know Selena."

Taimin felt a stirring of hope. "Can you find her?"

"Wait." Rei-kika lifted a hand.

Taimin paced impatiently, forced to wait while the mantorean searched. He saw the twinkling lights of campfires, marking out Blixen's army. Blixen and his escort of warriors had now been swallowed by the encampment. There would be no fighting today.

Then, even as Rei-kika farcasted, a piercing shriek split the air. Taimin lifted his head and a pair of wings grew larger and larger. Griff flew high above the rooftops and passed over the city wall to head directly for Taimin's position.

Relief flooded through Taimin's body. Griff's line of flight was clear, and his attention was focused on the man who had rescued him long ago. Taimin smiled, happy to be reunited with his friend.

But as Griff landed in front of him, and Taimin wrapped his arms around the wyvern's neck, Taimin's anxiety returned. Griff's back was empty.

"Where is she, Griff?" he asked. "Where is Selena?"

Taimin turned when he heard a clicking sound. Rei-kika shook herself. When she spoke, her tone was urgent. "The place where they watch fights . . ."

"The arena?"

"Yes, the arena," said Rei-kika. "She is in danger. We must hurry."

———

Selena was desperate. Arren's knife had moved forward another inch. Triumph lit up his eyes.

She and Arren faced each other on the sand. Arren's breath wheezed in his chest as he tried to bring his dagger just a little farther forward to end Selena's life.

Meanwhile sweat coated Selena's forehead. Fear made her want to turn and run, but she knew that if she did she would die with a knife in her back. Only her talent could save her life from an armed opponent. Yet what she was doing wasn't working.

She had to change strategy.

In order to survive, she would have to understand her enemy. As Arren's thoughts swirled around her, she had to find a way to break his will.

His memories. Rather than his thoughts, she had to focus on his past. If she could find something in there, something deep and full of turmoil, she would be able to cause him pain. She would find his weakness and destroy him.

She peeled up the layers to worm deeper into Arren's mind. The strongest memories were those attached to powerful emotions.

———

Arren was a skinny, frail boy. His mother was far bigger, with a wide body, thick neck, and beady, piercing eyes. Arren cowered in the corner but he couldn't retreat any farther. His mother loomed over him, fists bunched, ready to strike.

"I was cursed the day you were born. You think you're clever? Do you realize what you've done, with your lies?" She spoke scathingly as spittle flew from her lips. "You sniveling little worm. The door was closed. You didn't see me with anyone. I've never touched a man who wasn't your father. If you call me a liar again—"

Selena wanted to pull back from the memory; the accompanying emotion was too strong, too overwhelming. Arren had been just six years old. He hadn't yet begun to understand what the visions meant. He didn't know why his mother was angry. All he had done was ask her—in front of his father—why she had been lying on top of a strange man in the back room.

Arren had been beaten, first by his mother and then his father later on. He eventually learned to keep his mouth shut, but the beatings became a habit. Almost every time his parents argued, one of them saw him and came storming toward him, while all he could do was raise his arms in front of his face.

Selena didn't want to use the memory. It felt wrong, in every way. But she also didn't want to die.

She retreated from the memories and returned to the whirling storm of Arren's thoughts. She formed a thought of her own and held on to it with all of her power, feeling the radiance well within her as she slammed the idea home.

You are not talented, you're cursed.

Selena used the withering tones of Arren's mother. He would feel that his mother was inside his mind. For his entire youth, his mother's voice had made him feel fear, self-loathing, and anxiety.

Like a swordsman launching a flurry of blows, Selena continued.

All you do is hurt the people around you. Just give up. What do you have to live for? You might as well be dead.

Selena sensed Arren's anguish.

The last thought Selena drove home was one of contempt. *Worm.*

Then, once she was done, Selena retreated.

With a jolt, her eyes refocused as she found herself again within her body. She stood with her fists bunched at her sides. Her teeth were gritted so tightly that her jaw hurt. Arren was in front of her. The dagger was between them. A solid thrust would end Selena's life.

But, rather than stab, he blinked and stared in confusion at the knife in his hand. His gaze continued to move, to the tear in his tunic and the wide blood stain spreading across the material.

The dagger dropped out of his hand.

Arren's arm fell. His eyes slowly closed. His knees buckled underneath him as he collapsed to the sand.

Yet even in victory, Selena felt a sickening sensation. Every fiber of her being recoiled at what she had done.

To defeat her enemy, she had been forced to understand him and to use his fears against him. Her own upbringing had been far too similar to his. People had mistrusted her ever since her talent had surfaced. She had been beaten for trying to save a man's children. Settlers had abandoned her in the wasteland, only for her to find her way back to them. Her youth had been spent moving from group to group. All she had ever wanted was to remove her curse.

She was still holding on to her power, and had never taken on so much of it.

Her legs felt weak. She staggered and then crumpled to the ground.

Something inside her snapped.

She was thrown outside her body, but this wasn't like anything she had experienced before. She floated upward while the

412

stars above spun around and around with dizzying ferocity. The fighting pit fell away beneath her. She managed to glance down and saw that she was above the arena, which swiftly became smaller. The white-walled houses reflected the moonlight. The grid of streets and avenues blurred together. Soon the city was a pale, circular disc. A long line of campfires glittered outside.

The sense of horror stayed with her. Her very identity, her sense of knowing who she was, began to fade away, leaving a confusion of thoughts that jostled together so that none of them was able to take shape.

As she continued to rise higher and higher, she once more stared up at the sky. She was strangely drawn to the stars. They were so peaceful. Peace was what she desired most of all.

If she traveled high enough, she could leave the world behind.

Taimin shook Selena's body hard, but still she gave no reaction. She was perfectly motionless, legs folded beneath her as she sat with shoulders slumped on the sandy floor of the arena. Her eyes were unfocused. Her chest wasn't moving.

Taimin glanced at the thin-faced man's body and the dagger that lay flat on the sand. He tried to understand what was happening but couldn't. Selena hadn't been hurt physically as far as he could see.

Griff gave a growl that ended in a whimper. His lean body sprawled out with his wings fluttering. His sad eyes watched Selena intently; he knew that something was wrong. Beside Taimin, Rei-kika's antennae twitched in agitation.

Taimin put his ear against Selena's mouth. He looked imploringly at Rei-kika. "What's happening? Why isn't she breathing?"

"Selena fought for her life. She defeated her enemy, but her lifeline is broken," Rei-kika said. "She is no longer connected to her body."

"I don't understand," Taimin said. He had never felt so helpless.

"With her lifeline broken, her body will no longer breathe," Rei-kika said. "If she does not return quickly, she will die."

"Help her!" Taimin cried, staring at the mantorean, trying to read her black, prismatic eyes.

Rei-kika became still and Taimin watched, tensed and expectant. His pulse raced. He turned to Selena again. He could hardly breathe himself. She was so . . . absent. It was as if she was already dead.

The situation became even more hopeless when Rei-kika shook her head. "She is farther than I can reach. All I can sense is her despair."

"Can't you go to her?"

"I cannot," Rei-kika said. "My training is too much a part of me. My lifeline would bring me back." With a convolution of her limbs, the mantorean sat down beside him. "I cannot go to her." She was close to him as she stared into his eyes. "But you can."

"Me?" Taimin shook his head. "I'm no mystic."

"I am aware of that. Outside your body, you would have no lifeline at all. I can free your awareness. But you would be as Selena is now. You would cease to breathe."

"You can send me to her?" Taimin felt the faintest kindling of hope.

"No," Rei-kika said. "All I know is that she is high in the sky, and all I can do is help you leave your body. You have to find her. You must call to her."

"How would she hear me?" Taimin asked.

"Because, Taimin," Rei-kika said simply, "she trusts you."

414

45

Taimin burst free from his body and immediately knew that something was wrong. He was floating above the sandy floor of the fighting pit, but he sensed that he should return. He knew that he was dying.

He heard Rei-kika's voice. *Steady.*

Taimin was terrified but he had to face his fears with determination. *I can do this,* he said.

Be swift.

He stared up at a sky that was a shade somewhere between dark blue and deepest black. Brilliant diamonds of light glinted down at him, scattered across the heavens. He wanted to go there. He felt himself drifting upward.

He needed to go faster. Rei-kika had said that Selena was high. On cue, the moment he thought about it, his rate of travel increased until he was speeding toward the stars. He looked down. Rei-kika was antlike in size. Soon even Griff became tiny. The oval-shaped floor of sand grew still smaller. The arena itself started to shrink and was swallowed by the surrounding streets and buildings. The city of Zorn became a pale, perfect circle in the plain that enclosed it.

So this was farcasting.

Taimin again gazed up at the sky. The stars appeared just as distant. The next time he glanced down, he couldn't see the great city of Zorn at all, just a dark, shadowed landscape of deserts and valleys, mountains, and windswept plains.

He focused his attention on traveling as high as he could. The only constant was the cratered moon, which appeared to grow in size.

He felt dizzy. The stars were spinning. He kept the silver circle of the moon in sight and his vision stilled. He knew that looking down would be a bad idea. Even so, it took a great effort to prevent himself from doing it.

He started to call, even as he flew higher. Darkness swallowed him. Stars filled his vision, countless shining holes in the black curtain of night.

Selena? Selena!

———

Selena was at a place where the sky curved and cast a final blue glow before it met a horizon of perfect darkness. The world was a sphere, she realized, a layered sphere, with breathable air coating the land underneath. She was at the edge of the outer layer. Up above was a void of utter emptiness. It was both forbidding and strangely inviting.

More stars than she had ever seen dominated her vision. The moon was far brighter, clear enough that she could make out jagged circles, like the imprints of huge droplets of water.

She felt drawn to the void. The stars beckoned, beautiful and bright. Something told her that she needed to return, but she wanted to continue her ascent for as long as she could.

She heard a voice.

It was faint, as distant as a voice calling from the bottom of a deep canyon. At first, she wondered if she was really hearing it, but then it became louder. Soon, she heard it more clearly. It was a male voice, calling her name.

Taimin? She spoke with her mind into the darkness.

And then he was with her.

She could make out his ghostly silhouette; he was floating beside her. He was transparent but his face was nonetheless distinct. She knew she must look the same way to him.

Selena.

He spoke her name with desperation. In all the time she had known him, as they had traveled together across the wasteland, searching for a mysterious city, she had never heard such emotion in his voice.

Why are you here? she asked.

Because you need to come back with me.

Selena shook her head. She was confused. *I did something terrible.*

He spoke urgently. *Listen to me. That man tried to kill you. If you defended yourself, then you did the right thing.*

You're wrong. I'm cursed.

That's not true. Rei-kika is with me. She's a mystic. Is she cursed?

Selena looked for a moment at the moon and then faced Taimin's hovering silhouette. She considered his words. She liked and trusted Rei-kika.

You can't let them win, Taimin said. *If you believe the worst about yourself, that's what will happen. You're not cursed. Look at where we are: we're among the stars!*

Selena hesitated. Her shattered thoughts were starting to take shape again, with every word Taimin said.

Taimin continued. *You once told me that we can't group anyone together and label them the same way. There are good and bad humans, you said. What about mystics?*

Selena finally understood.

She wasn't a slave to her ability. She was in control of it. Her talent meant she could do things other people couldn't, but what she did was up to her.

Taimin reached out to put his hand against her face, although she felt nothing. *We searched together for a new home. We were looking for a city. But what we didn't realize was that we had already found what we were looking for, as soon as we found each other. Please. You have to come back with me.*

Selena reached out to touch him too, but then she realized with a sudden fear that neither of them were connected by a lifeline. The bodies they had left behind wouldn't be breathing. They were both in grave danger.

46

With such a long way to travel, Taimin wasn't sure if he and Selena would make it back before their bodies were starved of air. They had to return to the land below, leaving behind the moon and the stars and the curve of the sky's outer layer.

The world was dark. It was hard to make out the wasteland, that small part of the sphere that wasn't burned black by the effect of two suns. There was nothing beyond the firewall but death.

Or so Taimin thought, until the fiery edge of the red sun Lux burst over the rim of the world.

The crimson orb bathed the landscape in swiftly spreading light. The false dawn revealed something impossible. From his incredible height, Taimin couldn't believe what he was seeing.

A black line surrounded the wasteland, which was marked out as an oval-shaped region of rust-colored terrain. But outside the wasteland, there wasn't scorched earth. There wasn't death.

There was life.

Vast stretches of water pushed up against gigantic landmasses. Silver rivers carved their way through lush forests. Icy white caps crowned proud mountains. Taimin saw yellow deserts and grassy plains, blue lakes, broad highlands, and networks of islands. The color green was more dominant than any other.

Beyond the firewall, there was supposed to be nothing at all. That was what Taimin had always believed. Everyone believed it. It was such a part of ordinary life that the vista below went against everything he had ever known.

His world wasn't what he thought it was.

It was beautiful.

———

Taimin and Selena opened their eyes at the same time. They coughed and choked as their chests heaved with every lungful of air.

Rei-kika let out a sigh of relief. Griff raised his head and parted his jaws. His wings made a crackling sound as they fluttered.

But even as Taimin regained his breath and experienced a strange sense of reconnection with his body, there was one pressing thought overwhelming everything else.

He faced Selena. "Did you see?" he asked urgently.

"I saw it." Selena's expression was stunned. Taimin stood, taking her hand at the same time and pulling her to her feet. Rei-kika clambered up and looked from face to face, while Selena shook her head. "I still can't believe it," she said.

"What is it?" the mantorean asked. Her antennae twitched back and forth. "What did you see?"

"I could describe it to you, but better yet, I'll show you." Selena's eyes glazed, but then she frowned. "I can't reach my power." She looked worried. "What's happened to me?"

"You have been gone from your body for a long time," Rei-kika said. "It may have affected your power."

"Just tell her," Taimin said.

Selena explained what they had seen from the place where the sky met the void beyond. The firewall wasn't the boundary of the inhabitable part of the world, where the wasteland brushed against the area scorched by the two suns.

Instead, the firewall was an actual barrier, separating the wasteland from the world that surrounded it. On the firewall's other side was a paradise.

Rei-kika became pensive. "I have to share this with Blixen. It is right that all the races know. And . . ." The mantorean hesitated. "Selena, I have been too long from my eggs. I must leave you here."

"You should meet Elsa—" Taimin began.

Rei-kika shook her head. "For the moment, all I want to know is that my eggs are safe. But I may return. Be well. I hope to see you both soon."

Without another word or glance, the mantorean walked away with her curious gait. Taimin followed her with his eyes. It would be strange for people to see the mantorean walking alone to the city gates. A few would stare, but Elsa's followers would make sure that no one challenged her. Perhaps even soon, under new leadership, the other races would be a common sight in Zorn.

Taimin watched until Rei-kika was gone.

And then, moving at the same time, he and Selena faced each other.

Under the light of the moon and countless stars, Taimin took Selena's hands. She came forward and wrapped her arms around him, and he held her body against his. He thought about how much they had both been through.

At last, they were standing together in the white city.

They began to talk.

Taimin learned about everything that had happened to Selena. She told him about her time in the Rift Valley and then in the tower, and he learned about Ruth. In turn, he explained how he had searched for her after escaping the skalen, leading to his capture by Galen.

Blixen had found his wife and taken his vengeance. The Protector and Galen were dead.

They were both at the side of the sandy floor, and at first Taimin didn't notice some newcomers enter the arena. He heard voices and turned to see three figures walking toward them.

"You're not an easy man to find," Vance said. "If some people hadn't said they saw a wyvern, we'd still be looking for you. Elsa wants you. She said it's important."

Lars's eyes moved from Taimin to Selena and back again. Big and bald, with a thick black beard, he appeared the same as ever. Taimin realized that it was the first time that he, Selena, and Lars had been together in a long time.

"Good," Lars grunted. "You found each other. About time."

"This is Ruth," Vance said, indicating the young woman with short auburn hair beside him. "She says she's a healer."

"I am a healer." Ruth scowled at him.

Taimin smiled. His gaze took in the group of five people. He first considered Lars, who was selfish and hard-headed, yet had risked his life for him. Lars was by far the oldest, and all he had wanted was to find somewhere he could spend his winter years in peace. The skinner hadn't found what he was looking for, but perhaps now the city could become the place he had wanted it to be.

Vance's eyes were shadowed. Taimin saw a darkness that wasn't there before, and wondered if the former weapons trader had discovered the fate of the woman he had gambled everything to be with. No doubt his time in the arena had changed him. Could he return to his former life?

As Taimin considered Ruth, he realized that both he and Selena now had friends. The girl from nowhere was no longer alone in the world.

"There is something we have to tell you," Selena said. She glanced at Taimin and he nodded at her. "We saw something. I was farcasting. A friend, Rei-kika, helped Taimin to join me."

Selena gazed up at the night sky. Stars shimmered overhead. The cratered moon glowed pure and white. "We were high," she continued. "So high that we could look down and see all of the wasteland." She returned her attention to Ruth, Vance, and Lars. "We think that the world we know is all that there is, that the rest is burned black by the two suns. But beyond the firewall we saw something else. Large stretches of open water. Thick forests. Rivers. Islands. The land isn't black at all."

A perplexed silence greeted her words.

"It was like the stories we tell of Earth," Taimin said.

Lars spoke in a growl. "I've never believed in Earth," he said, "and I'm not about to start now. When you die, you die. I only trust what I can see with my own eyes."

"We saw it," Taimin said. "It's the truth."

"If the firewall is some kind of barrier . . ." Ruth said slowly. "Do you think it can be crossed?"

Lars looked up sharply.

"Wait," Vance interrupted. "Let's talk to Elsa. She wants to see Taimin right away."

47

Some semblance of normality had returned to the plaza surrounding the tower. Elsa's followers guarded the broken doorway, which Vance explained Blixen had kicked in. The men and women in blue armbands stepped aside when they saw Taimin. A few greeted him by name.

"Elsa's inside," an older man said. "She's downstairs."

Taimin was the first to walk through the doorway and found himself in a circular room. The red sun's crimson light poured through the oval windows. Selena followed, with the others behind her, as Taimin searched until he saw the curving stairway sunken into the floor. He exchanged a curious glance with Selena; something about her expression told him that she might know what he would find down below. He began to descend the steps.

The stairway wound down and then finished abruptly; there was only one level below ground. Now in darkness, Taimin pushed open a tall door.

He entered a huge stone-walled space, the same shape as the chamber above it. The floor was dusty and barrels lined every wall, stacked so high that they almost reached to the ceiling. There were no windows, and cool green light was the only reason he could see. He saw a few bowls filled with shards that glowed—aurelium lamps—dispersed throughout the room.

It was the center of the space that drew Taimin's attention. A circle of well-laid stones surrounded a deep hole. Elsa stood at the edge with a bucket in her hand, along with a rope connected to the bucket's handle. Looking at her, Taimin wouldn't have thought she had just led a successful rebellion. The wiry woman with gray-streaked hair had a scowl on her face as she stared into the round hole in front of her.

Elsa glanced at Taimin and saw Selena, Vance, Lars, and Ruth enter behind him, but she immediately returned her attention to the hole.

"It's true," she said bluntly. "This is the city's only well, and it's dry." She raised an eyebrow at Taimin. "How did you know?"

"Selena told me," Taimin said.

Selena spoke up. "Ruth and I have been here before."

"Well," Elsa sighed, "nothing has an effect quite so much as the truth. It certainly explains a lot about the Protector's actions." She gave Taimin a worried look as he came to stand by her side. "I have to say, though, part of me was hoping you were wrong."

Taimin gazed down into the depths but couldn't see to the bottom. The well was made with the same white stone as everything else in the city. Evidently it had been built at the same time as the tower itself.

"We get some water from the fields but not enough for so many," Elsa said. "I've known about the well here for a long time, but the Protector always kept it guarded." Her mouth tightened. "For obvious reasons."

Elsa frowned at Vance when he rapped the side of a barrel. The returning hollow sound made it clear the barrel was empty.

"Don't bother," Elsa said. "They're all the same."

"How long?" Taimin asked.

"How long can we last?" Elsa's frown deepened. "A few months? If we can establish trade with the Rift Valley, perhaps a little longer."

Her shoulders slumped. All of a sudden, she looked her age. "We left it too late. Our reserves are gone. We need water to grow food. The city can't survive."

Taimin saw Selena following the wall as she checked the barrels, tapping on the sides with her hands and listening to the hollow sound they made. She returned his anxious look.

"Even if the peace with Blixen holds, others will think we're an easy target," Elsa said. "And as we run out of water, we'll only get weaker. I refuse to cast anyone out of the city, but there are too many people here. What can I do? They have nowhere else to go."

Taimin threw a swift glance at Selena. "I don't know if it helps," he said slowly, "but there's something you should know."

He told Elsa about the paradise he and Selena had seen on the other side of the firewall, but her face registered only disbelief.

"It's true," Taimin said. "There is more open water than you can imagine. Perhaps there is a better life, not just for humans, but for everyone."

Elsa shook her head. "Sorry, Taimin. I can see that you believe what you're saying, but to me it sounds fanciful. We have two suns. The wasteland is all we have." She waved her hand. "And, at any rate, let's say for a moment that what you're saying is true. What use is dreaming of somewhere else if the firewall keeps us trapped where we are?"

Lars cleared his throat. "There might be a way to get to the other side."

Elsa shook her head, still dubious.

"Even if there was a way through, how would we find it?" Ruth asked.

"We could walk along the firewall," Vance suggested, looking from face to face.

Ruth scowled. "That's insane—"

"Then what do you suggest?"

As people began to speak over one another, a loud voice cut through.

"I think I've found something," Selena called out.

Taimin turned to look at her. She stood near the wall behind him, but while everyone had been talking she had been working alone to remove first one barrel, then another, until there was a growing number on the floor beside her.

Taimin hurried over. "What is it?"

Selena pointed out a faint line that traveled along the wall, a crack or contour, covered with dust and grime. It was just above head height, and she ran her fingernail along it, before the line disappeared behind the row of barrels.

"The wall is made of stone," Selena said. She glanced over her shoulder to address the group of onlookers. "It looks like something was carved into it."

Taimin turned to Vance. "Give me a hand."

Without waiting for his friend to join in, Taimin went to the next barrel in the row and picked it up. As he set it down on the floor nearby, Vance took his place beside him. Vance grabbed a barrel and gave Lars a meaningful look.

"Fine," Lars muttered and came over.

It took all their efforts to move the screen of piled-up barrels. Elsa stood back and said nothing; she simply watched with a perplexed expression as they removed barrel after barrel. Each time they moved a container they carried it away to keep the section of wall clear. Then, as they reached the bottom row, Selena inspected some of the barrels away from the wall, tilting them to the side, until she found one with a little water still in it. While Taimin, Vance, Ruth and Lars worked, she levered the barrel open.

"Here," Elsa said, tossing Selena a kerchief.

Selena dipped the cloth into the water. As Taimin took the last barrel away, she began to scrub at the wall, removing years of

427

dirt from around the long crack. She revealed the line engraved in the wall until it curved and formed a wide ellipse. Taimin now stood beside Elsa and watched. Meanwhile Selena continued to scrub. Lars waited and scratched his beard, while beside him Vance smoothed his neat moustache. Ruth frowned.

Shapes began to emerge.

There was no longer just one outer line to mark the edge of the ellipse. Selena's moving hand revealed multiple contours and indentations, all of them etched into the stone. She worked swiftly and then searched for more water. Another series of wipes in the center of the wall displayed even more detail.

She stopped when she was done. She turned toward the rest of the group with an expectant expression on her face.

"What is it?" Taimin asked.

Selena didn't reply. She just waited.

Lars stared at the wall. He gave a surprised grunt. "It's a map."

Taimin's mouth dropped open. He stepped closer to the wall and his eyes traveled over the lines carved into the stone. He realized that Lars was right.

"Look," Lars said. "That's where we are." He walked up to the wall and jabbed his finger against it to point at the symbol of a star in the middle of a barren plain. "This city is marked." Taimin stared at the star, and then the skinner's hand kept moving. "That's the Rift Valley. Here are the mountains." Lars walked farther along the wall. "That's where the three of us met up." He tapped an area and glanced at Taimin.

Taimin examined the map. "Wait. Who made this map?"

"Whoever built this city," Elsa said softly.

Taimin and Selena exchanged glances. Vance's brow was furrowed. Lars walked even closer, squinting as he inspected one feature after another.

Taimin stepped up to the wall to try to find the area where he had grown up with his aunt and parents. He thought he had found the right place when he saw the long barrier of cliffs, just where it should be. He waved his hand over the first contour Selena had discovered. "This boundary must be the firewall."

He studied the line. The curve that the firewall made was surprisingly smooth.

Vance looked puzzled. "How old is this city?" he asked Elsa.

"It's impossible to say," Elsa said. "The Protector's great-grandfather discovered it abandoned."

Taimin backed away to allow Vance to come forward. Vance had his eye on the line of the firewall that Taimin had just indicated. "If the other symbol is Zorn, what's this?"

As Vance stabbed the wall with his finger, Taimin realized it was true; there was a second star, located against the distant firewall, a great distance from the region of cliffs where Taimin had grown up. The engraved symbol was etched on the verge of an empty area, almost certainly a desert, given the fanciful ripples and the fact that it was even more barren than the plain surrounding Zorn.

Taimin examined the map, taking his time, making sure to check every portion of it. He turned to meet Selena's eyes. "There are no other markers. It's the only place given a symbol besides this city." He paused. "And look where it is."

"It's right on the firewall," Selena whispered.

"What are you saying?" Vance asked. "There's a second city?"

"No," Taimin said. "Look. Compare it to the symbol for Zorn. There's a small difference." He pointed out the two parallel lines that crossed the second symbol to intersect with the firewall. "I'm saying that there might be a path through the firewall. A way to the other side."

Silence met his words. Everyone scanned, looking for anything else put on the map or given special importance. There could be no doubt. There were only two symbols. No more. One was the city. The other was far away, directly on the firewall.

Taimin thought about what he knew.

The firewall that encircled the wasteland, that had burned his parents' bodies to ash, was nothing more than a barrier. He had always believed that the erratic movements of the two suns scorched most of the world, but the firewall had nothing to do with Dex or Lux at all.

He remembered gazing down from the heavens and seeing the rest of the spherical world. It was a place of beautiful, sweeping landscapes. He had seen white, swirling clouds—clouds that he had only heard about in stories of Earth, the paradise that some said people went to when they died. He had felt awe at oceans of deepest blue. Forests and grasslands, rivers and lakes . . . they were all there on the other side of the barrier. Everything enclosed within the firewall was dry, hot, and hostile. The world outside was completely different.

The wasteland was dangerous. Water was scarce. Predatory beasts roamed; only the foolish traveled far from safety. The few crops that could be grown were hardy herbs, tough cactuses, root vegetables, and razorgrass.

Whoever had built this city had abandoned it a long time ago. The city's builders couldn't have simply vanished. They must have gone somewhere.

Now there might be a way through the firewall. The marker was far away, but Taimin believed he could find it.

Elsa was the first to speak. "This changes everything. The news alone would give people hope." She met Taimin's eyes. "You're going to go there, aren't you?"

"I am," he said. He hadn't known he had made the decision until he spoke, but he knew in his heart that it was what he had to do.

He was surprised when Selena cleared her throat. "And I'm going with you," she said.

Taimin opened his mouth to try to change her mind, but then Vance interrupted. "We'll need supplies for the journey."

Ruth spoke up. "You'll need a healer."

Taimin glanced at Lars. The skinner was more thoughtful than Taimin had ever seen him. He combed his fingers through his thick black beard and then cleared his throat. "I'm going," he said. He scowled at Taimin. "But don't think for a second that I'm doing it for anyone but myself. I'm old. If there's a better life than this one, I want to live it, even for a short time. I want to see this paradise before I die."

"I suppose that's settled then," Elsa said. She gave Taimin a firm stare. "Don't forget what I told you. This city can't continue as it is. Give us hope."

Taimin realized that there was a great responsibility on his shoulders. "In the meantime, what will you offer Blixen?"

Usually swift to speak, Elsa paused for a moment as she thought. "First, trade—there's water in the Rift Valley and we have goods they will want. But perhaps . . . perhaps some members of the other races might come here. Zorn could be a haven for all."

"Do you think we can all work together, side by side?" Taimin asked.

Elsa gave him an unreadable look. "We have to try, don't we?"

48

The golden sun lit up the wasteland. On the opposite side of the heavens, the crimson sun gave a challenging glare. The sky was a perfect blue. Air shimmered on the rocky ground. There was no breeze to relieve the heat.

A long series of cliffs formed a jagged escarpment, high above a flat plain. Scorpions scuttled along the cliff edge, peering down from the heights, in turn under the gaze of scavenger birds that clung to the branches of gnarled trees and cawed to one another. Cactuses defied the insects that sought the sweet flesh inside their spiky armor. Lizards hid under the boulders that lay scattered along the top of the escarpment, checking anxiously for predators. Wyverns soared in the part of the cliffs where they made their nests. This region—close to the firewall, where the horizon shifted to red and a barrier of fiery air scorched any living creature foolish enough to stray near—was somewhere that most travelers avoided.

There were benefits, however, to following the firewall. In the barren land above the escarpment there was little game and water was difficult to find, which meant that there were fewer predators. Hunting was possible, just difficult, and the water was there, if one knew where to find it.

Five travelers skirted the escarpment and walked with the steady pace of people who had been traveling for a long time. Sweat beaded on their foreheads. Lips were parched and mouths were dry. They would need to find water soon, but fortunately one of the travelers knew the area well, and it had been his decision to follow this route.

As he walked in front, Taimin gazed out from the cliff's summit, to where the precipice plummeted in a sheer drop nearby. He watched the circling wyverns and the view stirred memories both good and bad. He was reminded of all the times his parents had lowered him down the cliff in search of wyvern's eggs. The plain below had always fascinated him; he had wanted to explore, to meet other people and to exchange news and goods. Then his parents were killed, and his life changed forever.

He saw Selena looking his way, and wondered what she could read in his face. He didn't tell her that this was where it had happened. It was a long time ago. As he limped along, the slowest in the group despite the fact that he was the one leading, his foot gave him more pain than usual.

Selena noticed him looking toward the winged creatures below the cliffs. "You must miss Griff," she said. She smiled. "I know I do."

Griff was now a wyvern, and would want to find a mate. Before beginning the journey, Taimin had known that the right thing to do was to say goodbye to his old friend. He had hugged Griff tightly, but at the same time, he felt safe in the knowledge that Griff would thrive on his own.

"Of course I miss him." Taimin returned her slight smile. "But he's now free to live his own life. I wasn't thinking about him. It was . . . something else."

"Where are we going to camp?" Lars called from behind.

Taimin glanced over his shoulder to meet the older man's dark eyes. "I know a path down the cliffs," he replied. "We'll find water in one of the caves at the bottom. There's just something I want to see first."

"Think it's worth making a try for one of those raptors?" Vance asked. Walking behind Lars, he had his gaze fixed on one of the distant trees filled with squawking birds. Like every member of the group, his skin was weathered and his clothing was dusty. Yet, as always, his beard and moustache were neatly trimmed. He held a fine composite bow and used every available opportunity to try his skill.

"There's better hunting below," Taimin said.

"Are you sure we shouldn't go there now?" Ruth tried to avoid looking at Taimin's leg. "We're all tired."

"I have to see this first."

Time passed as Taimin led the group of five away from the cliffs and past a field of rocks strewn across the landscape. As his foot ached and shoulders groaned from carrying his pack, he climbed up a low hill. Selena would be the first to join him. It would be a few minutes before the others neared.

While he waited for her, he blinked sweat out of his eyes and turned to gaze at the horizon, away from the cliffs, where the sky shifted from blue to become an angry strip of red. For a time he looked toward the firewall. He now knew what he hadn't known then, that on the other side of the barrier the wasteland ended, and the world became green and filled with life.

Selena climbed the low hill to join him and he faced forward once more. Together they took in a somber sight: the ruins of a homestead, with a ditch laid in a square around a broken fence. Within the fence were a few dry, withered plants, and the charred timbers of what had once been a house. The elements had taken their toll. It didn't look like a place that had once been filled with love and laughter.

"This is it," Taimin said without looking at Selena. "This is where I grew up."

He was lost for a few moments in memory. It felt like such a long time since his parents had told him stories and his aunt had raised him to survive.

Selena reached out and took his hand. "It must be strange to return," she said softly.

"It is strange," he said. "This now feels like the middle of nowhere." He cleared his throat. "I'm still glad I came." He slowly inhaled, and then let out a deep breath. He remembered his aunt, telling him that one day he might want to find love, and that sometimes people just fit together. He turned toward Selena, the woman standing beside him.

"Perhaps, in a way, this *is* nowhere," Selena said, indicating the entire wasteland. "The real world might be on the other side of the firewall."

Taimin fixed his eyes on the distant horizon. "This time, we're going to get there together."

ACKNOWLEDGMENTS

My utmost thanks to everyone at 47North and United Agents who has been so supportive throughout all stages of the publishing process, with special mention to my editor, Jack, and agent, Robert.

Eternal gratitude to Ian, for helping make sense of my crazy ideas. I'd also like to credit Jon's help with early development, and my amazing readers: Amanda, Amy, Nicole, Candida, Estrid, Sandra, and Rosa.

Thanks to all of you who have reached out to me and taken the time to post reviews of my books.

Boundless recognition must go to my wife, Alicia. We share these dreams together.

ABOUT THE AUTHOR

James Maxwell grew up in the scenic Bay of Islands, New Zealand, and was educated in Australia. Devouring fantasy and science-fiction classics from an early age, his love for books led to a strong interest in writing. He attended his first workshop with published authors at the age of eleven, and throughout his twenties he continued to develop the epic fantasy story he would one day bring to life.

The internationally bestselling four books of The Evermen Saga were published with 47North in 2014. James soon followed with his second series, The Shifting Tides, a sweeping tale of adventure, intrigue, and magic.

A Girl From Nowhere is the first title in his latest series, The Firewall Trilogy, with the sequel, *A World of Secrets*, out in 2020.

James lives in London with his wife and daughter. When he isn't writing, he enjoys French cooking, acoustic guitar, and long walks in the English countryside.

For free books and to learn about new releases, sign up at www.jamesmaxwell.com.